D0832383

Just One Season in London

LEIGH MICHAELS

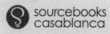

sourcebooks
casablanca

Published by Sourcebooks Casablanca, an imprint of Sourcebooks, Inc.
P.O. Box 4410, Naperville, Illinois 60567-4410
(630) 961-3900
FAX: (630) 961-2168
www.sourcebooks.com

Printed and bound in the United States of America
QW 10 9 8 7 6 5 4 3 2 1

For my mom
You taught me to reach for the dream

One

THE TOWN ASSEMBLIES WERE TOO SMALL TO HAVE much of an orchestra, so the music was most often provided by Miss Minchin at the piano. But this was all the young people had ever known, so they didn't miss the elegance of a London ballroom. Most of them would never have a London Season.

Including, Miranda thought with a wisp of sadness, the belle of tonight's ball.

Miranda's gaze rested on her daughter. Sophie's dark gold hair was a striking spot of color as she moved through the steps of the country dance. Miranda admitted she was partial to her own daughter. Still, everyone else faded into the background when compared to Sophie.

If only it was possible to get her to London... Even there, among the assembled lovelies of the nation, Miranda was certain that Sophie would stand out.

Sophie smiled up at her partner. It was a truly breathtaking smile, and Miranda wasn't surprised when the young man looked dazed, turned red, and missed a step.

Next to Miranda, Lord Ryecroft shifted his broad shoulders against a pillar. "I see my sister is at it again,

Mama. That will make three young popinjays whose pretensions I'll have depressed this month alone."

"It's only a dance. That doesn't mean he'll come to ask your permission to call on Sophie."

Rye looked down at her, one eyebrow raised. "If not, it will be because his father saw that smile too and put his foot down. You know as well as I do that Newstead wants someone with more of a dowry than our Sophie has when it's time to marry off his younger son."

"I wish…" Miranda bit her tongue, too late.

But it didn't matter, for the same thought was obviously already in Rye's head. "You can't wish it any more than I do, Mama. Get Sophie to London and she'd take the town by storm, marry a Croesus, and save us all."

He was joking, of course, Miranda knew. At least, he was mostly joking. But there was truth in what he said. Not that she wanted Sophie to choose a husband based only on wealth. But rich men fell in love too—and a young woman with Sophie's warm heart could surely find a wealthy man she could care about.

If only I could get her to London…

Rye smiled down at his mother—but though his expression was reminiscent of his sister's brilliance, she could see the shadow in his eyes. "I haven't the blunt to lay out for a London Season," he said, "and with the best intentions in the world, I can't find it this year."

"I know you can't, my dear." *But perhaps I can*, Miranda thought.

It would take sacrifice, and she would have to be careful not to let Rye and Sophie know. But for the sake of her children, Miranda would do anything.

Rye bowed to his mother and moved toward the refreshment room, where he helped an elderly lady to a glass of punch. She sipped the watery concoction and looked at him speculatively over the rim of her glass, her black eyes beady. "You're Viscount Ryecroft, aren't you?"

Rye admitted, warily, that he was.

She didn't favor him with her name. Instead she looked him up and down and asked, "Why isn't a young buck like you in the assembly room flirting with the young ladies? Not lack of interest from the chits, I'll be bound. Is there no one here tonight with enough juice to be worth your while to court?"

The comment stung Rye's pride—the more so because, in part at least, it was true. What sense was there in raising hopes among the young ladies at this assembly by dancing and flirting when he would never be able to form an attachment to one of them? Even worse, what if he were to meet a woman he *could* care about, but could not afford to marry her? Better to stay on the fringes.

What was true of his sister was equally true of him. If anything, his case was even more desperate—for Sophie needed only to marry a man who had enough money to support her. Rye needed to marry a woman who had enough money to support his estate and all the responsibilities that came along with it—including the tenant farmers, the servants, the retainers, his mother... In short, he needed an heiress of great magnitude—and generosity. Someone he was not likely to meet at this rural assembly.

Only in London...

Not that it was any sure thing, even if he somehow got to the city with enough brass in his pockets to make an impression during the Season. Sophie's beauty would draw the attention of any man, making her a bargain well worth having, despite her lack of a dowry—if only she could be brought to their attention. But Rye possessed nothing more than ordinary looks, along with a ticklish sense of humor. Neither attribute was likely to win over the sort of young woman who had a large enough fortune to take her pick of the Marriage Market. And he was still quite young for a man to be settling down—so the chits might not even take him seriously.

Not that he was about to discuss his situation with some elderly… lady.

As if the old woman had read his mind, she reminded him, "You have a title."

"So do many other men, ma'am."

"And many a woman covets one and is willing to pay for it." Her beady eyes rested on him for an uncomfortably long time, and then she said, "I like the look of you, Ryecroft." She dug into her reticule and handed him a pasteboard rectangle. "If you get to London, look me up in Grosvenor Square. I'd like to see more of you."

Rye's hand closed convulsively on the visiting card. Surely she didn't mean—surely she *couldn't* mean that *she* was one of those women who coveted a title and was willing to pay for it. She was older—far older—than his mother was, by Jove!

Her laugh sounded rusty. "No need to leap into the boughs, my boy. I know an heiress or two. That's all I meant. Come and see me, and I'll introduce you."

She set down the punch cup and walked away. She was spry for her age, Rye noted—though in fact, she might be anywhere from sixty to eighty, for he was no judge of such things. If she'd been a horse, now, then he'd have had a pretty fair guess.

He looked down at the card. *Lady Stone,* it said in neatly engraved type. *Tuesdays.*

So she already had a title, and her address on Grosvenor Square was in the most fashionable section of London—and she was at home to callers on Tuesdays. And she knew an heiress or two and would present him. That might improve his odds.

Not that he was foolish enough to count his chickens. It would take a fortune of massive proportions to rescue Ryecroft Manor, and there weren't many of those lying around for the choosing, even in London. But it was worth a try.

Perhaps he should make a trip to the city—for if he *could* catch an heiress, then next year Sophie could have her come-out and her chance at happiness. And he would be able to fix up the dower house for his mother so she could stop fretting about the concerns of running a large household on meager rations and enjoy her remaining years in peace. Then she would not have to deal day to day with the frustrations of living with a new Lady Ryecroft—one who might feel that since her money was paying the piper, she should be the one who called the tune. Of course, Rye would have to live with the as-yet nameless, faceless heiress...

It would take sacrifice for the rest of his life. But for the sake of his mother and his sister, Rye would do anything.

❧

They turned through the old-fashioned figures of the dance—bowing and curtsying, parading and wheeling. The sheer exhilaration of movement made Sophie smile up at her partner in delight. Instantly, however, she regretted it—for James Newstead's face went slack and then turned bright red. His hand tightened on hers, and he fumbled the next step of the dance.

Oh, fiddle, Sophie thought. *I hope Rye didn't see that.*

She looked past her partner's shoulder and saw her brother's face, just as he shook his head at her and shifted restlessly against the pillar.

Clearly, she was in for another scolding—and a scolding it would be, even though Rye wouldn't yell at her. He never did...

Well, Sophie thought with a reminiscent twitch of the lips, that wasn't absolutely true. There had been that time she'd taken his favorite hunter out for a gallop without permission, and the time she'd been trying to walk along the handrail of the bridge and had lost her balance and fallen into the creek.

But as a rule, Rye didn't yell. She almost wished he would; it would be so much easier if he were angry than when he seemed to be wounded by her behavior. As if it were her fault, for instance, that James Newstead didn't know the difference between a friendly smile and an encouraging one!

Sophie understood why Rye looked so sad these days. He really was the best of brothers, despite his many flaws. She knew that he would give anything in his power to be able to offer her a London Season and a chance to find a husband who was—as Rye would put it—worthy of her.

Which meant rich, of course. At least rich enough to provide her with the luxuries Rye thought she deserved.

It was all a bunch of twaddle, Sophie thought. Or at least, it would have been if not for Mama and Rye. It had been a long time since she'd seen Mama without that small worry line between her brows. And now Rye had come fully into his inheritance and realized just how bad things had gotten at Ryecroft Manor in the years since their father died...

Neither of them talked to Sophie about their worries. In that way, they obviously still thought of her as a child, even though she would be nineteen before long and Rye wasn't all that much older. She would have gone to London last year if Rye's trustees hadn't tightened the purse strings—and this year, it was clear, could be no different. Though she hadn't been told the details, only a dolt would fail to recognize that there simply wasn't money to rent a town house for a few months or buy a new wardrobe or purchase vouchers for Almack's. And without those things, as well as a reasonable dowry, no well-born English girl stood a chance of making a respectable match to a man with enough blunt to provide for her mother, and perhaps even to give her brother a helping hand in bringing his land back up to snuff.

Well then, what about a nonrespectable match? a little voice in the back of her mind inquired.

Sophie finished the dance with a curtsy to her partner and fanned herself as she waited for the next set to begin.

But the idea stayed in her head. Perhaps there were other ways to go to London.

She wasn't much of a hand at charades and such, so Sophie had no illusions about her chances of making a career as an actress. But she could sing, so perhaps she could be a chorus girl. And she was fond of dancing. Weren't there plays that needed dancers?

Of course, those weren't exactly respectable occupations. But what good was it to have a pure reputation and a sterling name if all she could do was stay at home at Ryecroft Manor, growing old while still a spinster?

At the least, if she went off to make her own way, Rye would be relieved of the expense of taking care of her. And if she were fortunate, Sophie might meet a gentleman—or even a wealthy tradesman—who would be intrigued enough to make her an offer.

Though probably not an offer of marriage.

She sighed. Perhaps it wasn't the best idea she'd ever had, but at least it was an idea. And if it came to that, she'd figure out how to convince Mama that she was happy. After all, Mama always said that the only thing she really cared about was for Sophie and Rye to be happy.

It would take sacrifice, of course, to pull it off. But for the sake of her mother and her brother, Sophie would do anything.

Two

RYE WAS USING A FRESH SLICE OF TOAST TO MOP UP THE juices from his plate of deviled kidneys when his mother entered the breakfast room. She shook her head when she saw his fingers in his plate, and Rye gave her his most charming grin. "If a man can't eat with his hands at his own table, Mama, where can he? There's a letter in the morning post for you from Lady Brindle."

Lady Ryecroft had opened her mouth to reprove him, but instead she turned to the pile of letters and began shuffling through it. "From Ann Eliza?" She sounded excited.

Rye had cherished a mild hope that the change of subject might distract her, but he was stunned at how well the diversion had worked.

He finished off the kidneys and popped the last bite of toast into his mouth. Even from across the table he could see that Lady Brindle had crossed and recrossed her lines. No wonder his mother was frowning as she worked out that puzzle.

"I know she's one of your oldest friends, Mama," he began finally, "but—"

"Don't use the word *oldest* to a woman of my years, dear," Lady Ryecroft said absently.

"That's a hum. You won't turn forty until next autumn."

She fixed him with a look he had long ago recognized as dangerous. "A *year* from next autumn, if you please, Ryecroft."

"Beg pardon, Mama. As I was saying, I never knew you to be so devoted to Lady Brindle that you would study her letter instead of noticing that poor Carstairs is waiting to pour your coffee."

Lady Ryecroft leaned back in her chair to let the butler fill her cup. "Carstairs, you're so silent and efficient that I had no idea you were there."

Her face was alight with appreciation, and Rye could almost see the butler relax under the warmth of her gaze. It wasn't difficult for Rye to see where Sophie had come by her beauty; their mother must have been a stunner in her day.

The butler smiled, set the coffeepot at her elbow, and took an empty chafing dish with him.

"You are the most complete hand, Mama," Rye said. "You can turn an abject apology into a compliment, and the servants adore you for it."

His mother, who had returned to her letter, made a little noise that might have been agreement.

Rye frowned. That sort of abstraction wasn't at all like her usual behavior. "I wanted to talk to you, Mama."

The pages of her letter rustled. "Oh goodness, Rye—how terrible for Ann Eliza. She has had a fall and sprained her ankle, and she is confined to the house. She would like me to—I'm sorry, dear. What was it you wanted to talk to me about?"

Perhaps she *was* listening after all. "I'm going up to London for a few days. To see my tailor."

It wasn't exactly a lie, for he *would* make sure to see his tailor—perhaps even before he dropped in on Lady Stone. He had let a decorous two weeks go by while he mulled over the advice the old lady had given him at the assembly. Now he felt it was time to act.

So he *wasn't* lying—quite. Still, when his mother's gaze sharpened, Rye felt much as he had as a child when he would put forth some outrageous whopper and hope to heaven she'd believe it. He had to restrain the urge to cross his fingers behind his back.

But all she said was, "When?"

"I thought I'd go today." He tried to make the notion sound careless, casual. "What is it that Lady Brindle wants you to do?"

"Come to stay for a few days, to keep her company while she recovers. She's sending a carriage for me"—she flipped the page over—"Oh, dear, it's to arrive this afternoon."

"In a hurry, isn't she?" But he felt sudden warmth for Lady Brindle. At the least her request should keep his mother too busy to wonder what he might be up to. "No reason you shouldn't go if you want to."

"Of course I shall go. Ann Eliza is my oldest friend."

Rye's jaw dropped. "But when *I* said that, Mama, you nearly bit my head off!"

"Nonsense, dear. I had thought to leave Sophie with you."

Rye was aghast. "With me? But I won't be here."

Lady Ryecroft's lips tightened.

Before she could ask why visiting his tailor couldn't possibly wait a week—a question for which Rye had no sensible answer—he said, "Why shouldn't she go with you, anyway? A little practice of her society manners wouldn't hurt Sophie."

"You being the authority on society manners, of course."

"Well, it's true. And it's not as if Lady Brindle's sprained ankle is contagious. Besides, you wouldn't want to leave Sophie here with me anyway," Rye finished triumphantly. "Not without a real chaperone in charge. As long as James Newstead is hanging around her…"

Lady Ryecroft frowned. "He hasn't asked your permission to address her, has he?"

"No, Mama—you wouldn't have missed out on that, I am persuaded. That's what worries me. If he would come out in the open, I could depress his intentions. But as long as he's only running into her by chance in the village, or when she's out riding, or when she stops by the vicar's to deliver some of Mrs. Carstairs's preserves…"

"James Newstead happened to be visiting the vicar at the same moment Sophie was there?" Lady Ryecroft looked horrified.

"To Sophie's credit, she told me about the encounter herself."

"And you didn't tell me? Rye…"

"She swore it was an accident, and she said she came to me because you would ring a peal over her head even though it wasn't her fault."

"As indeed I would have. As for it being her fault… do you think she planned to meet him?"

Rye didn't. Sophie was too transparent to be as cunning as that. And this was James Newstead after all—not someone she might seriously be interested in. But if it would distract his mother, he'd play along. "Now that I come to think of it, she must have known that her groom would report the incident to me."

"I should think he would if he values his employment. Do you suspect she only confided in you because she knew you'd find out anyway?" Lady Ryecroft didn't wait for an answer. "Very well. I'll take her with me."

She didn't look particularly happy about it, Rye noticed. But he put the niggling thought aside and comforted himself with the notion that whatever was going on with his mother, at least it had kept her from asking uncomfortable questions about his trip to London.

❧

Under other circumstances, Sophie would have enjoyed the drive, for Lady Brindle's carriage was well sprung and luxurious, and the countryside looked different from their usual surroundings at Ryecroft Manor. But it simply wasn't fair that Rye was going to London while she was stuck accompanying Mama to Sussex of all places. She was going to be farther from the city than when she was at home, and Lady Brindle didn't even live in the interesting part of the county.

Worse, it was likely to be a dull week. They weren't going to a house party, where she might at least meet new people. Not that Sophie had ever been to a house party—but she'd heard about them from her friend Emily. It wasn't even an ordinary visit where one might go calling or shopping or be invited to a party or a dance. With Mama's old friend lying upon her couch, they'd all be closed up together in Lady Brindle's house for days on end.

Sophie had only vague memories of a previous stay with Lady Brindle, when she'd been no more than a child. Of course, she'd been stuck in the nursery wing then, with Rye and with Lady Brindle's oaf of a son, but she feared this visit would be little better. She flounced back on the velvet seat.

"That is enough," Lady Ryecroft said. "It won't be as bad as all that."

"I didn't even say anything, Mama."

"You didn't have to, my dear. Your feelings are plain, and it's unladylike to display them so openly. I hope you will have a care not to do so in front of my good friend."

"But it's not fair! I've never been to London, and Rye's gone dozens of times!"

Lady Ryecroft's eyebrows raised. "*Dozens of times* is overstating it; pray do not exaggerate, Sophronia. Besides, patronizing your brother's tailor is not the sort of visit you have in mind, I'm certain, and you could hardly stay at Rye's club."

Sophie bit her tongue. It was useless to discuss the matter with Mama, who was so far past her own London Season that she probably couldn't even remember it.

There was, after all, no real reason Rye couldn't

have taken Sophie along. There would be nothing wrong with her going to the city, even staying at an inn—something Sophie had also never done—if she were traveling with her brother.

She suspected darkly that the truth was that Rye wasn't planning to spend much time with his tailor. When she'd confronted him in his library and begged to be rescued from Lady Brindle's sprained ankle, his expression had made her think he was up to something cagey.

A woman, perhaps. Though heaven knew Rye didn't have money for a highflier... whatever *that* really was. Sophie's friend Emily had overheard the term from one of her brothers, but he'd outright refused to define it more precisely. In fact, Emily said, he had turned red in the face when she'd asked him to elaborate. So Sophie knew better than to ask her mother or Rye for an explanation.

Still, it wasn't hard to deduce that whatever sort of woman a highflier might be, she'd require more money than Rye was likely to have at hand.

Sophie sighed as she caught the sympathetic eye of her mother's maid, who was sitting in the opposite seat, with her back to the horses. Mary glanced from Sophie to Lady Ryecroft, and Sophie tried to turn her sigh into an expression of appreciation instead of annoyance. "This is a nice carriage, isn't it, Mama?"

"Very nice," Lady Ryecroft agreed. "But I believe our journey is coming to an end."

"Truly?" Sophie pulled back the curtain just as the carriage turned into a long, sweeping driveway. At the end of it was the ugliest pile of dark brown brick she'd ever seen. She'd forgotten how frightful Brindle Park was—or perhaps on that years-ago visit she'd been too young to notice.

Sophie's heart sank. Their home might be battered by nearly two centuries of serving the family, followed by more than a decade when there hadn't been much money for repairs, but at least Ryecroft Manor was full of light and air. Brindle Park looked as if it had been built by someone who didn't understand the concept of a window.

No wonder Lady Brindle had fallen down the stairs. It was probably so dark inside that she hadn't been able to see her feet at all!

"Pray, Sophie, do not hang out of the window to stare."

Sophie sank back against the velvet again. The carriage stopped, then rocked as a footman jumped down from his perch, and Sophie could hear the crunch of his steps as he came around to the door.

Lady Ryecroft straightened her hat and took a deep breath. "Sophie—"

A last-minute lecture on manners, no doubt. "Yes, Mama. I'll be good."

The door opened, and the footman lowered the steps. Lady Ryecroft squared her shoulders—almost as if she was bracing herself for an ordeal, Sophie thought. But what would her mother need to gather her strength for?

As soon as Lady Ryecroft had descended, elegantly leaning on the arm of the footman, Sophie gathered her skirt in one hand and followed.

Just as she put her head out of the carriage, a horse

snorted so loudly it seemed his nose was almost against her ear. Startled, Sophie raised her head, knocking her hat on the carriage door and tipping it forward over her eyes. Her foot slipped, and to save herself from falling, she leaped from the top step to the crushed shells of the carriage drive. She landed lightly, pretending not to hear Lady Ryecroft's half-smothered sigh of exasperation—why, pray tell, could Mama sigh, when Sophie wasn't allowed to?—and raised one small gloved hand to push her hat back into place.

The horse snorted again, and she turned toward the sound and looked directly into the gaze of the rider.

He was scowling down at her—dark-faced and fierce-browed. He was obviously a gentleman, judging by the cut of his coat, the carefully arranged neckcloth, and the high polish on his boots. A fairly young gentleman too—not a particularly handsome one, but with an air that said he was used to getting whatever he wanted.

As Sophie watched, his eyes went wide and his jaw slack, as if he couldn't believe what he was seeing. With his rider's attention wandering, the horse side-stepped, and the gentleman tugged the animal back into line. Then he swung down, tossed the reins to a groom who had come running, and tipped his hat to Lady Ryecroft. "My apologies, ladies. I regret that my horse caused you to suffer a fright."

Sophie wanted to snort. What kind of a lily-liver did he think she was, anyway? As if she'd fall into a swoon because a horse made a noise!

The young man didn't take his eyes off her as he came closer. "Surely this can't be Sophie. My mother didn't tell me that you were coming to visit too."

Lady Ryecroft cleared her throat. "Sophie, you remember my dear friend's son, do you not? Lord Randall, Miss Ryecroft." The emphasis on the last two words was gentle but distinct.

Lord Randall looked abashed. "I beg pardon for the informality, ma'am. I was taken straight back to the days of your last visit, when Sophie—Miss Ryecroft, I mean, was—"

"Nothing but a tomfool nuisance of a girl, I believe you called me." Sophie tempered the words with a smile and a tiny curtsy. "But I shall not hold that against you, Lord Randall, if you promise in return to forget just how much of a tomfool nuisance I *was* back then."

He looked dazzled.

Sophie hoped her mother was watching closely. If only Rye could have been there, she thought—for if he could see this performance, he would never again dare to say that her society manners needed polishing. "I hope we find you well, Lord Randall. And how is your mother?"

"Very well indeed. She's somewhere around here, awaiting your arrival." He looked around vaguely. "Let me see you inside."

Lady Ryecroft said, "Don't let us interrupt your ride."

"No, no, that's not important at all now. I mean, I can hardly let our guests wait alone while the servants hunt down my mother." He gestured toward the stairs leading up to the front door, where a butler waited majestically.

"I shouldn't think she'd be at all hard to find, lying on a sofa with her ankle propped up," Sophie said.

Lady Ryecroft winced.

What? Sophie wanted to say. Was she not supposed to say the word *ankle* in front of a gentleman?

"Oh, my mother's never to be found on a sofa," Lord Randall said. "Ten to one, she's somewhere in the gardens. She's been out there for days already because the weather's been so pleasant this spring."

In the gardens?

"But I thought—"

"Sophie," Lady Ryecroft said. "Not now." She put her hand on Randall's arm and let him lead her up the steps.

Sophie dawdled for a moment, thinking. There really were only two possible explanations, she concluded. The first was that Lady Brindle's son was so oblivious that he wasn't aware his mother had suffered an accident—which seemed unlikely.

But the second was that there was no sprained ankle at all, and Lady Ryecroft knew it. Judging by her lack of surprise just now, she must have known it even before they had left home.

So why had Sophie's mother dragged her across half of Surrey and the better part of Sussex in order to visit an injured old friend, if the old friend wasn't injured after all?

❧

Grosvenor Square was lined with houses, and Rye had no idea which one might be Lady Stone's. But no one else on the street seemed to know either. The costermonger selling pies at the corner goggled at him when he asked, and said he'd like to know how he was supposed to know who was whom in the quality—at least, Rye thought that was what he said; he'd had to disentangle the man's Cockney accent. A flower girl walking along the pavement only giggled and offered to sell him a bunch of violets. He gave her a coin and tried in vain to refuse the flowers, but she pressed them into his hand anyway.

So he was holding a tight little handful of blooms when he turned round from talking to the flower girl and almost ran down a lady who had just stepped from a carriage onto the pavement. The violets burst from his hand and sprayed over her, catching in her hair, in the basket she carried, in the dark braid that trimmed her deep blue cloak.

She gave a gasp of annoyance and glared up at him.

"I beg your pardon," Rye said. His gaze swept over her. She was young, though hardly a schoolgirl—twenty perhaps, or even older. She was not dressed like a young lady either. Her hair was caught up in a neat, not-quite-schoolmarmish chignon, under a plain dark chip of a hat—not one of the elaborate creations the young ladies of the *ton* commonly wore. Her gloves were serviceable rather than elegant—tan leather, but not the finest-grained kid. As she brushed at the violets on her shoulder, he saw that the fingertips were worn. Her cloak was fastened with an ordinary frog, not buttoned with gold.

Even more telltale was the fact that her face was not fashionably pale; this woman had been kissed by the sun. There were a couple of freckles on her nose, something that would likely have sent a society miss and her mother into strong hysterics the moment they were noticed.

Rye thought they were charming.

There was a violet caught in her lashes, right at the corner of her eye. She put up a hand to brush it away, and Rye found himself stepping forward. "Let me. It seems to be tangled, and if you pull at it, you might get pollen in your eye."

She stood still as he leaned closer yet. No wonder the flower had caught; he'd never seen lashes so long and full, so curly and so dark. They were a shade darker than her hair—which wasn't simply brown, as he had thought, but a rich mixture of chestnut and honey, glinting in a sudden shaft of sunlight.

For a moment the noises of the square faded away—no costermonger's call, no rattle of carriage wheels—and he was caught up, surrounded by the scent of violets and the brush of his finger against her temple, where the skin was so soft that even through his glove he knew he had never touched anything so fine...

The violet came loose, and he stood holding it and feeling foolish.

"Have you finished?" she said coolly, and Rye realized he had grasped her arm, as if it had been necessary to hold her closely while he plucked at the flower with his other hand.

"What's this, Portia?" said a gravelly voice beside him.

Rye felt as if he'd been drifting away on a slowly ebbing tide until the grating voice jolted him back to the square. Too late, he realized he was standing far too close to the unknown young woman—closer even than if they had been waltzing—and that she hadn't been alone in the carriage after all.

The woman who had followed her was short and spry, with a beady black gaze that rested on him with a familiar glint.

"Lady Stone!" he said. "I… I was just…"

The young woman pursed her lips as if she was anxious to hear his answer. Rye stumbled to a halt.

"Accosting my companion?" Lady Stone said coolly.

Companion. So she was not a friend or a relative, but an employee. It all made sense now. The young woman's plain hat and cloak and the way her hair was styled so as not to draw attention to herself. Even the freckles—they were far more typical on the face of a woman who was expected to go and fetch her employer's parasol rather than being free to twirl her own. A woman who would read aloud the books her employer wished to hear, not those of her own taste. Who would run her employer's errands, not shop for herself.

He let his hand drop to his side and stepped back from the young lady—quickly enough, he hoped, that Lady Stone wouldn't begin to think her companion was at fault and blame the poor girl. *Portia*, Lady Stone had called her. It suited her somehow. But now was not the time to be thinking of that.

Accosting my companion… Lady Stone had sounded almost angry. Was an accident with a bunch of violets about to cause him to lose his one real hope of bettering himself? Sacrificing the only source of help that had been offered to him? Better that, he supposed, than if the companion were to suffer because of his clumsiness. At least he would be no worse off because of their encounter, while her situation might be dire indeed.

"I beg your pardon, Lady Stone," he said. "I was calling to leave my card to let you know that I've arrived in town, when I... encountered... your companion."

"*Encountered?* Is that what you young bucks are calling it these days when you're practically embracing a young woman on the pavement?"

"I assure you, ma'am, I was not—"

"Lady Stone," the companion said quietly. "Nothing happened. The... gentleman... moves very quickly."

It didn't sound to Rye as if she meant it as a compliment.

"Oh, very well. If you say nothing happened, then nothing happened. But be warned, I'm keeping an eye on you, girl." The old woman's gaze raked over Rye, from the hat he had belatedly touched in respect, to the toes of his well-polished Hessians. "I wondered if you'd actually turn up, Ryecroft. But here you are, and looking as impressive in daylight as you were at the assembly. Don't you think so, Portia?"

"Since I did not attend the assembly, ma'am, I am unable to make a comparison. But if you are asking me in the abstract whether the gentleman is attractive, I should have to agree that he makes a passable figure."

What a prim, smug, opinionated, *conceited*... Rye ran out of adjectives.

"There's a facer for you, Ryecroft." Lady Stone made a vague gesture of introduction. "Viscount Ryecroft, Miss Langford."

Rye swept the companion a bow. "I am honored by your regard, Miss Langford." He managed to let only a trace of sarcasm oil his words. But he knew she'd heard the edge in his voice, for she inclined her head and made no comment.

Lady Stone said, "I'll expect you to call tomorrow morning, Ryecroft. Be ready to tell me exactly what you're looking for in a bride. There's no sense in wasting time with girls who haven't enough of a dowry to be acceptable to you. But I think as long as you're not unreasonable, we can fit you up nicely. What do you think, Portia? Summersby's eldest, perhaps?"

"I am unaware of any assets that make Lord Ryecroft eligible—apart from his title. Therefore, I'm sure you are a far better judge of the matter than I could be, ma'am." Miss Langford's tone was almost colorless.

Rye knew she was only doing what a companion did best—agreeing with her employer and deferring to her opinion. Besides, what she said was no more than the truth. How would Miss Langford know anything of his family, his character, his habits, his assets? Yet the words rankled.

"Ryecroft could grab her before the rest of the young bucks have the opportunity," Lady Stone said thoughtfully. "Her coming-out ball is still a couple of weeks away, and as yet she's barely been seen outside Berkeley Square. Or perhaps he'd do better with the Mickelthorpe girl. Hers is not as well-bred a family, of course, but that might be all to the good. It's a much larger step upward for her to become a viscountess than for the Summersby chit, so she'll appreciate it more. And she has an even larger portion, I understand."

"I'm certain she would be honored to be chosen," Miss Langford agreed.

Rye sketched an ironic bow at Lady Stone. Why had he ever thought this was a good idea? *Once I escape from this harpy*, he thought, *I will never set foot near Grosvenor Square again!*

"Come, girl." Lady Stone turned on her heel and marched up the nearest set of steps without bothering to check whether her companion was following.

The younger woman obeyed without so much as a glance at Rye—and without a hint of resentment or irritation. Of course, when her employer issued an order, no matter what the words or the tone, a companion had no option but to comply.

She was half a dozen feet away from him, with one foot already on the lowest step, when Rye said, "Miss Langford." He had no idea why he'd spoken, except that the careless note in the old woman's voice had jolted him.

She paused and half turned to face him, her head tilted to one side. Her foot was still on the step. He noticed how small her foot was and the slenderness of her ankle in the high-buttoned boot.

"I crave your pardon, Miss Langford, for any difficulty this incident might cause with your employer. I hope she does not blame you."

"How kind of you to notice." The irony that laced her voice was deft, almost delicate. "But of course, whether she blames me or not, you'll still call on Lady Stone tomorrow—because she can help you choose the richest heiress."

It wasn't really a question, and he didn't owe her an answer, anyway. Who was she to question his motives or his reasons? But before Rye could even consider explaining, she had reached the top of the stairs, and the door closed firmly behind her.

At least now he knew which house was Lady Stone's.

And tomorrow Lady Stone expected he would come to give her his specifications for a bride. Namely, how much money an heiress must bring with her in order to become the next Viscountess Ryecroft.

Well, Lady Stone would be disappointed—for he would not appear tomorrow.

Except, he reminded himself, there was still Sophie to think of—and his mother—and that left him with no choice but to comply.

Three

LORD RANDALL'S PONDEROUS EFFORTS TO MAKE THEM welcome set Miranda's teeth on edge. She felt easily eighty years old because of the way he tucked her solicitously into a chair and inquired whether she would like a hot brick or a shawl or a tisane to help her recover from the long journey.

The way he treated Sophie, though entirely different, was not much better. He kept apologizing for his horse and assuring Sophie that riding was the best pastime in the world. He even told her that if she would only give a try to a gentle old cob, one his father kept in his stables solely for the use of ladies who had been frightened by equines, she would soon get over this foolish prejudice of hers.

Miranda, keeping a careful eye on Sophie for signs of steam rising from her dainty ears, was pleased to see that her daughter resisted the temptation to set him straight.

Fortunately it was only a few minutes before Lady Brindle bustled in. If Lord Randall had kept it up for another quarter of an hour, Miranda thought, all bets would have been off. Sophie, despite her youth, *might* have been able to hold on to her temper, for she was clearly taking care to be on her best behavior. Miranda was fairly sure she herself would not have. One more offer of a pastille for her headache and she'd have given the young man an aching head of his own.

There was no doubt who the authority was in Lady Brindle's house. Within five minutes of her arrival, Lady Brindle had firmly dispatched Sophie to the guest room that had been set aside for her, in the care of the housekeeper, for a rest—without inquiring whether her young guest felt in need of one.

It was soon clear why she had done so, however. Without Sophie present to hold her son's attention, Lady Brindle was easily able to persuade Lord Randall to resume his interrupted ride. And soon thereafter Miranda and her old friend were settled in the drawing room with a glass of ratafia and a tray of cakes for what Lady Brindle called *a comfortable coze*. Miranda suspected it would be anything but comfortable.

Within moments of picking up her first cake, Lady Brindle said, "Now, Miranda, you must tell me what this is all about. I'm happy to have you visit of course, at any time, but why in heaven's name did you write to ask me to make up some ailment that would require you to come and stay for a few days?"

Miranda sipped her ratafia. It wasn't as though she hadn't anticipated the question or given thought to how to answer it. But she'd forgotten how like a bulldog Ann Eliza could be when there was something she wanted to know.

Perhaps, she thought wryly, she had *wanted* to forget.

"Since when," Ann Eliza persisted, "aren't you free to come and go exactly as you like?"

"When one has children, it's hardly as easy as—"

"Oh pish. It's not as if they're still in the nursery. And you've had years to get used to the situation. That must be one of the best things about being a widow—not having to be accountable to a husband." She sounded almost wistful, and not for the first time Miranda wondered whether Ann Eliza's determination to marry Brindle all those years ago had been such a wise thing. She seemed to have let herself run to seed.

But to an extent, Ann Eliza was right. There was definitely something to be said for the independence that came with being the widowed mother of a son who had achieved his majority and taken on the responsibilities left to him by his father.

If only, Miranda thought, the freedom she enjoyed had included an independent *income*, she would truly be a happy woman!

Ann Eliza hadn't stopped talking. "From everything you've told me, Ryecroft is the best of sons. Why wouldn't he agree for you to visit a friend just because you wanted to do so?"

"I didn't wish him to feel I was trying to avoid my responsibilities."

Ann Eliza looked at her narrowly. "Do you mean by leaving Sophie at home with him as you said you were going to do? Did Ryecroft object to being left in charge of a young lady? Or did you not ask him? Miranda, you must give me leave to tell you that if you've trumped up this visit merely in order to bring your daughter to the attention of my son—"

"I most certainly have not! Ann Eliza, I'm shocked. Why you should think that I would do such a thing… I have *no* desire…" Miranda swallowed the rest of the sentence. *To see my daughter married to your selfish oaf of a son*, she had been starting to say. What in heaven's name was wrong with her tongue today that she'd almost insulted her hostess?

"Because I would have you know that his father and I have made plans for his marriage already," Ann Eliza said firmly. "Summersby's eldest daughter—a considerable heiress in her own right. The money comes from her mother's side of the family, and the house that will be settled on her is only ten miles away from here."

"How convenient," Miranda managed to say.

"Yes, isn't it? Eventually Randall and Flavia will join the two estates."

"Why haven't I heard this happy news before, Ann Eliza?"

"Oh, well, Lady Flavia's only seventeen. She will make her formal come-out in a few weeks, as soon as the Season gets well started. It's only fair for the girl to make her curtsy, after all, and have a bit of fun before settling down. But there's been an understanding for years now between Summersby and Brindle. I expect that by June we'll have a wedding."

"My congratulations."

"Yes, I'm well pleased to have that settled. She's such a biddable girl too—delightfully accommodating. I only wish I had a daughter of my own. Such fun it would be to match her up. After all, there's young Carrisbrooke, right here in the neighborhood. He's not reached marriageable age, of course, but in another year or two, when he reaches his majority—"

"And *his* estate is even closer—and larger—than Lady Flavia's," Miranda put in acidly before her common sense kicked in.

"Yes, just three miles away… and an abbey. It would be so convenient to have my daughter right at hand and to have her be a countess as well. However, there's no sense crying over spilt milk; it wasn't meant to be. But I shall enjoy having a daughter-in-love— helping her set up her household, advising her as to the best way to go about things."

Miranda couldn't help wondering if Ann Eliza's assistance would be as welcome as she expected.

Ann Eliza refilled her glass and selected another cake. "It seems to me you'll have your hands full presenting your Sophie, when the time comes. Surely you're not going to try this year, Miranda? It seems to me that more seasoning would be wise. Of course she's old enough and foolishly pretty—just as you were. But Blackett tells me she's something of a hoyden as well. He said she actually jumped from the carriage."

"I'm surprised your butler thought it necessary to mention that Sophie *slipped* on the carriage step."

"*Jumped*," Ann Eliza went on ruthlessly, "and she practically knocked her hat off as well. My word, Miranda, how you are going to deal with a young miss like that one…"

At least, Miranda thought, Ann Eliza had distracted herself from the original question. "She only slipped because Lord Randall's horse startled her."

"You mean she isn't familiar with horses? I thought

he must be funning when he said that. I never thought a daughter of yours would be anything but a bruising rider."

"She rides very well indeed. Speaking of riding," Miranda added carelessly, "I wonder, Ann Eliza, if you will lend me a mount and a groom. Tomorrow, perhaps? I have a fancy to ride over some of the old paths and revisit the places I knew as a girl."

"By all means. I'll send a message to the head stableman. But your plan sounds like fun, my dear. Perhaps I'll come along. We can take the carriage out and relive our youth together. No?" She laughed. "You looked quite put out for a moment. What are you up to, I wonder, Miranda Ryecroft? Something dodgy, I'll be bound. But as long as you swear on your mother's Bible that you're not trying to match up your ridiculously pretty Sophie with my boy—"

"I swear it," Miranda said. And she had the virtuous reassurance that she was, at that moment, telling the absolute and complete truth.

For a change.

‍☙

Portia took off her outdoor things, neatened her hair, and plucked a wayward violet from under her collar, where it had lodged somehow when that fortune-hunting oaf had almost knocked her into the street.

She had to admit the collision had been only an accident—the sort of thing that could have happened to anyone. But the way he'd let go of her and ducked away the instant he'd realized she was nothing more than a paid companion… now *that* had been intentional.

Insulting, even, because he wouldn't have dropped her arm like a hot coal if she'd been one of the heiresses Lady Stone had promised him. He'd have bowed and scraped and begged her pardon and flattered her...

And you'd have hated it, she reminded herself.

So it was just as well that he knew right up front she was a mere companion. And it was just as well that she knew he was a mere fortune hunter. Because otherwise...

Because otherwise she might have kept believing that eyes as dark and warm and sincere as his were, in that long instant when he'd looked down at her, must belong to a true gentleman. She might have kept thinking about how strong his grasp was when he held her, and how soft his touch had been against her temple as he untangled the violet from her eyelashes, and how his height had made her feel as fragile as a flower...

"A violet, perhaps," Portia jeered at herself. "Just like that bunch he was holding. And look what happened to them—trampled in the street." Except for the one that lay on her dressing table now.

She smiled at her foolishness, dismissed the thought of Viscount Ryecroft, and tapped on the door of Lady Stone's boudoir to ask if her employer would like her to read the next chapter of *Mansfield Park*.

"Not just now," Lady Stone said. "Come and talk to me instead."

Portia took a chair near the chaise where Lady Stone was reclining. "What shall I talk about, ma'am?"

"Whatever is on your mind. Lord Ryecroft, I expect."

"Why would I be thinking about *him*? What inspired you to take him up, anyway?"

Lady Stone shot a shrewd look at her. "Do you think him too young for me?" she simpered.

"I think he'd be too young for your daughter, if you had one," Portia said under her breath.

"I heard that, miss. My ears are as sharp as they ever were."

"Yes, ma'am. Are you certain it's not misplaced maternal instincts that you're feeling?"

Lady Stone gave a rusty laugh. "You might be right. He did seem to treat his mother well, so perhaps I felt envious. At the time, however, I merely thought it might be amusing to have a tame young man around the house."

"The blush having worn off the idea of having a companion?"

"Indeed it has. You've been here all of six weeks, Portia, and you're no longer showing me proper respect. I should turn you off and find someone new."

"No one else would put up with you for six weeks, ma'am. But I still don't understand why Viscount Ryecroft has commanded your attention."

Lady Stone shrugged. "When I met him at that assembly down in Surrey, I felt sorry for him. He's got this huge manor house that's falling to rack and ruin, or so it's said in the neighborhood. In short, he needs to marry an heiress, and a whomping great one too."

"So you decided to be his fairy godmother and introduce him to Summersby's eldest daughter?"

"Not exactly."

"You don't intend him for Summersby's daughter after all?"

"No, I meant I don't fancy myself as a fairy godmother—I wouldn't look at all good prancing around in wings, waving a magic wand. As for Summersby's daughter, her marriage portion may not be large enough to meet his needs. But she would thank me in the end if I did make a match between them."

"Being married solely for her dowry? What an honor that would be."

"Ryecroft's a great deal more interesting than Lord Randall is."

"That," Portia said, "is hardly a challenge. The last climbing boy who came out of the flue in my bedroom was a great deal more interesting than Lord Randall is."

"Portia, my dear, you could make something of him, you know."

"Ryecroft?"

"Certainly not. I told you, *he* needs an heiress. I meant Randall."

"What could I make of him, pray tell? A leather wallet from his thick hide?"

Lady Stone's laugh pealed through the room. "It can't be denied that Randall's a dull stick, though a lively woman could keep him on his toes. But there's sufficient money there and a decent title. True, the estate is in Sussex, but..."

"There are worse places," Portia conceded and regretted her momentary lapse into agreement when she saw Lady Stone's gaze sharpen.

"He's an only son, and there's not even a sister who needs a dowry funded. Besides, once I've peeled away Summersby's daughter, Randall will be ripe for the plucking for a lady who possesses some diplomacy. What do you think?"

"I think, my lady, that you have exceeded the bounds of good taste in matchmaking."

"I'm only trying to make your life easier, my girl, but if you don't appreciate my efforts, I'll move on. If you're positive you don't want Randall—"

"I'm certain."

"Then he can have Summersby's daughter with my blessing. Let's go back to Ryecroft."

"Must we?" Portia muttered.

"There's Juliana Farling."

"She seems sweet. Too sweet to waste on him. I thought you mentioned Miss Mickelthorpe."

"I did. No family connections to speak of, but she'd be moonstruck at the idea of being a viscountess."

"So moonstruck that she wouldn't even mind if Ryecroft had a mad aunt concealed in the attic of that crumbling house of his. Or if he had a previous wife or two who died under mysterious circumstances."

"He's hardly old enough for that."

"Or to be married at all."

"When one has to marry for money, there's nothing to be gained by waiting." Lady Stone waved a dismissive hand. "I want you to write a letter for me."

"Certainly." Portia went to a small writing table in the corner of the boudoir, got out a sheet of Lady Stone's hot-pressed notepaper, and trimmed her pen. After a while she glanced over at her employer, who was staring abstractedly out the window. "It would be helpful, Lady Stone, if I knew to whom the letter should be addressed and what information you wish it to contain."

"You've a pert way with you, miss."

"You knew that when you hired me, ma'am, and you said it suited you right down to the ground."

"And so it does. Mealymouthed young women give me an ague. The letter's to Robert Wellingham. I want him to call on me tomorrow."

"Robert Wellingham? The merchant banker? Why do you—" Portia bit her tongue.

"Because," Lady Stone said blandly, "I find myself in need of financial advice."

"I suppose that means the merchant banker has a daughter?" But instead of waiting for an answer she knew would not be forthcoming, Portia began to write.

❧

Miranda had to admit that Lord Randall was correct about one thing—for late March, the weather was uncommonly fine. When she rode out from Brindle Park the next morning with only a groom in attendance, the air was cool and fresh. She could smell damp earth just coming to life with green spikes that would quickly become daffodils. And she could hear the chatter of birdsong in the newly budded trees.

Escaping from Lady Brindle had not been difficult, for it was clear that Ann Eliza much preferred her carriage to a saddle these days. Escaping from Sophie had been a larger problem. Explaining why she couldn't come along on a simple ride, without raising her suspicions about why Miranda wanted to be alone, had been a challenge.

Sophie had grown up a great deal in the last year. She was no longer a self-centered child, and now the risk was far greater that she would notice and wonder and observe and—unless Miranda was lucky—draw conclusions.

The longer their visit went on, and the more bored Sophie became, the more likely she was to speculate about what her mother was up to. So Miranda's errand had to be done today. In any case, there was nothing to be gained by putting off this all-important interview. The sooner she acted, the sooner Sophie would have her Season.

"'Twere well it were done quickly," she mused, and the groom who was waiting to assist her into the saddle looked at her in puzzlement as he helped her up, then shrugged at the ways of the quality and went to mount his horse, so he could follow at a respectful, protective distance.

Miranda took a wandering, casual sort of path that was, in fact, not casual at all. They rode through the tiny village and forded a river that was almost too small for the name. A few miles from Brindle Park, Miranda slowed her horse's pace and waited for the groom to catch up. "I've lost my bearings," she said innocently. "What's that great house up there?"

"That's Lord Carrisbrooke's estate, that is."

"Is he in residence?"

"Doubtful," the groom said. "The young earl's still at Oxford most of the time. But his uncle's there just now."

I know, Miranda thought. "That would be Mr. Winston?"

"That's the one. Saw him myself at the Blue Boar in the village last night. He sometimes drops in for a pint when he's down from London."

"Very democratic of him."

The groom shot her a look. "P'raps it's the years he spent in America." His tone was flat.

Miranda let the silence draw out, wondering if he would take the opportunity to fill in the other, less savory details about Marcus Winston.

"The men like him," the groom said finally. "The ones from the village *and* from the estate. Any rate, that's Carris Abbey up ahead. There's a nice view from up on the hill if you'd like to see it."

Riding up that hill would get her much closer to her goal, so Miranda clucked to her horse and took the direction the groom had indicated. "The young earl doesn't care if the locals trespass on the abbey's grounds?"

"The young earl's too new to the duties to give much thought to it. It's only been a year since he inherited from his grandfather, and the trustees are in charge till he reaches his majority. But Mr. Winston's one of the trustees, and he don't care."

"I knew him, years ago." Miranda hoped it sounded careless, like an afterthought. "Mr. Winston, I mean. Perhaps... Oh, it's a silly idea, I suppose, only I might not get the chance again. I believe I'll ride up to the house and leave my card."

The groom looked at her askance, but he obviously knew better than to comment.

Miranda felt herself color. It simply wasn't done, of course, for a woman to call on a man socially—even a man she had known from her youth. Only if she had business to take up with him or professional dealings might it perhaps be forgiven. Otherwise she paid her formal calls on a gentleman's wife or mother or sister or hostess, but never directly to a gentleman himself. And never alone, without a friend or maid in attendance.

Ann Eliza had told her, however, that there were no women in residence at Carris Abbey, so there was no one to form a social screen. And in any case, she *did* have business to take up with Marcus Winston.

It just wasn't the sort of business she wanted anyone, except for herself and Marcus Winston, to know about.

Four

SOPHIE KNEW THAT A REAL LADY WOULDN'T ALLOW herself to droop over the breakfast table, but she was entirely alone. Even the butler had gone about his duties after refilling the warming dishes with food Sophie had no intention of eating. Lady Brindle was already in her garden, and Lord Randall had not yet come downstairs.

What a slug-a-bed he was—though on second thought, Sophie decided it was just as well; if he'd been breakfasting with her, he'd probably have been prosing on again about why she should really learn not to be afraid of horses. She'd told him twice that she wasn't, but he hadn't listened.

But Sophie's biggest aggravation was that her mother had gone out for a cross-country ride by herself, even though Sophie had begged to go along. *But I'd like to see where you used to go as a girl,* she'd said—and she hadn't been entirely untruthful, even if her more important reason was simply to escape the dark pile of brick that was Brindle Park.

However, Lady Ryecroft had said only that perhaps

tomorrow she could go, and briskly—before Sophie could scramble to find another line of argument—she had gathered the train of her black riding habit over her arm and gone out.

There had been something distinctly havey-cavey about her mother this morning. Sophie was still mulling over the way Lady Ryecroft hadn't met her gaze when Lord Randall exclaimed from the threshold, "Miss Ryecroft! What a sad thing that I find you here alone!"

Finally, Sophie thought, *he's said something I can agree with.* "Good morning, Lord Randall. I was just finishing, I'm afraid." She crumbled her last bite of toast.

"What a pity it is that you do not know how to ride," he observed as he filled his plate. "I myself stay to break my fast only because my mother insists I eat before I go out."

"If you're offering a lesson, I am pleased to accept."

He seemed taken aback. "Well… I… I suppose…"

Before he could weasel out of it—and cost her a ride she sorely coveted—Sophie barreled on. "Lord Randall, you have convinced me of two things—the need for a lady to ride well and your skill in teaching. I am most happy to accept your generous offer, and I'm certain that by the time you finish your breakfast, I shall have returned, ready to undertake a lesson." And before he could do more than stammer, she had left the room.

She was still trying not to laugh—half in glee at the look on his face, half in satisfaction that, all going well, she would be out in the open air for an hour or two—when she reached her bedroom and startled the pert little housemaid who was tidying up.

At least, that was no doubt what the girl was supposed to be doing. In fact, she was holding Sophie's favorite silk dressing gown and rubbing her cheek gently against the fine fabric. She caught sight of Sophie in the mirror and jerked to attention. "Oh, miss. I'm that sorry, truly I am. I was putting your wrap away and… and…"

"And you were overcome by temptation," Sophie agreed easily. "It feels wonderful, doesn't it? Let's make a bargain. Help me into my habit as quickly as we can manage, and you can stay and touch whatever you like."

The girl's eyes rounded. "You don't wish to wait for your maid?"

"I do *not*." Mary would fret and scold and remind her that her mother must have had a good reason not to take her riding, and if Lady Ryecroft didn't approve of her going out…Well, Lady Ryecroft couldn't be consulted at the moment, and Sophie was in no mood to sit in a dark and dismal morning room and wait for her to come back. Not when it was perfectly acceptable according to anyone's society rules to ride out with her hostess's son.

The housemaid's hands shook with nervousness as she buttoned Sophie's riding habit. "Oh, miss—I've never felt such fine wool. You have lovely things."

It was odd, Sophie thought, that until recently, she hadn't wondered how Lady Ryecroft had managed to eke out a respectable wardrobe for each of them from nothing more than her housekeeping money. "Nice, yes—but nothing next to what a girl needs for her first Season."

"Will you be on your way to London soon, then?

Lord Randall will be there, and Lady Brindle plans to spend the Season in the city this year too. Her maid has already started packing, and they go in a few days, I believe."

Sophie paused, her fingers frozen on the brim of her hat. Then she finished adjusting it to show off her curls to best advantage and reached for her gloves and crop. "Perhaps."

Lord Randall is going this year... Why hadn't it occurred to her that he was of an age to look for a wife? Despite his pompous attitudes, perhaps he was worth a little attention after all. She wouldn't be the first young lady to subtly encourage a suitor—and if Lord Randall *was* looking around for a bride, why shouldn't he look at Sophie and perhaps make a decision before he ever got to London?

He was an only son who would inherit a sizable estate... sizable enough, perhaps, to lend a hand to assist Rye with Ryecroft Manor. And his mother and her mother were already bosom friends. It was perfect.

She pushed aside the thought of having to listen to his prosing ways day after day and made up her mind to be congenial, charming, and captivating. And, as she ran lightly down the stairs to join him, Sophie decided that her first action—if the choice were ever hers— would be to rip down this dark and dingy pile of brick and build something light and fresh and airy in its place.

❧

The footman who opened the huge and creaking door at Carris Abbey looked startled to see a woman alone, but he quickly composed his face as Miranda pulled a folded sheet of paper from her sleeve and held it out. "Please see that Mr. Winston receives this immediately," she said. "I'll wait for an answer."

She could almost see the thoughts clicking in his head, but a moment later he stepped back from the door. "If Madam would care to come in…"

He showed her to a small reception room which was chilly despite the coals burning merrily in the grate, and disappeared. Miranda held her hands out to the fire and noted that her fingers trembled. Now that it was too late to back out, she was so nervous that her stomach was turning flips.

Think of Sophie, she told herself. *Think of Rye*.

What she wouldn't allow herself to think of just now was that message—how long it had taken her to compose it and how many sheets of hot-pressed paper she'd wasted and how much she now wished she hadn't sent it off with the footman.

If she left right now, slipping quietly away to the front door and letting herself out…

But she had sent the groom around to the stables with the horses, not only so he wouldn't be able to overhear, but because she'd had no idea how long she would be inside and didn't want to keep the animals standing in the chilly air. She could hardly go chasing after him. Besides, the abbey was huge—it could be half a mile or more to walk from the front door all the way around the far wing and the stables.

A step sounded in the passage. *Not the footman*, she thought and tensed. But it wasn't Marcus either. Instead a butler, stiff and correct in a black morning coat, came into the room. "Mr. Winston will see you," he said and stood aside to guide her down a long hall to a big square library at the back of the house.

Then she was inside, and the butler was closing the door as he went out.

A man rose from behind a desk that seemed the size of a cricket field. Miranda stopped dead on the carpet halfway across the room, as if she'd run into a glass wall.

Marcus Winston had been an uncommonly handsome young man—but maturity, she thought, suited him even better. When he was eighteen, he'd been almost too good-looking, with the classically perfect features of generations of Carrisbrookes mingled with the dark, exotic beauty of the woman who had been his mother. It had seemed that fortune, while cheating Marcus of a father's name—for his mother had not been the wife of the earl when her son was born—had tried to make up for it by giving him every other advantage.

Now, however, he was thirty-nine. The Carrisbrooke nose no longer looked too perfect to be real; his shoulders were broader, and he was taller than he'd been in her memory. But his hair was just as dark and, she suspected, just as inclined to wave if he would let it grow long enough. Though she had found him behind a desk, there was an air of energy about him. He seemed to have alighted there only because he was required to do so. He seemed more a creature of the outdoors, where he could act and move and breathe freely.

"Miranda," he said. His accent had shifted ever so slightly. Perhaps the years he'd spent in America had added an extra note to what had always been an extraordinarily deep and rich voice. "Lady Ryecroft, I should say. To what do I owe this pleasure?"

The spell was broken, and she went forward, offering her gloved hand. "I am visiting my friend Lady Brindle—you remember Ann Eliza, of course?"

He bowed over her hand. "Of course." There was a faint note of irony in his voice. "She must approve of me more now than she did when we were children, if she too has come to visit me." He looked past her, as if expecting to see Lady Brindle in the doorway.

Damn the man—even as a youngster he'd been acute to every hidden meaning, to every half-truth, and particularly, to every hint of a slight. But then, he'd had reason. From the time he'd come to the abbey at the age of ten, he'd been passed off as a sort of undefined cousin who was being housed and educated by the sixth Earl of Carrisbrooke because the nobleman had a generous heart. But the entire county had known the truth—that Marcus was, in fact, the unacknowledged son of the earl by one of his many flirts.

While Marcus's half brother, the legitimate heir, was referred to as *my lord*, Marcus himself was allowed the benefit of the Winston name only because it was impossible to deny the family resemblance. And there were so many branches of the Winston family that it was easy enough to lose one nondescript twig on the tree…

"She was unable to accompany me this morning," Miranda said. "I came only because I was riding past and I did not want to let slip the opportunity to pay my respects, in case you were departing again soon."

"Unable?" he said softly. "Or unwilling? Or does

she have no idea you're here? I'm willing to wager the latter, my dear. You've come without a companion or a maid, to see me. I must wonder why."

The butler came in with a tray, and Miranda moved aside to stare at a stack of books on a nearby table so she could keep her back turned until he departed again.

As the door closed behind the servant, Marcus said, "Come and have some tea and bread and butter. Or"—she heard the splash of liquid against crystal and turned to see him holding a goblet full of deep red wine—"would you prefer to join me?"

She reached out for the goblet.

His eyes darkened; Miranda suspected he was feeling satisfaction. "Sit down," he said, gesturing to a settee, "and tell me what you want."

Her throat was so dry that the wine seemed to stick as she swallowed. She settled on the little sofa, perching on the edge of the cushion. He took the seat beside her, turning to face her, his big hand cupping his wineglass.

"You spent a long time in America," she said.

He shrugged. "There was nothing for me here. An illegitimate son has no expectations."

Was there just the faintest note of bitterness in his voice?

"The newspapers say you made good there."

His eyebrow quirked. "I did well enough, as it happens."

Miranda felt incredibly clumsy—but there was no tactful way to ask the question, so she might as well be direct. "Well enough to be in a position to lend me money?"

He sipped his wine, and for a long moment she thought he wasn't going to answer. Finally he said, "So I was right all those years ago, when I told you that you were a fool to marry Henry."

She didn't look up, but her voice was firm. "No, you were *not* right. I have my children, and not for the world would I give them up."

"Your children. Yes. An heir and a spare, I believe?"

"A son and a daughter. It is only for them that I ask."

He sprang to his feet with a sort of coiled energy that almost frightened her, and strode across the room to refill his glass from the decanter on the corner of the big desk. "So you come to me for funds because their father was improvident. How ironic, Miranda. My apologies—Lady Ryecroft."

"Please, Marcus. It's been a long time ago. Henry died when Sophie was barely a year old and Rye was only three."

"I wrote you with my condolences when I heard. You didn't answer."

She bent her head. "I should have done, I know."

"I asked you to come to me then." There was an edge to his voice.

"But how could I, Marcus? I had my son's heritage to think of. I couldn't simply take him away from all that."

"A heritage of entailed land, mortgaged houses, and debts acquired to keep up appearances for society. Yes—what a heritage it is, the way our English nobility lives."

"It wasn't entirely my husband's fault," Miranda said. Then she shook her head. "It hardly matters now how the situation arose."

"But it is dire, or you would not be here. I suppose your son has asked you to come to me for a loan?"

"Of course he hasn't," she flared. "Rye has no notion I'm here. He's in London just now, and he thinks I'm simply visiting Ann Eliza. He would never agree to let me..." Her voice trailed off.

"Ask for money from the illegitimate son of a peer?"

"Ask for money from an old friend," Miranda finished. She turned the goblet between her fingers, watching the dregs of the wine swirl against the cut crystal.

"Why do you need the money?"

She swallowed hard. "My daughter is soon to be nineteen."

His gaze rested on her face, dark and unreadable. "Does she look like you?"

"She is said to."

"A beauty, then." His tone was careless, the observation offhand.

It was apparent, Miranda told herself sternly, that he hadn't intended to flatter her. So there was no reason for her to be flushing like a schoolgirl at the mere possibility he might still think her attractive. "I want to take her to London."

"So she can make a good marriage."

Someone who didn't know him well might have thought the wry twist in his voice was humor. Miranda knew better.

"To someone just like her father." Now there was no doubt he was being sarcastic.

She felt herself flush with embarrassment and with fury—not so much at him as at herself. She hadn't anticipated how her request would sound to him—as if she thought he was good enough to pay for a come-out, even though someone with his background would never be considered eligible to marry her daughter.

Any more than he'd been eligible to marry Miranda herself.

"Except, no doubt, you'll be looking for someone who's wealthier than Henry was," Marcus mused, "now that you're more experienced in the realities of life."

She wanted to deny it, but her innate honesty wouldn't allow her to do so. She clenched her hand tightly under the concealing folds of her habit and stayed still. He would never be convinced she wasn't aiming to sell her daughter to the highest bidder. He wouldn't believe that while she *did* want more for Sophie than she had achieved for herself—a great deal more, in fact—she was not thinking of material things, only of giving Sophie the widest possible opportunity to find a man who suited her.

The silence dragged. Miranda counted the ticks of the tall-case clock in the corner of the library and wondered if he would speak again or simply throw her out.

Finally Marcus said, "What security do you offer that the loan will be repaid?"

She looked up at him in shock. "You'll do it?"

"I haven't agreed to anything yet. I'm merely taking a sensible approach to the question, as any good businessman would. You must admit, if nothing else, that I *am* a good businessman, or I wouldn't have the funds at my disposal to make such a loan. A London Season does not come cheaply."

Miranda hesitated. "It's only... She *is* a lovely girl and a delightful one. If I can simply show her off in London..."

"You're making things worse, Miranda. Stick to business. If you have no resources to pay for this endeavor yourself, then what assurance do I have that you will be able to repay the loan after the Season ends? Will you, for instance, ask your daughter's husband to include the necessary funds in the marriage settlements?"

"I..." She stumbled to a halt.

"Or hadn't you thought that far ahead? You considered, perhaps, that I would think it so flattering to be tapped for this honor that I wouldn't require repayment?"

Miranda felt something snap inside her. She had hoped it wouldn't come to this—that the bonds of long-ago friendship would be enough to persuade him. But there seemed to be no option left. "I have nothing," she said flatly. "Except... Once upon a time you wanted me, Marcus. Give me the funds to provide my daughter with her chance, and..."

"And...?" he asked softly.

She looked into the chasm that waited for her, and closed her eyes to take the leap. "And I'll be your mistress."

⤳

On the following morning, Rye presented himself at Lady Stone's door as ordered. The butler, without comment, led him up the first set of stairs and into a drawing room that overlooked the corner of Grosvenor Square. "I will tell Lady Stone you have arrived," the butler said grandly and departed, closing the door.

The drawing room was surprisingly light and airy—not at all the sort of crowded, cramped, and overheated space he had expected Lady Stone to prefer—and he looked around with satisfaction at the pale-blue-and-cream furnishings.

Until he saw someone move. Miss Langford had been sitting quietly on a damask-covered sofa in front of one of the twin fireplaces. She was wearing a dusty shade of green, with some sort of tapestry thing spread across her lap.

She laid down her needlework and said, "So you did come back, just as I predicted you would." She added, just a little too late to be respectful, "My lord."

"I considered not returning, Miss Langford, but I found the idea insupportable."

"You mean you could not support the thought of seeking out an heiress on your own?"

"No. The thought of never again hearing the dulcet tones of your being rude to me was more than I could bear." Rye suspected she had to bite her lip to keep from smiling, and suddenly he longed to say something so amusing that she wouldn't be able to help herself.

He asked, with honest curiosity, "Why is it, Miss Langford, that you dislike me so much? I am certain we have never met before yesterday. What have I done to annoy you so greatly?"

"It is not personal, Lord Ryecroft. I simply don't appreciate men of your type."

"Ah. *My type*. You are referring, I suppose, to tall, handsome, titled gentlemen?"

"You're tall and titled at least," she said. "But... no."

"Sadly, then, you must be referring to fortune hunters."

"Indeed I am. Though, Lady Stone aside, it's rare to meet with such plain speaking when discussing the subject. Most gentlemen who seek wealthy brides prefer not to admit it. They are devious instead, denying their real motivations while pretending to be in love."

"I see no point in attempting to conceal a fact that must be self-evident to all of society, Miss Langford, and no shame in admitting the truth. I *am* a fortune hunter. There are, I believe, a number of us."

He had startled her; that was clear. Her eyes were wide and her face less guarded than he had seen it before. It made her far prettier somehow—as well as softer and more approachable. Not that he wanted to approach her. He swallowed the odd tickle in his throat.

"But will you make your reasons for marriage clear to the young woman you eventually choose?" she challenged. "Or will you dazzle her into thinking you care about her instead of only her wealth, until you are wed and it is too late for her to escape?"

"I believe it will be possible to choose a person I can learn to care for."

"With her marriage portion as nothing but a welcome bonus?" She dismissed that possibility with a firm shake of the head. Her hair shimmered in the firelight.

"There must be a reason you so dislike fortune hunters, Miss Langford. Do you have a friend, perhaps, who was pursued for her money, not for herself?"

"How perceptive of you to think it, my lord." She bent her head to her needlework once more, and her voice grew soft. "While I was at school, there was a young woman… Her father had gone out to the West Indies to work in the sugar industry. Just after she left school and went to live with an aunt, her father died. Soon a careless comment from her aunt caused a rumor to spread—unknown to the young woman herself—that she was an heiress. She thought the young gentleman who said such pretty things to her was telling the truth about his growing attachment for her, until his mother came to make a formal call and asked straight out what her financial circumstances were."

"And when the facts were revealed, the young gentleman broke off his attachment?"

"When she told him her father had been a book-keeper on the sugar plantation, he made an excuse—and she never heard from him again."

"How fortunate," Rye said.

"That he discovered the truth, you mean, before he had committed himself to her?"

"No. She was lucky to have discovered he was no gentleman before she had committed herself to him."

"True enough, though it was hardly an adequate consolation for being duped. We shall see, whether you will do better." She set another stitch and held the tapestry up to study the effect. Though the bits of gold thread caught the light, they paled beside the gleam of her hair.

He tore his gaze from her and glanced around the room. "Lady Stone seems to have been delayed."

"She has not yet come downstairs this morning. Is

finding your heiress so crucial that it could not wait until after breakfast?"

She was obviously regretting the momentary lapse in control that had made her confide that sad little story about her friend. Now she was back to being prickly Miss Langford... but the sharper she was, the easier it was for him to remember this woman was nothing like the one he was searching for.

"You may recall that your employer didn't specify a time—and I did not wish to be rude by keeping her waiting. Shall I come back later, or stay and let you sharpen your claws on me until she appears?"

"She always breakfasts in her room, and I expect she will be down before long. I asked you a question, my lord. Is finding an heiress truly so important to you?"

This time she sounded as if she really wanted to know. A polite inquiry from her made a nice change, Rye thought. "I'm afraid it is. In my defense, however, I should point out that my mother relies on me to provide for her future, and my sister is of a marriageable age and must make her curtsy no later than next year."

"Then seek employment, my lord." Her tone was crisp.

"I *have* employment, Miss Langford. More than three hundred people connected with my estate depend on me."

"How selfless of you to take such pains to care for them. What a sacrifice it must be for you to have to marry a wealthy woman."

So much for politeness. And a snap of the fingers for the idea of wanting to make her smile. Why had such a nonsensical notion even crossed his mind? "And I suppose if a wealthy man offered for you, Miss Langford, you would reject him out of hand simply because his pockets were too plump?"

"Of course not."

"Then what is the difference between you and me?"

"I am not trying to marry a wealthy man, my lord. Or, indeed, any man at all."

"Probably wise of you," Rye said.

Her gaze lifted to his for a moment, and he saw turbulence in her big hazel eyes—why had he not noticed how fine her eyes were yesterday? Was it only because he'd been so caught up in untangling those long, curly lashes? Something made him take a step closer to the sofa where she sat, but she merely picked up her needlework again.

"If I *were* trying to marry," she said gently, "and if any man at all would suit my purpose, the only thing I would have to do is call out for the butler right now. By the time Padgett arrived, I could muss my hair and undo the top buttons of my dress—and no matter how much you protested your innocence, my lord, the evidence would say otherwise."

Rye could almost feel his face going pale. If Lady Stone believed her companion had been compromised, she would insist that he instantly come up to scratch.

Marrying an heiress was one thing; at least it would still be his choice of whether to make an offer and when and to whom. But the possibility of being forced into marrying a termagant like Portia Langford was another thing entirely.

He didn't realize he'd taken yet another step toward

her until she held out her palm to warn him off. "No, my lord, do not threaten me—you need have no fear for your reputation. I was merely having fun at your expense by pointing out the threat. I have no wish to be trapped in a scheme like that"—her gaze swept over him as if she was taking stock, before she finished levelly—"with a man who has nothing to recommend him but his title."

Relief surged through him, mixed with a good dose of aggravation. He'd *never* threatened a woman... though he had to admit if there was one who could drive him that far, it was likely to be Portia Langford. She had the tongue of an adder—making it sound as if he was the last man on earth who could possibly interest her.

Not that he cared what she thought.

She rethreaded her needle with a different shade of wool. "Still, it's a trick you might wish to remember, my lord. If the heiress you choose is not agreeable to your suit, you could always manage to trap her in a room alone with you and arrange to be discovered by her mama."

"I'll keep that in mind." He went to the farthest corner of the drawing room to stand by the window, pretending to study the traffic down on the square. But even though his back was turned, he could feel her there. He could sense the movement of her hands as she plied the needle in fine, small, rhythmic motions. He could almost feel the cool touch of her fingertips—as though his skin were the canvas she was so carefully stitching.

Nothing to recommend him, hmm? He had half a notion to go over there and show her it wasn't just his title he could offer to a woman. It might be satisfying to kiss her senseless, to make her incapable of speaking, to leave her panting for his touch. To turn the stiff and upright Miss Langford into a puddle of femininity who would beg him not to stop…

It wasn't until the door opened and Lady Stone rustled in that Rye realized he had started across the room to act on the impulse. He cleared his throat and thanked heaven that she hadn't waited another two minutes to make her entrance.

Lady Stone ignored Miss Langford altogether and crossed directly to Rye, offering her hand. He bowed over it and apologized for being early.

She gave a rusty laugh. "Not at all, Ryecroft. Your eagerness to get started makes me feel important. Come and sit down, and let's discuss our strategy. For one thing we will need to consider how to play down your weak points and build on your strong ones."

Rye thought he heard a murmured "if he *has* any strong points," from Miss Langford.

"Perhaps," Rye said, "we should excuse Miss Langford from this discussion, since she does not appear likely to enjoy it."

"Oh, I'll enjoy hearing about your weaknesses. Would you like me to keep a detailed list as you uncover them, ma'am?"

Lady Stone had gone straight on. "Heiresses can be temperamental sorts, so we also need to plan out how best for you to approach them. If you're aloof, they will pay no attention at all. Yet you must not appear too eager, for nothing makes a girl less interested than a gentleman who presents no challenge. And you must not be too particular to any one of them until you've definitely made up your mind and are certain your offer will be accepted."

There was a small, genteel sniff from the direction of the sofa.

But Lady Stone seemed to have heard nothing. "You face troubling competition this year as well. It's too bad you didn't come up last Season, Ryecroft."

"He must still have been with his tutor then, ma'am."

Rye told himself to ignore her, but with no effect. "It is true that last Season I had not yet reached my majority, Miss Langford, but the lessons to which I have applied myself in the past year are those of estate management."

"No one could have outshone you." Lady Stone sighed. "I vow, every bachelor on the Marriage Market last year had a cast in one eye or needed corsets or couldn't dance a step."

"While this year, there's the Earl of Whitfield." Miss Langford ticked off points on her fingers. "Good family, young, nice looking, a respectable estate, and just back from Italy, so he's got an air of romance about him."

"Yes," Lady Stone said gloomily. "All the girls will be after him."

"And there's Swindon as well," Miss Langford went on with an appreciative-sounding sigh. "He's a great deal older than Whitfield, but I understand he's declared his intention to set up his nursery at last. Don't you agree, Lady Stone, that there's something about a rake that is irresistible to young women?"

Rye couldn't stop himself. "Including you, Miss Langford?"

"Certainly," Miss Langford said calmly.

"Then I won't fret about *him*, since your attractions will no doubt keep him too fully occupied to notice any young woman I might be interested in."

To his regret, she refused to be drawn. "It is not I whose help you need in order to draw off the competition, my lord. The answer to your difficulty is plain."

It might be plain to her, Rye thought, but there was no understanding the logic of the woman. He let his gaze linger on the way her neck curved as she bent over her tapestry once more. "I must beg you to clarify."

"I recommend you consider your sister."

"Sophie?" Rye said warily. "What about her?"

"Lady Stone has said she is beautiful. And you told me she is of a marriageable age."

"True enough, on both counts. She's eighteen. But I don't see…"

"Bring her out now instead of waiting till next year. If she is indeed as lovely as Lady Stone believes, she will command the full attention of every gentleman who comes near her."

Lady Stone began to laugh. "I see what you're up to, miss. All the other girls, seeing every man in London jostling for position round the Beauty…"

"…will naturally turn to the *only* male on the Marriage Market who cannot possibly be in love with Miss Ryecroft or interested in making her an offer," Miss Langford said.

"Her brother! Portia, I vow you're a prodigy. That's the ticket, Ryecroft. Go home right now and fetch your sister."

"My lady…" The confession that he couldn't stand the nonsense wasn't going to come easy—especially not under Miss Langford's cool, judgmental gaze.

"Oh, I know," Lady Stone said with a wave of her hand. "You haven't a town house, and it's too late now to go looking for one to rent. All the really good addresses have been bespoken already, and the few that are left will command a king's ransom. It doesn't signify. Bring her to me, and Miss Ryecroft can make her debut from Grosvenor Square. Oh, Portia, my sweet—what fun we're going to have this Season!"

Five

MIRANDA THOUGHT FOR AN INSTANT THAT EVEN THE tall-case clock had paused in shock at her offer. But no, time had simply drawn out endlessly as Marcus looked at her and as her words seemed to echo in the still air of the library.

Give me the funds to provide my daughter with her chance, and I'll be your mistress...

Marcus took her goblet from her hand and set it down on the small table beside the settee. He turned toward her, his fingertips warmly cupping her chin and lifting it so he could look directly into her face. His eyes were so dark that she could barely see the difference between pupil and iris and so intent that her breath caught painfully in her chest.

Slowly, he bent closer. She could feel the heat of his skin burning away the air that separated them. His lips brushed the corner of her mouth almost tentatively, as if he expected that she would move away or protest. But she stayed still.

His hands slid over her shoulders and eased her back against the velvet cushions of the settee. He leaned over her, nibbling at her mouth. The tip of his tongue slowly traced the lines of her lips, exploring as carefully as if he were the first to see a new continent and needed to notice and remember every instant.

She could feel her heartbeat in her throat and in her ears. She was having trouble breathing, so she opened her mouth slightly. Instantly, he deepened the kiss, his tongue slipping easily between her lips. She could taste the wine on him, and the sensation shot straight to her head, making her dizzy and weak in a way the wine she had drunk would never have done.

She sighed, and his mouth grew more demanding, while his hands moved from her shoulders down the front of her riding habit, until he cupped her breasts. Even through the fine wool, her nipples peaked eagerly at the circling brush of his thumbs, and she arched her back, pressing into his palms. Heat seeped from her breasts down her body, pooling between her legs, an embarrassing, warm rush of desire. She shifted, trying to ease the pressure, and he whispered against her lips, "This is what I wanted to do all those years ago, Miranda."

She nestled closer to him, and he eased her down farther on the settee, using his knee to nudge her legs apart. Her fingers spread across the hard plane of his back, urging him closer and closer yet, until her body was cradling his in a mimicry of the act of love. Only a few layers of cloth held them apart, and even those seemed to vanish as he pressed against her. She wasn't certain if the heat she felt came from his body or her own, but she was melting, desperate, hungry for him to possess her, to supply what she was missing…

Her skirt seemed to be dreadfully in the way. She tugged fitfully at it.

Against her lips, Marcus whispered, "I deeply regret that I must refuse your very flattering offer."

For a moment she didn't even take in what he had said. Then it hit her with the force of a hammer blow. *Refuse?* When he was lying on top of her, practically making love to her already? When his erection was jutting proudly—insistently—against her?

Her voice was husky. "This jest isn't funny, Marcus."

"I was not trying to amuse."

Suddenly she was free. His weight was gone, her hands were empty, and she lay sprawled across the settee alone. She blinked up at him in confusion. "Marcus?"

"I find myself unable to take advantage of your offer, Lady Ryecroft."

"But why?" She struggled to sit upright. She felt disheveled, so mussed that she suspected she might never feel neat again. "Don't tell me you're being self-righteous and moral! You're hardly a primer of good behavior—you've had mistresses."

"I have," he said levelly. "A fair number of them."

"And they've been all kinds of women too, or so the gossip says. Beauties and bluestockings, widows and wives…"

He rose and went to refill his glass. "Only *unhappy* wives."

"But all Americans, were they not?"

"It has to do with living there all those years, you see."

He was laughing at her. Miranda gritted her teeth

and plunged on, "So why not revenge yourself on the society that has turned a cold shoulder to you and refuses to admit you?"

"By taking one of their own as my mistress? It's an interesting bargain, I must admit. I could complete my collection." Then he shook his head. "But no. It wouldn't do."

"Why not? Because I've grown too old to interest you?" She knew she sounded bitter, but she didn't care any longer. She had gambled and lost. What did it matter, now, what he thought of her?

"Oh no. You're hardly old, my dear. And you do interest me—quite a lot, in fact. I thought that much would be obvious to a woman of your… experience."

Of course it was obvious, she thought irritably. He had, after all, been pressed against her so intimately that if it had not been for a couple of layers of fabric they'd have been lovers already. She had felt the size and the heat of his erection against her. And even now, as he stood there leaning negligently against the corner of the mantel, she could see the telltale bulge in his pantaloons that said he was anything but indifferent. "Then what's the problem?"

"You're proposing to be my mistress for pay. There's a name for that, though it's not a pretty one, I'm afraid."

Miranda closed her eyes in pain.

"I don't buy favors from women, Miranda. I only make love to the ones who want me as much as I want them, without money added into the equation. So I must decline your bargain."

That was it, then. All that was left to her was her

dignity—and there was precious little of that. She stood, shaking her skirts back into place. "Then I must ask you to ring for the butler to show me out, and to summon my groom."

He gave a tug to the bellpull. "It's been entertaining, Miranda, as well as educational." She was already on her way to the door when he added, "I look forward to our affair, my dear."

She stopped and wheeled to face him. "But you said we aren't going to have an affair."

"I merely said I wouldn't pay you for your favors. But we will make love, Miranda. You will be my mistress on my terms, not yours." He paused just inches from her and brushed his thumb lightly but possessively across her lower lip. "Because you want me as much as I want you."

❧

Lord Randall politely suggested that Sophie wait outside the stables for a suitable horse to be brought to her rather than take the risk of another fright by getting too close to the beasts.

Instead Sophie marched into the stables to run a practiced eye up and down the big old cob that was being saddled for her. "I'm sure you're sweet," she murmured to the animal, holding out a carrot in her palm, "but I outgrew hobbyhorses years ago, and now I prefer something with more spirit. Like… that one." She pointed at a nearby stall, where a dainty gray mare with four white feet and a blaze on her forehead tossed her head and nickered.

Lord Randall remonstrated. Sophie strolled into the

mare's stall to feed her a carrot, while she pretended to listen to him. By the time the second carrot was gone, she and the mare were fast friends.

"She is a bad choice for a rider who's afraid of horses," Lord Randall said firmly.

Sophie smiled at him. "But just look at how perfectly her gray coat sets off the powder blue of my habit. We'll make a nice picture together."

He sputtered. "Color? You chose her because of her *color*? That's by far the liveliest mare in the stable!"

The head stableman cleared his throat. "Beg pardon, sir, but it do seem that the young miss knows what she's doing, handling horses as she does. And while Moondust is frisky, she's not a bad actor."

"Thank you," Sophie told him. "I can saddle her myself if you wish—and then it's not your responsibility at all." Her smile at the nearest stablehand was just as effective as it was on other men, however, and even before Lord Randall had finished his lecture, the groom had led the mare to the mounting block and Sophie was springing up into the saddle.

Lord Randall looked horrified. He scrambled onto his own mount and followed, rattling away about how she should have more sense. By the time they had crossed the carriage drive and threaded through a copse of lime trees, however, he was nodding and smiling.

Clearly, demonstration was far more effective than argument where Lord Randall was concerned. She filed that bit of information away for future reference, patted the mare on the neck, and pulled up at the edge of a recently mowed meadow, unsure which direction to turn.

"Wonderful sense of humor you have," Lord Randall called as he rode up. "You had me convinced for a while that you were afraid of horses. What a jester you are, young lady, but you must be careful that people don't take you seriously!"

"Yes," Sophie said, her eyes downcast in what she hoped looked like modesty. "Levity is something my mother frequently warns me about."

"We'll ride down toward the river, to the village," Lord Randall said and pointed with his crop.

Brindle Park sat on the brow of a hill. The view was the best part of the entire estate, with a sweeping vista spreading out before her. She touched the mare with her heel and fell in beside Lord Randall, riding down the long slope toward a glint of water in the distance, where a river made a lazy turn. Houses nestled into a group in the little valley, surrounding a small stone church. Far on the other side of the river, halfway up another hill, a huge old stone block of a house nestled into a grove.

Sophie noted that once he was in the saddle, Lord Randall was a reasonably good horseman, with solid form and light hands. His assessment of the mare called Moondust was accurate too—or else he had listened more closely to the head stableman than he had to Sophie. Moondust *was* lively, and she had a way of making her wishes known—and it was clear that the mare would really like a gallop. Which, Sophie had to admit, was exactly the sort of morning she'd prefer too. But Lord Randall seemed to be content to jog along quietly, so she reined in the horse and rode sedately beside him.

"Will you be going up to London soon?" she asked. She knew the answer already, but there was no sense in letting him know the servants had been talking about him.

"Of course. There are certain expectations of one, you know. The Season is about to begin in earnest, and my presence is required."

He made it sound as if the *ton* couldn't function without him! Sophie wanted to roll her eyes. "It must be such fun," she said and knew she sounded wistful.

"There are moments that are enjoyable. This year in particular it is important that I be at hand." He paused. "I do not wish to sound inhospitable, and indeed I am pleased that my mother's good friend has come to visit her, but I must admit surprise at Lady Ryecroft's timing. My mother's arrangements have already been made, and I came to Brindle Park this week in order to escort her to town."

"And instead you find us here." All the suspicion Sophie had felt when she discovered that Lady Brindle was not, after all, recovering from a sprained ankle mingled with the unease that had swept over her this morning when Lady Ryecroft had insisted on going out for a ride without her. What exactly was her mama up to?

"And a great pleasure it is," Lord Randall added hastily, "to have such a dear old friend and her daughter in the house."

"But you're anxious to be off to town and afraid that your mother won't tell us that it's time for us to be going home?"

"You see, there is a lady… and our intentions to

wed are soon to be announced. It is necessary that I be in attendance for her official presentation, and my mother must be there as well."

So much for the plan to ensnare him with her beauty, her charm, and her innocence.

She couldn't for the life of her feel sad about it, however. In fact, a little bubble of glee rose inside her as she realized it was no longer necessary to behave in the strict pattern that Lord Randall obviously seemed to think ladies should. The sudden relief was like a weight lifted from her shoulders, and she laughed merrily at her foolishness in thinking that he might be the answer to her problem.

Then she leaned forward, whispered to the mare, and touched Moondust's side with her heel—and they were off, horse and rider of one mind as they careened down the gentle slope in a wild, joyous, headlong flight. She reached the outskirts of the picturesque little village and was reluctantly beginning to slow her pace when a rider darted from between the stone church and the shop next door directly into her path and, it seemed, no more than inches away.

Sophie's heart leaped into her throat, but Moondust was already turning with a flash of white feet, and Sophie felt only the brush of a hard thigh and the scrape of the edge of a high-topped boot through the skirt of her habit as the other rider pulled his gelding aside.

Moondust skidded to a halt in the middle of the narrow street, leaving Sophie breathing hard. She was still frightened, but she was exhilarated as well—for what a display of horsemanship that had been. She patted the mare's neck in appreciation. "You're a good girl, Moondust!"

Lord Randall galloped up beside her and stretched out a hand to grab the mare's reins from her hand.

"What are you doing?" Sophie gasped, guiding the mare to one side so his fingers closed on thin air.

"How fortunate you were not thrown, Miss Ryecroft, because of her running away with you like that! And then to nearly unseat another rider... I shall lead her all the way home."

"You shall do nothing of the sort," Sophie snapped. "She didn't run away with me—I wanted to have a good gallop. But I'm afraid the rest is true, though it is entirely my fault and not Moondust's." She turned the mare toward the rider she had almost collided with.

He was yards away, taking time and space to bring his mount under control. Wise of him, Sophie thought, to keep some distance from an unknown rider and an unfamiliar animal. Now, however, he pulled the gelding around and came back toward her, and she nudged the mare and met him halfway.

"It was rude and thoughtless of me not to stop well before I reached the edge of the village," Sophie said. "I do beg your pardon, sir, but you have the most wonderful command of your mount, not to have knocked me into the dust as I deserved!"

She was looking at the horse as she spoke—he was a glossy black gelding, big enough to have bowled Moondust over entirely. Big enough to have seriously injured both of them, in fact.

Sophie raised her eyes to the gelding's rider and had

to smother a gasp. She had never seen a young man who was so handsome. Beneath the stiff brim of his hat, his hair curled in ringlets of an even brighter gold than her own, and his wide-set eyes were an unusual shade of greenish blue. His features were regular, his profile perfect, his shoulders broad, his face lean and youthful… He might have been a classical statue come to life. He was older than she was, she decided, but not by much.

The handsome young man controlled his horse with ease, turning him in the street and bringing him up alongside Moondust. He touched his hat respectfully and smiled, which made his features seem even more like those of an angel.

Sophie felt a little dizzy. "Oh," she said feebly and wondered if this was how men felt when she smiled at them. Was she acting as besotted as most males seemed to do around her?

"It is an honor to encounter you," he said softly. "*There be none of Beauty's daughters with a magic like thee.*"

His voice was just as beautiful as the rest of him— like bells on a crisp spring morning, Sophie thought, even though he wasn't making a whole lot of sense.

He must have seen her puzzlement. "Byron," he said simply. "It seemed the only thing to say."

Lord Randall pulled up beside them once more. "I must apologize, sir." He sounded both appalled and breathless, as though he had been the one involved in the near collision. "I trust no lasting damage has been done to you or your mount through Miss Ryecroft's heedless action?"

How dared he interrupt that beautiful voice when

all she wanted to do was listen? Before she could stop herself, Sophie said sharply, "I've already expressed my regret, Lord Randall. And I'm not some pet puppy whose behavior you are responsible for!"

"The fault was not yours, Miss Ryecroft," the Greek god said, "but mine. I was not watching when I burst out from between the buildings." Somehow he had managed to get hold of her hand—no mean feat with the two horses sidling and flirting.

Lord Randall was finally silenced, and he seemed to be paying her no heed. Sophie turned to look over her shoulder, interested to see what could possibly have drawn his attention away from her and the gentleman she had almost run down.

Riding straight toward her down the village street was her mother, with Lady Brindle's groom trotting along a couple of lengths behind. Sophie felt her stomach turn over.

Lady Ryecroft had obviously seen the chase down the hill, as well as the encounter at the edge of the village, *and* the hand-holding—for her mouth was a tight line and her spine was so rigid that Sophie didn't see how her mother could stay in the saddle without shattering.

Sophie knew she was in for it now—though with a last feeble hope of heading off trouble, she said brightly, "Hello, Mama. Did you have a good ride?" It was a foolish question, for anyone could see that no matter how pleasant her ride might have been at the start, Lady Ryecroft was no longer having a joyous morning. Sophie gave a tiny tug and pulled her hand away from the Greek god's.

Her mother's gaze seemed to burn. "Sophronia," she said firmly. "I believe I indicated that you were to stay at Brindle Park."

Sophie's jaw dropped with the injustice of it. "But you *didn't*, Mama! You said I wasn't to come riding with you, but—"

"Ma'am," Lord Randall said, "I must take all the responsibility. I should not have allowed Miss Ryecroft to coax me into taking her out."

"*Coax* you?" Sophie protested.

"But having done so, I own it was my duty to have maintained control of her mount, and—"

"What an utter hum!" Sophie said. "As if you could!"

The gelding's rider bowed to Lady Ryecroft, then to Sophie, and touched the brim of his hat with his crop. "No damage done, ma'am. Miss Ryecroft, I'm Carrisbrooke." Sophie felt as if choirs were joining in a hallelujah for the sheer joy of hearing him speak.

Carrisbrooke. Wasn't that the young earl she'd heard Lady Brindle mention at dinner last night? So that explained why Lord Randall was treating him with humble respect, despite the earl being so much younger. She really should not have given in to a temper like that in front of him, no matter how aggravating Lord Randall had been. Her mother's frown was no surprise.

"Carrisbrooke," Lady Ryecroft said tightly. "How pleasant to meet you. We must return to Brindle Park immediately, however, as we will be going home today."

Sophie goggled at her. "Today? But, *Mama*…"

Lady Ryecroft gave her a quelling glance, and

Sophie subsided. She'd been on the receiving end of that look frequently enough to know there was no ignoring it.

The moment I meet someone interesting, Sophie thought. She let self-pity wash over her for a moment before she tugged on Moondust's reins and obediently fell in beside her mother.

But she darted a look back over her shoulder and was pleased to see that Carrisbrooke was watching her as she rode away.

❧

Portia held her tongue until the front door had closed behind Lord Ryecroft and his curricle had pulled away from the house and headed east from Grosvenor Square. Once she was absolutely certain he was gone, she turned from the drawing-room window to face Lady Stone. "You cannot be serious, ma'am."

"...forty-nine, fifty," Lady Stone said. "It took less than fifty seconds for you to break down. What a disappointment you are, Portia. I wagered with myself that your nerves were so strong you weren't going to say anything at all. But as it happens, you didn't even hold out for a full minute."

"If you think making fun will keep me quiet, ma'am, I must tell you that you are deceived indeed. You, introduce a debutante? Sponsor her appearance in society?"

"I am certainly able, you know. I fancy I know everyone who is anyone in this city."

"Take her all over London, to every ball and rout and party, day after day and night after night?"

"I go to many of them anyway."

"And how long has it been since you attended an assembly at Almack's?"

"A while," Lady Stone conceded. "Two or three years, perhaps. But I might enjoy it again."

"You would have to give up the card room and spend every moment chaperoning her."

"But you see, that's the best part of the idea, because I won't have to give up anything at all. That, my dear Miss Langford, is why I have *you*."

Portia was speechless.

"As my companion, you're the ideal chaperone for a young woman in her first Season."

"But you told Lord Ryecroft that you would personally see to it!"

"As I have done, by putting his sister in your capable hands."

Portia had to admit, as she thought back over the conversation, that Lady Stone had not lied; she had merely allowed Lord Ryecroft—and Portia—to believe whatever they wished.

"You're the perfect chaperone, in fact." Lady Stone sounded pleased with herself. "You're young enough to mix into her crowd, so you can stay close at hand and see exactly what she's up to. You can even hear what she says to the other chits when they're chattering to each other in the withdrawing rooms at balls. That, you must admit, would be difficult for someone like me to accomplish."

Portia had to bite her lip hard at the image of Lady Stone surrounded by giggling young women—trading gossip with them, admiring new hats, tying their ribbons and corsets, mending rips… and sharing confidences along the way.

"Yet you have that air of respectability that every chaperone requires."

Portia sighed. "And how do you think it's going to look to society—your bringing out Lord Ryecroft's sister?"

Lady Stone sighed sentimentally and clasped her hands together under her chin in a gesture worthy of a charade. "I suppose society will fondly think I'm a childless lady who wishes to recapture lost opportunities by pretending, for a Season, to have a daughter."

"No," Portia said bitterly. "They'll think you're an old woman who is trying to curry favor with an impecunious but handsome young man because you feel an unnatural attraction for him!"

Lady Stone looked into the far distance for a moment. Her index finger tapped gently against her jaw.

Portia didn't know if she should feel pleased that her employer seemed to have understood her point at last, or concerned because the work of canceling this odd start of Lady Stone's was bound to fall on her companion's shoulders. The one thing Portia looked forward to even less than presiding over Sophie Ryecroft's come-out was telling her brother the entire idea had been called off.

She was thinking how best to break it to him when Lady Stone said, "Do you truly think he is?"

"Poverty-stricken? My dear ma'am…"

"No. You called him handsome."

Portia stared at her. "We're talking about you here, Lady Stone—not me."

"Are we, my dear? But what an innocent you are if you do not realize there's nothing at all unnatural about a woman of *any* age feeling attracted to a young buck like that one. He's not only handsome; he has a winning way about him—unusual for a man his age. Inheriting so young—and facing such financial strictures—has matured him beyond his years."

Portia opened her mouth, thought better of what she'd like to say, and closed it again.

Lady Stone laughed merrily. "Oh, don't look at me like that—and don't be such a ninnyhammer. Have you not even stopped to think? The girl has a mother, after all. Lady Ryecroft will hardly allow her daughter to be launched into society without her assistance."

"Oh," Portia said feebly. "Of course."

"One might think you had your mind so firmly upon Lord Ryecroft that you'd forgotten all else... It will appear to the public that Miranda Ryecroft and I are the best of long-lost friends, especially since I've just returned from the corner of Surrey where she lives."

"And you think people will believe you're giving Lady Ryecroft and her family houseroom only for *her* convenience?"

"Perhaps not. But I'll tell everyone I'm inviting them in order to make your life more lively."

"Mine?"

"A dull existence you have of it, Miss Langford, being a companion to an old lady like me. But never let it be said that I'm not a thoughtful employer. With some young things about the house, you can't possibly be bored to extinction."

Overworked, Portia thought. *Annoyed... put-upon... aggravated beyond reason...* But no, Lady Stone was right; with the Ryecrofts in the house, she would absolutely not be bored.

"Yes, indeed," Lady Stone mused. "It's you I'm thinking of."

"I am honored beyond reason, ma'am."

Lady Stone didn't seem to hear the ironic twist in Portia's voice. "As well you should be, my girl, because the sort of man who will seriously court Sophie Ryecroft is exactly the kind you're looking for."

"I am not looking—"

"Then you should be. And since she can't marry *all* of them..."

"You believe that perhaps a crumb or two might fall my way?" Portia said dryly.

"And why shouldn't it? You're presentable enough, and your pedigree is nearly as good as hers."

"If one leaves aside the fact that I earn my living as a companion."

"Irrelevant. Of course, you'll need some new dresses too, if you're to go about in the lovely Miss Ryecroft's wake and help to keep her on the straight and narrow. You'd best get started on that right now so the dressmakers will be free by the time the Beauty arrives. I wonder how long Ryecroft will be about bringing them? Better inform the housekeeper that we'll need the guest rooms opened and polished too." Lady Stone yawned. "I believe I'll have a nap; I was wakeful last night."

For a moment Portia feared Lady Stone intended to tell her exactly what had kept her awake. She'd been mooning over handsome young Lord Ryecroft, no doubt—perhaps picturing him in her boudoir or visualizing him shucking his clothes in her bedroom... Portia could see the details of that vision with no effort at all. Lord Ryecroft's face alight with interest, with humor, with delight... with desire...

Only it wasn't Lady Stone he was looking at, in Portia's imagination. And it wasn't Lady Stone's boudoir that he seemed to fill to capacity, but her own smaller bedroom. She could actually see his hand, strong and tanned against the pure white of his cravat, as he began ever so slowly to unfasten it, revealing his throat... A little shiver ran over her. *Of distaste*, she told herself firmly.

"I won't need you for the rest of the morning, so you may start straightaway on arrangements for the ball."

"Ball?" Portia was surprised she could speak at all.

"Yes, I'll be giving a ball to formally introduce Miss Ryecroft—and her brother, of course—to the *ton*. In about three weeks, I think."

Portia was only surprised that Lady Stone had remembered Miss Ryecroft, and not her brother, was supposed to be the star of the show.

"That should be enough time to build a buzz of expectation and to get them both properly fitted out with the right clothes. Oh, what fun *that's* going to be!" Lady Stone gave a wicked chuckle. "Such a fine figure of a man he is. If his coats were only cut a wee bit closer to show off those magnificent shoulders, and his pantaloons just a *shade* tighter..."

"Ma'am!" Portia wanted to clap her hands over her ears, but interrupting—even though it was also rude—would have to do. "You *cannot* be thinking of advising his tailor? Or sitting in while Lord Ryecroft is measured?"

She wondered how broad his chest really was… and how much measuring it took to fit a gentleman's pantaloons… The room was feeling a little too warm.

"Of course not." Lady Stone's tone was virtuous, though there was a hint of laughter underneath. "My goodness, Miss Langford—such an idea for a lady to express. Do take your mind out of the chamber pot!"

Six

RYECROFT MANOR MIGHT BE SHOPWORN, EVEN VERGING on threadbare, but it was home, and Miranda was relieved to be back in her familiar surroundings.

For about half a day.

Once she had made the rounds of her domain, answered the questions that had arisen during her absence, and settled a minor tiff between the crusty old gardener and the cook over which herbs to add to the kitchen garden this year, she felt curiously at loose ends.

Whenever she tried to sit quietly and read or sew or even plan a menu, she found her mind drifting back to that quiet library at Carris Abbey and that mortifying instant when Marcus Winston had rejected her.

No. If she were honest, it wasn't the moment of mortification that she recalled most clearly, but the few minutes that had preceded that embarrassment. The minutes in which she had let him hold her, caress her, touch her breasts... Even now, all she had to do was be still and she could feel his hands against her skin and the heat of his body as he pressed against her. She once more felt the tingle of desire in her breasts, along with a new rush of heat between her legs, reminding her that if he had not turned away from her, she would have become his lover right there on the settee…

And she had to admit that part of her wished the moment of madness hadn't ended.

In a feeble attempt to wear herself down enough to rest, she announced—to the housekeeper's horror—that she was going to turn out every room and cupboard at the manor. She began with a linen press that hadn't been entirely emptied since before she'd arrived as a bride. She put Sophie to work counting towels, while Miranda sorted the sheets that could still be mended from those that should be cut down into pillow covers instead.

But even as she handled the smooth linen and felt it warm under her hands, she remembered the way his crisp shirtfront had felt against her fingertips…

On the third day of her cleaning spree, Miranda came downstairs early after a fitful sleep and found Sophie already in her riding habit, munching toast as she tiptoed across the hall toward the side door that was closest to the stables. Obviously she had intended to escape the house before her mother came downstairs, but she had been tripped up by her always-healthy appetite.

"Oh, do come and sit down like a lady for a proper breakfast," Miranda said crossly. "And after you've finished, you may ask Cook for some beef jelly to take to Mrs. Curtis at the gate cottage. Mrs. Carstairs tells me that the baby has arrived."

"Perhaps Mrs. Carstairs hoped that you would deliver it yourself and stop poking into her responsibilities,"

Sophie offered as she perched on the edge of her chair to gulp her food. She was not exactly ladylike, Miranda noted.

"If you don't want the excuse for a ride," Miranda began.

Sophie shook her head and jumped up, still clutching the last of her toast. "No, I'll do it." The next moment she was gone, her boot heels clicking on the marble of the hallway, and Miranda was too glad of her absence to fuss about her daughter's lack of manners.

After Sophie had gone, Miranda turned over the pages of the newspaper, hardly seeing the stories, while she drank her coffee.

You will be my mistress, Marcus had said.

But of course that was laughable. How could she possibly become his mistress, when she was in Surrey, with no intention of leaving Ryecroft Manor anytime soon, and he was a hundred miles away?

Because you want me as much as I want you...

She simply must get over this nonsense; that was all. She felt like a violin string, tensed and taut as she waited for the bow to come to rest and draw forth a melody—which was completely foolish, since there was no possibility she would see him again. *Ever*.

And the low feeling that gave her was the most ridiculous thing she'd ever experienced.

She spent a couple of hours sorting out the contents of a drawer in her morning room. There were letters from girlhood friends whom she hadn't heard from in years now, a calf-bound journal she'd received for her twelfth birthday and kept fitfully for a few months, and sentimental keepsakes of her childhood—including a red paper valentine that Marcus had given her when she was sixteen.

She sat down, hard, her fingers trembling as she held the card. Not only had it slipped her mind that he had made it and given it to her, but she didn't recall bringing it along with her as a bride. But here it was, tucked among her most precious mementos.

At the door, Carstairs cleared his throat. "My lady, a… gentleman… has called and requests to see you." The hesitation in the butler's voice sent a flicker up Miranda's spine. Carstairs never missed; if he said a man was a gentleman, then indeed he was. But if Carstairs wasn't certain…

Was it Marcus? Not that she expected even Carstairs could sniff out Marcus's exact origins, but there had been an air of informality about Marcus when she'd seen him at Carris Abbey that she'd never noticed before. Perhaps it had been born of the years he had spent in the New World. Carstairs wouldn't miss that.

Still, it couldn't be Marcus, for he wouldn't dare to call on her at her home.

You will be my mistress…

But why wouldn't he come to Ryecroft Manor? Even though a morning call at her home would violate the rules, it was no worse than the way Miranda had barged in on him at Carris Abbey…

"He asked for the master," Carstairs said, "but when I told him that Lord Ryecroft was not at home, he begged to have a moment with you, ma'am."

Marcus would not have asked for Rye. Relief swept over her, followed instantly by a sensation Miranda refused to admit—the barest sense of disappointment.

She realized Carstairs was looking at her with ill-concealed curiosity and holding out a tray, and she picked up the visiting card that lay on it. *Robert Wellingham*, it said. It was not a name she recognized, though somehow there was a flicker of familiarity about it. But she had been away from society for so long it would be no wonder if she had grown rusty. For all she knew, he might be part of a distant branch of one of the nation's most eminent families.

She turned the card between her fingers. "Very well. I'll see him. Show him into the drawing room in five minutes."

Carstairs inclined his head and went away.

Miranda sat still for another few seconds, then put the valentine safely back in the drawer and went down to the drawing room. She glanced around to be certain everything was in place, though there was no need; the maids had obviously not cut corners in their regular duties while she was gone. A fire blazed in the grate, and the velvet draperies had been pulled open to admit the spring sunshine that reflected off the early green of the gardens.

Miranda noted that the strong rays fell across a thin spot on the carpet, and she sighed as she pulled a chair forward to mask the flaw. Of all the rooms in Ryecroft Manor, this one was least used, and despite the furnishings being dated and tired, it was still the most impressive. That was why she had chosen it to receive her unknown guest, though exactly why she had the odd sense that it was important to impress this man, she did not know.

Carstairs brought in her caller, and she surveyed

Robert Wellingham with curiosity. He was tall and broad-shouldered; his deep blue morning coat had obviously come from the hand of a fine tailor, and his neckcloth, though not elaborately tied, was of the whitest and best linen. His hair was dark, and there was the slightest touch of silver at his temples. More than that, however, the way he stood told her that he was nearly her own age, for he had an air of command that few younger men possessed. Even Rye, who had been born to rank, hadn't quite mastered that attitude yet, though inheriting so young—and coming into an estate in such disarray—had matured him well beyond his actual age. She sensed, however, that Robert Wellingham had come by his aplomb the hard way— through work, not by inheritance.

She nodded politely but did not invite him to sit. "Good morning, sir."

"Lady Ryecroft, thank you for receiving me." He bowed over her hand. "I had the pleasure of meeting Lord Ryecroft in London several days ago. He indicated that he would soon be returning home, and we arranged that I would come to Surrey to discuss some business with him. But I must have misunderstood, for I am told he is still away."

"Yes." Miranda kept her voice level. If Rye had intended to come home several days ago, where was he now? It was a matter of just a few hours' drive to London… "I have not received word from him, so I regret that I cannot tell you more than that."

Then the rest of his words registered, and a chill slid down her spine. *What sort of business?* she wanted to ask. Only now did she recall the odd expression she'd seen on Rye's face the morning he had announced he was going to London. *To see his tailor*, he'd said—as if she was likely to believe that tale. He'd had the same look on his face at the age of four, one day when he'd sworn to her that he did *not* have a snake in his pocket—*Indeed, Mama, I do not!*—right up to the instant when the snake had slithered down his leg and onto the carpet. Right about where Robert Wellingham was standing now, as a matter of fact.

But on that last morning at breakfast, she'd been concentrating on how to finagle a trip to see Ann Eliza without taking Sophie along, so Miranda hadn't pressed to find out exactly what had put that mulish look on Rye's face. In any case, she'd believed that whatever Rye was up to in London, it was no worse than the average young gentleman's pastime.

Now she wished she had insisted on knowing. He was of age, which meant that technically he was no longer answerable to his mother, but surely he wouldn't have lied to her.

What was it about Robert Wellingham's name that nagged at her?

He looked around appreciatively. "You have a lovely home, Lady Ryecroft. This is a most pleasant room."

Carstairs had left the drawing-room door open, and from the corner of her eye, Miranda caught a flurry of activity in the hallway outside.

Then Sophie spoke, her clear voice resounding. "You said Mama's in the drawing room, Carstairs? Do please bring us a tray—I could smell Cook's lemon cakes baking as I came in, and I'm famished from being out in the air all morning." She burst into the room. "Mama, I met Emily in the village, and she says her aunt is arranging a picnic party to—Oh, I beg your pardon."

She stopped on the threshold, almost poised on tiptoe. One small hand clutched the long skirt of her riding habit, while the other was raised to her lips in apology.

"My daughter," Miranda said ruefully. "Sophie, this is Mr. Wellingham."

"Have I interrupted? Well, of course I have. I am so sorry to have interrupted you and your caller, Mama." She curtsied. "It is lovely to meet you, sir."

"Do not distress yourself, Miss Ryecroft; I was just taking my leave."

"But you must not let me drive you off! Mama so seldom has gentleman callers..."

Sophie's eyes widened as she spoke, and Miranda could almost read her daughter's mind as she put the pieces together. A gentleman calling, alone, on her mother... Sophie's powers of observation and deduction might be improving, but she obviously had a long way to go yet.

"I see you've not been here long enough for her to offer you refreshment," Sophie plunged on, "but Carstairs will be bringing a tray at any moment." She perched on the edge of a sofa cushion. "Have you come from a great distance, sir?"

"I live in London—at present."

"Really? How exciting. But then how did you meet Mama? Have you known her long?"

"Sophie!"

"Yes, Mama? Oh, do you mean to say I should

go and change? Indeed, I must smell of horse." She wrinkled her nose and jumped up again. "And then there will be no need for Mr. Wellingham to go away, and you can have the most comfortable chat together."

Miranda could not stop herself. "Sophie, Mr. Wellingham is not that kind of caller!"

The instant the words were out, Miranda would have given anything to call them back. Wellingham's dark gaze met hers, and the challenging glint in his eyes left her breathless, for she understood only too clearly how he had interpreted her thoughtless remark.

What she had said was literally true; she'd simply meant that his call was business, not a social event, as Sophie obviously believed. But he had heard an insult—deliberate and crude. Carstairs had been right; he was *not* quite a gentleman, and he knew it. Therefore, he thought she must be warning Sophie that he did not belong in their world. That he was not a fit person for the sister and mother of a viscount to know...

"I regret that I have disturbed you, ma'am." But the apology was no more than words; it was apparent to Miranda that he didn't mean it.

"Mr. Wellingham, it is I who must beg your pardon. I did not mean to imply..."

He cut her off crisply. "It is of no importance. I shall return to the village now. I shall be at the inn if Lord Ryecroft returns today."

Repeating his name, however, had finally jolted Miranda's memory loose. "You're a banker," she said slowly. Fear slithered along her veins. *What has Rye done? Why has he gone to the moneylenders?*

A chill ran down her spine. *You have a lovely home*, Mr. Wellingham had said. But had it been an appreciative comment or an acquisitive one? *I live in London—at present.* Had there been a hidden meaning in that brief hesitation?

Was it possible that Rye had put a mortgage on the manor? He could not sell it, of course. The estate was entailed and had to pass along with the title. But borrowing against the land or the house—he might have found a way to do that. Now that he had full control of his affairs and his money—what there was of it—he would no longer even have to consult trustees before taking such a major step.

"A banker?" Sophie asked. All thought of going off to change her clothes seemed to have vanished. "What do you do as a banker, exactly? Do you have to sit and count money all day? How perfectly dull."

Wellingham smiled. Under other circumstances, Miranda might have thought it a charming smile, but in her current frame of mind, it appeared more predatory than amused. "Not usually, Miss Ryecroft."

"Do you ever lose your place when you're counting and have to begin all over again? I do. Not when I'm counting my pin money, because I haven't that much. But just yesterday, when I was counting towels for Mama…" Sophie settled herself on a couch. "Do sit down, Mama, so poor Mr. Wellingham can too."

"Why are you here, Mr. Wellingham?" Miranda blurted. "What is it you want from us?"

His face hardened. "I have told you my errand, Lady Ryecroft. I have private business to discuss with Lord Ryecroft, whom I expected to have returned

home by now. I am sorry to have troubled you."
He turned to Sophie. "It seems we must discuss my
profession at another time, Miss Ryecroft." He bowed
once more and departed, his step firm and unhurried.

Miranda sank down onto the sofa. Her head was
buzzing. Had Rye lost a fortune at the gambling tables
while trying to win a stake to take Sophie to London?
Would a banker even loan money if it was to settle a
debt of honor? And if he did, what would he demand
as security?

Where *was* Rye? Was he ashamed to tell her what
he'd done?

In the same moment Sophie bounced up again.
"Beg pardon, Mama—I'm going to see what's keeping
Carstairs with my tray," she announced, and before
Miranda could draw a breath to scold her, the
thoughtless child had gone.

❧

As she rounded the corner from drawing room to
hallway, Sophie heard the rattle of Wellingham's
curricle pulling away from the manor. Carstairs
began to speak, but she raised her finger to her lips,
cautioning silence, and slipped past him through the
still-open front door.

She could never catch up with the curricle if she
tried to chase it down the drive, but if she took the
shortcut to the gate, she might—with luck—get there
in time to intercept him.

She had no idea what she'd do then, but she
wanted some answers. What had this stranger said
to her mother that had made Lady Ryecroft nearly

faint? Why had he avoided a simple question about his reason for coming? What sort of business did he have with the Ryecrofts?

And why, Sophie asked herself wryly, was there never a horse saddled and waiting by the front door at the moment when she needed one? The boots she wore for riding were not intended for this sort of hurried cross-country walking.

The carriageway wound and turned for more than a mile from the manor before it reached the gate, but the distance was not nearly so long by the footpath Sophie took. She was panting, however, when she reached the last turn in the carriageway, still several hundred yards from the gate, just as Wellingham's horses came into view around the last bend.

She strode out into the center of the path and faced the team, with her head up, shoulders back, and arms outstretched.

The team came to a gentle halt just a few feet away from her, and he looked down at her from the driving seat with polite inquiry.

"I need to speak with you, sir," Sophie said. "Kindly come down from there so I do not have to shout."

He didn't move. "The word *please* would not come amiss."

"Please, Mr. Wellingham. I would like to speak with you." There was the slightest breathlessness in her voice, but that must be from walking so far and so fast.

"Take them, Henry." His groom climbed down from the back of the curricle to take the horses' heads, and once they were controlled, Wellingham leaped lightly down from the carriage and came toward Sophie.

She hadn't realized how tall he was. Or perhaps it was only the cut of the capes on his driving coat that made him look so imposing. In the drawing room, she'd thought he might be as old as her mother, but out in the open air, with his hat concealing the few silvery threads in his hair, he looked far younger. His mouth was a firm, straight line, and there was no humor in his eyes. He looked dangerous... but how ridiculous of her to think so. What could possibly happen to her within sight of the gate cottage?

"I suppose I ought to have anticipated that a holdup would be exactly your style, Miss Ryecroft, though I observe you seem to have mislaid both your mask and your pistol."

He sounded different too. His tone was deeper and more melodious; perhaps being outside let him expand somehow. It made her feel all shivery, as if his voice had gotten inside her and was vibrating.

"What is it you wish to discuss with me? Or shall I guess? Let us walk while I contemplate." He strolled a few steps and paused. "I have it. You have decided to seek employment in banking, and you would like my advice as to how to go about establishing yourself."

Sophie was momentarily diverted. "Could I?"

"Doubtful. Banks—at least my banks—do not generally employ young ladies."

She frowned at him. "Well, then it was ill done of you to lead me on by suggesting it. Because, as a matter of fact, it sounds as if it would be ever so much more pleasant than dancing in a theater."

"*Dancing in a...* You are not like your mother, are you, Miss Ryecroft? Looks aside, of course."

"You are laughing at me, sir."

"Indeed no." But there was a catch in his voice that belied his words. "Let's get on with it, shall we? What is it I am to be taken to task for, Miss Ryecroft?"

"Why did you upset Mama just now?"

"I assure you it was not my intention to do so."

"Why didn't you answer her questions?"

"Perhaps if she had been as insistent as you, I should have done. However, once my word is given on a matter of business, I do not make a practice of telling others the details."

He meant he'd promised Rye. But what about? Sophie chewed on that as they strolled.

Wellingham seemed to think he'd said too much already. "Unlike you, it appears Lady Ryecroft has taken a strong dislike to my profession."

"I don't understand what's wrong with being a banker."

"Moneylenders, in general, are not well thought of, Miss Ryecroft."

"Oh, well, if you're talking about the cent-per-centers, no. They're rapacious and greedy, and they drive people into debtor's prison. But that's different. I'm convinced *you* don't do that."

His eyebrows rose. "What makes you so certain?"

She had to pause to consider why she was so positive. "I suppose because when you said you don't talk about matters of business, you seemed so… firm about it. As if you have high standards and you keep to them always."

"I am flattered," he murmured.

"And you said something about *banks*—surely if you are associated with more than one, you don't need to be rapacious and greedy. At any rate, if you wish my mother to think well of you…" She looked up at him through her eyelashes. "*Do* you?"

"Somewhat to my surprise," he said slowly, "I find that I do. I'm sure you're about to recommend a course of action, Miss Ryecroft; I await your advice with breath held."

"You're laughing at me again. So I shall not offer my assistance after all."

"I am humbled," Wellingham said gently. "But *not* ready to beg."

She noted a twinkle in his eyes. She smiled up at him and wondered how she could have thought him dangerous. He was *nice* really. What was wrong with her mother, not to see that?

"Will you be going back to London soon?" she asked.

"Perhaps tomorrow. I had planned to return today."

"You'll go even if Rye hasn't come home yet?"

"I have obligations, you see. And there will be another opportunity for discussion with your brother. Why do you ask?"

She took a deep breath. "I want you to take me with you."

For the first time, she saw surprise in his face. "Miss Ryecroft, only a moment ago you offered to point out to me how I might maneuver my way into Lady Ryecroft's good graces. Now you suggest that I abduct you? It hardly seems the way to win your parent's heart."

"It's not abducting if I ask you to do it."

"Perhaps not, though the finer points seem to elude me."

"And Mama needn't know that you had anything to do with it."

"I beg pardon for my no doubt limited understanding. But we have been walking and talking for some time within sight of the gatekeeper's cottage, and I note that the gatekeeper himself has been paying particular attention."

She glanced over his shoulder toward the cottage. He was right; though Curtis, the gatekeeper, seemed to be stacking wood behind the back door, he kept looking in their direction.

"It seems likely that your departure from the estate in an open carriage would not go unnoticed, Miss Ryecroft."

Sophie said crisply, "I hardly intended that you should boost me up into the curricle and drive away right now!"

"I am relieved. How did you... er... intend to go about the matter?"

"Well, I hadn't entirely figured that out. It just seemed to me that I should seize the opportunity when it presented itself and work out the details later."

"If you run away to London now, you would miss out on the picnic party."

Sophie sighed. "Yes, and I would regret it. I do love picnics, though it's apt to be chilly as yet, and I do hate getting my hems wet on dewy grass... But I don't see that it can be helped."

"Your willingness to make the sacrifice is noble indeed," he murmured.

Sophie eyed him narrowly. Yes, there was that twinkle again. "If you're leaving tomorrow, I could ride to the village as I usually do in the morning, and Mama would not even know I was gone for hours and hours. You would have to hire a post chaise, I'm afraid, but I could manage to climb into it in the inn yard, where no one would see."

"I don't doubt you could. I had anticipated the need for a closed carriage, and fortunately I am well supplied with ready cash."

"Well, that's good. I would offer to pay for it myself, but…"

"But you have a shortage of pin money at the moment, I believe."

She nodded, pleased that he understood how things were. "And I could hardly arrange to do the hiring for myself, you see, because everyone in the village knows me. So it is agreed?"

"Do you feel you can wholeheartedly trust me, Miss Ryecroft?"

"Yes," she said, but she had to own that there was something about the deep rumble of his voice that made her just the slightest bit nervous. Which was foolish, for it wouldn't be at all like going off with one of Rye's friends. Wellingham was old enough to be her father… near enough.

"You would be comfortable being alone with me in a closed carriage for some hours, without even your maid in attendance?"

"Absolutely not," she said.

"You relieve my mind."

"Because you wouldn't be in the carriage. You'd be driving your curricle instead."

Wellingham gave a burst of laughter. "Indeed I

must, in order to draw off suspicion that I was the one behind your abrupt disappearance! Miss Ryecroft, I congratulate you—and I would be honored to take part in your grand scheme. Only—will you give me your word that you will allow me to make all the arrangements? I shall leave word for you... Where? Is there an establishment you frequent in the village?"

"The baker. I stop in for a sweet bun whenever I ride through."

"The baker," he repeated, as if he was not surprised. "Very well. When I have news, I shall bribe the baker to insert a message into a sweet bun and reserve it for you. However, do not be disgruntled if I am not able to make arrangements as quickly as you would like."

"I suppose it will take some careful handling," Sophie admitted.

"In the meantime you must promise me to be perfectly natural and go about your regular routine so that you do not attract undue suspicion. Do you promise that you will not disappoint me, Miss Ryecroft?"

Was he quizzing her? She asked suspiciously, "Do you *swear* that you'll take me to London, Mr. Wellingham?"

He folded his hand over his heart. "Indeed, I swear I will see to everything. Now I must be on my way—and I am reminded that you have been away from the manor for some time, so you had better hurry back to partake of Cook's lemon cakes before they are all gone."

He kissed the air above her hand, climbed back into his curricle, and drove off.

It was really too bad that he couldn't have driven

her back to the manor, for Sophie suspected she had a blister forming on her left heel. But being delivered to the front door in Wellingham's curricle would hardly have been following her regular routine.

She limped slowly down the path, stopping now and then to rest her foot. She was still several hundred yards from the front door when she heard the rattle of hooves and wheels coming up the carriageway. She looked up, half in anticipation and half in concern. Had he thought better of his promise and returned to withdraw his offer? Or worse, had he come back to inform her mother?

A moment later a familiar gold-and-green curricle took the curve with Rye's characteristic casual style. Sophie raised a hand in greeting, and he smoothly drew in his horses so the curricle's seat was exactly level with her as she stepped out onto the carriageway.

"So you're finally home," Sophie said.

"I broke a wheel near Staines and had to wait to have it fixed, or I'd have been here yesterday." Rye looked her over. "What's going on, and what mischief should I be looking out for now?"

Sophie managed a casual shrug. "It's only Mama. She's turned into a madwoman. She's intent on keeping me locked up forever inside the house, sorting sheets and counting towels."

Rye looked intrigued, but he said, "You don't seem to be locked up at the moment."

"She sent me down to the gate cottage with beef jelly for Mrs. Curtis. The new baby's arrived." It was, she told herself, not *really* a lie—even though the errand had been completed a couple of hours ago.

"Is that a new riding habit? What's up, Soph? Did you lose your horse somewhere?"

"No, I did *not* lose my horse. When was the last time I let a horse throw me? But I wouldn't turn down a ride the rest of the way."

Without a word, Rye's valet climbed down from the curricle and took a seat at the rear beside the groom. Rye shifted the reins, then reached across to clasp Sophie's wrist and, without noticeable strain, pulled her up into the vehicle. It was hardly an elegant maneuver, and Sophie thought their mother might have had a fainting spell if she'd seen it.

Rye clucked to the horses. "Now tell me what you've been doing to get Mama all in a fuss."

"*Me?*" Sophie said indignantly.

"Well, it must have been something you did if she set you to counting towels. What are you doing home from Lady Brindle's already? I thought it certain I'd have to come all the way to Sussex to find you."

"The Season started," Sophie said glumly.

"You know, I'd heard that somewhere."

Was he laughing at her? "Well, of course *you* can be amused about it. No doubt you've had a great deal of fun in the city, and you're ready to rusticate again, but for the rest of us…" She frowned. "Why would you have come to Sussex to fetch us? You must know that Lady Brindle would send us home in her carriage when our visit was done."

"Because I have matters to discuss with you and Mama, and they won't wait."

Matters to discuss… That sounded ominous. He'd spoken in what she thought of as his head-of-the-family voice, the one that always sent shivers up Sophie's spine, and her conscience gave an uncomfortable ping. "Did you... happen to meet anyone on your way from the village?" she asked cautiously.

"No. Should I have done?"

"Oh no. Not at all."

"Then why should it matter... Never mind. You're *not* going to tease me about what could be so important that I would have traveled all the way to Sussex to find you? Perhaps I should warn Mama you must be sickening for something. Sophie, you're going to London—tomorrow!"

Seven

RYE WOULD NEVER, IF HE LIVED TO BE A HUNDRED, understand women.

That much was clear, he told himself a few minutes later as he munched another of Cook's lemon cakes and wondered how long it could possibly take for the kitchen to deliver some real food. He'd been so anxious to get home that he'd left Staines as soon as his wheel was repaired, without even waiting for breakfast—so excited to hear what his mother and Sophie would say about his marvelous news that he'd been prepared to pause at Ryecroft Manor only long enough to change to the traveling chaise and pick up some clean shirts.

The news that they were going to London—in fact, were commanded to appear in the city as soon as humanly possible—should have been greeted with rapture. Instead he was suffering an inquisition worthy of the Middle Ages.

Of course, he'd expected Sophie to look stunned by her good fortune—as indeed she had. But once the news had registered, she should have started to glow with happiness and exhilaration. Instead she'd looked at him with something close to fear, as if he were threatening to hit her over the head with a log. She'd sunk into a chair in the corner of the drawing room, and even now she was sitting bolt upright, not saying a word. Her almost-frozen demeanor was so unlike his little sister's normal behavior that he wondered if she truly *was* ailing.

But perhaps there was a simpler explanation staring him in the face. *James Newstead must be hanging around again*, Rye thought grimly. The way she'd asked so casually if he had met anyone on the road had been a tip-off. That, followed by her obvious reluctance to leave Ryecroft Manor...

Well, the sooner he got Sophie to London and safely married—and off his hands—the better.

But though Sophie's reaction had startled him, his mother's was enough to give a man the shakes. Honestly, he thought, females were impossible. He'd given his mother exactly what she wanted—precisely what she'd been hinting at all year—but she hadn't fallen on his neck with tears of joy and gratitude as he'd expected. Perhaps Sophie was right, and their mother had turned into a madwoman...

"Where have you *been*?" Lady Ryecroft asked. "*Three days* to get home—"

"It wasn't three days. It wasn't even two. I had to have a wheel mended in Staines, and... Wait a minute. How did you know I was even coming home yet? I told you when I left I'd be at least a week in the city, and it's only been..."

"Mr. Wellingham told me," she admitted.

Wellingham. Well, that was something of a facer. That

broken wheel had been even more of an inconvenience than he'd thought. "You've met him, then?" Rye said warily. "What... what did you think, Mama?"

"What should I think, Rye? My son is consorting with moneylenders..."

"It's not at all like that. He's not a moneylender; he's—"

From the corner of his eye, he saw Sophie give a little nod. It was the first sign of life she'd shown since she'd staggered into the drawing room and perched on the edge of that chair like a plaster statue. "A banker," she murmured.

"That's what I said," Lady Ryecroft went on. "You had an appointment with him, Rye; he called on me when you did not keep it. If that is not consorting with moneylenders—"

"It wasn't an appointment exactly. He said he'd like to look the house over first, that's true, but he seemed confident, just from my description..."

Lady Ryecroft made a noise that Rye had never before heard coming from anything except a teakettle. She sat down on the nearest sofa with her hands over her face. "Oh, my dear. I never intended you to do anything so rash. I know how much you want to give Sophie a Season..."

Finally she'd come round to something easy—a subject where he knew the correct answer. "I certainly do, Mama."

"But to borrow money against the manor to fund it, Rye... To risk your heritage! I *cannot* allow—"

"How dare you accuse me, ma'am! I did no such thing. I would never risk the manor." He took a deep breath. This next bit wasn't going to be easy. "But if Wellingham's still interested after seeing the place, then I *am* going to rent it to him."

Lady Ryecroft's head came up with a snap. "You're going to… *what?*"

She looked so horrified that he quailed for a moment. "Lease the house. But only for the Season, Mama."

"To a *moneylender?*"

Rye was beginning to see the humor in the situation. "At least with a moneylender there's no question his pockets are deep enough to afford it. You see, Mama, Wellingham's banks have made him so wealthy that he's thinking of retiring and buying an estate. So he's been looking for a house in the country that he could lease for a while…"

"But why *this* house?"

"…to decide whether he really wants to move out of London. Since we're not going to be here anyway, I offered to lease him the manor." He added hopefully, in case the main point really hadn't sunk in for her yet, "And we truly can use the rent money, because even though Lady Stone has invited us to stay with her, Sophie will need gowns and whatnots. As you will too, if you're to chaperone her round to all the parties. For that matter, Mama, you might even find someone in London who's to your taste."

She glared at him.

All right, Rye thought, that joke had gone sadly wrong. He ran a finger under his neckcloth in an attempt to loosen it. Where in the devil had he lost his way? For the life of him, he couldn't see it.

Women! He would *never* understand them.

Though Rye had told her flatly they would leave for London the next day, it was plain to Sophie that their departure could never be carried out so quickly. For one thing, even after Lady Ryecroft had stopped ranting at the idea of leasing out their home, she went on at some length about how impossible it would be to pack in less than a week.

Rye pointed out once more that they were bidden not only to come immediately, but to bring only enough clothes to get by for a few days, since they would need everything new anyway. And, he added cheerfully, he had better leave the ladies to it and get over to the village right away to finalize terms with Robert Wellingham, who—he said—was truly the most friendly and approachable of men.

That comment sent Lady Ryecroft off again, and she shrieked something about how moneylenders always presented themselves as the best of pals—until it was time to collect what was owed to them.

Sophie was too busy feeling ill to pay much attention. What if, during his comradely chat with her brother, that *most friendly and approachable of men* backed out of his offer to rent the manor, because he'd promised to take Sophie to London instead? She'd only been trying to relieve Rye of the expense of her care and start making her own way in the world, but what if she'd managed to ruin everything for all of them?

Or what if Wellingham slipped up and mentioned the conversation he and Sophie had had by the gate-keeper's cottage? Not only would Sophie never see

London then, she'd count herself lucky if Rye didn't dig a deep, dark dungeon and lock her in it forever.

And even if Wellingham didn't mention Sophie's plan to Rye…

That, she thought, might be even worse. For that might mean he expected her to keep to their agreement despite the changing circumstances—*do you swear that you will not disappoint me, Miss Ryecroft?*—and turn up in the village in the morning, ready to go.

And if that was the case, what would he expect from her?

She thought the afternoon would never end—and the longer her brother was absent, the more certain she was that Wellingham must have told Rye everything. Perhaps they were even laughing together—Rye and that *most friendly of men*—about how silly she'd been.

No. If Rye had any inkling of what she'd been plotting, he wouldn't be laughing. It would be the dungeon, for sure.

But finally Rye returned, slightly worse for wear—having made serious inroads into the innkeeper's stock of brandy, Sophie thought darkly—but plainly delighted at being able to reach an even better deal than he'd hoped for. "For, once he saw the surroundings, Mama, he felt even more compelled to carry through the bargain," he said triumphantly.

But surely bankers weren't in the habit of giving out more money than was strictly required of them… Had he made a higher offer because he expected something from Sophie?

The next morning she managed to get out of the house for a ride, pleading to her mother that, despite the press of impending departure, it would be only good manners to deliver the news to her friend Emily in person.

Once at Emily's house, however, Sophie could barely concentrate. Fortunately Emily laid her friend's absentmindedness to excitement, and Sophie was able to excuse herself after just a few minutes.

On her way back through the village, she stopped at the baker's shop. *Just in case*, she told herself. Not that she expected there would be any message, for surely Rye had made their plans known to Robert Wellingham…

"A sweet bun as usual, miss?" the baker's daughter said with a smile and a wink. "There's a special one set aside for you today."

Sophie's heart sank. Sure enough, she noticed as she took the bun, there was a tiny slit on the bottom of the dough.

She waited till she was well out of the village before she bit carefully into the bun, and her mouth went dry as she felt a slip of paper catch in her teeth. She rode as far ahead of her groom as she could, then reined in her horse and paused to read the message.

I did assure you, Mr. Wellingham had written, *that I would make arrangements for your trip.*

So now he was trying to take credit for the entire thing. As if it had been his idea in the beginning. As if Rye had had nothing to do with it.

Well, that told her all she needed to know about Mr. Robert Wellingham—and glad she was indeed that she wasn't going to be relying on *his* good nature to get her to the city!

It was a good thing she'd stopped at the baker's,

however—for now she could go to London without a care. She could have a good time and not give another thought to Wellingham.

Not another single thought.

Ever.

❧

Almost before Miranda could catch her breath, it seemed, they were on their way.

Packing for a three-month stay would normally take weeks, but Rye had been firm—and in fact, Miranda could scarcely argue with Lady Stone's advice. The Ryecroft ladies would need entirely new wardrobes if they were to be fashionable; there was no sense in dragging along things that they could never be seen wearing in the city.

As a result, they had almost no baggage—just a few trunks in the second coach, along with Rye's valet and her own lady's maid.

It wasn't until she was in the carriage, forced to sit still and with time to think, that Miranda began to fret about leaving Ryecroft Manor to the care of a tenant about whom they knew so little. "We didn't even have time to put away treasures," she mused as they paused at an inn for refreshment and to change the horses.

"What treasures?" Rye asked bluntly. "Carstairs will defend the silver with his life, and as for the rest, you can send him a list of things to hide, if you must. In any case, Wellingham isn't going to hurt anything, and he's not the sort to snoop. Plus, there's no managing wife to upset the servants by counting all the linens."

Miranda shot him a stern look. It was true, she had to own, that Mrs. Carstairs had seemed relieved when Miranda had stopped turning out the darkest cupboards and begun packing to leave instead.

Rye went on blandly, "...and no wild children to break things. The man is a perfect tenant."

"One wonders, if he intends to be entirely alone, why he wanted so much space," Miranda said tartly. "And what if he decides to hold house parties? Anything might happen if he brings in a rabble of guests."

"Then I'll dun him for repairs, and the moment we return home, you can order all the new curtains and carpets your heart desires, Mama. He can stand the nonsense." Rye drained his tankard and paid the innkeeper for the ladies' tea, and they went back out to the carriage.

Miranda had to admit that the payment from Rye's tenant for a three-month lease had been generous indeed. *Is it too generous?* she wondered and admitted to a lingering fear that Rye wasn't telling her the entire truth. Why would a man like Robert Wellingham even want to take a house in the country, all by himself, much less be willing to pay such a startling amount in order to do so?

But she had to admit the money would make things far easier. Rye had declared that the entire lease payment was to be available for Sophie's come-out. "And you're not to go cheeseparing now," he had told Miranda. "It's ready money we weren't counting on, so we can invest every penny of it in Sophie's future without hurting the estate. Sophie's to have the best—and so are you."

Miranda had to admit that a new dress or two for herself wouldn't come amiss, and being able to choose fabrics and styles without considering how much the garment cost would be even more welcome. But of course it was Sophie who mattered, not herself. She was dreaming of dressing her daughter in lace and ruffles and tulle—pink would be insipid with Sophie's vibrant coloring; Miranda made up her mind to try a minty green instead, as well as a soft lilac—when they reached Grosvenor Square.

Sophie had been peeking out the window since the outskirts of the city had come into view, wide-eyed and eager. But now she settled quietly back into her seat, looking pale as she gathered up her bits and pieces and stuffed them into her reticule.

Rye had obviously noticed Sophie's change in attitude too. "Don't go thinking that you're not as good as any of the other girls, for you're a whole lot better than any of them. And you'll do fine with Lady Stone and her dragon of a companion too. The first time you let fly at me in a temper—"

"I won't, Rye," Sophie swore. "At least, I'll try not to."

He laughed. "Go right ahead, for that's the one thing guaranteed to get you on good terms with Miss Langford."

The carriage door opened. Rye swung out to help them descend and ushered them up the steps to the front door.

A painfully correct butler opened the door. "Lady Stone has gone out, but Miss Langford is awaiting you in the drawing room."

"And no doubt she's thinking we're late." Rye handed his greatcoat to the butler. "I'll go up and brave the fire first, Padgett—just in case."

Miranda took a deep, steadying breath and reminded herself once more that accepting Lady Stone's offer was not the same as taking charity—even though at the moment she'd have been hard-pressed to explain the difference.

"If Miss Langford is such a dragon as Rye seems to think she is," Sophie remarked, handing over her cloak and giving her head a careless shake to settle her curls into place, "I must wonder why he is in so great a hurry to greet her."

"Indeed," Miranda said. She noted the sudden stiffness in the butler's face. "However, Sophie, your brother spoke in jest, and you must not allow him to lead you a merry dance." She smiled at the butler, inviting him to share the joke, and was relieved when his face relaxed.

So Padgett liked Miss Langford... which left her wondering why Rye, who wasn't typically hard to please, did not. Miranda made a mental note to warn Sophie to be careful what she said in front of Lady Stone's servants. Then she linked her arm in her daughter's, and together they followed the butler up the stairs to the drawing room.

Rye must have taken the steps two at a time, Miranda thought. Though they were barely half a minute behind him, he had already crossed the long room to a table set by the front window. The table looked as if the entire contents of a stationer's shop had been dumped atop it, and behind the stacks of white paper sat a young woman who was dressed in a plain teal gown with a high neck and long sleeves. Obviously, this was the female Rye had called the *dragon of a companion*. One glance set her intuition tingling, for Portia Langford was both younger than Miranda had expected from Rye's laconic mention and far more attractive. The warm tone of Rye's voice as he spoke—and the slightly acerbic note in Miss Langford's as she answered him—served as confirmation. Intentionally or not, they were flirting.

No, Portia Langford was no dragon. She wasn't even a mere companion. Unless every maternal instinct Miranda possessed had just gone out the window, Portia Langford was going to be a *complication*.

સ≈

Portia had asked Padgett to set up a table by the drawing-room window in order to capture the best light as she wrote out the invitations for this blasted ball Lady Stone insisted on holding—in just under three weeks' time now. She had settled herself there directly after luncheon, and she was still working her way down Lady Stone's scrawled list, writing out the last of the addresses, late in the afternoon when a carriage drew up in Grosvenor Square.

Portia put her pen down and watched. Perhaps it was someone calling on one of the neighbors. With any luck, it might be another four or five days before the Ryecrofts took up residence…

But she knew better. From this distance, she couldn't clearly see the crest on the carriage door, but she could tell by the prickle at her nape who was inside, even before the footman climbed down from his perch at the back to open the door.

Lord Ryecroft, of course, was the first to appear. Portia noted dispassionately that her breathing had gone shallow. *Not*, she told herself, because he was looking particularly handsome today. She was merely anticipating the next outrageous thing he would say to her. She was forced to admit that she'd gotten in a few good jabs herself during their last conversation. No doubt today, with Lady Stone gone out, he would seize the opportunity to take her to task for them.

Still, he had been straightforward about his intentions to marry an heiress. He hadn't tried at all to pretty up the facts or to make his goal sound noble. Furthermore, he'd been sympathetic to the plight of the young woman she had told him about, the one who had been courted when it was thought she had money, and dropped when it was clear she had none. The average fortune hunter, in her experience, was more likely to blame the young woman for raising hopes...

He said all the right things, she reminded herself. *That doesn't mean he truly felt them.* Men who set out to marry for money never lacked for charming things to say—up to and including Ryecroft's canard about how he hoped to care more for the woman he married than for her money. Pretty words—but what did they mean, really?

As if he could feel her watching, he looked up at the drawing-room windows, and Portia shrank back behind the brocade draperies. Gawking out the window at a handsome young man—she could just hear what Lady Stone would have to say about *that*.

But he turned back toward the carriage, and Portia tore her gaze away from the breadth of his shoulders—because of the capes on his greatcoat, she couldn't get a good look anyway—and craned her neck to look at the young woman Lady Stone was so certain would be the Beauty of the Season. The young woman that Portia herself had goaded Lord Ryecroft to bring to London...

Yes, she admitted; she would have no one but herself to blame there if Sophie Ryecroft turned out to be as spoiled and temperamental as she was said to be beautiful.

But the next person to appear was a woman who was definitely not in the first blush of youth. Lady Ryecroft was small and slender, and she managed to descend from the carriage without showing even a hint of ankle—something Portia herself had never once managed.

Portia's heart sank. If Lady Ryecroft was in any way as exacting and proper as she appeared at first glance, it would be a long three months. She wondered, not for the first time, whether her employer truly knew *anything* about the three people she had so casually invited to share her house for the Season... except, of course, that the slapdash Lady Stone found young Lord Ryecroft to be utterly fascinating.

And, of course, she had Portia—so any unpleasant duties could simply be pushed off to her companion.

Portia looked down at her pen and the next sheet of fine stationery and considered writing a letter of resignation instead of yet another invitation. Being left in the lurch was exactly what Lady Stone deserved.

Still, Portia had to admit that having a front seat at

the most exciting show of the Season would be some compensation for all the work and tact that would no doubt be required of her. And if Sophie Ryecroft really was the lodestone Lady Stone expected her to be... well, perhaps Lady Stone was right, and one of the crumbs that fell undesired from her plate would be exactly what Portia herself could appreciate.

Not that she was looking for a husband. But if the right man should come along...

Her gaze drifted back to Lord Ryecroft, who was once more reaching into the carriage—and an instant later Portia's thoughts scattered like pigeons in the park as the Beauty appeared, looking around Grosvenor Square as though she had expected an appreciative audience to be awaiting her.

Indeed, Sophie Ryecroft *was* a beauty—and clearly she knew it, judging by the way she carried herself and the smile she bestowed on her brother as he helped her down.

Lady Stone would be unbearable as she watched all her predictions come true, Portia thought. For there was no doubt her ladyship had been correct; Miss Ryecroft would have all the gentlemen of the *ton* at her feet the moment she made her first appearance in society. Lord Ryecroft would need to equip himself with a cricket bat to fend off all the offers. He'd likely have difficulty finding leisure to do his own courting by the time he dealt with all his sister's suitors...

Portia sighed and turned back to the invitations.

But before she had finished even one more address, she had spoiled two—one with a huge blot because, while she was holding her newly inked pen over the paper, her thoughts had wandered to the image of Ryecroft besieged by a line of would-be suitors; the other because she'd absentmindedly addressed it to Ryecroft himself, as if his name was the only one with the power to stick in her mind today.

Just as she put her pen down to flex her fingers, he spoke from the doorway. "I see you are keeping up with your correspondence, Miss Langford." He strolled across the room to stand over her table. "Are *all* these love notes to... What was the rake's name?"

"Lord Swindon. And they are not love notes." Portia patted the foot-high stack of finished invitations. "I have, on the contrary, been making a comprehensive list of your flaws, my lord."

Too late, she realized that the ladies had not lingered belowstairs but had followed him into the room. Had they been in time to hear her comment? There was no way to tell from Lady Ryecroft's expression, though there was a set to her mouth as if she'd seen something distasteful.

Miss Ryecroft, on the other hand, gave a little crow of laughter.

The young woman didn't even giggle inanely as most girls her age would do, Portia thought irritably. Even her gurgling laugh was beautiful.

"A *comprehensive* list?" Miss Ryecroft said. "If that's your aim, Miss Langford, please do let me help. But we'll certainly need more ink!"

Eight

IT WASN'T THAT MIRANDA HAD MISSED GOING INTO society, for she had been content and busy at the manor, with life spiced by the occasional local party or assembly. She had told herself it was entirely for Sophie's sake that she longed for London.

And yet she had to admit it was pleasant to be surrounded by gaiety and—for the first time she could remember—not to have to make every single penny do double duty.

Her new dress, in a figured silvery-gray lace, was the finest thing she remembered owning. It made her feel almost young again, and even Rye gave her an appreciative look when she descended the stairs to attend the first party of their stay in London. "Mama, you're looking lovely tonight!"

Sophie, coming along behind her, gave an irritable sniff. "That is the last thing Mama needs to hear from *you*, Rye."

Rye looked his sister up and down. "What's the matter, Soph? As long as you're cadging compliments, I must own you look fairly nice tonight too, though you'd do better to take that sour look off your face. But I'm used to that. Mama, on the other hand—"

Sophie didn't wait for him to finish. "*Mama, on the other hand,*" she mimicked, "is not nearly as lovely as she could be if she were wearing something both stylish and colorful. You should also be made aware, my dear brother, that your tone of surprise is not as flattering to her as you seem to believe it is."

Rye looked as taken aback as if a brand-new puppy had bitten his hand.

"Every new dress she has bought," Sophie went on, "is either dowager gray or the faintest, most sickly shade of lavender. When you tell her she's lovely in it, you merely encourage her to choose more of the same. The next thing you know she'll be wearing lace caps around the house. If she had bought the green silk I told her to instead—"

"I should look like an unripe apple," Miranda finished. "To say nothing of appearing to compete with my daughter rather than chaperoning her. But thank you for the notion of the lace caps, Sophie. I shall keep that possibility in mind the next time we go shopping." She glanced past Sophie to catch Miss Langford's eye, expecting her to share the joke. Instead Miss Langford was looking from Sophie to Rye as if she'd never seen either of them before. Miranda gave a small sigh. "Now a smile if you please, miss—and no squabbling with your brother at the ball, mind."

Sophie obliged. She really was breathtaking, Miranda thought, in violet silk with a gauze overskirt embroidered in purple. Matching ribbons were woven through her hair. Her eyes were bright with excitement, and she looked more beautiful than Miranda had ever seen her appear before.

The only reason Sophie was making such a fuss about her mother's wardrobe, Miranda was certain, was to distract herself from the importance of this first evening party. They had met a few people, of course, as they made the rounds of the dressmakers and the shops. Some of Rye's friends had come to call on Lady Stone on her regular at-home days. And they had attended a few small parties and a dinner or two. Sophie had begun to make friends, gently guided by Portia Langford.

But tonight was Lady Flavia Summersby's coming-out ball, and Sophie was making her first official appearance before the *ton*. It would be no wonder if the girl was nervous, even though her dance card had already been half spoken for by Rye's friends.

Lady Stone's ball was now less than two weeks away—and it was crucial that Sophie make a good impression tonight. If society's elite found her unappealing and made excuses not to appear in answer to Lady Stone's invitation, then Sophie would be ruined and all their efforts would have been in vain. The mere idea made Miranda shiver as she put on her new charcoal-gray cloak and allowed Rye to hand her into Lady Stone's carriage.

The press of traffic around Berkeley Square was immense. "I don't remember it being this crowded when I was a girl." Miranda peered out at the long line of vehicles waiting to drop off their passengers.

"I didn't expect anything like this," Portia admitted. "I fear this evening sets a standard of success that every hostess for the rest of the Season must aspire to."

"Nonsense," said Lady Stone. "It's the first ball of any size of the Season; that's all. I say our affair will be even more of a crush—would any of you care to wager on it?"

By the time the ladies had left their cloaks, touched up their hair, and made their way to the ballroom to be announced, the dancing was about to begin. Bright dresses and dark coats filled the floor, and a young friend of Rye's who had been hovering anxiously near the door exclaimed in relief when he spotted Sophie.

"I thought you were never going to get here." He gave Rye a friendly grin. "You could have walked from Grosvenor Square in the time." He swept Sophie away into a set that was still forming.

"We're more fashionably late than I intended." Lady Stone looked around. "It appears all the young ladies I was planning to introduce to you are already partnered, Ryecroft. Miss Langford, you may do the honors and step onto the floor with Lord Ryecroft."

Miranda felt Miss Langford's sigh, but the girl didn't utter a word of protest. Rye guided her into a nearby set, and the music started.

Miranda said quietly, behind the dainty silver lace of her fan, "Do you think it wise, ma'am, to pair them up like that?"

Lady Stone's beady eyes grew even brighter. "Do *you* think it wise to leave him standing on the edge of the floor, looking as though he cannot find a willing partner?" Before Miranda could think of an answer, Lady Stone went on, "We can go over by that pillar in the corner. Look at the ripple across the room—all the men's heads are turning already, despite their partners, to look at your Sophie."

Miranda couldn't help feeling a glow of satisfaction.

"There's Whitfield," Lady Stone said. "On the far side of the floor, in the blue coat, dancing with the girl in pink ruffles. Is it that color that is so bad for her, or is the style even worse? She looks like a half-melted ice."

Miranda let the prattle slide gently over her ears, picking up a name here and there from previous conversations about possible suitors for Sophie, while she admired the brilliant, shifting patterns as the dancers moved in the stately grace of the country dance.

"Swindon is the dark gentleman in purple," Lady Stone said. "That coat of his will look lovely with Miss Sophie's dress tonight. I must make sure to introduce them straightaway… What is Carrisbrooke doing at a ball? He's barely out of the nursery himself—still at Oxford, at any rate. I suppose they invited him since he's a neighbor of the Brindles and not far removed from Summersby's country home."

Miranda spotted Carrisbrooke's golden head at the far side of the ballroom. Such a young man he was, and how much his features looked like Marcus's—though, of course, he was angelically fair, while his uncle was dark. But Carrisbrooke need not concern her. She let her gaze drift on across the ballroom, back to the Earl of Whitfield.

"Well," Lady Stone said in a different tone. "I'm surprised to see *you* here."

Miranda pulled her attention back from the ruffled lady in pink who was dancing with the Earl of

Whitfield—that dress wasn't just unfortunate; it was a disaster—and turned to see who had drawn that tone of asperity from Lady Stone.

Before her, sweeping deeply into a formal bow, was Marcus Winston.

Miranda's fingers went numb, and she dropped her fan.

Marcus swooped it up and returned it to her, balanced on his outstretched palm. "What a shame it would be to let this be stepped on and broken."

Miranda willed herself to reach out casually and pick it up. To do so, she would have to touch him, but that was nothing to quail at. She was wearing gloves, and so was he. It would be nothing like touching his bare flesh…

She hesitated an instant too long, and she saw a gleam spring to life in his eyes as if he had read her mind. With his other hand, he took hold of hers, turning it over until he could lay the silver-and-lace confection in her palm. As he released her, his fingertips stroked gently down the back of her hand, a touch that was featherlight but burned nonetheless, sending an arc of sensation through her glove and deep into her flesh. As if he had touched her breast instead, her nipples tingled.

And he knew precisely what effect he was having on her, she thought. His eyes grew darker, and the barest hint of a smile tugged at the corner of his mouth—that strong, hot mouth that had so easily conquered her in the library at Carris Abbey…

"Lady Stone, Lady Ryecroft. A pleasure as always to see you… both."

"And what gives us the honor of your company

tonight, Winston?" Lady Stone's voice held a touch of acid.

Her tone sent a chill up Miranda's spine. Was this what society was like for Marcus—a sharp edge to every question, a slight hesitation from everyone who spoke to him? And what was she to do about it? Speak up and risk offending the woman to whom she owed so much? Or stay silent and allow it to seem as if she agreed with Lady Stone in thinking Marcus was out of place here? "I'm certain Mr. Winston is a valued guest wherever he goes," she said tightly.

"Of course he is," Lady Stone said. "When he deigns to appear, that is, which he seldom does. The Season started two weeks ago, but I don't recall seeing him at any society event until now."

"Perhaps you simply overlooked me," Marcus suggested.

Unlikely, Miranda thought. How could anyone overlook Marcus?

Lady Stone gave a disappointed grunt. "Don't be fatuous, Winston. I must wonder, therefore, what brings you out tonight." But she wasn't looking at Marcus; her beady eyes were focused squarely on Miranda, who played with her fan and tried not to meet that searching gaze.

"Why does any man come to London in the Season, ma'am?" Marcus asked easily.

"To find a bride, of course," Lady Stone said promptly. "But don't expect me to fall for that sort of faradiddle—not from *you*. At any rate, Flavia Summersby is spoken for already—or at least that's what Lord Randall believes. So why choose this ball, Winston?"

"Why not? We are neighbors, of a sort. But I am wounded to the quick, my lady, that you think my intentions anything but honorable. I see that I shall have to prove myself truthful." He turned to Miranda. "My nephew informs me that you have a most beautiful daughter, Lady Ryecroft. I beg that you will introduce me to her."

∞

Though Rye had visited London many times, he had never been to a ball during the Season, and though he told himself this evening was really no different from the assemblies in Surrey, he couldn't make himself believe it. The Earl of Summersby's ballroom glittered with candlelight and mirrors, the music was provided by a small orchestra, and the dancers gleamed in their finery.

The figures of the country dance partnered him with each of the other ladies in the set in turn, then brought him face-to-face with Portia Langford. She danced much better than any of the others, he noticed, and she looked quite elegant in her dark bronze dress tonight. He started to tell her so as they went down the set together, but she didn't give him the opportunity.

"Notice the young woman in pink, just over there," she said as they circled and once more retreated.

He tried to glance without being obvious and caught a glimpse of a young woman who looked like an overgrown bonbon coated in pink icing. A moment later, as he and Miss Langford waited their turn, he said, "It doesn't seem like you, somehow, to call attention to such an appalling choice of dress."

"It's not the dress I was pointing out, you mutton-head, but the woman wearing it. That's Miss Amalie Mickelthorpe."

Ah. One of the heiresses Lady Stone had listed—and if his memory was correct, the most likely of them all to find a debt-burdened Surrey estate attractive, so long as a viscountess's title was attached to it. Rye did his best to keep his face expressionless.

Apparently, however, he was not successful, for as the dance ended and he offered his arm to escort her off the floor, Miss Langford said sweetly, "But do not let her choice of dressmaker put you off. If she would agree to take instruction from your mother's exquisite taste, she might do you proud."

She sounded less than convinced, however. Rye nodded at the other dancers as they passed.

"And that was the Earl of Whitfield she was dancing with. One of your more serious competitors in the Marriage Mart this year, you must recall."

Rye took a careful look at the earl. What was it Miss Langford had said about him? Oh yes, he'd been to Italy and had an air of romance... He couldn't see what would make her believe Whitfield would be a catch. "I thought you said he looked the romantic sort."

"Perhaps not at this moment. I doubt he's thinking as seriously about Miss Mickelthorpe as she is thinking about him."

"There's a comfort."

She gave him a sharp look, but she didn't pursue the subject. "Lady Stone likes to stay at the corners of the room, by the way. At any ball, look for a group of pillars, and that's where you're likely to find her."

"I shall keep that in mind."

"You should indeed, and not only so you can vanish in the opposite direction. Tonight I believe she intends to put you on display."

Rye suppressed a shudder. All this was necessary, he knew—and he had, after all, asked for it. With the advantage of his extra height, he looked over the crowd. Near the group of pillars Miss Langford had pointed out, there was a bustle of bodies and voices, and as he and Miss Langford drew closer, he saw his sister's bright hair in the center of the group, with Lady Stone performing introductions. Off to the side, his mother stood, looking like an icicle in her silvery-gray gown.

"I see your sister has already been discovered," Miss Langford said. "But it appears you won't have Lady Stone's assistance in finding a partner for the next dance, since she is fully occupied at the moment. Come, and I'll introduce you to Miss Mickelthorpe myself."

Miss Langford, Rye thought with a tinge of regret, seemed a great deal more eager to get him off her hands than he was to leave her presence.

❧

Sophie was afraid she would never remember all the names Lady Stone was tossing at her. She only hoped that the gentlemen who were vying to fill in the remaining lines on her dance card would write legibly. If the names were readable, tomorrow she could study the card, think back over the evening, and try to remember whether the Earl of Whitfield was dark or fair, what color coat Lord Swindon had been wearing, and which of Rye's acquaintances had danced with her because they had really wanted to versus which ones had asked her only because it was a duty to a friend.

She was almost relieved when her mother beckoned to her, so she could break free of the group. "Yes, Mama?"

"I wish to make you known to an old friend of mine, Sophie," Lady Ryecroft said.

Sophie had never heard her mother's voice sound so brittle. And she looked almost ill—her face was nearly as colorless as her dress. Sophie took a step forward, concerned that Lady Ryecroft would faint right there, but her mother shook her head slightly.

"Mr. Winston, Miss Ryecroft," Lady Ryecroft said, and for the first time, Sophie looked at the man her mother was presenting. He was tall and very elegant in a plain black coat and snowy-white linen that made every other man in the room look overdressed. He was handsome too—no question about that. But there was something about him that made Sophie feel odd.

"Miss Ryecroft," he said. "May I beg the pleasure of a dance?" He stretched out a hand for her dance card.

Sophie was glad to see, when she glanced down at the small paper booklet listing the evening's dances, that there were no empty lines. She held it up with a tiny shake of the head.

"My misfortune," he said.

His smile was singularly attractive, and she wondered if her first reaction had been wide of the mark. Then she glanced at her mother again, and that odd, shivery feeling came back.

"Perhaps another time, Miss Ryecroft."

"Certainly, sir," Sophie said politely. She was relieved when her next partner came up to suggest that they go and get a cold drink before the music started again.

She tried to remember her new partner's name, but her mind had gone blank. Was this the Earl of Whitfield, she wondered, or Lord Swindon? Or someone else entirely? She wished she'd had a moment to look more closely at her dance card and refresh her memory about who was next.

It was another country dance, and after the music ended, the young man ushered her to the edge of the floor and stood beside her, silent and stiff, obviously waiting only for her next partner to appear so he could hand her over.

"The next dance is a waltz, is it not?" Sophie asked.

A light feminine voice cut in, "What a pity you have not yet been to Almack's and, therefore, are not yet approved to waltz, Miss Ryecroft. Perhaps that is why your next partner has yet to appear."

Lady Flavia Summersby was strolling by with her hand on Lord Randall's arm as they prepared to take the floor together for the first waltz of her coming-out ball.

Lady Flavia had been presented to Sophie at Hookham's last week. In the bookshop, she had been ordinary looking—small and dark and almost plain. Tonight she was all in white—from the pearls in her hair to her soft dancing slippers—as befitted the debutante, and there was a haughty look on her face.

"I imagine you're right," Sophie said earnestly.

Lady Flavia looked disappointed that she hadn't risen to the bait.

Sophie had to admit, however, to a tinge of envy. Since she had not yet been approved by the patronesses of Almack's to waltz there, her mother and Lady Stone felt it was wiser for her to err on the side of caution tonight, even though this was a private party. So Sophie would be left on the sidelines while Lady Flavia waltzed.

As she looked past Sophie, Lady Flavia's eyes widened with shock. Only a moment later a young man with golden hair and a truly monumental neck-cloth bowed before Sophie. "Miss Ryecroft, I am here to partner you for this dance."

Carrisbrooke. But his name could not be on her dance card, Sophie was certain, or she would have remembered. And of course Lady Flavia was right there to see... "Then I'm afraid you're mistaken, Carrisbrooke." Sophie lifted the card that dangled from her wrist. "I don't see your name here."

The young earl's smile made it seem as if the sun had risen right there in the ballroom. "I am on your dance card now, for I bribed your partner to give up his place to me."

Lady Flavia looked as if she'd swallowed a lemon whole.

"Oh, well," Sophie said lightly, "in that case..." She thanked her previous partner with a smile. "That's not entirely flattering, however. That my intended partner would give up a dance with me, I mean; not the part about bribing him. *That* fact is flattering indeed. How large a bribe did it take?"

"I told him he could drive my new pair of grays through the park tomorrow."

"Horses? And a mere drive around London—not even a good run out in the country?" Sophie sighed in mock distress. "I suppose it's just as well that I know where I rank."

Behind her, Lady Flavia gave a little snort, but just then the music began, and Sophie heard her rustle away.

"I'm glad you don't waltz as yet," Carrisbrooke confided. "I'm not good at it myself." He guided Sophie to a nearby corner with an overstuffed seat just large enough for two.

Sophie hesitated. But surely the seat wouldn't have been placed there, so invitingly close to the dance floor, if it was not considered suitable to use it. She perched at one end, and Carrisbrooke took the other, sitting almost sideways so he could look directly at her.

"I trust you took no harm from our little encounter in the village," he said. "I could not bear it if something as lovely as you were to be injured through my fault. Truly, you *walk in beauty, like the night.*"

More poetry? Sophie's heart gave a funny little flutter. "That's Byron again, isn't it?"

"You know your poets well, Miss Ryecroft. Did your governess share them with you?"

"No, my mother was my first teacher. No one has ever quoted poetry to me before, Lord Carrisbrooke, but you've done it twice now."

"Then it is their loss and their shortsightedness. *For you are…*"

But Sophie's gaze had been suddenly drawn to the dancers swirling around the floor. Surely her eyes deceived her—that spot of silvery gray simply couldn't be her mother's new dress; she must be seeing things. The dancers were, after all, moving quickly.

But she kept looking, just in case.

There was Rye, partnering a girl in horrid pink ruffles... and Portia, in the arms of a gentleman in purple. And...

No, she hadn't been mistaken. This time Sophie could see Lady Ryecroft's partner; she was dancing with the man she had so stiffly introduced to her daughter barely half an hour ago.

"That gentleman," Sophie said abruptly.

Carrisbrooke looked affronted that she had interrupted his poem. "Which gentleman?"

"The one dancing with my mother. Who is he?"

"Oh, that's just my uncle Winston. I expect he felt obligated to dance with her, since I asked him to scrape an acquaintance with your mother. Because of you, of course, Miss Ryecroft. For *thy fair hair my heart enchained*. That's a line from Sir Philip Sidney." And as he smiled at her once more, Sophie felt her heart melt.

Nine

HE WANTED TO BE INTRODUCED TO HER *DAUGHTER*? Because he was looking for a *bride*?

Miranda almost burst out laughing, for the idea was so insane that it couldn't possibly be real. Then she looked more closely at Marcus and realized there was no glint of humor in his eyes. His expression was calm, interested, almost sober.

She felt much the same way as she had once in Rye's childhood when he'd been learning to skip stones on the lake and let fly with a rock that had hit her instead of the water. But this time she couldn't decide whether she was frustrated, furious, or simply stunned. All she knew was that she wanted to scream at the notion that Marcus Winston could nearly make love to her, then ask—in that so polite tone—to court her daughter.

Nearly, she reminded herself—for he *hadn't* made her his mistress. Quite.

Had this scheme been in his mind even then, when she'd told him she wanted to take Sophie to London and give her a Season? Had he been laughing at her?

Even plotting to seek revenge because all those years ago Miranda had turned him down and married Henry Ryecroft instead?

Miranda barely noticed when Lady Stone moved away to intercept Sophie and introduce her to the young gentlemen who crowded around. She faced Marcus squarely and demanded, "What is your intent, sir?"

"Only what I said. I wish to be introduced to your daughter." His gaze drifted to the little knot of eager suitors surrounding Sophie. "She has the look of you, ma'am, and your beauty."

Miranda glared at him. "If you think to bring me around with flattery…"

"I pay no compliments I do not mean, Miranda. When I tell you that your daughter is lovely, it is the truth." He let the silence draw out. "You have no reason to refuse my request. None, at least, that society will accept."

He was only asking for an introduction, after all—for now at least.

Miranda caught Sophie's eye and beckoned. She felt sure her voice would crack as she presented them, but long training held firm. She couldn't help the satisfaction she felt on finding that Sophie's dance card was full, but Marcus didn't look as disappointed as she had hoped he would.

Portia Langford came up just then, looking abstracted. She was standing next to Miranda before she seemed to see Marcus at all. "Lady Ryecroft, Mr. Winston. I beg your pardon—it was not my intent to interrupt your conversation."

"Not at all, my dear." Miranda purposefully turned her back on Marcus, hoping he would take the hint and go away. Sophie had gone off with her next partner, so there was nothing left for him here. He'd accomplished his main purpose anyway—for, now that he'd been properly introduced, he could lie in wait and ask for a dance any evening for the rest of the Season.

"Did you enjoy your turn around the floor, Portia?"

"Yes, of course. Lord Ryecroft is an accomplished dancer. I'm sure all the young ladies will appreciate his talents."

Miranda noted the carefully casual tone of Portia's voice, and her heart sank.

The sets had formed again, and the music was well under way by the time Lady Stone waved off the last of the gentlemen she had gathered and returned to the shadow of the pillars. "You do not dance, Portia?"

"I thought perhaps you would have need of me, ma'am."

"Yes, indeed. What a good idea. I shall lean on your arm as we walk about the room."

Miranda noted that Miss Langford did not turn a hair at the notion that the spry and lively Lady Stone suddenly found herself in need of a human cane. She offered her arm instead, and they strolled off.

"That young woman is really a delightful companion," Marcus murmured. "She displays an incredible amount of patience."

Miranda sighed. "Are you still here?"

"Since I may not have a dance with your daughter, I find myself at loose ends."

"Well, go find someone else to dance with, then. There are plenty of eligible young ladies here. Surely you don't expect me to believe that, based on less than a minute's acquaintance, you've made up your mind to pursue Sophie and only Sophie."

"Of course not," he said.

Miranda relaxed.

"I'm not acting on a minute's acquaintance. I have already heard a great deal about her, from my nephew."

"Your nephew has spent little more than a minute with her himself. What are you plotting, Marcus? You are all wrong for Sophie, and you know it."

"Indeed? What makes you say so?"

"You're too old for her. If you're trying to get even with me for rejecting you all those years ago by courting my daughter…" She bit her tongue. There was no point in telling him how best to annoy her.

"To marry your daughter would surely be an odd way to exact revenge on you," Marcus observed. "Since I'm most likely wealthier than any other suitor who is apt to come Miss Ryecroft's way, and since your stated goal is for her to be financially secure, I'd be playing straight into your hands."

"If your intent was to marry her, perhaps, rather than to ruin her." She knew she sounded breathless, worried. She really must get hold of herself. "At any rate, money is far from the only consideration in choosing a husband."

"If you're still concerned about my unorthodox birth, Miranda…"

"I was *never* concerned about your birth, and you know it!"

"…then you might be interested to know that my father went to a great deal of trouble, in the last years of his life, to make me legitimate."

Miranda goggled at him. "How in heaven's name did he manage that?"

"Lied through his teeth, I should imagine," Marcus said calmly. "Though since I was still in America at the time, I don't really know. Perhaps he faked a set of marriage lines naming him and my mother."

"But *why*?"

Marcus shrugged. "It must have begun after my brother died. My father seems to have been singularly unimpressed with his grandson, so perhaps he wanted a second heir on hand in case young Carrisbrooke continues to be more interested in poetry than in continuing the family line."

"So of course you're being received by everyone in society now, because if something should happen to Carrisbrooke, you'd be the next earl."

"Even Ann Eliza Brindle bowed and spoke to me this evening. She must have heard the news the moment she reached town." There was a note of self-deprecating humor in his voice. "I was honored by the… well, I can't honestly call it the *warmth* of her regard, but…"

"So you really are looking to marry."

"It seems an option I should consider."

"Very well. Find a bride. But not Sophie." Too late, she realized that protesting might only spur his interest. "Marcus, you're not at all the right man for Sophie. I beg of you, don't do this."

His eyes gleamed. "Oh, Miranda, you don't know

what the idea of you begging does to me. Do carry on. What sort of bargain are you offering? If I give up the idea of courting your daughter, what will you do in return?"

She lifted her chin. "If you're attempting to blackmail me into being your mistress..."

He looked thoughtful. "What a flattering opinion you have of my character."

Why had she let her tongue run away with her? She should have acted instead as if she had no memory of those few minutes she'd spent in his arms at Carris Abbey...

He added softly, "Would it work?"

"Of course not!"

"Then I shall not waste the effort."

"You're too old for her. Too sophisticated."

His eyebrows arched. "Is there such a thing as being too sophisticated? I believe I am insulted. As for being too old, Swindon is only two years younger than I. I remember him well from our time at Eton, when he tormented the weaker boys. Yet I am convinced Lady Stone has arranged for his name to be inscribed on your daughter's dance card."

"We're not talking about him," Miranda said stubbornly.

"Very well. Let's not talk at all. Speaking of dancing, you suggested I find a partner. Shall we share a dance for old times' sake?"

"I'm here as a chaperone."

"And you're behaving as if you're in your dotage—dressed in gray like the dowagers."

"I *am* a dowager."

"Only by the strictest of definitions. I thought perhaps that dress of yours was intended as a message for me."

"I do not dress to please—or displease—you."

He smiled. "You have no need to *dress* to please me."

Undressing seemed to be more on his mind; that was true enough.

"Gray is not at all your color. But it does make clear that you're past being interested in society and fun and men, so of course a man's thoughts turn to younger women... You know, Miranda, it would be no wonder if a man, looking at you tonight, would think your daughter old enough to marry."

"She *is* old enough."

He slanted a look down at her.

"Just not for someone with your... experience."

He smiled. "Stop quarreling and come and dance with me. Surely you will not begrudge me a dance. Or do you truly wish to be a dowager and live only to marry off your daughter?"

She glared at him, but before she could find an objection, he slipped a hand to the small of her back and escorted her out onto the floor just as the orchestra struck up a waltz.

A waltz, she thought. Of course, it would have to be a waltz.

She hadn't waltzed in what felt like ages—not since Sophie had made her first appearance at the local assemblies at least—but one never forgot how. And she hadn't forgotten how it felt to circle the floor in Marcus's arms either, even though it had been more than twenty years since she had danced with him.

Only... she didn't remember him being so imposing,

so strong, so powerful. She didn't remember feeling like thistledown in his arms, as he made the steps light and quick and effortless.

It wasn't entirely the exercise or the beat of the music that made her breathless, she admitted. It was being held so closely, with the light scent of his cologne and clean linen surrounding them. It was the warmth of his hand clasping hers, of her skirt brushing his legs as they danced.

One waltz, she thought. She would put it into her drawer of memories along with the valentine he had made her so many years ago. She closed her eyes to soak up sensations.

"I shall have to put a stop to *that*." Marcus sounded annoyed and not at all breathless, as if to him the dance was nothing special at all.

Miranda's eyes popped open, and for a moment she wondered what she could possibly have done to displease him. But then he took them on a sweeping turn, and she saw Sophie sitting in a corner of the ballroom, on a settee that was far too small for two. And bent close over her was a set of golden ringlets that could only belong to Carrisbrooke.

Miranda missed a step as she tried to move to the edge of the dance floor, the better to reach—and scold—Sophie.

Marcus steadied her. "Stay. You will only call more attention to them if you storm off the floor and make a scene." His arms tightened, pulling her just a fraction closer than was proper.

"So you're intending for us to create a scene right here instead?"

He smiled at her and drew her nearer yet. "It would at least keep the minds of the *ton* away from your offspring."

The light scent of his cologne caught at her senses, and his knee, slipping between her legs in the steps of the dance, sent heat through her body.

"Would it be such a bad thing if we were to enjoy each other, Miranda?" he whispered into her ear.

How, she wondered, had he managed to get close enough to do *that*?

Then they turned again, and she frowned at the sight of Sophie's bright hair and Carrisbrooke's ringlets.

"Don't fret. I will handle Carrisbrooke's infatuation," Marcus said firmly.

But would he act only because he wanted Sophie for himself? Despite all her efforts to dissuade him, he hadn't clearly said he *wouldn't* pursue her daughter... Miranda's heart felt like a lump of lead.

❧

When Portia introduced Lord Ryecroft to the heap of pink ruffles otherwise known as Amalie Mickelthorpe, she could have sworn that the young woman licked her lips at the sight of him. But when he asked if he might sign her dance card, Miss Mickelthorpe was coy about showing it to him. "I am already bespoken for this dance," she said sweetly, "but the next is free."

The dance she was offering, Portia calculated, would be a waltz. Of course Miss Mickelthorpe wished to be the first to take the floor with the dashing young Lord Ryecroft for a waltz, for it was the most intimate and romantic of dances. It was the most meaningful as well, for dancers reserved the few waltzes of an evening for the most special of partners.

Portia would dearly love to get a look at the dance card Amalie was protecting. She'd have bet her next quarter's wages there was already a name on the line next to the first waltz, and that as soon as Portia's back was turned and Rye had moved off into the next country dance, Amalie would be scrambling to disentangle herself from whomever she'd originally promised.

And why should it matter to you? It's the way the game is played.

The sooner Lord Ryecroft found his heiress and made his intentions known, the better. Certainly Portia's life would be more peaceful.

She matched Lord Ryecroft up with Juliana Farling for the next country dance and, with a sigh of relief, returned to the pillared corner for some peace and quiet. *That's where you belong anyway*, she told herself. *In the corner with the dowagers and the companions.*

But she was still thinking of the look on Amalie Mickelthorpe's face as she'd watched Lord Ryecroft— as if she'd been admiring a particularly savory cake she was about to bite into. Portia knew exactly how the girl felt. How lovely it had been to dance with him, to swirl through the figures with his strong arm to lean on, even if she had only been a placeholder until he could begin to meet the girls who really mattered. Portia could still feel the thrum of the music; her head felt muzzy yet from the quick turns and spins he had guided her through without ever making a misstep.

She didn't realize that Lady Ryecroft was not alone

until she'd barged into the middle of what was obviously a tense moment.

"Did you enjoy your turn about the floor?" Lady Ryecroft asked.

It was only a polite question, Portia knew. She managed to say something bland and began wondering how to extricate herself. Whatever Lady Ryecroft and Mr. Winston had been discussing, it seemed to have left them at odds—yet he wasn't going away, despite the fact that Lady Ryecroft had turned her back on him...

Lady Stone returned. "You do not dance, Portia?"

"I thought perhaps you would have need of me, ma'am." *Please*, Portia wanted to say.

"Yes, indeed. What a good idea. I shall lean on your arm as we walk about the room."

As soon as they were at a safe distance, Portia looked down at her employer. "Doing it up too brown, ma'am. It's not like you to hobble—and if you can't walk easily, why did you not just sit down in the corner?"

"You mean you would have preferred to stay and play gooseberry to those two?" Lady Stone's face brightened. "You there—Randall. Why aren't you dancing?"

Lord Randall bowed. "I dance only with Lady Flavia tonight."

"Well, that's romantic. Also foolish to let her conclude, before she is firmly committed to you, that you have no possible interest in anyone else. But if you prefer not to dance, then take Miss Langford for a turn around the edge of the ballroom."

"Ma'am," Portia protested, "there is no need."

"But, my dear, as you just told me—if I cannot walk easily, I must sit down and rest. Surely someone will come and talk to me; I have many old friends in attendance. Do go and enjoy the spectacle. Or take a breath of fresh air on the terrace. Lord Randall, Miss Langford was just mentioning how warm it is in here." She winked.

Portia would have made a face at her, if only there weren't half a hundred potential observers. But Lord Randall had obediently offered his arm, so she laid her hand on his sleeve with the lightest possible touch. "Of course Lady Stone is joking about fresh air on the terrace."

"I should hope so. Though I have the greatest respect for your employer…"

What a hum, Portia thought.

"She has little understanding of the implications of such an act."

Oh, she understands perfectly well.

"A gentleman might as well declare his intentions if he were to take an unmarried lady out to the terrace alone." Belatedly, he seemed to realize that he was not flattering her. "I do beg your pardon, Miss Langford, but surely you must see—"

"Oh, don't go on, my lord. There is no need to explain to me that I don't begin to reach your exalted level of society or that you're doing me honor in simply walking about the room with me."

"That is true," he said after a pause, as if he had given it a great deal of thought.

Portia felt like pinching him. Instead she turned her attention to the dancers, only to meet the frowning gaze of Lady Brindle from across the ballroom. *Now Lady Brindle will think I'm trying to flirt with her son.*

"But the dance is finishing," Lord Randall said with unmistakable relief. "I must find Lady Flavia, for I am promised the honor of leading her out for the first waltz." He bowed and left Portia at the edge of the floor. It was rude of him to abandon her there, but Portia couldn't work herself up to be irritated. At least it should be clear to Lady Brindle that her darling was in no danger of having his head turned by Portia Langford...

In any case, Portia realized, they had made nearly a full circuit of the ballroom, for from a dainty chair nearby, Lady Stone beckoned to her. For a moment Portia considered pretending not to have seen her, but Lady Stone was remarkably difficult to ignore. Her employer was not alone, she saw; a gentleman in purple stood by her chair.

"Lord Swindon has no partner for this waltz," Lady Stone announced. "And I have assured him you are a talented dancer."

Portia dropped a small curtsy. "Lady Stone exaggerates. Having never danced with me herself, she has inflated notions of my skills."

Swindon's eyes gleamed.

With humor? Portia wondered. Or something else?

"But Lady Stone is never wrong." His voice was low, with a rough edge. "I must test your skills for myself."

A chill slid up Portia's spine. "I'm certain any of the young ladies would be delighted to honor you with a dance."

"But I want you. Come, the music is already starting."

With Lady Stone beaming at them, Portia could see no means of escape. Besides, it was only a dance. What was wrong with her tonight, anyway, that she was seeing hidden meanings in the most innocuous of phrases?

The floor was less crowded than before, with the youngest girls not yet permitted to waltz and many older dancers preferring the slow and stately country figures to the exertion of this newer, more daring, more active dance. Across the room, Portia caught a glimpse of Lord Ryecroft with Amalie Mickelthorpe. His sober deep green coat looked like a leafy background to her petal-pink ruffles. Portia had to stifle a chuckle at the image.

Lord Swindon had apparently followed her gaze. "I noticed you arranging partners for Ryecroft. Is that a companion's duty now, to find enter-tainment for her employer's"—his pause drew out significantly—"guest?"

Was he implying that Ryecroft and Lady Stone were carrying on some kind of personal intrigue? *And where is the surprise in that? You warned her yourself that people would talk.*

The only surprise was that Swindon would come so close to saying it. And to her, of all people—Lady Stone's companion... She'd been right in thinking that the sooner Ryecroft chose his heiress, the better it would be for everyone.

And there was no reason at all for her to feel low about it. "Lady Stone requested me to make him known to some of the young ladies."

Swindon chuckled. "Especially the ones with fortunes, I collect. Lady Stone is an untraditional lady."

"Indeed. I find her refreshing."

"No doubt, for you seem to be refreshing and untraditional as well. You are a mysterious companion, Miss Langford. Quite... unusual."

A quiver ran through her. "There's no mystery about me."

"How did you come to meet Lady Stone?"

Oh, why had he asked her for a waltz, where it was possible to chat all through the dance? "She was taking one of her treks up and down the country. I believe she spends her winters going from one house party to the next."

"And you were a guest at one of these house parties?"

"Not precisely. But my aunt lives in the neighborhood of one of them, and we were invited to a dinner party at the great house."

"Where was that?"

Portia pretended not to hear. The patterns of the dancers had shifted, and suddenly Lord Ryecroft was next to them. Swindon drew her closer, as though to avoid a collision, but Portia suspected he had only been waiting for an opportunity. She was sure of it when she tried to pull away and found his arm to be like steel.

"Lady Stone and I found ourselves to be compatible, and as I wished to see the city, we came to an amicable arrangement for my employment."

"Your aunt must have been devastated to lose you."

"I believe she has come to terms with the loss."

"And of course you could always go back to her."

"Of course." It was a casual answer to a casual comment, but Portia couldn't help but wonder whether there had been a reason he had said it.

She tried again to pull away, without success. Over Swindon's shoulder, she caught Lord Ryecroft's eye. He frowned a little, and she felt a bubble of annoyance rise inside her. What business was it of his whom she danced with or how she conducted herself on the floor? Why wasn't he paying attention to the heiress in his arms, anyway, instead of sending disapproving looks in her direction? On the other hand, the fact that he'd noticed made her feel warm somehow. Perhaps she wasn't the only one who was still feeling the aftereffects of that first country dance…

She stopped resisting and let Swindon draw her half an inch closer yet into his arms. So much for Lord Ryecroft's scandalized sensibilities.

The next time she met his gaze, she sent a smile in his direction.

Swindon's arms tightened. "Ah yes. You are skilled indeed."

Portia smothered a sigh. How long could this waltz possibly continue? It already seemed to have been going on forever.

Ten

It was long after midnight when the carriage delivered them to Lady Stone's mansion on Grosvenor Square, and Rye expected that the ladies would not rise until well into the morning.

He, however, found himself in the breakfast room at the usual hour, feeling more irritable than usual, for he had barely slept. He'd tried counting heiresses instead of sheep, only to realize too late that dwelling on a parade of moneyed females was hardly a soothing sort of pastime for a man who was going to have to choose one of them, and soon.

He didn't feel like eating, but he finished his coffee, then continued to sit at the table, feeling as empty as his cup.

Perhaps, he thought, if Sophie were to make the brilliant match they all hoped for, then he wouldn't have to choose from the heiresses after all. But a shaft of disgust shot through him at the idea. What sort of man was he, to wish for his little sister to rescue him?

A rustle in the hallway made him paste a smile on his face. It wouldn't fool his mother, he suspected, but it might get by Sophie and buy him some time to talk himself round again.

But it was Portia who came into the breakfast room. *Portia.* He wondered when he had started thinking of her that way. Not that it was surprising; after a couple of weeks of living under the same roof, of attending and discussing the same parties, even of standing about waiting for dressmakers and milliners to finish what Sophie insisted would take *no more than a minute*, it would have been difficult to maintain strict formality. Not that he would ever call her by her first name to her face, of course... She would freeze him in a minute if he tried.

"Good morning, my lord," she said lightly and helped herself to toast and scrambled eggs from the chafing dishes on the sideboard. "And congratulations."

Rye had risen automatically when she came in. He held her chair, noting how neatly turned out she was in a green morning dress that somehow made her hair glow. He wondered if the glossy strands felt as soft and warm and smooth as they looked, and clutched his cup a little tighter to keep himself from reaching out to explore. "Regarding what?" He knew he sounded grumpy. He didn't care.

She looked a little startled. "I expected you'd be totting up your successes from last night. Your sister is a Sensation indeed, and did you meet three heiresses or four? I'm afraid I lost count." She briskly buttered her toast. "Which of them impressed you most?"

Rye filled her coffee cup. "That's hard to say," he mused. "Miss Mickelthorpe, I suppose. She looked at me as if I were a particularly luscious tidbit she was about to crunch between those strong, horsey teeth, and her bray of a voice definitely made an impression."

"That is unkind of you, sir." But he thought she had to struggle not to laugh. He wondered for a moment why she was in such a good mood, then remembered she had waltzed last night with her favorite rake. No doubt she was bubbling this morning because her dreams had been filled with Swindon. Perhaps she looked so utterly delicious because the rake had maneuvered her out of the ballroom for a kiss... No, Rye would have noticed if she'd been gone.

"Did you not think Juliana Farling pretty?" she asked.

"Oh yes. But she barely spoke a word all through the country dance we shared. And when I attempted to pay her the smallest of compliments, she turned beet red and looked as if she wanted to cry."

"What did you tell her?"

Rye admitted, "That her blue dress matched her eyes."

"Yes, indeed," Portia said gravely. "That is what I would call the *smallest* of compliments. You'll have to do better than that if the young ladies are to take you seriously."

"And you're an authority on what young ladies like to hear? Perhaps I should have danced Miss Mickelthorpe closer, so that I could have listened to what Swindon was whispering in your ear."

Her eyes had turned to granite, but all she said was, "If Lady Stone were to hear about your lack of finesse, she'd immediately start you on a course of lessons until your style improved to her satisfaction."

"Lessons? Do you mean she'd make me practice by flattering her?"

"Or worse, *me*."

As lessons went, Rye thought, that would be far more pleasant than Latin declensions—at least until he had to share his work. He suspected Portia might be a tougher taskmaster than any Oxford don.

"You'll need to work on your skills if you wish to escape that fate."

Eyes, hair, lashes, smile… Rye tore his thoughts away from the mental list he'd already started. He'd need to be more original than that to please her. "Sophie said something similar last night. She told me I'd insulted our mother, when I'd meant to praise her instead. Damned if I can see it, for all I said was—"

Portia wrinkled her nose. "That you were surprised to see Lady Ryecroft looking pretty. Imagine how wonderful *that* must have made her feel—as though you think her an antidote the rest of the time."

"Oh." There were three freckles on the bridge of her nose, Rye noticed. They formed an off-balance triangle that made his finger itch to connect the dots.

"And your sister is correct. With Lady Ryecroft's looks and figure and coloring, she would show to far better advantage in rust and periwinkle and bronze rather than gray and silver and lavender."

He looked again at the brassy green of Portia's dress. "You mean she should wear the same sort of colors that look so good on you?"

"There, my lord—you *are* able to turn a pretty compliment when you put your mind to it." She smiled, and Rye wanted to lean closer, until he could discover for himself whether her lips were really as warm and sweet and soft as they looked just now.

He refilled his coffee cup instead. He knew he should have excused himself and left the room. He should have simply gone away—anywhere at all.

Instead he stayed in the breakfast room, where her scent tickled his nose and the light that shifted on her dress with each breath she took made him want to touch her…

No. At least he should be honest with himself. It wasn't the light and it wasn't her scent that made him long to touch her. And he wouldn't be satisfied with a touch either.

Last night, when he had been struggling through that waltz with Amalie Mickelthorpe and Portia had swept past him in the arms of Lord Swindon, Rye had felt as if someone had smacked him across the head. She'd looked so damned pleased with herself—smiling at him from that libertine's arms, letting him hold her so closely.

It was none of Rye's business how she conducted herself, of course. *He* had to marry an heiress.

But there was something about Swindon he simply didn't like. He hoped Portia knew what she was doing.

&

When the little maid who had been assigned to look after Sophie brought in her tray of chocolate, she was grinning so broadly that Sophie was startled. "Oh, miss, you won't believe the drawing room!"

Sophie yawned and sat up, pushing a pillow behind her back. "What's wrong with it, Susan?"

"It's so full of flowers delivered already this morning that Mr. Padgett's had to send to the storerooms for more tables to set them all on, and he's turned out every vase and container in the house. Flowers for *you*, miss. You're a… a *Sensation*, that's what I heard Miss Portia tell him. Do hurry and drink your chocolate, so you can come and see them all."

The maid set the tray across Sophie's knees and went to pull the curtains open. A tap on the door made Sophie sit up a little straighter. "Come in."

Her mother, already neatly attired in a charcoal walking dress despite the hour, came in. "Did you sleep well, Sophie? You were not too excited to rest?"

Sophie stretched luxuriously. "Oh, wasn't it a *grand* ball? Susan tells me I'm being sent flowers. Loads and loads of flowers, she says. Have you seen them?"

"I have not."

"And she tells me that Portia says I am a *Sensation*… Susan, please bring another cup so my mother may join me."

Lady Ryecroft picked up Sophie's dance card, which had slipped off the chair where Sophie had dropped it last night along with her gloves. She ran her eye down the list of names before she laid it aside.

"Sophie," she said as soon as the door closed behind the little maid. "It's one thing to be the belle of Surrey, but I should hate to have you expect the same reaction here in London, where there are many pretty girls."

"And every last one of them has more of a dowry than I possess. I know, Mama."

"Perhaps I should speak to Portia. Calling you a Sensation…"

Sophie laughed. "Oh, Mama, don't be silly. Of course I'm not getting a big head over this. I expect if there are three nosegays downstairs, Susan would consider them a roomful, for surely Lady Stone doesn't receive flowers regularly. And as for Portia—well, most likely she said I was *sensitive* instead, and Susan simply heard her wrong. But I must own to being relieved that I can hold up my head with confidence. Just think of the shame if I had made so small an impression that I didn't receive even one single rose!"

"Speaking of shame…" Lady Ryecroft's tone of voice was a warning.

"What did I do, Mama?"

"I find it hard to believe you don't know. Sitting out a dance with Lord Carrisbrooke, in a chair meant for one person…"

"Mama, it was not so small as that! And if it was improper to use it, why was it right there, at the corner of the ballroom?"

"Perhaps so a fatigued dancer—*one* fatigued dancer, Sophie—could sit there. Your behavior last night in allowing him to pay you such particular attention…"

"It was only a dance, Mama."

"How is it that I do not see his name on your card?"

"He traded…" Sophie bit her tongue, but it was too late.

"He *bargained* for your hand in a dance?"

"Mama, it wasn't like that at all. He did nothing improper… he merely stepped in for a friend." Sophie watched her mother's brows draw together and hurried on, hoping to distract her. "And he has the most beautiful way of speaking! He recited poetry to me entirely through the waltz, as the dancers circled before us. It was *so* romantic."

Lady Ryecroft's lips were tight.

"Did you enjoy dancing with his uncle?" Sophie ventured. "Carrisbrooke asked him to do so, he said."

"We will discuss this later, Sophronia." As Susan came in with the cup, Lady Ryecroft went out—and for once, Sophie noted, her mother did not so much as pause for a smile or a kind word for the servant.

I must really be in for it. Sophie set her chocolate cup aside untouched and pushed back the blankets. She might as well face the day.

❧

The distance from Grosvenor Square to Bloomsbury, where the gossip columns reported that Marcus Winston had bought a house shortly after his return from the New World, was not great in miles. But the surroundings could hardly be more different, Miranda thought as the hackney carriage took her eastward. The farther the carriage went, the smaller and closer together the houses were. Though they were still sizable and solid, these homes were nothing like the elegant edifices that surrounded the great squares of the West End. And the occupants were likely to be bohemians—artists, writers, successful businessmen— rather than members of society.

Which made it an appropriate location for a man like Marcus Winston. She wondered if this neighborhood reminded him of his home in America. She knew so little of what he had done there, where he had lived, how he had gone on, what his business was...

"And I don't care to know," she reminded herself. The only thing she cared about—and the only reason she was here today—was his promise to put a stop to his nephew's infatuation. Miranda aimed to hold him to it.

She half expected, when the front door opened, to see Marcus himself standing there; it seemed the sort of thing he might do. But she was greeted by a proper manservant instead. Neither a butler nor a footman, however; perhaps he was something in between.

He looked skeptical at the sight of her, and Miranda wished she hadn't been so cautious in choosing a bonnet with a dark, obscuring veil. She had no desire to look interestingly mysterious, only to be over-looked altogether.

She held out her card. "I wish to see Mr. Winston."

The manservant showed her into a small reception room where no fire had yet been laid, and returned only a few minutes later to say, "If my lady will follow me." He led the way up the first set of stairs.

Miranda's heart skittered madly as she followed in his wake, and even more so as his careful, steady tread passed by what must be the doors of a drawing room and went on toward the back of the house. Where was he taking her?

He tapped on a closed door, but rather than open it immediately, he waited at attention, and only when she heard Marcus's voice calling permission from inside did he turn the knob. "Lady Ryecroft, sir," he said formally, and Miranda found herself frozen on the threshold for an instant before she could gather herself and step into the room.

At least, Miranda thought, he had not brought her to a bedroom. Though it was close enough, truth be told; there was a chaise longue, and a sofa that was larger and looked even more comfortable than the one in the study at Carris Abbey.

I'm not going to think of that right now, she told herself.

She heard the door close softly behind her, and for a moment she was utterly alone. There was not even a sound except for the soft crackle of coals settling in the grate. Marcus was nowhere to be seen. But she *had* heard him speak, had she not?

A door opened across the room, and Marcus came in, one hand lifted as if he was still adjusting the pearl stickpin in his cravat. "What a pleasure to receive you so early in the morning, Miranda. Would you care to join me for breakfast?"

She couldn't prevent the picture that sprang to her mind. The two of them, sitting at a small table that stood in a bay window overlooking a garden. Herself in a soft morning gown, her hair caught up under a cap. Marcus passing the toast rack, commenting on a tidbit from the newspapers, rising from the table to go about his day, but pausing to brush aside the lace edge of her cap to kiss her nape… then—with his business forgotten—pulling off the cap to release her hair… kissing her throat and her lips and her breasts… taking her back to bed…

How utterly foolish. You might as well picture him making love to you right there on the breakfast table, among the coffee cups and the toast crumbs.

The trouble was she could visualize that with no difficulty at all.

"How long did it take you to train your manservant to knock at doors before entering?" she asked.

"A while. I never could abide the way the servants slithered around Carris Abbey, popping up when they were least expected—or wanted. Never a moment of privacy."

"And of course that's important to you. It must make things far more convenient when you wish to… entertain."

He smiled. "If you came to discuss with me the intricacies of having an affair, Miranda, I'd be happy to demonstrate how all things are possible to those who have both the desire and the imagination."

"That is not why I came."

"A pity," he said. "I gather you do not wish to share my breakfast after all? Or my bed, it seems. Then pray, do sit down and tell me what I may do for you."

She perched on the edge of the sofa. "Only what you promised—you said you would put a stop to Carrisbrooke's paying court to Sophie."

"I have every intention of doing so. I spoke to him last evening, in fact."

"For all the good it did. He sent Sophie flowers this morning."

"Surely he's not the only one who thought of that trite gesture."

"Four dozen red roses—at least four dozen, I didn't actually count them. I saw the bouquet delivered, so I came directly to talk to you."

Marcus braced his elbow on the mantel. "How unimaginative of my nephew. I expected far better from the poetic soul that he would like to appear."

"I do wish you'd take this seriously. He is far too young for her."

"As cases of puppy love go, I take it seriously indeed. But the way to handle puppy love is *not* to forbid it. Miranda, you didn't scold your daughter, did you?"

"Of course I did. She should know better—she was nearly sitting on his lap!"

Marcus shook his head. "You would do far better to tell her how much his childish antics amuse you."

"Childish!"

"Well, he is, you know. He's not yet nineteen—barely dry behind the ears."

"The same age Sophie is, give or take a few months."

"Exactly. But young women of that age are far more pragmatic than the boys are. Given time, Carrisbrooke will fall out of love with your Sophie and into it again with some shockingly inappropriate opera dancer. But if you make him a romantic hero to her by forbidding contact between them, don't be surprised if she climbs down the drainpipe some night and runs off with him before he has a chance to get over her."

Was it possible he was right? "I do not doubt that you know your nephew better than I do, but—"

Marcus's eyes widened. "Do I hear aright? Lady Ryecroft admits that someone else might have the advantage of her? If only I had a witness to swear to this occasion!"

"...but you do not know my daughter."

"I should like to, Miranda." There was a thread of steel under the soft baritone.

Her eyelids prickled, and she blinked hard. She would *not* cry. "No, Marcus. You're too old for her."

"You say I am too old," he said philosophically, "and Carrisbrooke is too young... Will anyone ever be satisfactory, in your mind?"

"She is special."

"I don't doubt it, my dear. She's your daughter."

"I mean it, Marcus. I can't bear it—you and Sophie." Her voice caught, and she realized too late that she had given herself away. Primly, she added, "Or Carrisbrooke either."

"There's a way to fix this, Miranda. But it requires your cooperation."

There was a long instant where everything seemed to stop. Each muscle in Miranda's body went as rigid as if she had frozen solid. "Be your mistress, you mean. If I become your mistress, you'll leave Sophie alone."

Marcus looked thoughtful. "You told me last night it would be impossible to blackmail you into such a thing."

"But of course you would try it anyway," she said bitterly. "If that's the price..."

His eyes gleamed. *With triumph*, she thought. Very well. She had made her bargain, and she would live with it.

But he didn't move. He didn't swoop on her to claim his prize.

No doubt he was savoring his victory and drawing out the satisfaction of her surrender.

He crossed the room and sat next to her on the big sofa. *Too close for propriety*, she thought, before she remembered that what was proper had now changed—utterly, completely, and forever.

But he did not touch her, only sat with his head tipped a little to one side and looked at her. Finally he stretched out a hand and tugged at the ribbon that held her close-fitting bonnet in place. In the quiet room, the sound of the satin ribbon sliding against itself seemed as loud to Miranda as the beat of her heart. Then the knot gave way, and slowly he lifted the bonnet from her head and tossed it aside.

"That," he said quietly, "was not what I meant, my dear. My plan does not involve courting your daughter, for I have concluded you are correct and she is indeed too young for me. So there is no need for the offer you have made."

Miranda was horrified at herself. He had made a fool of her once before; had she learned nothing at all in the library at Carris Abbey? "I… bed your pardon." Her voice cracked. "I mean… *beg* your pardon."

"Since you now wish to become my mistress, Miranda… I accept." His fingertips brushed over her hair and then flicked against her cheek. "But I intend to have things absolutely clear between us. I want no misunderstanding of how—and why—we become lovers. You are not sacrificing yourself for the sake of your daughter. You are going to make love with me because you want me as much as I want you."

Miranda sat frozen as his thumb traced her lower lip, and she felt herself tremble against his touch. "I do *not* want—" But she couldn't finish, for her words were caught between his mouth and hers. The tip of his tongue brushed the corner of her mouth—slowly, as though he were tasting a new dish.

"Don't you?" he whispered. "Isn't this exactly why you came here today, because you want me to make love to you? You could have merely spoken to me about Carrisbrooke tonight at the Farlings' musicale."

"How was I to know you would be there?"

He smiled a little at what she had to admit had been a feeble protest. "Or at Almack's tomorrow. Surely you don't think I would miss that. But you didn't wait; you came here today instead. Alone—without even your maid to chaperone you. What else could you have had in mind, but this?"

Somehow—Miranda was uncertain just how it had happened—she was lying back on the sofa, and he was beside her, big and warm and strong, with one hand at her nape and the other cupping her jaw to turn her face up to his.

"Ever since the first time you suggested we have an affair, I have regretted letting you go." His voice was soft, but there was a rough edge underneath. "And since you have renewed the offer, I shall not insult you by refusing again."

"No," she managed to say. "That's not why..." She stopped, too confused to go on. Why *hadn't* she waited until this evening, when she could have spoken to him without putting her reputation at risk? Why hadn't she dispatched a note asking him to call on her?

"Then why did you rush to accept a bargain I did not offer?" He nibbled gently at her lower lip, tasting, then traced the edge with the tip of his tongue.

Was it possible that he was right?

"Tell me you don't want me, Miranda, and make me believe it, and I'll let you go." He kissed her throat, slowly working his way down to the tiny ruffle that edged the neckline of her gown.

She tried to say the words, but they seemed to stick in her throat. She couldn't deny it any longer. She hadn't realized it, hadn't admitted it, hadn't planned it, but this had been her intention, or she would have found another way. A way that did not involve being alone with him, privately and intimately…

Marcus seemed to read her mind. He ran a possessive hand over her body, pausing over her breast, cupping her hip for a moment, sliding the length of her leg to where the hem of her skirt had slipped higher than was proper, and lingering a couple of inches above her ankle, where her boot top ended.

There was an instant when she could have stopped him. An instant when he paused, as if waiting for her to object.

But she didn't want to. Miranda felt herself quivering, but was it with shame or anticipation?

The instant passed, and Marcus began to work his way back up—under her skirt this time. His fingertips were firm against the silk of her stocking, gentle against the bare skin above her garter and masterful as he found the slit in her drawers and cupped his palm over her mound.

His eyes blazed with satisfaction and desire, and heat ran through her at the confirmation that he wanted her. He had not put her aside so easily after all that day at Carris Abbey when he had sent her away. And just as she had been thinking of him ever since, perhaps he had been thinking of her…

He kissed her again, long and deep, his tongue

delving into her mouth even as his fingertip sought another warm, moist place. She whimpered a little and opened her legs for him.

"So lusciously wet," he whispered against her lips. "So deliciously eager. Show me, Miranda, how much you want me."

He slipped his finger inside her and began to stroke softly, and she moaned and let her head fall back against the velvet cushions. She could feel her heart pounding, her muscles tensing in anticipation, her mouth going dry as he nudged her closer to the brink. All she could do was feel, but she was afraid to, for she had never felt this way before.

She opened her eyes and realized he had pulled back as if to watch her. Miranda felt embarrassment sweep over her at the idea of the spectacle she was presenting—skirt hiked up, head thrown back, breath rasping...

If only, she thought, he weren't *looking* at her! If it had been dark, she wouldn't have minded. Or at least—if she were being truthful—she wouldn't have minded so much. Instead here she was. In the middle of the morning, with sunlight pouring in through the windows, she was spread out across a sofa like a trollop as she took her pleasure...

She was taking, she realized belatedly, but she was not giving in return. Was that why Marcus had withdrawn ever so slightly—because she was doing something wrong? Exactly what was expected of a mistress, anyway? For surely it must be different from what was appropriate for a wife.

Enthusiasm—yes, that much was obvious. And of

course a mistress should show concern for her partner's needs... Yes, that must be where she had fallen short. Too focused on her own unfamiliar sensations, she had forgotten his.

She reached up to him, clutching his cravat and tugging. His pearl stickpin went flying as the neckcloth came loose, and she caressed his bare throat, then slid her hands down the front of his shirt to the waistband of his pantaloons, trying to release his buttons. But her fingers didn't seem to work.

"Stop," he said gently. "This is for you this time."

She wasn't certain she'd heard him correctly. "But that's not... not fair. You can't enjoy..."

"We've only begun, Miranda. I will be satisfied, I assure you, before we've finished. For now, look at me. I want to watch you come apart in my arms." His caresses grew firmer, more demanding.

Miranda whimpered, and everything around her seemed to turn slightly blue. "I want..." Her voice was so ragged that she couldn't finish. She reached for him instead, brushing her palm across his nape and tugging him down to her so she could bury her face in his shoulder—a rock to cling to as the storm broke deep inside her.

～

Sophie paid particular attention to her toilette, just in case her mother was still in a mood to be critical. By the time she went downstairs, feeling as bright as the sunshine in a butter-yellow muslin morning gown, a good part of the day was already gone. The first thing she heard as she descended the stairs was Rye sneezing, so she looked around the newel post to wish a blessing for him.

"The place has turned into a damned conservatory," he said irritably.

Sophie came face-to-face with a row of floral arrangements that stretched from the drawing-room doors at the front of the house to the round window that looked out over the garden at the back.

"Oh my goodness," she whispered. "Are all these for me? Maybe I *am* a Sensation." There were big bouquets and tiny nosegays, roses of every shade, along with daisies and violets and bachelor buttons and flowers Sophie had never seen before. Not only was there a rainbow of colors, but the multitude of blooms gave off a clash of scents that threatened to make her head ache. And she'd only had to smell them for a couple of minutes; no wonder Rye was cranky.

He sneezed again, his whole face disappearing into a large white handkerchief.

Portia bustled out of the drawing room, holding a china pitcher full of golden-yellow roses, which she held out to Rye. "Take these while I shift the others to make room on that side table. Good morning, Sophie—I'm trying to make space in the drawing room for the callers who will no doubt begin arriving at any moment."

He didn't take the pitcher. "Now that she's finally up, Sophie can help you," Rye pointed out. "They're her flowers. I'm going to my club."

Portia paid no attention to his protest but thrust the roses into his hands. The pitcher lurched, and water sloshed over the lip of the container as Rye hastily held it away from him to keep from drenching his neckcloth. A small card that had been tucked in between the stems fell out.

Sophie picked up the card from the carpet at Rye's feet and read it. "Or perhaps I'm not such a Sensation. This bouquet is for you, Portia." She held out the card.

Portia looked startled. "Surely not. That must be a mistake."

Rye's eyes narrowed. "Let me see that card."

"If it's mine," Portia said, "then I am able to read it myself."

Rye held the pitcher out of her reach with one hand and tried to seize the card from Sophie's grasp with the other. Sophie danced away, and the bouquet overbalanced and tipped out of his grasp. For what seemed endless seconds they all watched as the pitcher cartwheeled through the air; then it shattered on the marble floor, spraying bits of china and broken roses across the hall.

"Now see what you've made me do, Sophie," Rye said.

"Me?" Sophie was incensed. "I'm not the one who was trying to snatch a card that's not mine." She bent to scoop up a handful of wounded roses before someone stepped on them.

"Leave it, Sophie," Portia said. "Here comes Jane now—she'll get the rest."

As a housemaid hurried up to deal with the mess, the sound of the front door opening rose from the lower floor, followed by a peal of girlish giggles. The first callers had arrived.

Portia cocked her head to one side. "That sounds

like Miss Mickelthorpe. I think we can assume you made a favorable impression last night on her at least, my lord."

"Though you'd think," Sophie said, "if she's seriously interested in you, Rye, she'd know better than to come here today. She should be at home, hoping you'll call on her, not seeking you out the morning after you met."

Rye looked gloomy.

"Or else," Portia suggested cheerfully, "perhaps she does know the etiquette, and this is her way of making it clear that she's *not* interested in you."

"I'm not even supposed to be here. I'm going to my club—remember?"

"Too late for that," Sophie said. "Padgett's bringing them up, and you can't simply brush past Miss Mickelthorpe and leave. Unless Jane's willing to smuggle you down the servants' stair…" The little maid giggled from the floor, where she was gathering shards of the china pitcher.

Sophie handed the card to Portia, who glanced at it and tucked it under a nearby vase. Sophie was impressed that her expression didn't even change.

"Swindon, eh?" said Rye, who'd been looking over Portia's shoulder. "Well, well. It seems I'm not the only one who made an impression last night."

"I'm sure that's an opening gambit to get Sophie's attention," Portia said with a shrug. "To whet her interest in him by making it seem he's not interested in her."

"Did you send Miss Mickelthorpe flowers this morning, Rye?" Sophie asked brightly as she brushed a few stray droplets of water from her gown. "You should have done, you know."

"No. I'll use Swindon's strategy and send them to her chaperone instead. I'm sure that will get her attention."

Sophie advanced to the top of the stairs just as Padgett came into view. Directly behind him was Miss Mickelthorpe, who was wearing a confection in ruffled blue, topped by the most ridiculously overtrimmed hat Sophie had ever seen, full of ribbon roses and feathers and lace. She was flanked by Lady Flavia Summersby, and bringing up the rear was Lady Brindle.

Sophie put on the widest smile she could summon. "I am so glad you've come to visit, ladies. What a lovely ball it was, Lady Flavia."

Lady Brindle stopped on the top stair and raised a quizzing glass. "Are you trying to start a new fashion, Miss Ryecroft? Carrying a sheaf of broken-stemmed roses that match your dress?"

Sophie let the sarcasm pass. "Only a small domestic accident, I'm afraid. It's entirely under control." She handed the flowers she had rescued to Jane.

Portia said, "Do come into the drawing room, ladies."

Lady Brindle swept down the hall and paused on the threshold of the drawing room. "But where is Lady Stone? And your mother, Miss Ryecroft? I was hoping to spend the morning with my good friend Miranda while you girls enjoyed chattering about last night. I was so caught up in dear Flavia's ball last evening that I had no time even to greet Miranda. Of course, your party was very late in arriving, I noticed... Surely your mother hasn't left you to receive guests alone this morning—without a chaperone?"

Rye stepped forward. "Miss Langford is here."

"Oh. Yes. Miss Langford," Lady Brindle said with a notable lack of enthusiasm.

"Where *is* Mother, do you suppose?" Sophie whispered to Rye. "She rang a peal over me before breakfast"—too late, she realized it might not have been wise to share that information with her brother—"but I haven't seen her since."

He stepped aside in the hallway for Lady Flavia and Miss Mickelthorpe to precede him, then followed Portia and Sophie into the drawing room, where Lady Brindle had already chosen the most comfortable chair. He waited for the rest of the ladies to choose seats, and then—deliberately, Sophie thought—went to stand near Lady Brindle.

For an instant Miss Mickelthorpe looked annoyed. She had obviously, and carefully, chosen the long sofa and seated herself at one end in order to leave plenty of room for a gentleman. So much for the idea that she might not be interested in Rye after all.

"I'm glad to see your injury has healed, Lady Brindle," Rye said.

Sophie winced, but there was nothing she could do.

"My injury? Oh, you mean that Banbury tale your mother was telling about my ankle and why I needed her to come to Brindle Park. I never did find out why she was so determined to come, you know... No, I'm pleased to say my ankle is as sound as ever."

Rye looked daggers at Sophie, who tried to ignore him as she started talking nonsense with Miss Mickelthorpe.

It's not my fault, Sophie thought. She would have

remembered to tell him the strange tale of the unsprained ankle, if it hadn't been for things like Robert Wellingham coming to visit and Rye renting out the manor and Lady Stone inviting them to London… Did he expect her to remember *everything*?

Lady Stone came bustling in just then and flung herself down next to Lady Brindle. "Late to my own visiting hours," she crowed. "But of course you started without me. Do tell me the latest *on-dits*, Ann Eliza, before we're overrun with other visitors. What are the gossips saying this morning? And better yet, is any of it true?"

Eleven

THE MOST POWERFUL CLIMAX OF HER LIFE LEFT MIRANDA trembling, almost whimpering, and clinging to Marcus. He held her close, nestled in the safety of his arms…

What an odd way to put it, Miranda thought. As if there had been anything *safe* about the way she had spiraled out of control!

He kissed her temple, her eyelids, her mouth, catching her sigh of satisfaction on his lips as the last tremors died away. "You hid your face and didn't let me watch you after all," he whispered. "Next time… Come to bed with me, Miranda."

Sanity returned. How could she possibly parade through the hall and up the stairs to Marcus's bedroom as if she didn't care who knew what they'd been doing here?

It was bad enough that his manservant, trained not to intrude, must have a good suspicion of what was going on in this quiet, private room. But to go out into the public areas of the house and confirm it…

Some people might not mind if the staff saw—or even if they gossiped. But Miranda did. And right now she felt so mussed that anyone who saw them would have to know what she had been doing.

Yet the tension within her was so strong that she suspected if she left him now, she would be in agony. And what kind of a mistress even considered leaving her lover with his desires unsatisfied?

"You've lost your cravat."

"No, darling, it's not lost. It's right over there on the floor." He kissed her, slowly, and withdrew his hand from under her skirt. She felt cold suddenly, and abandoned.

He took her hand, but instead of leading her back to the hallway, he took her across to the door where he had entered and opened it with a flourish.

The room beyond might have once been a music room or perhaps an extra parlor. Now it was, in all respects, a bedroom—complete with a huge and elaborately carved four-poster bed, neatly draped in deep blue velvet.

So neatly draped, in fact, that it seemed never to have been used. How perfectly convenient, she thought, to have this snug little hideaway ready at a moment's notice.

"Who but a rake would have thought to put a bedroom on the same floor as the drawing room?" she said.

"Someone who finds it a pointless waste of energy to run up and down extra flights of stairs every time I need to change clothes. *Not* to make it easier to entertain—though, at the moment, I am grateful for the inspiration. Miranda…" He drew her close.

She couldn't stop herself from melting into his

body, where she seemed to fit perfectly. His chest rubbed hard against her breasts, and her nipples peaked in eager response. His hands slid down her back and came to rest on her hips, pulling her so tightly against his erection that she could feel his heat even through the fabric of her dress and chemise, and her response to it shocked her. She should have been sated; instead she felt an aching emptiness and an almost overwhelming urge to rip away the barriers that separated them. She tried to unfasten his shirt and settled for pulling it loose so she could at least slide her hands under the crisp linen and caress his skin.

"Let me deal with your buttons," he said gently, "or we'll never get you put back together afterward."

How accomplished he was in the practical aspects of carrying on an *affaire*, she thought. Thinking ahead so clearly, not letting passion get the better of him, not for an instant forgetting that she would have to appear again in public without arousing suspicion…

But then he must have done this many times, while it was only her first. She should, perhaps, be pleased that he was taking steps to protect her from her own shortsightedness.

But she would not have been human if part of her hadn't wanted him to lose control, to forget everything except her… and his desire for her.

His fingers worked with a great deal more efficiency than hers were capable of doing, but it still seemed to take a long time to free Miranda of the charcoal walking dress—mostly because he kept stopping to kiss her collarbone and nip at her shoulder and taste the rosy circles around her nipples.

By the time they were finally together on his bed, free of all restrictions, there was not a square inch of her that had not been caressed, and Miranda felt as if her entire body was aflame. The brush of his lightly haired chest against her breasts only served to heat her more, and the emptiness inside her had grown torturous. When at long last he parted her legs and moved over her, she pulled him closer, demanding with her body what she couldn't bring herself to put into words.

As carefully as if she'd been a virgin, he probed and slowly entered, looking deep into her eyes as he took her an inch at a time. He was hot and hard and big, and she realized that his breath was rasping with the effort he was making to be careful, to take his time. *How sweet*, she thought. She abruptly tilted her hips, moaning with satisfaction as she succeeded in pulling him deeply inside her.

"Wench," he said and held still for a moment, as if to savor the sensation, before he started to move. Each long, deliciously firm thrust filled her completely; each withdrawal left her aching. Ever so slowly, the pace increased, each stroke just a little quicker, a little deeper, a little more forceful.

She caught his rhythm and met him eagerly, until—with her gaze locked with his—she lost herself once more just as he thrust hard and exploded deep inside her.

∽

Lady Stone's offhanded prediction had been correct— within minutes more callers began to arrive, and inside half an hour they were overrun. Every few minutes Padgett trudged up to the drawing room to announce a new contingent of visitors. Young ladies with their mothers. Young men in small groups, as if clustered together for courage. Older men one at a time.

Rye kept on the move, greeting everyone and exchanging a few words in each small group. Portia, he noticed, was doing much the same thing as she tried to find chairs for everyone who wanted to sit, and once, they nearly collided near the windows overlooking Grosvenor Square. "You're supposed to be buttering up heiresses," she said quietly. "Not making engagements with your friends to go inspect horses."

So she'd been eavesdropping on his conversation, not paying attention to the matron who had been talking to her… Satisfaction surged through him. "I'm applying Lady Stone's advice not to seem too eager to please."

"Not appearing overenthusiastic is one thing. Being stiff and unapproachable is another. You've barely exchanged a word with Miss Mickelthorpe, and Lady Brindle will excuse herself any moment now, because she's already overstayed the polite length of a visit. You'll lose the opportunity."

Good, thought Rye, before he could stop himself. Unfortunately, Portia was correct that he must not let this chance pass altogether. In this group, only Amalie Mickelthorpe was on Lady Stone's list of potential eligible brides.

He glanced around the room and noted that Lady Brindle had indeed slid to the edge of her chair as if she was about to say her farewells. Miss Mickelthorpe was still sitting on the long sofa where she had planted herself on arrival, and he was headed in that direction to do the pretty, when Padgett came into the room once more. This time the butler was ushering Lord Swindon. Rye couldn't help it; he looked over his shoulder to see how Portia would react to the sight of her favorite rake coming to make a morning call.

She had paused in midstep as if her attention was arrested for a moment by the mere sight of Swindon on the threshold. Then she turned to Sophie, who happened to be standing nearest her, with a brief comment. Rye was too far away to hear, but Sophie frowned a little, and he couldn't help but wonder whether Portia had been warning his sister to keep hands off. But surely not—a mere companion would not assume a nobleman was her property, much less caution a Beauty to stay away.

Between the scent of the flowers that seeped in from the hallway as each visitor entered, the shrill giggles of the young ladies, and the posturing of the men—young and not so young—who were trying to impress the ladies, Rye's head was beginning to ache in earnest. *And I don't even have to run up and down the stairs through that cloud of pollen.* "Poor Padgett."

He wasn't aware he'd voiced his opinion until Amalie Mickelthorpe said, "Did you say 'poor Padgett'? You mean the butler, my lord? But surely he should be thankful to have such a position."

"I'm certain he is grateful to be employed. I only meant he can't be accustomed to Lady Stone receiving this sort of crowd. It must be hard on him at his age, having to tramp up and down every time the knocker falls."

Miss Mickelthorpe looked puzzled. "But think of the honor—the house being so busy." She pulled her ruffles aside, making room for him on the sofa, and for the first time he realized that she'd been holding that space open all morning. Rye glanced around, noting that—for a wonder—every lady in the room was seated at the moment, so he could sit too. Lady Stone caught his eye and nodded her approval, her beady black gaze sparkling over him and his companion.

As he sat down, Miss Mickelthorpe leaned toward him and dropped her voice to an intimate murmur. "Do tell me about Surrey, my lord. I have never been there, but I understand the countryside is pretty and that your home is close enough to the capital for easy visits."

What he wouldn't give to go home to Ryecroft Manor right now, and stay there in peace and quiet. Only, he reminded himself, he would have to take this young woman—or one much like her—home with him. Forever.

At least, he thought philosophically, his father had not only built a good wine cellar, but stocked it well. Once he was back at Ryecroft, he could just go through his regular routine in a port-induced haze and not even notice Miss Mickelthorpe...

"Perhaps," she went on, "with the days growing longer now, you will host a luncheon party there? I should so love to see Ryecroft Manor."

The hair on Rye's nape stood up. "It's only a few hours' drive, true enough," he admitted, "but it's not close enough to go all the way back and forth in a day and still enjoy the visit."

Lady Flavia came up behind them. "In any case, since Ryecroft Manor is rented out for the Season, you can hardly go nosing about the place, Amalie."

Automatically, Rye popped to his feet, wondering how that news had gotten out and why Lady Flavia had thought the fact important enough to notice.

"It's time to go," Lady Flavia went on. "Lady Brindle is saying her farewells."

Rye thanked heaven; his timing had been well-nigh perfect. "It is my bad fortune to have you swept away just as I'm finally free to join you, Miss Mickelthorpe." He offered his hand to help her rise. "I shall see you this evening at the Farlings' musicale, I believe?"

"Oh yes. I do so appreciate music, though I have little talent in that direction myself."

Somehow that announcement didn't surprise Rye.

"My gift is more in the arts. My watercolor teacher says I have an incredible feel for color and proportion."

Rye's gaze fell on Miss Mickelthorpe's hat, loaded down with such a variety and number of trimmings that it must make her neck hurt to hold up the weight of it all, and he wondered whether the watercolor teacher was an incompetent artist or a master of ironic understatement. *Incredible* could have several interpretations…

Silence fell across the room, and for an instant Rye wondered if his expression had given away his thoughts. That would be untidy, if anyone happened to be watching him closely.

From the doorway Padgett cleared his throat and said, "Mr. Wellingham, my lady."

Oh, that explains it. A moneylender appearing in the drawing room of a peeress, during her regular visiting hours... In the eyes of society, Lady Stone might as well invite the butler himself to sit down and chat with this roomful of guests!

Robert Wellingham paused on the threshold and looked about him. Rye was close enough to see the ironic twinkle in the banker's eyes as his gaze swept over the crowd, and he liked the man even more for that humorous glint. He also wondered how many of the *ton* who had gathered in this overheated, over-scented room were uncomfortable to see the banker there, not because of his social station, but because they owed Robert Wellingham money.

Probably not many, but Rye suspected it wasn't because they hadn't tried to borrow; it was more likely Wellingham had found them to be bad risks and turned down the bargain.

The silence stretched out. Lady Brindle broke it finally, her voice almost echoing through the drawing room. "Lady Stone, I declare—you do have such *amusing* taste in acquaintances!"

Lady Flavia gave a nervous titter.

Rye, feeling militant, stepped forward and offered his hand. "Wellingham, it's good to see you again. What brings you up to town? Nothing wrong at the manor, I hope?"

Robert Wellingham smiled. "No, my lord, though I have been entrusted with messages from your household staff for you and for Lady Ryecroft and for Miss Sophie." His gaze flicked across the room and then returned to Rye's face. "Your mother is not present?"

That was quick. And interesting too; there must be thirty people in the room, but in no more than a few seconds Wellingham had apparently noted that Lady Ryecroft wasn't one of them. "No, it appears she had... other obligations this morning."

Wellingham's forehead creased.

It *did* sound odd. "Padgett," he said quietly, before the butler could depart once more. "Have you seen my mother today?"

Padgett's gaze shifted. "I believe she went out, my lord." He slid through the door into the hallway before Rye could ask anything else. Not that he'd have known what to ask. She'd gone *out*? What errand could possibly be more important to his mother than watching Sophie's triumph?

He recalled, vaguely, that Sophie had said something about being on the receiving end of a scolding this morning, and then his sister had turned pink, as if she regretted mentioning it. Perhaps he should have asked what she'd done to deserve a tongue-lashing.

"I'm keeping you from Lady Stone, Wellingham," Rye said. "And she doesn't like to be kept waiting. Perhaps we can talk later about those messages from the manor?"

"Of course, my lord." Without hurry, Robert Wellingham moved across the room toward the tall-backed chair where Lady Stone was ensconced, pausing courteously along the way to greet Sophie and to nod to a number of other visitors. The hum of conversation picked up once again.

Lady Brindle went out, with Lady Flavia and Miss Mickelthorpe—the latter drooping and looking wistfully over her shoulder at Rye—in her wake. Rye, still standing near the drawing-room door, heard Lady

Flavia's voice on the stairs. "Carrisbrooke! What a shame we're just leaving."

The earl didn't seem inclined to pause on the stairs for conversation, because a moment later he bounded into the room ahead of Padgett. *Something like an undisciplined puppy*, Rye thought, and was amused at the comparison until Carrisbrooke's gaze came to rest on him.

He made a beeline straight for Rye. "Lord Ryecroft, I hardly dared to hope, when I came to call on Miss Ryecroft this morning, that you would be present. I should like to arrange an appointment with you at your earliest convenience." Carrisbrooke lowered his voice. "I'm sure you understand that I cannot, in this public setting, disclose my reasons for needing to speak with you, since it involves a lady who is dear to both of us."

Rye felt as if he'd stepped into some kind of storybook; Carrisbrooke's flowery language made him want to sneeze every bit as strongly as all Sophie's bouquets had earlier today.

Only it felt as if someone had torn out the middle pages of this fairy tale. There had been no doubt in Rye's mind that Sophie would be well received in London, but for him to field a request from an earl to court her, on the morning after she'd made her first official appearance… "Later today, if you like." There was no point in putting it off, Rye supposed.

Carrisbrooke beamed at him and headed straight toward Sophie, cutting his way through the crowd.

Rye wandered toward to the windows, where Portia and Robert Wellingham were having a low-voiced conversation. At least she wasn't chatting privately with Swindon.

Portia looked up as he approached. "Is it my imagination, or have you just received the first request for Sophie's hand?"

"It appears that's what the pup has in mind. If so, I suppose I'll have to give my permission for him to press his suit. There's nothing about him to find objectionable. Good land, good family, plenty of money…"

Portia's small, pearly white teeth closed so firmly on her lower lip that Rye wouldn't have been surprised to see blood well up. He started to reach for her, intending to make her let go before she hurt herself. Then—annoyed because he had even noticed—he said, "I thought you'd be happy to have her out of your way, where Swindon is concerned. Isn't that who Lady Stone has in mind for you?"

Portia's gaze should have turned him to a cinder. "The question has nothing to do with me. But in my mind, a young man who is barely old enough to be out of the care of his governess does not seem to be the best candidate as a husband."

Lord Swindon, Rye thought uncharitably, was probably old enough not to even *remember* his governess, which in Portia's view would seem to make him a wonderful choice as a husband. He reminded himself that whomever Portia Langford chose, it would be in no way his concern. Thank heaven.

"Especially for a girl Sophie's age," she went on.

"I suppose you think there's an even more brilliant match in the offing for her?"

"I simply think you should not rush to approve this

one. I recognize, of course, that you are eager to have the matter decided, so you can begin negotiating the marriage settlements."

Despite the sparks in her eyes, her voice was calm and even. Rye had learned to be wary, however, for when Portia Langford's voice took on that sweetly reasonable tone, there would be hell to pay for someone.

"If Carrisbrooke is truly as infatuated as he appears," she went on pleasantly, "and willing to make a huge settlement on Sophie, then your troubles will be over. If he comes through, you can look well beyond Miss Mickelthorpe and her sort for a match for yourself."

Rye's jaw tightened till the muscles threatened to snap. "If you believe I will leap at the opportunity to sell my sister in order that I may choose a bride who has no dowry…"

"Oh no. I would *never* expect you to settle for a bride with no dowry, my lord. After all, you have a position to maintain."

Rye had forgotten Wellingham was standing there until the banker said, "I'm certain Miss Langford did not mean to imply that anyone was for sale here."

Rye wasn't certain of any such thing, but he was glad the man had spoken up and kept him from adding even more fuel to the fire.

"I'm sure she meant only that it would be wise to take your time and investigate the young man before giving consent," Wellingham went on. "It is possible Carrisbrooke is not free of vices, but has simply had no opportunity as yet to get himself into trouble."

The banker had a point, Rye had to admit. Carrisbrooke's uncle was some sort of adventurer,

after all; that didn't bode well for the nephew he was
shepherding around town. "I'd hardly be giving my
approval to a match. I'd simply be allowing him to
court Sophie to see if they suit."

Portia looked unconvinced. "That's close enough
to being the same thing that it will please all the
other girls."

"What? Why would it please them to have
Carrisbrooke off the Marriage Market? They ought to
look on him as a prize."

"I mean, it would please them to have Sophie
settled. The only reason there are so many young
women here today is to befriend her, in the hope that
the odd crumb will fall from her plate, but the sooner
she is spoken for, the more rapidly all the other young
men in town will look beyond her."

Wellingham spoke up again. "On the surface, it
would appear to be a brilliant match—Carrisbrooke
and Miss Ryecroft. Such a pretty couple they are." His
tone was meditative, and his gaze, Rye noticed, was
resting on the pair of bright heads as Carrisbrooke raised
Sophie's hand to his lips and she laughed up at him.

"I'd better go break that up," Portia said. "At least
until you've given your permission, my lord, Sophie
must not allow Carrisbrooke to behave as if he's been
accepted." She nodded at Wellingham and drifted off
toward the couple in the center of the room.

Rye couldn't help but notice that Lord Swindon
was standing near Sophie too. As Portia neared the
group, she smiled and spoke to him even before she
casually linked her arm into Sophie's to draw her away
from Carrisbrooke.

"A foresighted young woman, that one," Wellingham said.

"Sophie? Obviously you don't know my sister, or you wouldn't say that. No more sense than a soaked goose."

"If that's the case, I wonder that you intend to leave Miss Ryecroft's choice of a husband entirely up to her."

Rye was stung. "I don't."

"My mistake. It sounded for a moment as if any man who was not objectionable to you would be allowed to pay her court—so she could be free to choose among them all. In any case, I was not refer-ring just then to Miss Ryecroft, but to Miss Langford."

"Foresighted? *Managing* is the word I'd use," Rye muttered.

"And you must be grateful for it, I believe." Wellingham turned away from the room. "As for the messages I bear, perhaps now would be an acceptable occasion to share them?"

Rye, too, put his back to the room so they would have some privacy. "What has broken at the manor this time?"

"There was a matter of a tree limb that came down in a strong wind, directly through the roof of the greenhouse. But it has been seen to, and the bill has been paid."

"How? Carstairs can't have had that sort of money put aside."

"I believe not." Wellingham didn't sound interested.

"Well, if you paid the reckoning yourself, you're to send me the bill." Rye's gaze was caught by a curricle pulling up in front of the house. A groom leaped from the back of the vehicle and ran to take the horses' heads. A moment later the driver—tall, dark-haired, wearing a greatcoat cut in the latest fashion—jumped down and turned to lift a lady from the high seat. A lady who was wearing a close-fitting bonnet and a dark gray cloak.

A lady, Rye thought, *who looks an awfully lot like…*

No, he told himself. *It can't be.*

Beside him, Sophie's voice was high and strained. "Rye, is that *Mama*? I wonder where she's been—and why is Mr. Winston bringing her home?"

❧

Every bone in Miranda's body seemed to have melted away in the wake of that incredibly powerful orgasm. Not only did she not want to move, she was incapable… and Marcus seemed equally reluctant. He shifted position only enough to snuggle her against his side, resting his chin against the top of her head. Her hair had come undone, of course; he lifted the end of a curl from where it sprang madly across the pillow, and used it to caress the tip of her nose.

"Miranda, you are incredible." His voice was richer than before, even more like honey spread across warm toast, and it reached so deeply inside her that it made her want him all over again.

Even though she shouldn't. She *couldn't*.

Despite the lassitude that dragged at every muscle, her mind was finally starting to work again, and Miranda was horrified at herself. What had come over her? What had made her act like a wanton, fixated only on her pleasure—and his? What had caused her to think, for this fleeting hour, only of what she wanted and not of what was sensible or right?

Lust, she admitted. Just as a thick layer of cotton wool would deaden sound, the lust Marcus had fanned inside her had, for the first time in her life, quieted every whisper of common sense.

It wasn't as though she didn't know the rules, for Marcus had made them plain. All he was promising was an affair… and though she'd have been lying if she denied how wonderful it had felt to make love with him, she was clear-eyed enough to know there was no future in this.

She didn't blame him, for she had let this happen. She had *wanted* it to happen. In a moment of weakness—well, all right, an hour of weakness—she had given in to the demands of her body and to the memories of a young man she had been fond of long ago.

He lifted a lazy hand and traced the line of her jaw. "My sweet," he said. "My lover…"

While his touch was gentle, it was also possessive, and though desire began to build in her again, it warred this time with wariness. She knew if she didn't make a move, she would once more lose herself in that rising hunger. And though half of her longed to make love with him again, the other half feared it would be all too easy to forget that this was temporary.

So she must end it herself, now. The fact that she had surrendered once didn't mean it would happen again. It certainly didn't mean she'd agreed to continue this… whatever *this* was. It was not technically an affair, surely, if it had only happened once…

His hand slipped to her breast, his thumb teasing

lazily at her nipple. But when he roused himself to bend his head to taste the hollow between her breasts and then nibble his way up her throat, Miranda turned her head away. "I must go home. The girls will be receiving visitors this morning."

"*The girls?* You have more than one?"

"I suppose I do, in a way. I like Miss Langford a great deal, and I admire her." *If things were only different, Portia would make a good wife for Rye—and then she'd be my daughter too.*

Marcus kissed the hollow at the base of her throat and sat up, reaching for his clothes. "Very well. If you must reappear, then you must. I haven't a lady's maid at hand, so I'm afraid you'll have to make do with me to help you back into your dress."

He seemed not at all concerned or regretful that she was leaving. Miranda knew it was illogical to wish that he hadn't been so agreeable. But part of her, she had to admit, had hoped he would try to persuade her to spend the rest of the day in bed with him.

Not that she would have agreed to do so, of course. But it would have been nice to be asked.

Perhaps you were just an amusing distraction for an hour, but now he has other obligations.

That must be at least part of the reason that men had mistresses—because they could be ignored when the timing was not convenient. A wife, on the other hand, could not always be put aside so easily.

But that was too dangerous a direction for her thoughts to be allowed to flow.

"I suppose your man can find me a hackney?" she said as she wriggled into her chemise.

"My man will order my curricle, and I shall drive you home."

"Drive me…" She paused until she had pulled her dress over her head and could see him once more. "You can't, Marcus!"

"On the contrary, my dear—my taking you home will confirm your story."

"What story?"

"You stepped out this morning to shop before the press of visitors descended on you. But you were jostled—nearly pulled to bits—in the crowd. I happened to see you in Bond Street, just in time to prevent worse damage. But you were so shaken"—he turned her away from him and began to fasten buttons up the back of her dress—"and ruffled by the experience that I insisted I must see you safely home."

"A truly convenient tale."

"Have you a better way to explain why this bow at the back of your gown does not look as it did when your maid sent you out this morning? And as for your hair…" He looked her over thoughtfully and handed her a hairbrush. "You *should* have been shopping, by the way."

"Instead of coming here?" She felt as if he had struck her.

His eyes lit up. "No, my dear. I meant in addition to coming here. This dress is an abomination. I am not referring to the style, for the cut flatters you. In fact, it makes your figure even more enticing than the lace you were wearing last night. But the color…"

"I don't recall asking for your opinion."

"Indeed you did not. But if you believe that

dressing in drab colors will lessen my demands as your lover, think again. Seeing you wearing gray only makes me want to take your clothes off. When will you come to me again?"

Warmth swept over her—and then she remembered that she wasn't cut out to be a mistress. "I won't. This was a mistake, Marcus."

He was buttoning his shirt, and she thought for a moment that he wasn't going to answer at all. "How could something so wonderful be a mistake? Or are you going to tell me it wasn't wonderful for you?"

She couldn't, of course—not without being struck dead for lying. "Well, yes, it was." She kept her voice cheerful. "I'm thinking much more clearly, now that I'm no longer confused and doubting myself. But it's obvious to me that as enjoyable as this morning has been, it just isn't what I want to continue."

"You don't wish to be my lover." He retrieved a fresh neckcloth from a drawer and arranged it with swift, efficient motions, as if creating perfect folds was every bit as important as their conversation.

"Exactly. And you did tell me, you know, that you would not pursue Sophie and that you will stop Carrisbrooke from doing so—even though I don't become your mistress."

"Indeed I did." He shrugged into his coat and reached for the bellpull. "But the question isn't whether you *become* my mistress, it's whether you *remain* so."

She thought he might go sullen and silent and send her home in a hackney, despite his offer to drive her—for she had, after all, rejected him. But when the manservant appeared, Marcus ordered his curricle to be brought around. And on the drive, he chatted easily of ordinary things, like the musicale that evening—"I own I have no desire to hear young ladies warbling through their repertoire of songs."

"Oh, it won't be as bad as all that," Miranda said bracingly. "No doubt some of them will play the harp instead."

He groaned a little, and she was pleased.

The curricle swung round the corner and into Grosvenor Square, and Miranda gathered up her reticule and said, "Thank you. It was kind of you to bring me home."

"I'm coming in. I need to speak to…" He paused as he feathered his horses neatly between two carriages that had stopped in the middle of the street.

Miranda's heart went to her throat. Was he threatening her? Surely he would not tell Lady Stone about what she had done this morning. But if he did—if he were to let slip even a hint…

She could see her world—Rye's future and Sophie's—crumbling around her. Oh, *why* had she not realized that she had handed him a weapon—a perfect tool for blackmail?

"I must speak to my nephew," Marcus went on, sounding abstracted. "That's his curricle being walked up and down the street. One can't miss it, with that ridiculous magenta-and-gold color scheme he insisted on."

He pulled his pair to a stop in front of Lady Stone's house and turned to look at Miranda, while his groom dismounted from the perch at the back. "Why, my dear—you've gone pale. I wonder… who did you think I meant to speak to? And what did you think I was planning to say?"

Twelve

WHATEVER CARRISBROOKE WAS TALKING ABOUT—HE was reciting a poem, if Portia's ears hadn't deceived her—it made Sophie laugh. And Sophie's laugh— that delightful, effortless gurgle—in turn attracted attention from the entire room, which only served to make everyone notice that the young Lord Carrisbrooke and the beautiful Miss Ryecroft seemed to be on excellent terms. Even from halfway across the room, Portia could see speculation on the faces of several matrons. At least the crowd was greatly diminished now, as the fashionable hour for calls slipped away.

Still, with so many eyes focused on the pair in the center of the room, Portia knew that if she simply burst on the twosome and snatched Sophie away, the gossip would fly. She looked around for something— or someone—that might serve as a distraction.

Lord Swindon caught her eye, his gaze full of irony. "What a pretty child she is."

"Indeed. And she's as charming as she is beautiful." Portia wished—not for the first time—that it was possible to speak her mind. Sophie *was* charming, but she was hardly the perfectly prim miss that Portia made her sound.

"So sweet, in fact, that she's apt to give the sugar sickness to anyone who gets too close," Swindon added.

Portia gave him a vague smile—one that said she was listening no more than was polite—and moved on toward Sophie. Why, she wondered, was it no fun at all to cross blades with Swindon? If Lord Ryecroft had said the same thing—about little Juliana Farling, for instance—Portia would have been struggling to keep from snorting with amusement.

"My dear," she murmured into Sophie's ear. "Your brother wishes to speak to you. *Now.*"

"Is Lord Ryecroft free?" Carrisbrooke said eagerly. "I wish to speak with him myself." With a grand gesture, he offered his arm to Sophie. She flashed a look up at him and gave him her hand. Carrisbrooke tucked it into his elbow with care and strolled across the room with regal arrogance.

Portia sighed. Her effort to peel Sophie away from her suitor had only made things worse.

"Yet another duty for the put-upon companion," Swindon murmured. "Minding the children and sending them to Papa for discipline. Are you paid extra for acting as a governess on top of your other responsibilities?"

Portia thought, *There's no pleasure in sharing a joke with him because Swindon says everything with a cruel twist. Rye would have made a simple observation of human nature, too true to be considered rude…*

"I beg your pardon, Lord Swindon. My attention

wandered for a moment. You were saying, I believe, that Miss Ryecroft has excellent manners?"

"I was saying that I prefer my companions to have more spirit." His gaze lingered on her mouth.

Portia was relieved when Padgett appeared once more in the doorway. "Mr. Winston, my lady."

With an air of leisure, Marcus Winston crossed the room to kiss Lady Stone's hand. He murmured something that made her laugh, and then turned as if he was magnetically drawn toward the small group by the window.

Carrisbrooke drew himself up to his full height as he faced his uncle. Unfortunately for him, he was still a couple of inches shorter than Mr. Winston and not nearly so impressive. "I should have known you would pursue me here," he announced dramatically.

Marcus Winston laughed. "Pursue you? My dear boy, if you were trying to elude me, you should not have left that arrestingly painted vehicle of yours in the street outside. Not that it was difficult to predict your movements this morning. Lord Ryecroft, may I have a word with you?"

"If you want to talk to him about me," Carrisbrooke began, belligerence in his tone.

Sophie stepped closer. "Where is Mama, Mr. Winston, and why did you bring her home?"

At least the girl had the good sense to keep her voice down. But why she was asking such a question when Lady Ryecroft was right there near the door...

She blinked. *And just when did she come in?*

"This house is far more interesting than a circus," Swindon reflected. "In fact, it appears that at any moment we might have a bout of fisticuffs, for Miss Ryecroft is looking militant. It seems perhaps she is not so sweet after all, but is far more interesting than I thought."

"Leave her alone," Portia snapped. She saw the gleam of interest in Swindon's eyes and wished she had bitten off her tongue. She turned away from him and went to join the group at the window. "Sophie, my dear, come with me a moment to bid good-bye to Lady…" She mumbled something that she hoped resembled a name.

Sophie tore her gaze away from Marcus Winston. "Who, Portia? I don't see anyone leaving just now."

"Well, they won't *ever* leave if you carry on in this manner." Portia kept her voice low. "Your mother's right there by the door, but don't ask me how long she's been here, because I don't know."

"Not long," Marcus Winston said easily. "She merely stepped upstairs to take off her bonnet."

Sophie shot him a fuming look and went straight to Lady Ryecroft. Portia glanced around the room, hoping to see no other fires that needed to be extinguished before they could flare up into disaster. Robert Wellingham had moved away from the group at the window and was watching her thoughtfully from near the fireplace. "Being a companion seems an exhausting business, Miss Langford."

"Some days are worse than others."

"Miss Ryecroft appears to be a handful." His eyes twinkled as if he was challenging her to disagree. "And her brother is too, I should think."

Portia sighed. "Rye's all right. And Sophie's a dear, really."

The twinkle grew into a gleam. "You're very informal."

"Well, I am chaperoning her, so using her Christian name is…" But that, Portia realized, was not what Wellingham had referred to. When, she asked herself, had she started thinking of Lord Ryecroft as *Rye*?

It's only because Sophie calls him that, and his mother. I hear it all the time.

"I understand that he must, of course, marry an heiress," Wellingham went on.

"If you're trying to tempt me into gossiping, Mr. Wellingham…"

"Oddly enough, Miss Langford, I was not. I must go and say my farewells to my hostess now or risk being thought to be a hanger-on."

Portia realized that the drawing room was now almost empty. Carrisbrooke and Marcus Winston were still standing with Rye by the window, Sophie and her mother were near the door, and Lady Stone was beckoning to Wellingham. Everyone else had gone.

Portia congratulated herself for surviving the morning and strolled toward Sophie and Lady Ryecroft, stopping to plump a pillow that Lady Brindle had sat on and squashed.

"Robert," Lady Stone demanded, "what brings you up to town again? I thought we had you comfortably settled at the manor for the duration."

"Business, of course. But I also thought it might be amusing to see the Season unfold."

Rye glanced around the room. "Lady Stone, may I trouble you for the use of your library for a few minutes to hold a private conversation?"

Portia felt Lady Ryecroft, standing next to her, go as rigid as a lamppost.

"And I was right," Wellingham said under his breath. "It's amusing indeed."

Lady Stone waved a careless hand, causing the diamonds that lined her fingers to sparkle. "Of course, dear boy. No need to ask; use anything in the damned house anytime you care to."

As the three gentlemen crossed the room on their leisurely way toward the library downstairs, Carrisbrooke paused to bow gracefully to Sophie, kiss her hand, and tell her that he would call on her again on the morrow.

Lady Ryecroft glared at Mr. Winston, who seemed unmoved.

Rye said, "Mama, Mr. Wellingham was looking for you earlier."

"Was he?" Lady Ryecroft said without taking her gaze off Mr. Winston.

"I believe he has messages to deliver from the manor—from Carstairs."

Finally Lady Ryecroft seemed able to focus on her son; then she looked past him to the banker with her most charming smile. "It is so nice to see you again, Mr. Wellingham. How delightfully thoughtful of you to bring messages, but I hope you did not have to make a special trip to do so?"

Good God, Portia thought. *She's flirting with him.* She wondered what Rye would have to say to that, but apparently he was already out of earshot.

Wellingham bowed over Lady Ryecroft's hand. "It would cause me nothing but pleasure, my lady, to bring you word from your home—even if business had not required me to return to town for a few days."

Lady Stone was looking from one of them to the other. "You must come to dinner tonight, Robert, and entertain us." She settled back in her chair and crooked a finger to summon Portia closer. "Send word to Cook that we'll have a small dinner party tonight, before the musicale. Let me think who else to invite. Carrisbrooke, of course, now that little matter is nearly settled... and Winston. That's easy, and it makes the numbers just right. This plan of mine is all going *wonderfully* well, Portia—don't you agree?"

❦

Sophie, already dressed for dinner in an apricot gown trimmed with deep green bows, sat patiently at the dressing table while the little maid anxiously wound matching ribbons into her upswept curls. Portia tapped on the door and came in.

"You're not dressed yet," Sophie said. Portia's hair had been gathered back smoothly into her usual chignon, with a few loose tendrils softening her face for evening, but she was wearing a wrapper, not a dinner gown.

"It will take only a moment for me to finish. I wanted to talk to you privately before we go down, Sophie, and while everyone is dressing for dinner seemed the only time we're likely not to be interrupted."

"Oh, please don't scold, Portia. I know I shouldn't have spoken up to Mr. Winston that way, but I was worried about Mama, and—"

"It's not that, dear—and in any case, your mama has

no doubt had a few words to say about the subject, so there's no need for me to do so."

Sophie frowned. "That's just it. She *didn't*. Not a word."

Portia looked as confused as Sophie felt. "She didn't? That *is* odd, but perhaps she was convinced—as I am—that you have already learned the required lesson. At any rate, what I wanted to talk to you about is entirely different." She eyed the little maid. "Don't repeat this to anyone, Susan. Not to the other maids and not belowstairs."

The maid bobbed her head. "I know my place, miss."

Portia took a deep breath, opened her mouth, and then seemed to think better of whatever she'd planned to say. "Sophie, you'll no doubt receive permission to waltz tomorrow when we go to Almack's."

Susan looked disappointed, and Sophie couldn't blame her. This was hardly the rich sort of gossip Portia's warning had led her to expect. Why had she bothered to come along the hall for a private talk, when she could have made that announcement in front of a crowd?

"Sometimes gentlemen attempt to hold you too closely when you waltz with them," Portia went on. "A young woman's reputation can be severely damaged if she allows it."

Sophie looked straight at her. "You're referring to Lord Swindon, when he was dancing with you last night. So how does one prevent it?"

There was a scratch on the door, and Rye put his head in. "Sophie? I wanted to talk to you about..." His gaze focused on Portia, running over her from head to foot, and he seemed to have trouble swallowing. That was interesting, Sophie thought. "Oh, *you're* here. I should have known." He closed the door behind him and crossed the room.

He looked wonderful tonight in his deep blue coat and all-white embroidered waistcoat. If he hadn't been her brother, Sophie would probably have thought him handsome. "What brings you in, Rye?"

He pushed aside Sophie's hairbrushes so he could sit on the corner of her dressing table. "How do you feel about the men you've met so far, Sophie? Whitfield... Swindon... Carrisbrooke?"

Sophie considered. "Lord Whitfield hardly matters, does he? He didn't come to call this morning, and he didn't send flowers, so I must not have impressed him any more than he impressed me. To tell the truth, I barely remember what he looks like."

"One dance—even one ball—is hardly enough to form a valid impression of a man," Portia said. "You should not assume that he wouldn't suit, based on such a small acquaintance."

"Because, of course, Miss Langford knows all about such things," Rye put in smoothly. "What about Carrisbrooke?"

Sophie fiddled with a jeweled hairpin that Susan had dropped on the dressing table. "Lord Carrisbrooke is amusing—and handsome. Why?"

Rye shifted his weight, the dressing table creaked a little, and Susan sucked in a breath as if she expected it to collapse under him. "Because he has asked to pay you particular attention, Sophie."

"You mean, he's asked to court me? Already?"

"At least *she's* being clearheaded about this happening too quickly," Portia said, not quite under her breath.

"Sophie, I'm only telling you now because I want you to be thinking, as you get to know him better, about whether the two of you suit."

Sophie considered. "Does it matter so much? If he truly wants to marry me, and if he really is as wealthy as Lady Stone says, then that would save the manor and take care of Mama, and you wouldn't have to pay court any longer to Amalie Mickelthorpe."

Portia rolled her eyes. "There you have it. Sold to the highest bidder."

Rye fixed his gaze on Portia. "Charming as you look in your wrapper, Miss Langford, I must ask whether you are planning to go down to dinner in it. The gong will be going off in ten minutes."

Portia made a face at him. She closed the door behind her with unnecessary force.

"Sophie." Rye's voice was deeper than usual. "You must not think it is up to you to save the manor. That is my responsibility."

"But it would make things easier for you if I made a good marriage, would it not?"

"Of course it would. But that has nothing to do with whether I plan to wed Miss Mickelthorpe."

"Now there you're out, Rye. It was apparent this morning that you'd rather face a hangman's noose than even look at her."

"It's not going to come to that, Soph. There are other heiresses."

Sophie shrugged. "Someone has to bring some

funds into the family, and promptly. If it comes down to a choice between my marrying a gentleman who amuses me and who actually seems to like me, or your marrying Miss Mickelthorpe, then, to my mind, the answer is clear."

"Sophie, I did not give Carrisbrooke permission to court you—only to get to know you better. I have also asked him not to speak to you about it yet, but to let you have your Season first."

"That was thoughtful of you, Rye."

"There's no need for you to be in a hurry to decide, and there are plenty of other gentlemen you should consider before making up your mind. Lord Swindon, for instance. He's well established and has a nice estate…"

"Well, he doesn't enter into the picture at all," Sophie said absently. She was still thinking through Rye's list of heiresses, considering whether there was one who might be more bearable than Amalie Mickelthorpe. "From what Portia said about him…"

Rye stood, assuming his head-of-the-family look—the one that always made Sophie quake in her boots while she hastily thought back over everything she'd done lately. "What was Portia telling you about him?"

"Nothing, really. I figured out on my own that he's arrogant. And he's so *old*, Rye. In any case"— she sneaked a look at him from the corner of her eye—"remember that pitcher full of yellow roses you dropped this morning? Portia's flowers?"

"I wish I'd walked all over them while I was at it," Rye muttered. "Did she have the infernal gall to warn you away from him because she thinks he's going to offer for her?"

"No. But why should it matter if he does? If Carrisbrooke intends to offer for me, then I won't be pining after Swindon, so—"

"It doesn't matter," Rye said. "Not at all."

He spoke far too quickly to be convincing. Sophie had learned long ago that when Rye was stretching a point, he was often in a hurry to make his case and get back to safer ground. But did that mean Rye was interested in *Portia*?

If so, it was even more important that Sophie do whatever was necessary to save the family.

Thank heaven, she thought, that it was Carrisbrooke— handsome, charming, *young*—who had offered for her, and not Lord Swindon!

"Just think about it, Sophie. I only told you because I don't want you to be taken by surprise if Carrisbrooke forgets the agreement we made. He seems impatient to have things decided."

"Well, *that's* flattering."

"Perhaps it would be if he knew you better," Rye muttered.

Sophie laughed. "Touché. But I assure you, I'll stay on my best behavior in order to bring Carrisbrooke up to scratch."

"Dammit, I don't *want* you to—unless marrying him is truly what you wish."

She raised her eyebrows. "What young woman wouldn't wish to marry him?"

"He'll recite poetry at you over the breakfast table."

"But I *like* poetry." Sophie stood, and Susan

draped a deep green cashmere shawl over her shoulders. "We must go down now, or we'll be late." She settled the shawl, thanked Susan, and led the way out of the room into the wide, drafty hallway. She was glad for the shawl and pulled it a little tighter about her nearly bare shoulders. "And here I thought that private talk you were having with Mr. Winston in the library was about Mama and why she was coming home this morning in Mr. Winston's curricle!"

"Oh, that," Rye said. "It seems he rescued her from a—"

He stopped abruptly, and Sophie looked past him to see Lady Ryecroft standing in the hallway, her hand on the knob of Rye's bedroom door.

"Hello, Mama," Rye said. "Were you looking for me?"

"I can think of no other reason I'd be visiting your bedroom, Rye."

"Are you feeling quite the thing, Mama? After your experience this morning…"

"What experience are you talking about?" Sophie demanded.

"Mama was roughed up by a crowd while she was shopping, Mr. Winston told me."

"And that's why he brought you home? *Mama*…"

"I do not wish to discuss it," Lady Ryecroft said firmly. "About this… arrangement you've made, Rye… I'd like a moment of your time. Alone, please."

"It's all right. I told Sophie—"

"*Alone*," Lady Ryecroft repeated.

"I'll just run along downstairs." Sophie was careful

to keep her tone cheerful. "Carrisbrooke might have already arrived."

Lady Ryecroft's brows drew together, making a frightful line down the center of her forehead.

That was puzzling. Shouldn't her mother be over the moon with delight?

Sophie walked on along the passage and down the stairs. Despite what she'd said, she wasn't looking forward to seeing Carrisbrooke just yet. But that was only because if things were settled quickly, there would be no reason for her to finish out the Season. That would be the sensible course, regardless of what Rye had told her—for if she were to be married right away, then he could save the rest of the money he'd planned to spend to launch her and use it for the manor instead.

It was silly of her to feel cheated simply because her time as a Sensation might be cut short—as if *that* was important!—when she had so swiftly accomplished everything she'd hoped to do in London.

More than she'd hoped for. Had it only been a few weeks ago that she'd bargained with Robert Wellingham to sneak her out of Surrey and take her to the city? Back then, she'd half expected to end up as some rich old man's mistress in order to earn enough to save the manor. Compared to that fate, what in heaven's name did she have to feel mournful about? *Carrisbrooke...*

Of course she was pleased to have some time to get better acquainted with her prospective husband, and of course she was grateful that her brother cared enough about her wishes to insist on a delay so she could consider her choice. But the fact was that Sophie had already decided. If Lord Carrisbrooke offered for her, she would accept him.

And as for feeling let down...

Sophie sighed. She hadn't expected to mind things like not going to parties night after night or receiving loads of flowers from admirers. But then, her success was so new and exciting that she hoped it wasn't *entirely* shallow of her to feel some regret at what she would be giving up.

In any case, by the end of the Season, she'd no doubt have grown tired of all that. One couldn't dance till dawn every day and still find it amusing—especially if, as Portia had warned, it was necessary to be on guard all the time, lest a gentleman take liberties.

And surely marriage to Carrisbrooke wouldn't be the end of everything fun, anyway—as it might have been had Rye made a match for her with some elderly earl who suffered from gout and a bad temper and lived all the way up in Yorkshire. If that had been the outcome, she'd probably never get to London again in her life.

No, Carrisbrooke was young enough to want to have some fun himself. He was a good match, and Sophie would do her best to seal that bargain.

Ages ago, up in her room, Rye had said that the dinner gong would go in ten minutes. But he'd obviously been mistaken or exaggerating—or perhaps he'd simply been trying to remove Portia so he could talk to Sophie alone—for it still lacked a few minutes to the hour, according to the chiming clock in the hallway.

Sophie was the first of the entire party to reach

the drawing room. Fires burned briskly in the twin
fireplaces at each end of the room, waiting for the
dinner party to assemble. Candlelight gleamed,
reflecting from the mirrors above each mantel. A
sherry tray stood ready near the chair Lady Stone
liked best.

Sophie had never before been completely alone in
Lady Stone's drawing room, and the room seemed
to echo. She hovered on the threshold, hearing the
steady thump of footsteps coming up the stairs from
the entrance floor as Padgett showed a guest to the
drawing room. But which guest had arrived?

Her heart was pounding even louder than the footsteps. She tried to tell herself it was excitement, for if
it was Carrisbrooke coming up the stairs...

If it was, Sophie admitted, she wasn't ready to be
alone with him. She was too excited just now, and she
might say exactly the wrong thing.

Though *excited* wasn't quite the right word...

She darted through the drawing room and into the
music room beyond, leaning just far enough around
the door to see who came in.

It was Robert Wellingham. Padgett showed him
into the drawing room, poured him a glass of sherry,
and withdrew.

Wellingham. At first she felt relieved to see the
banker, not Carrisbrooke. But as she pressed her eye
to the narrow slot in the door and watched him make
himself comfortable by the fire, Sophie's aggravation
level began to rise.

She had, after all, gone to him for help. Her plan
had been foolish, but she had been sincere. But instead

of helping, he had patronized her and indulged her. He had pretended to go along, while all the time he must have been struggling to contain his amusement. No doubt he continued to enjoy a good laugh at her expense now and then, whenever he happened to think of the incredibly silly Miss Ryecroft.

Since she had not expected to see him ever again, with him well established at Ryecroft Manor and her in London, Sophie had not allowed herself to give much consideration to the questions of what Robert Wellingham thought of her or how he had conducted himself. But now he was here, appearing in the middle of visiting hours and coming to dinner, and it was past time to get things clear between them. It was providential that he was alone and that she had been the first to come downstairs.

Sophie reached for the door handle.

Wellingham took the first sip of his sherry with evident enjoyment and said, without looking toward the music room, "The butler is out of earshot, Miss Ryecroft. You may as well come out now."

Irritated to have lost the element of surprise, she pulled open the door and emerged. "How did you know I was there? I am certain I made no sound at all."

He raised his glass toward the mirror over the fireplace. She tilted her head to look at it.

"From here," he said, "I had a clear view not only of the door, but of the big bright brown eye peering through the crack. Since Miss Langford's eyes are hazel, and since neither Lady Stone nor Lady Ryecroft would have felt it necessary to retreat, I was certain of the identity of the lady who lurked within."

"I was not lurking. And I did not feel it necessary to retreat. Not from *you*."

He paused in midmotion as he poured a second glass of sherry. "You were avoiding some other person, then? If someone has been annoying you, Miss Ryecroft…" He handed her the glass.

"If I had a problem, sir, you are hardly the person I would come to for help. After the last time—"

"Oh yes, the last time you approached me for assistance… Pardon me for thinking, for just a moment, that you might have been lying in wait to hold me up *again*. I observe, however, that since you have still not equipped yourself with a mask and a pistol, acting the highwayman must, in fact, not have been your intent."

Sophie felt herself color at the gentle irony in his voice.

"But we were speaking of problems," he went on, "and why you would not feel able to confide in me if you indeed faced a difficulty."

"Because last time you lied to me," she accused.

"I beg your pardon?"

"You agreed to transport me to London!"

He waved a hand. "And here you are."

"But not because of you! You said you would arrange… You *agreed*…"

He smiled, and the twinkle in his eyes that had so disarmed her as they walked together along the road at Ryecroft once more sprang to life.

Sophie felt herself begin to sputter in frustration.

"Surely you would not have preferred for *your* plan to be the one that was carried out," he said softly.

"The notion of running away with me, weighed against that of being the Sensation of the Season—it hardly compares."

"I… Well, no, of course it doesn't. But you played me for a fool, Mr. Wellingham. You let me talk of closed carriages and post chaises and… and you planned to make an assignation with me via a sweet bun—and all the time you didn't mean a word of it."

"Not an assignation, exactly," he said, sounding aggrieved. "I only promised to send you a message in a sweet bun."

"And in that message you had the supreme arrogance to suggest that *you*, and not my brother, were the one who arranged for me to come to London after all!"

"I did not bring about the trip itself, but you must admit I had a rather large hand in the details."

"What are you talking about?"

"Tell me, Miss Ryecroft, what was the source of the funds that paid for that elegant gown you're wearing and the cashmere shawl wrapped around your shoulders?"

Sophie closed her mouth with a snap. "Oh. You mean the money you paid to rent the manor."

"I wondered if you had contrived to forget that."

"No… but you must realize it's rude of you to comment about my gown, other than to tell me how pretty I look in it."

He only raised his eyebrows inquiringly.

Sophie waited a moment for him to continue, but he obviously intended to ignore the hint. She reminded herself that she received plenty of compliments without needing to ask for them from people who obviously didn't know any better.

"And it's rude of *you*, Miss Ryecroft, to instruct your elders in matters of etiquette, so shall we consider that exchange a draw and move on? Without my renting the manor, your Season would be quite different, I believe. When your brother explained to me why the house would be available, and mentioned that he had a good use for the funds, I—" He broke off.

Sophie was startled. "Rye told you all that?"

"Since it was Lady Stone who introduced us, I believe he viewed me as a friend."

She studied him thoughtfully. "What were you going to say just then? *When your brother explained to me*, you said, and then you seemed to be intending to add something."

"Not at all."

But he looked the slightest bit uncomfortable. "What sort of bargain did you and my brother make?" Sophie asked slowly. "What is it you want in return for all that money?"

Wellingham sipped his sherry. "My dear Miss Ryecroft, generally when a man rents a house, it's because he wants the use of the house."

"But Rye told me you paid a great deal for it, which hardly seems a good investment, considering that you're not even in Surrey now, but in London."

"I have business to conduct in town."

"Exactly. So what do you want with a great house in the country when you're not even there?"

Rye came into the drawing room. Sophie thought

he looked a little frazzled, but she understood; a discussion with their mama could do that.

He strode directly across to the serving tray and poured himself a sherry. "Evening, Wellingham." He tossed off his drink, spotted Sophie, and looked around the room. "You—the two of you—you've been in here alone?"

Sophie's heart dropped into her toes. She'd been so eager to confront Robert Wellingham that she'd entirely forgotten the rules. She hadn't even realized that she'd been alone all this time with a man, unchaperoned. "Oh, for heaven's sake, Rye. Don't be so cork-brained."

Wellingham's lips twitched. "I believe Miss Ryecroft is saying that she regards me in the light of a... shall we say, father figure?"

Sophie stared at him. *Father figure?* What was the man talking about?

With a swish of her skirts, Portia swept into the room. It was apparent she'd been close enough to hear Rye's question, for she glanced at each one of them in turn and then said briskly, "So sorry I had to step out for a moment to check on dinner. I trust you haven't found Miss Ryecroft a nuisance, Mr. Wellingham?"

Sophie waited tensely for him to say something about her want of conduct.

Instead he gave her a brilliant, breathtaking smile. "On the contrary. I have found her conversation enlightening, for she has given me entirely new directions to consider."

"That's lovely," Portia said, obviously preoccupied. She shot a look at Sophie and said softly, "Just be glad it wasn't Lady Ryecroft who discovered you alone in here. Good heavens, child—"

"Another sherry, Wellingham?" Rye asked. "I've been meaning to ask your opinion about something, if you will…"

"Thank you, my lord," Wellingham said, taking his refilled glass. As the two men moved toward the fire at the far end of the room, Wellingham paused to look back at Sophie. "Miss Ryecroft, I would be remiss not to tell you that you look quite pretty in that gown."

Portia frowned. "What was that all about?"

"Nothing," Sophie muttered. The instant glow the comment had caused her was fading already—for as she untangled his words, she realized he had not, in fact, paid her the compliment it seemed. He had *not* said that she was pretty—only that good manners required him to tell her she was.

Well, she thought as Padgett announced Lord Carrisbrooke and Mr. Winston. *We'll see about that, Mr. Wellingham. This isn't over yet.*

Thirteen

THOUGH THE UNCONVENTIONAL MAKEUP OF THE Grosvenor Square household meant that there was no male head of the house to preside over the dinner table, Lady Stone had solved the problem in her inimitable way. On the first night the Ryecrofts had stayed in Grosvenor Square, Lady Stone had asked Miranda to take one end of the table, while as the hostess, Lady Stone herself occupied the other.

In general, Miranda approved of the plan, for though it was unusual, it was better than having Rye pretending to be the host in Lady Stone's dining room. The messages that would send to society were too complicated even to consider.

Tonight, however, as Rye escorted her to her chair, Miranda had to smother a sigh as she looked around the dining room. What had possessed Lady Stone to put together this combination of people? At Miranda's right, Marcus Winston seated Portia with due care between his chair and Rye's, then waited with perfect manners until all the ladies had sat down. At Miranda's left, Robert Wellingham was making certain that

Sophie was comfortable beside him, while beyond Sophie, Lord Carrisbrooke was fussing over Lady Stone. It was all correct in terms of etiquette, Miranda knew, but it felt like a disaster about to happen.

Padgett and the pair of footmen served the first course, and Miranda picked up her soup spoon and turned to the gentleman on her right, as protocol demanded. "I hope I see you well, Mr. Winston." She hoped he would take the hint and keep their conversation on a mundane level.

"I was concerned when you were the last to arrive in the drawing room this evening, Miranda. I thought perhaps you would make an excuse and stay away."

"I am not such a chickenheart as that."

"Then the demands of your day did not exhaust you? I am glad to hear it."

Whatever she said, he would no doubt find a way to turn it into suggestive banter. Obviously he intended to use this entire dinner party as a long attempt at verbal seduction—for all the good it would do him. She should just let him continue wasting his breath, while she listened with only half an ear as she drank her soup.

But she could not help feeling agitated at the risk he was taking, murmuring sensual nonsense within earshot of a group of people who would be agog if they knew what was going on. Even more important, she could not help but feel that he was keeping the banter flowing simply to keep her off balance, as a defense against the subject he must know she would bring up at the first opportunity.

"Stop it," she ordered.

"No, I don't think I shall, my dear. Because when you color up like that, it reminds me of how you look when—"

Miranda interrupted. "I must speak with you."

"You *are* speaking, Miranda." He smiled. "Or do you mean privately? I am at your service. Where might we find a quiet enough location, I wonder? Shall I take you for a drive tomorrow morning?"

"And end up at your house? I think not. I spoke with my son before dinner, Marcus. He tells me that you and he and Carrisbrooke had an involved conversation about Sophie's future—and that you are of the opinion that Carrisbrooke should be allowed to pay court to her."

"I am."

Miranda kept her voice low, but it took effort. "After you promised me you would keep him away from her."

"I promised you that he will not marry her," Marcus corrected.

"And how do you plan to do that? By forbidding the match? Surely you can, because he's underage. But if that was your intention, why allow…?"

Marcus shook his head. "As I told you this morning, forbidding a thing only makes it more appealing. The youngsters deserve a chance to get to know each other better, to see if they suit. I know quite well they do not, and given time, I am convinced they'll see that too—unless your objections make it such a star-crossed romance that they don't realize how unhappy they would be together until it's too late."

"And you plan to make them see this… *how*?"

"By encouraging them to spend plenty of time together, so they see past the froth and the romance to the real people underneath. All the while keeping them properly chaperoned, so it doesn't appear to society that their attentions are becoming too particular. In fact, it might be just as well if it appears they meet by accident."

"You are surprisingly well acquainted with society's rules, considering that you choose not to live by them."

"Thank you," Marcus said smoothly, and Miranda had to bite her tongue to keep from pointing out that she had not intended the comment to be flattering.

"I've always thought it a good idea to thoroughly understand the conventions," he went on, "so one can effectively circumvent them."

"I don't see how you expect to carry out this plan."

"That's because you didn't listen when I started to explain this morning, but… ahem… distracted me instead."

There's a way to fix this, Miranda. But it requires your cooperation. She had thought he was blackmailing her…

"You have Miss Ryecroft's best interests at heart, and I wish only for my nephew to be happily settled. So, together, we can chaperone them everywhere they wish to go."

Miranda thought she was going to choke. "*Together?*"

"Starting tomorrow. I thought perhaps the four of us could meet—coincidentally, of course—on horseback along Rotten Row and ride through the park together. Shall we say nine o'clock?"

"If you think I'm going to help with this scheme of yours—"

"If you're saying you would prefer to spend our time together in other ways, I am at your command. Left to my own wishes, I would far rather drive than ride, and with only you beside me, not a couple of young nuisances. And we would reach a different destination as well… But it's entirely up to you, Miranda. Shall we keep control of our cubs—or indulge ourselves?"

❦

As the footman set a plate of soup in front of Sophie, she contemplated Robert Wellingham—who would be her captive audience until the next course required her to turn to talk with Carrisbrooke instead. She gave him a smile so charming that anyone who happened to be watching would think she was the world's most intriguing dinner partner, and said quietly, "You are no gentleman, sir."

He seemed unmoved. "That, Miss Ryecroft, has never been in question. My father was a clerk in a banking establishment; my mother was the daughter of a moneylender, who did not make his fortune through offering generous terms to his clients. Being a gentleman is something that lies entirely out of my reach."

"That was not what I meant, and you know it. Paying compliments that aren't meant as compliments…"

"What on earth did I say that wasn't true?"

Knowing that an explanation was beyond her, Sophie gave it up as a bad job. "I still want to know what bargain you and Rye made—because there must be something you want besides a few months' lodging at the manor."

"You make your lovely home sound like the lowliest of inns, Miss Ryecroft."

"I wish you would stop changing the subject."

"You have reminded me, however, that I have not yet delivered all the messages entrusted to me by the staff at the manor. One of the maids asked me to inform you—"

"One of the maids? I thought it was the upper staff that had sent messages."

"Do you mean to say I should not have allowed the rest of the servants to speak to me? You see, I'm hopeless at this entire business of being a gentleman."

There was something about his tone of voice that said he was poking fun at her again, but he chatted on easily throughout the soup, and she could do little to redirect the conversation. As the soup plates were removed and her mother, in turning the table, claimed Wellingham's attention, Sophie prepared herself to listen to poetry from Carrisbrooke for a while.

But instead of admiring Carrisbrooke's polished delivery, she found herself thinking about Wellingham. What *did* he want with a house in the country?

After the fish course had been removed and the meat brought in, Lady Stone smoothly made some comment to Carrisbrooke, claiming his attention. Sophie turned once more to Wellingham, determined that this time she would get answers.

But before she could do more than open her mouth, he murmured, "Did you enjoy that lovely paean to your eyes? Now I understand what you mean by meaningful compliments, Miss Ryecroft, and I shall study hard to emulate Lord Carrisbrooke."

"Oh, don't be ridiculous. It would sound foolish coming from you."

"Perhaps you're right. It would hardly be a proper thing for someone you regard as a father figure to say to you, would it?"

Sophie felt a cold shiver run over her. It was the second time he'd said it. *Father figure*... But that meant... *Could* he mean...? Surely not—but she would not be able to rest until she found out what his intentions really were.

"Actually," she said, trying to sound casual, "there *is* a way for you to become a gentleman, you know. You could marry a lady."

"Easier said than done. Both the *marrying* and the *becoming*."

His answer came so quickly and calmly that Sophie knew her suggestion had been no surprise. He must have thought it over. "I don't see why it should be difficult. Other than a certain levity, you have lovely manners. You dress well..."

"I am humbled," he murmured.

"See? There's that levity popping up again. You're obviously educated. And you measure up nicely against the gentlemen of the *ton*—you're taller than Lord Whitfield is, for instance, and more athletic looking than Lord Swindon."

"I suppose it would do no good to ask you to spare my blushes, Miss Ryecroft?"

She plunged on. "And Lady Stone says you're very wealthy."

"I assumed you would, sooner or later, get to that particular qualification. I'm only surprised it took so long for you to work your way down the list of my assets. So which lady do you believe I should pay my addresses to? Lady Stone herself, perhaps?"

"Must you be nonsensical? Why should she marry again? She has a home, and there's no question of an heir. What would marriage offer at her age?"

The corner of Wellingham's mouth twitched. "What, indeed? Though there *might* be other reasons to wed besides homes and heirs."

Sophie had moved on, unheeding. "Portia—Miss Langford—seems to like you." She shot a sideways look at him to gauge his reaction. "But she is not of a high enough rank, I'm afraid. Marrying her would not vault you above your current station."

"Then I agree we must strike her off the list."

He'd taken the comment so calmly that Sophie's heart sank. He must have given a good deal of thought to the problem, to be so sanguine. "And that, unfortunately, leaves out Amalie Mickelthorpe as well. I was so hoping to find someone to match her up with, in order to dissuade Rye from the notion of marrying her."

"Have you consulted your brother, to be certain he wants to be dissuaded?"

"Oh, that goes without saying. Do you *know* her?"

"I have not the honor." His voice quivered just a little. "Are you certain it's Lord Ryecroft's welfare you're thinking of and not your own?"

He was laughing at her again, but at least this time he had reason. "All right, I admit it. I should not like to have Amalie Mickelthorpe as a sister."

"Then by all means, if it would make life easier

for you, Miss Ryecroft, I shall not hesitate to throw myself on my sword and offer for her."

Sophie narrowed her eyes at him. "What a noble offer you make it sound! You know you're perfectly safe in suggesting it, because she simply won't do. You need someone of impeccable lineage. It would be best if she's at least the daughter of an earl, so she already has a title that will remain her own forever."

"I am in awe of your reasoning."

"Lady Flavia Summersby would be perfect. Perhaps I could introduce you at the musicale tonight."

"I must stand excused, Miss Ryecroft, for I have not been invited to the musicale."

"Oh, that doesn't matter. Lady Stone will take whomever she likes. And surely…" She paused, suddenly ill at ease. *Surely, with all your money, you'd be welcome anyway,* she'd been about to say.

"Regrettably, I have a business appointment after dinner."

"Oh. Well, I suppose Lady Brindle wouldn't much like it if Lady Flavia didn't marry Lord Randall after all. But"—Sophie's gaze wandered around the dining room and came to rest on her mother. She could deny the facts no longer—"you said I looked at you as a father figure… You've set your cap at my mother, haven't you?"

"I cry pardon, Miss Ryecroft, but all I meant when I used that phrase was that we are a generation apart."

"Oh no, you're not going to catch me out this time."

She had, of course, seen it coming long ago—she simply hadn't wanted to admit it. Not only had he been hinting as much this evening, but there had been indications even before that. As they'd walked down the road together at the manor on that first afternoon, Wellingham had said he wanted Lady Ryecroft to think well of him... Perhaps that even explained why he'd been willing to pay such a high rent for the manor.

"If you're trying to convince me I'm the one who gave you the idea," Sophie said, "simply because I suggested how you might win her good wishes..."

"You didn't suggest anything of the sort. You offered to, but before fulfilling your promise, you changed your mind."

"Because you were laughing at me. And now you're doing it again."

"I fear I cannot help it, Miss Ryecroft. You are an amusing child."

"I'm not a child. This is a foolish notion, of course. I understand how you would have got your hopes up, but you must not misinterpret my mother. She is always gentle with..." Sophie stopped, feeling suddenly awkward.

"Social inferiors? I did not find her gentle when we first met at Ryecroft Manor."

"Oh, that was when she was terribly worried that Rye might have mortgaged the manor to borrow money from you. Once she understood that he hadn't... At any rate, today she was much more like her usual self, and I understand how it might have seemed that she was... well... flirting with you."

"Flirting? With *me*? My dear Miss Ryecroft, I assure you I had no such understanding."

"That's all right, then." Sophie felt a great wave of relief engulf her.

His eyes twinkled. "But now that you bring the

possibility to my attention… Perhaps it is fortunate that my business here will require several days, during which I will need to call on Lady Stone from time to time. I can only hope to be fortunate enough to encounter Lady Ryecroft during my visits. I shall, of course, take pains to keep you informed of my progress…"

From her other side came a plaintive voice. "Miss Ryecroft," Carrisbrooke said. *Oh, do stop whimpering at me!* she wanted to snap at him. Instead she smiled and pretended to listen as he once more launched into verse—Shelley, this time.

He'll recite poetry at you over the breakfast table, Rye had warned her. And, it seemed, a great many other places too.

There were worse traits in a prospective husband, she told herself philosophically. Far worse traits indeed.

At least he wasn't laughing at her.

❦

The Farlings lived off Cavendish Square, in a street that was no longer quite fashionable. But the house itself was lavish, large enough to accommodate a surprising number of people who had come to listen to the youngest ladies of the *ton* show off their talents at singing and instrument playing.

The first thing Rye spotted when they were shown into the great drawing room—turned into a performance hall for the night, complete with a small platform at one end—was a harp. Apparently he didn't succeed in swallowing his groan, for Portia, walking along in front of him, glanced over her shoulder as if to ask what was wrong with him.

"Only an unpleasant memory," he said quickly. "Sophie tried to play one of those once, until she broke so many strings that she was persuaded to give it up. Worst fifteen minutes of my life."

Portia's laugh rang out, and the tilt of her head, along with the candlelight falling across her face, made her look enchanting. For a moment Rye forgot all about the harp and the excruciating evening that awaited and wished there were a silhouette artist at hand to recreate her profile, so he could admire it forever.

Sophie poked him in the side, not at all gently.

"Well, it *was*," Rye said. "I still think those strings broke just to escape from you."

"You had better give up making fun of my harp lessons and pay attention."

Rye blinked and found himself standing in front of Lady Farling—a large lady who was holding a small quizzing glass that, at the moment, was focused directly on him. "My lady." He swept her a magnificent bow.

With the formalities satisfied, they moved farther into the room to look for seats. Rye's preference would have been to sit at the back—since spending the evening out in the square wasn't an option—but by the time he'd looked over the crowd, his mother was moving purposefully toward a row of seats near the front of the room, with Portia on one side of her and Sophie on the other.

"I think we've been left to fend for ourselves, Ryecroft," Marcus Winston said, "since there is only room for the ladies there in the front. Unless… Yes, I believe Miss Mickelthorpe is beckoning to you from the far corner."

"Damnation. I don't suppose I can pretend not to see her and retreat to the card room instead."

"If there were a card room on offer tonight, there would hardly be a crush here."

"And if I'm to comment sensibly on Miss Farling's performance, I suppose I should listen to it," Rye admitted.

Winston's smile was sympathetic. "I don't see why. 'Charming performance, Miss Farling… You have an amazing talent… Such an impression you have made on me.' Simple, once you get the hang of it."

Rye grinned. "It's that easy, is it?"

"Well, perhaps not for you tonight—since you're paying court to two young women at the same time, and one of them seems to be a possessive sort. Take Carrisbrooke with you. He can stare at Miss Ryecroft just as well from that corner of the room, and at least then it won't look as if you and Miss Mickelthorpe are a pair."

"Thank you, sir. But what about you?"

"Oh, I'll manage. I see a friend I must speak to."

Rye succeeded in maneuvering Carrisbrooke ahead of him into the row so that Rye ended up one seat away from Miss Mickelthorpe rather than directly beside her. She didn't look particularly pleased, but instead of making a fuss about it, she began chattering to Carrisbrooke, who responded mechanically without ever looking at her. His gaze was focused on Sophie, across the room.

Rye settled back in his chair. Winston had been right, he thought absently. From this angle, Carrisbrooke had a perfect view of Sophie as she sat with her head bowed. Next to her, Portia was perfectly still, until Sophie murmured something. Then Portia's face lit up, and she laughed once more.

It wasn't a loud laugh; her enjoyment didn't ring out above the rattle of conversation around him. But somehow to Rye her laughter was far clearer than Miss Mickelthorpe's harsh voice, almost next to him. It wasn't until Miss Mickelthorpe cleared her throat forcefully that he even heard her.

"As I was saying, Lord Ryecroft," she began.

But just then a hush fell over the crowd as three young women stepped onto the small platform. One sat down at the harp, and one raised a violin. Miss Farling stood between them, her hands clasped over her midriff as if she was about to burst into an aria.

The first notes of the violin sounded like a tortured cat. Rye tried his best to tune it out. From the corner Miss Mickelthorpe had chosen, he at least had a good view of the crowd, so he settled back once more to watch instead of listen.

And if his gaze rested more frequently on Portia than on anyone else... well, there was no harm in looking. Or in remembering the fresh scent of her or the warmth of her as he had helped her to don her cloak as they left Grosvenor Square...

He applauded with enthusiasm when the noise stopped, and he was just thinking that the concert hadn't been too awful after all—and was a great deal shorter than he'd expected—when Miss Mickelthorpe said, "There's time to go and get an iced drink before the next performers begin."

Carrisbrooke's face was alight at the idea, and he

jumped up so quickly that he almost got his feet tangled with Rye's as he plunged off toward the front row and Sophie.

Miss Mickelthorpe smiled sweetly at Rye, who could do nothing but take the hint. "I shall be pleased to bring you something, Miss Mickelthorpe."

"Oh, it's so warm in here," she murmured. "Even the hallway must be cooler. A breath of fresher air would be welcome."

Few people seemed to agree, however, for there was no bustle in the hallway. In fact, Rye was startled to see that they were almost alone. He heard a trill of voices but couldn't tell where they were coming from; for the moment no one was in sight.

Carrisbrooke must not have offered to fetch Sophie refreshments after all, Rye thought idly. He'd probably preferred the opportunity to worship her from nearby.

"Here, I think," Miss Mickelthorpe said, pausing beside a closed door across the hall from the drawing room. "I'm certain Miss Farling said the food and drink would be laid out here because it's so much more convenient than having to go all the way downstairs."

Rye turned the knob, and Miss Mickelthorpe whisked past him into the room. Which, he realized too late, was dimly lit and far too quiet.

Convenient, he thought.

"But perhaps I was mistaken." She hovered just inside the door, smiled at him coquettishly, and laid a hand on his chest. "Oh, do come in, Lord Ryecroft. We've had no chance at all to be alone."

Rye tried not to gulp in dismay. If he went into that room, he knew he was committing himself to Amalie

Mickelthorpe. Even if no one discovered them alone together, she would expect a proposal—and with good reason. Despite the fact that she'd arranged the tryst herself, a gentleman did not sweep a lady off into a private room for an interlude without coming up to scratch.

Clearly he could not cross that threshold. But if he turned down her invitation, she would be offended. Possibly so deeply offended that any chance he had to woo the Mickelthorpe fortune would be gone...

Perhaps if he told her she was far too tempting, that being alone with her was more than any man could bear...? No, for then she really *would* expect him to be calling on her father tomorrow.

You are truly in the soup, Ryecroft.

A clear, crisp voice behind him said, "If you are looking for the *usual* sort of refreshments, Lord Ryecroft, they are being served later in the dining room, downstairs."

Portia, he thought with a gust of relief. *Bless the woman.*

"That, I believe, is Lady Farling's private sitting room," she went on, looking past him. "The performance is about to start again, Miss Mickelthorpe. Perhaps we should go back into the drawing room now." She linked her arm in the heiress's and led her away.

"How silly of us to get confused." Miss Mickelthorpe giggled.

"Indeed," Portia said coolly, and then they were out of sight.

Rye pulled the door closed and sank back against the stair railing, feeling too relieved to move. From across the hall, the caterwauling started up once more, and he edged into the very back of the drawing room.

That had been an uncomfortably close call. But it wasn't Amalie Mickelthorpe he found himself thinking of as he listened to Juliana Farling butcher yet another song. If it had been Portia who had led him into a quiet, dim room…

But it hadn't been. And she was never going to let him forget this one.

Fourteen

Miranda had been careful to choose a section of the room where there were only three open seats, though she wasn't pleased to note that they would be sitting right in front—under observation by the entire crowd. Being watched would likely only become an issue if Miss Farling's performance was worse than usual and Sophie's sense of humor got out of hand— but even that, she knew, she could deal with more easily than she could have withstood another hour with Marcus Winston beside her.

As it was, even though she had escaped his constant presence, she could still feel him in the room as clearly as if he were standing beside her. The light aroma of his cologne seemed to have stuck in her mind, for each breath she took reminded her of his scent. The sensation was so pervasive that she looked up to make absolutely certain he wasn't standing next to her.

He was more than ten feet away, bending over an elderly lady who was sitting at the end of a row and clutching his sleeve as if she intended never to let him go. Miranda relaxed and smiled at the gentleman on

her right. He smiled back and then looked at something beyond her.

Just as the harpist took her place, the violinist raised
her bow, and Miss Farling opened her mouth and
clutched her hands together in an operatic pose, the
gentleman sitting next to Miranda rose abruptly and
made his way over to the doorway.

A moment later Marcus slipped into the empty chair.
He shifted slightly, and his sleeve touched Miranda's
elbow. Though it was the faintest of contacts, she felt
it as clearly as if he had jostled against her, and despite
her long kid glove, she could feel his body warmth.
Until that moment Miranda hadn't realized exactly
how spindly the chairs were or how closely they were
crammed together. Now she felt as if she didn't have
room to take a full breath, for fear that she would
brush against him—and he would think she had done
it deliberately.

"That seat is taken," she said quietly.

"Not any longer. Your neighbor has gone to
join my good friend George Kingsley for what will
probably be a lengthy chat." He seemed to turn
his attention to the little stage, but Miranda knew
better. She could feel the vibrations of his body—or
was it her own tension that made every muscle feel
tight and hot? Worse, she knew exactly what would
make her feel better. The only thing that would
soothe the ache was the long, slow caress of his hands
against her skin, and then his body stroking inside
hers, as he brought her again and again to the brink
of orgasm...

Stop it, she told herself.

Her hands had gone nerveless, and her lace-edged handkerchief dropped soundlessly from her fingers. Without seeming even to look at it, Marcus reached down and snagged it from the floor before she could react.

She watched helplessly as he spread the dainty white lawn over his palm and rubbed his fingertips across it, smoothing out the creases where she had clutched it too tightly. He folded it with just as much care as he had used to undress her…

Her mouth went dry.

Only when the folds seemed to satisfy him did he turn his attention back to Miranda. She stretched out her hand to take her property. But rather than simply lay the fabric in her palm, he cupped his hand under hers—as if she would not be able to support the weight without assistance—and used the lace edge of the handkerchief to brush the spot where the buttons of her glove left a tiny sliver of her wrist uncovered.

She felt naked.

She barely heard Miss Farling's performance; the rasp of her own breathing drowned out the music. She applauded mechanically with the rest of the audience.

And when Marcus said, "Come with me for a breath of air before we have to listen to more of this," she rose as if she had no will of her own and went with him.

They didn't go far—only across the hall. He paused just long enough to be certain no one was in sight; then he opened the door for her, and Miranda stepped into a small, dimly lit room where a fire had burned down to embers and not even a candle glowed.

But the lack of light seemed to be no problem for Marcus. His hands went unerringly to her shoulders, then slid urgently down her back to her hips, pressing her against him until the length of her body was molded into his and the heat of his erection prodded firmly against her belly. He took her mouth with a sureness that made her hunger even more explosive, and she answered with a silent demand for satisfaction. Surely she'd seen the dim outline of a sofa... Though right now a wall would do just as well.

Abruptly he let go of her—and only then did Miranda hear a telltale creak. Silently Marcus drew her into the even darker shadow of the slowly opening door, and she tried to still her panting breaths and at the same time to smooth her skirt, which she was nearly sure had been gathered up in a most unladylike manner only a moment ago.

Light cascaded in from the hallway, and a young woman said, "Perhaps I was mistaken... Oh, do come in, Lord Ryecroft."

Only Marcus's finger across her lips smothered Miranda's gasp, and she felt her stomach twist. It was bad enough to be discovered in such a compromising position at all, but the incident could be passed off, perhaps entirely overlooked, if they had been surprised by a stranger. But to be found by her son...

Even before the full weight of what she had done settled over Miranda's heart, Portia's crisp, clear voice rang out in the hallway. "If you are looking for the *usual* sort of refreshments, Lord Ryecroft, they are being served later in the dining room, downstairs."

Miranda held her breath until she heard footsteps retreating toward the drawing room. The door closed almost silently, and the room was once more dark.

But by now her eyes had adjusted, and she could see Marcus shaking his head, though she wasn't certain if his expression was consternation or amusement.

"That was Rye," she whispered. "If he had walked in and found us—"

"Then he'd have been mightily startled, considering what *he* was up to! But he does seem to have spoiled the mood. The hell with riding tomorrow—let the youngsters deal with their own affairs and come to my house instead."

"No. This must stop, because…"

His eyebrow quirked. "Because?"

What would he accept as a reason? And what would make it impossible for her to forget herself again and give in to base desires?

"Because"—her voice felt strange, and the words seemed to tear at her throat—"I intend to marry."

"Do you, darling?" He sounded a little out of breath. "Ah, is it anyone I know?"

He could not, Miranda thought, have made it more obvious that it did not matter to him.

"Yes. I am going to marry Robert Wellingham." Where the name had come from, she did not know; only when she opened her mouth, it popped out.

Marcus looked at her for a long moment. "Then," he said gently, "I shall dance at your wedding."

❧

After the musicale was over, Portia rode back to Grosvenor Square sitting across from Rye in Lady Stone's carriage. She made a random answer now and then to Lady Stone's comments, but Rye was entirely silent. Once inside the house, Lady Stone sighed in relief and started up the stairs, but as Portia handed her cloak to Padgett, Rye caught her eye and jerked his head toward the library.

Portia thought about ignoring him, but something told her they were going to have this conversation sooner or later, and perhaps it would be better to keep it private. "If you don't need me right now, ma'am," she called after Lady Stone, "I believe I'll go and choose a book to take up to bed with me."

"Of course I don't want to chat about this evening; I only want to forget it," Lady Stone said without looking back. "A book? My dear, the music wasn't boring enough to put you to sleep?"

Portia, glad that Lady Stone obviously didn't expect an answer, didn't look at Rye as she picked up a candlestick from the hall table and crossed to the library. "I'll only be a minute, Padgett."

Rye had obviously had to wait for Padgett to go away before following her, for by the time he came in a couple of minutes later, Portia was wishing she'd kept her cloak on. Her thin gown had been perfect for the Farlings' overheated drawing room, but in the dark, chilly library, it was hopelessly inadequate.

When the door opened, she ran a finger along the leather spines, pretending to browse the shelves, until she was certain there were no servants in view.

"You're freezing," Rye said. "We need a fire."

"How perfectly noble of you. But it would be half an hour before the chill went off this room, so don't bother to summon a footman. Let's just make this quick, shall we?"

"I wasn't going to call for a servant. I can build a fire myself, you know."

"Well, don't let any of the heiresses see you do it, or she'll think you're hopelessly lower-class. At any rate, you seemed to want to speak to me." She set her candle down on the desk and held her hands over the feeble warmth it offered. "What kind of a gudgeon are you, my lord—to let yourself be drawn into a room alone with Amalie Mickelthorpe?" She couldn't keep herself from shivering—from the chill, she told herself firmly, not from the vision of what would have happened tonight had Miss Mickelthorpe succeeded and someone like Lady Brindle had happened to find them.

It was none of her affair, after all.

Rye stripped off his coat and draped it around her shoulders. If Lady Flavia had seen him do that—especially without waiting for his valet to assist—she'd no doubt have swooned at the shock.

But he still hadn't answered, and Portia frowned, trying to puzzle out why he hadn't just come straight out with the thanks he so clearly owed her. "Unless it was your scheme and not Miss Mickelthorpe's. And if that is the case, then you truly are a fool. So if you expect me to apologize for interfering…"

He smoothed the wool across her shoulders, wrapping the coat more tightly around her. The silk lining snuggled closely against her bare arms, and the wool collar was warm along the arch of her throat. But the transferred heat from his body did not make Portia more comfortable; the warm wool seemed only to drive the shivers more deeply into her body, until every bit of her was quaking.

"It was my intention to express my appreciation for your timely intervention."

Portia felt the knots of tension inside her loosen. "I accept your gratitude." She should have stopped there, she knew, but the shivers seemed to have driven out common sense. "Of course, you must be more careful in future. The next time I may not be available to come to your rescue."

"*Rescue?* You do want a lot of credit, don't you?"

She should have done the ladylike thing and demurred. Instead she told the truth. "As it happens, I saved your reputation tonight, my lord."

"Yes, you did."

"There. Was that so hard to admit?"

"And very flattering it is to know that you were paying such close attention to my actions this evening that you knew with precision exactly where to find me and exactly when to strike for the maximum effect."

Portia found herself stammering. "I didn't! Watch you, I mean—or notice!"

"Are you certain of that, Miss Langford? Never mind; we'll leave it there for now."

"Well then. If that is all…" Reluctantly, she took his coat from around her shoulders and handed it back. The air in the library seemed even colder now. He was watching her so closely he could probably count the goose bumps rising on her skin.

The sensation frightened her, and his silence even more so.

Without taking his gaze off her, he shrugged back into his coat.

"Lady Stone would no doubt say that your tailor

should be rebuked for making your coat too loose-fitting," she said.

"Because, unlike the dandy set, I don't require a valet to pry me into it? I'm inclined to believe that Lady Stone would more likely think fondly back to her salad days."

Portia frowned. "What do you mean?"

"Simply that there are advantages to being able to get in and out of one's clothes without waiting for a servant to help, and I'd bet a pony Lady Stone knows that firsthand."

She could feel herself turning pink. Lady Stone's affairs of the heart were a subject Portia preferred not to dwell on.

"Run along now," he said softly, "before you freeze. I'll wait before I come out."

So the servants wouldn't see them together, of course. "I'm glad to see that you're wiser now than you were at the start of the evening." She smiled at him in approval, but it wasn't easy to do.

"Though in this case it's hardly necessary, since—unlike Miss Mickelthorpe—you have no designs on me."

Portia was already on her way to the door. "Of course I do not."

"Then there's no reason for me not to do… this."

She turned back in surprise. Rye was standing closer to her than she'd realized, and before she could react, he reached out and cupped his palm under her chin, then tipped her face up to his.

In the shadowed dimness of the library, his eyes were dark and intense. She could feel his warm breath on her face, and his fingertips seemed to burn her cheek. He had taken off his gloves. She did not recall ever before being touched in such a way, by a man's naked hand…

She didn't move. She couldn't move. But she wasn't cold anymore.

His mouth brushed hers so softly that, for a moment, she would have thought she'd imagined it—if it hadn't been that she could taste him.

They stood there for a timeless moment… and then Rye dropped his hand and stepped back. "My apologies, Miss Langford."

He just remembered the heiresses. "I should think so, my lord."

"I only wanted… to thank you." His voice had a rough edge.

Portia gave a curt little nod and rushed out of the room.

In the entrance hall, Padgett was greeting Lady Ryecroft and Sophie, who had just been delivered to the door by Marcus Winston's carriage. Portia hoped that Rye could hear the commotion through the library door, so he would stay there a moment longer and not walk straight into his mother while Portia's kiss was still warm on his lips.

Not that she had kissed him; *he'd* kissed *her.*

Or perhaps, she thought, it hadn't counted as a kiss. After all, there had barely been any contact.

Yes, that was it, she told herself hopefully. It had been more like a nudge, really; it hadn't truly been a kiss. Though she suspected she would remember the taste of him forever.

❧

Rye waited impatiently at the base of the stairway, shifting from one foot to the other and rhythmically slapping his riding gloves against his palm. If Sophie was so keen on riding at the crack of dawn, she could at least have the decency to be dressed on time. But then their mother was late as well, and that wasn't like her.

At the sound of boot heels on the stairs, he looked up to see Portia coming down. She was wearing a riding habit the color of dull copper.

This morning she was obviously the same rigid maiden who had been insulted by his kiss. Last night, for just a moment, she had been soft and yielding and willing in his arms. And then, in his dreams, she had come to his bed and made love with him so sweetly that he had tried to stretch the illusion out to last for hours...

But he must not think about that.

"You?" he said, too startled to consider how it would sound.

"It wasn't my idea to join this party. Your mother has a headache, so she asked me to take her place."

Rye grunted. "All these late nights must be taking a toll on her. I'm not surprised, at her age."

Portia raised an eyebrow. "I doubt that's the problem, since Lady Stone keeps up the pace. Lady Ryecroft didn't tell me you were riding, but since a brother is a perfectly adequate chaperone under these circumstances, there is no need to for me to go."

Sophie called from the landing, "Oh, do come, Portia. You've been stuck in the house for days, arranging the details for our ball."

"Many of which remain to be settled," Portia pointed out.

"What you need right now is fresh air. The ball is still a week off. You can put Rye to work on it when we get back from our ride."

Portia's gaze was full of irony. "I think I'd do better to take care of things myself."

"And me too, of course, but I've already offered to help," Sophie went on. "Oh fie—I forgot my riding crop." She started up the stairs once more.

Portia paused on the bottom step. "Regardless of Sophie's opinion, it is not necessary that I come along."

"And if my mother thought I alone would be an adequate guardian, then she wouldn't have asked you to take her place."

Portia looked at him steadily for a long moment. "I can well believe *that*," she said at last.

"In any case, I was merely startled to see you, not displeased. Unless you are afraid of riding?" He intended it to sound like a challenge and was pleased when Portia's eyes blazed and her hand tightened on her crop as if she'd like to take a swing at him.

As they picked their way through the morning traffic toward Hyde Park, she made it a point to stay on the opposite side of Sophie, who kept up a steady stream of chatter. Rye held his big bay at a comfortable gait; because the women were so preoccupied, he was the first to spot Marcus Winston and the Earl of Carrisbrooke, trotting easily toward them down Rotten Row.

The moment they met, Carrisbrooke edged Sophie's horse away from the others. Rye and Portia exchanged a glance, and Portia nudged her horse with her heel and followed them.

Winston turned his gelding and came up beside Rye. "Lady Ryecroft does not ride this morning?"

"I am told she has a headache. From the music last night, no doubt."

"Is that what it was called?"

Rye laughed as he looked toward the trio of riders just ahead of them. He had no doubts about Sophie's skill in the saddle, but he watched Portia for a minute, until he was certain she was nearly as much at ease on the back of a horse as his sister was. "I don't know why my mother thought Sophie needed two chaperones today. On horseback, she's perfectly able to take care of herself."

Marcus Winston smiled. "Who knows what goes through a mother's head?"

"Not much of a conversationalist, your nephew," Rye observed, "but he's a good horseman—cutting Sophie out of the pack like that. Of course, she allowed it, or he'd never have managed."

"Riding was one of the few skills my brother imparted to his son."

"Not much impressed with him, are you?"

"My nephew? Oh, he'll do well enough—when he's had a chance to grow up. Miss Langford rides well."

Rye jumped as he realized his gaze had drifted back to Portia once more. Her copper-colored habit was a colorful splash against the greenery of Hyde Park...

"You don't mind if I ride ahead with her?" Winston asked casually. "Only to keep a better eye on our cubs, of course."

And Rye could say nothing to object—no matter how much he would have liked to.

❧

It seemed to Miranda that Almack's remained exactly as it had when she made her own debut there. As they came into the assembly rooms, she could almost feel time folding in around her.

Only the fashions had changed, she thought wryly. In her day, the ladies had still been wearing frilled tuckers, and nearly every skirt had sported a train...

Within moments they were surrounded, and Sophie was filling out her dance card. Rye went off to arrange his partners for the evening; Lady Stone claimed Portia's assistance in getting settled in the most comfortable chair the assembly rooms boasted, and Miranda was once more left to her memories.

But she did not indulge herself for long, for she could feel Marcus approaching even before she saw him. She braced herself for his smile, for his touch.

"I missed you this morning," he said with a conventional bow. But rather than merely brushing the back of her hand with his lips, as politeness dictated, and then releasing her, he stroked her palm with his fingertips. "You would have enjoyed the ride, I think, for it ended up being a lively group. Lady Flavia and Lord Randall joined us... and Robert Wellingham."

There was the faintest flicker in his voice. It wasn't amusement, surely, Miranda thought. Was it challenge, perhaps? Satisfaction that she had missed an opportunity to cement her standing with the banker? Regret that he hadn't been able to watch her try?

She shrugged. "I thought it less likely to cause comment if Sophie went out with her brother and her friend instead of making a foursome of it."

Marcus didn't comment.

Sophie came up to them. "Mama, I have to take my place now for the first set. But if Lord Carrisbrooke comes to talk to you, tell him I kept my promise from this morning and saved the first waltz for him."

She was off before Miranda could answer.

"I hope you were not going to protest," Marcus said.

"No. You're right about opposition only making her more determined. And she does seem to be set on having him; even Rye was taken aback by how firmly she says it."

"That might work to our advantage. Even young men who are head over heels in love prefer being the pursuer, not the prey."

"Well, I could almost wish the tiresome boy would come down with... not measles, I suppose; I don't wish him anything that's dangerous. But can you not find an excuse to take him home to Sussex?"

"I could. But I will not."

"Because that would only increase the attraction between them; I know."

"No. Because taking him down to Carris Abbey means I would have to leave you behind, Miranda, and I would regret not being able to see you every day."

There was a sensual note to his voice that told her he wasn't thinking of formal visits, but of a much more intimate sort of contact—and the reminder of the morning they'd spent in his bed created a rush of warmth and wetness between her legs.

"I've told you I have no intention of repeating that."

Marcus gave her a long and lazy smile that was as intimate as a caress—and she realized that she'd given herself away. She should have made the conventional reply, as she would have done to any other gentleman, merely expressing regret at missing a formal call.

"I did not think you a coward, Miranda—until this morning. But refusing to ride? What other explanation can I believe, except that you are too afraid of your feelings to trust yourself around me?"

"Arrogance is hardly your most attractive attribute, sir." But part of her whispered, *He's only telling the truth.*

"My dear, I assure you that no man can seduce a lady while she's on horseback—though it's flattering of you to think I might be the exception to that law."

Miranda would have said it was impossible to seduce a woman while standing at the edge of the dance floor at Almack's under the watchful gaze of all the patronesses, but he seemed to be doing just fine with that. The air sizzled between them, even though he'd finally let go of her hand and was standing at a distance that was perfectly polite.

"Leave Carrisbrooke to me," he suggested.

"I don't see you doing much about it!"

"On the contrary. My nephew and I had a lengthy conversation about beauty this morning on our way to Hyde Park."

"And he quoted Byron to tell you that it walks like the night, I suppose?" Miranda knew she sounded waspish, but she no longer cared.

"No, my dear. I imparted the wisdom of my many years of experience and pointed out that a Beauty is always arrogant, spoiled, self-satisfied, and notoriously difficult to manage. And since good looks never last as long as arrogance and self-satisfaction do, it is far more sensible to choose a woman who will show gratitude for the honor of a man's name, not make his life miserable with her whims."

"Do you believe that's true?"

Marcus looked down at her, his eyes gleaming. "Of course not. You, my dear, are remarkably beautiful and will no doubt remain so—without being arrogant, spoiled, or self-satisfied." He added thoughtfully, "Though you *are* perhaps just a trifle difficult to manage. As for your whims, it would be my pleasure to—"

"I wasn't talking about me. I meant, do you think Sophie is spoiled and... all those things?"

"No." The tinge of humor had faded from his voice. "I think you've done a marvelous job. But Carrisbrooke already believes that he ought to listen to me—"

"Because of the incredible breadth of your experience with women, I suppose?"

"Of course," Marcus said easily. "And every time Miss Ryecroft shows impatience with him, he's going to have even more faith that I am a fountain of wisdom."

"You're remarkably certain she'll do so. But if she truly is determined to snare him..."

"You would have enjoyed the ride this morning, Miranda, particularly the moment when your daughter cut Carrisbrooke off midline in his peroration about love—I think it was Shelley he was quoting—so she could listen to Wellingham talk about banking."

"I would have liked to see that," Miranda admitted.

"Then we must set up another opportunity. Not tomorrow, perhaps—there is a risk of having too much of a good thing. But we could ride the day after that."

The first country dance ended, and just as Sophie's partner brought her back to Miranda, Carrisbrooke turned up as well. He greeted Miranda politely, spoke respectfully to his uncle, and bowed to Sophie. "This is my dance, I believe," he said, and she laid a hand on his arm.

Marcus intervened. "But this is a waltz, isn't it?" Amusement crept into his voice. "Miss Ryecroft, I'm sure Carrisbrooke has told you about the last time he waltzed. It was at a private party, with Lady Jersey."

Miranda saw an awkward flush sweep over Carrisbrooke's face and felt sorry for the boy.

"What happened?" Sophie asked suspiciously. Her gaze flicked from uncle to nephew.

"She… she told me not to take the floor at Almack's until I finished dancing lessons," Carrisbrooke admitted.

Miranda winced in sympathy. All the patronesses were known for sharp tongues; it seemed to be a requirement for the position. But for anyone to tell a young man *that*!

"But I've saved this dance for you," Sophie burst out. Then, to Miranda's relief, she regained control of her temper. "We'll just sit it out, then."

"Nonsense," Marcus said. "A Beauty must not be seen sitting out such an important dance—your first waltz at Almack's. Will you accept me as a poor substitute, Miss Ryecroft?"

Miranda's jaw dropped. Before she could recover, Marcus and Sophie had moved onto the floor, and she was left with Carrisbrooke.

"I've *had* dancing lessons," he said. "They didn't help. But Miss Ryecroft was so set on this waltz…"

"Ah yes." Miranda recognized a cue when she heard one. "My daughter is"—what was that string of adjectives Marcus had used?—"difficult to manage. It's like her to assume that you should bend to her wishes without ever considering yours." She hoped that Sophie would never hear what she'd said.

"But she's so beautiful," Carrisbrooke said wistfully. "I wish I could learn. She deserves someone who doesn't dance as if he has two left feet."

Miranda felt so sorry for him that she forgot herself. "I taught my son to waltz, though I thought for a while that he *did* have two left feet. But look at him now." She glanced across the floor to where Rye was sweeping past, with Juliana Farling in his arms.

When she looked back at Carrisbrooke, she was stunned at the hopeful—almost worshipful—look in his eyes. "Will you teach me, ma'am? Please?"

She took a long breath and let it out. The Carrisbrooke men, she thought, were absolutely impossible.

Both of them.

Fifteen

TAKING THE FLOOR WITH CARRISBROOKE'S UNCLE WAS scarcely the way Sophie had pictured her first waltz ever in London society. It was apparent that Marcus Winston understood, for as the first notes sounded, he clasped her hand lightly and said, "You will not crush me by admitting the truth, Miss Ryecroft. I must seem a poor substitute for my nephew, but I assure you, I am the better dancer. Of course, he will learn, given time and practice."

Sophie admitted, "I'd prefer my partners *not* fall over my toes."

"I shall endeavor to give satisfaction. Are you enjoying Almack's?"

Sophie gave him a pert smile. "That's a dangerous question, sir, for if I say no, I'll appear spoiled and tiresome, and if I say yes, I'll appear unfashionably easy to please."

He laughed. "Then I beg you will tell me the truth."

"It's old looking, isn't it? Not at all grand, as I had expected."

"It is the reputation, and not the surroundings, that

makes these assemblies so exclusive. I'm afraid I cannot tell you much more than that about Almack's, as this is my first visit in many years. Since I danced here with your mother, in fact, the winter before she married."

"Truly? That was her only Season. Do you remember it well—dancing with her?"

"Very well indeed," he murmured. "Tell me, Miss Ryecroft, which of the gentlemen you have met so far capture your fancy?"

Sophie shot a look up at him and almost said, *Carrisbrooke*, before she remembered that she must be discreet. It would hardly be wise to tell him that she'd made up her mind to have Carrisbrooke when no offer had been made. Was he testing her somehow? Trying to find out how she felt about his nephew? "I can hardly say. I do not know any of them well enough as yet."

He smiled. "It is circumspect of you not to declare a favorite."

She felt rewarded somehow, but not yet entirely out of danger. "But there is someone I'd like to know more about, and I believe you could tell me—if you will."

"It would please me a great deal to be the confidant of the Season's premiere Beauty. Though I must warn you, after so many years away from England, I have not memorized the dossiers of every gentleman of the *ton*, so if that is the sort of information you seek, you would far better apply to Lady Stone or to Miss Langford."

Sophie was startled. "Portia? But she's nearly as new to London as I am. She only came to Lady Stone right before the Season started."

"Nevertheless, it seems she is wise in the ways of the world. Who is it you wish to know more of?"

"Mr. Wellingham. I see he is not here this evening, but is it true, as Portia told me, that he would not be allowed in?"

"I don't read the patronesses' minds, and their restrictions are sometimes eccentric rather than logical, but I believe it likely."

"Just because he made his money himself instead of inheriting it?"

"In fact, he did inherit a large chunk of it."

"I know. He told me about his grandfather."

He looked at her oddly. "Did he, now?"

"So there is a difference between moneylending grandfathers and estate-owning ones? Yet they allowed Mr. Brummell to come to Almack's, and his father was a valet."

"True—but the Beau was a different sort of case. What the prince regent fancies is by definition fashionable. What fascinates you so about Mr. Wellingham?"

She considered the question for a moment. "Only that he is different from anyone else I've ever met." It was true enough, as far as it went. And even if someday Marcus Winston might be family if she married his nephew, he was still a stranger now. She couldn't throw herself on his mercy and share her deepest suspicions about Mr. Wellingham having designs on her mother. She smiled brightly at him.

"Miss Ryecroft, you are unique. Tell me about your home."

She seized the change of subject gratefully, and she was startled when the dance was finished and she found herself once more in front of her mother and Carrisbrooke.

The young earl rushed toward her. "I am certain Miss Ryecroft would like a glass of lemonade," Marcus Winston said.

Sophie put her hand on Carrisbrooke's arm. "Thank you, Mr. Winston."

He bowed.

"Lady Ryecroft has agreed to give me dancing lessons," Carrisbrooke said eagerly.

He reminded her of something, Sophie thought idly. A newborn colt, perhaps...

From the corner of the ballroom, Portia waved at her. Sophie sent Carrisbrooke off to the refreshment room for them and sank into a chair next to Portia's, fanning herself.

"Are you having fun, Sophie?"

"These things are such a bore," Sophie drawled, in her best imitation of Lady Flavia Summersby. Then she grinned. "Of course I am. And you?"

"What do you think, silly goose? There is a vast difference between coming to Almack's as the companion of an elderly lady and attending as the friend and sometime chaperone of the Season's most acclaimed Beauty. There's an enormous benefit to being the one standing next to you when your dance card is filled up, you must know. The young men simply turn to me next."

"Not all of them," Sophie pointed out. "I saw you waltzing with Lord Whitfield, and he didn't ask me, you know. Only you."

Portia gave her a sideways glance. "Does that upset you?"

"That he's not interested in me? No." She wrinkled her nose. "Well, perhaps a little. Did you see Rye waltzing with Juliana Farling? I wasn't sure she'd have the nerve to go out onto the floor. I think her mother may have pinched her. I know, I'm behaving badly."

Portia glanced around to be certain no one was close enough to hear. "I think it wasn't a pinch from her mother, but the look on Amalie Mickelthorpe's face when she realized Juliana was Rye's choice for the first waltz."

"What a difference a few days makes. Even Lady Flavia was eyeing Rye before the dancing started, and I think she put him down for a waltz as well."

"Lord Ryecroft is making a dent in society…" All the liveliness drained out of Portia's voice. "My lord."

"Miss Langford." Lord Swindon bowed deeply. "Surely you have not been abandoned by your partner so soon after the waltz was over? How unflattering of him. I would not have so lightly left your side."

"I'm honored by your regard, of course," Portia said coolly.

"I've come to beg a dance—if I am not too late?"

"Regrettably, my card is full."

"Then I must act earlier next time." His gaze slipped to Sophie. "Miss Ryecroft."

Sophie, still admiring how much Portia had conveyed by the tone of her voice, was surprised to be noticed. "My lord, we missed you at the Farlings' musicale."

"There are limits to my endurance." Seemingly oblivious to Portia's set-down, he took a chair beside her. "But had I known that you wanted me there, Miss Langford…" He was no longer looking at Sophie.

Carrisbrooke came back with three glasses of lemonade balanced between his hands, then stood, looking foolishly between the drinks and the ladies as if wondering how to divest himself of them. His first attempt sent lemonade over the rim, narrowly missing Portia's hem and Lord Swindon's breeches. The earl rose, his jaw tight and irritation evident in his voice. "You oaf!"

"No harm done," Portia said quickly. She extracted a glass from Carrisbrooke's hands and thanked him. "Perhaps we could take a turn about the floor, my lord, while I sip my drink."

Carrisbrooke managed to shift a glass into Sophie's hand without drenching her and sat down beside her. "Calling *me* an oaf," he said bitterly. "I was tempted to draw his cork."

"That would have put paid to your hopes of waltzing at Almack's. You can't punch a gentleman in the face *here*, you sapskull!"

Carrisbrooke looked stunned. "But for him to speak that way in front of you, Miss Ryecroft…"

Sophie remembered—too late—that telling one's intended he was a dolt was no way to move a romance forward, and drew breath to apologize.

"It's just a good thing Miss Langford wanted to go for a stroll, or I would have planted him a facer."

"But she *didn't* want to go off with him. She took him away so you wouldn't create a scene." And Portia had done it so smoothly that Carrisbrooke would never have dreamed he was being treated like a child, if it hadn't been for Sophie opening her mouth. "Never mind. Next time, my lord, have a waiter bring the glasses on a tray."

"Oh. Didn't think of that."

Shallow brooks murmur most, Sophie thought and wondered if he would recognize the line. Wellingham would, she was almost certain, and he wouldn't mistake it for flattery either. The corner of his mouth would twitch, and his eyes would twinkle, and then in that dry way of his, he would top her comment with something just as sly…

It occurred to her that her question to Marcus Winston had garnered her precisely no new information about Robert Wellingham, but like Portia, Winston had turned the conversation so smoothly that she hadn't noticed until now.

Toast of the Season or not, she told herself, *you have a lot to learn.*

❧

Miranda tapped her toe impatiently throughout the first waltz. When it was finally over and Marcus returned her daughter to her, Sophie's face was alight with laughter and the two of them seemed to be on the best of terms.

Carrisbrooke jumped up from his chair next to Miranda's. "Lady Ryecroft has agreed to give me dancing lessons," he told Sophie.

Marcus raised an eyebrow and sent the children off in search of lemonade. "Miranda, what inspired you to do such a thing?"

"I might ask you the same question."

"Don't be a goose. You know why I danced with your daughter."

"You didn't have to flirt with her!"

"Do you think it likely that Miss Ryecroft will get the wrong idea from a single waltz? If you wish, I'll go and flirt with all the other young ladies present tonight, so she doesn't feel she's been singled out."

Miranda's jaw snapped tight.

"My darling, green only looks good on you when it's in the form of a gown."

"I am not jealous."

"Of course not. There's a secluded little corner not far from the ballroom, just large enough for you and me. Perhaps we should take this discussion there."

"I didn't know there were any such corners at Almack's."

"Neither did I, the last time we were here together. If I had—"

"You wouldn't have dared."

"Perhaps not. Your father was a force to contend with in those days." He paused. "He's why you married Henry, isn't he?"

"Not entirely," she admitted. "My father wanted me to be settled well, yes, but he didn't push for the match, because he didn't believe Henry would offer for me."

"But when Henry came up to scratch, both of you leaped at the chance. Oh, I don't blame you, Miranda—he was everything a girl dreams of. Good looks, charm, title, estate, fortune." There was a cynical twist in his voice. "Or at least it appeared that way at the time."

"And I was in love with him," Miranda said softly. "I didn't know then that first love doesn't last. I have often wondered…"

"Wondered what, Miranda?"

"Nothing," she said firmly. "At least, nothing that pertains to the problem we face. But that's why I don't want Sophie to marry Carrisbrooke."

"Because first love doesn't last?"

"Exactly." She looked across the floor, where the sets were forming for the next country dance. "If you're going to flirt with every young lady who's here tonight, Marcus, you'd best get started. I imagine all the ladies adore your accent. Even I find it fascinating to listen to the combination of Eton, Oxford, and Boston."

"If you will only slip off with me to that secluded little nook…"

"I am absolutely not going to repeat what happened last night."

He smiled. "Don't get starchy on me, Miranda. I was only going to offer to whisper in your ear." He kissed her hand. "Since we're not riding tomorrow, may I expect your visit in the morning?"

"Certainly not."

"One can but try." He bowed and took himself off, and a few minutes later she saw him partnering Amalie Mickelthorpe in the country dance.

Miranda swallowed hard and turned away. Of course she had made the right decision. It would be even more difficult to watch if she was his mistress in truth.

But she couldn't help but wonder where that hidden little corner was to be found—and if he would take another woman there tonight.

❧

On the day before Lady Stone's ball, Portia carried her notebook into the ballroom to check on the final preparations. She was looking at her list instead of around the room, so she didn't see the young footman who was zooming around the dance floor as if it were a frozen lake, using rags for ice skates, until he plowed into her. She went flying backward, expecting to hit the edge of the still-open door. Instead a pair of arms closed round her, holding her safely. Breathless with relief, she let her head fall back against Rye's warm, solid shoulder.

From just above her ear, he demanded, "What the *hell* do you think you're doing?"

"Making certain the greenery is—"

"Not you," he growled. "I wouldn't swear at you. *Him.*"

The young footman gulped and hung his head.

"Exactly what I told him to do, Lord Ryecroft," Portia said. "Polish the wax on the dance floor. If he has fun while he's doing it, that's not my affair."

"Nevertheless," Rye said sharply, "watch where you're going from now on."

The footman's voice cracked. "Yes, sir."

"Now, really," Portia said as the young man tiptoed away. Suddenly becoming aware that the room was full of interested servants, she reluctantly disentangled herself from his arms. She'd felt warm there and safe and… *Better not to think about it.* "Lord Ryecroft, I've never seen you yell at a servant before."

"He might have hurt you." He retrieved her notebook and handed it to her.

Portia led the way across the hall into the drawing room. "But he didn't. You were there to save me."

She saw his brows draw together and added hastily, "All right—I didn't want to terrify the boy, but I'll admit that could have been a disastrous accident. As I was falling, all I could think of was that if I hit the door, I'd likely not be able to wear my new ball gown after all, because of the bruises."

Rye grunted. "*That's* what you were thinking as you fell?"

"Well, not quite. Thank you, my lord. You did save me from a nasty fall."

"Anytime. Where is everyone, anyway?"

So much for the moment when she'd felt important to him; apparently *everyone* didn't include her. "Lady Stone is still in bed, Sophie went riding with a party of young ladies, and Lady Ryecroft has gone out to shop." Portia flipped the notebook open to her checklist.

"Shop? What can she possibly need?"

"It's different for men. You could wear the same dark blue coat to every event all Season, and no one would pay much attention. But ladies can't be seen to wear the same gown more than a few times, especially when they're the center of attention, as Sophie is. Already her wardrobe needs to be replenished."

"But what's Mama shopping for?"

"How should I know? Perhaps she's going to take Sophie's advice and come to the ball wearing scarlet. Or perhaps she's shopping for Sophie—the dressmaker has all her measurements, so Lady Ryecroft could simply choose the fabrics without Sophie even being present." She ran a finger down her checklist. *Wax and polish floor—Done. Replace candles—Done. Hang greenery...* "You're usually gone to your club by this time of the morning—or you're out calling on heiresses. Why are you hanging around here and being such a bear this morning, anyway?"

For a moment she thought he wasn't going to answer. Then he said quietly, "It's the idea that Sophie needs more clothes."

"Oh. Because that means more money to be laid out."

He nodded. "The quarter's rent that Wellingham paid for the manor—it's almost gone." He ran a finger around his collar. "It seemed like such a lot, at first. But then the bills starting coming in."

She stepped a little closer to him, laid a hand on his lapel, and looked up, intending to make some comforting comment about things turning out all right in the end. But the words felt so inane that she couldn't force them out. How *could* it be all right, when Sophie's best chance of a rich marriage was an infatuated boy who wasn't yet out of his teens? When Rye's best chance of a rich marriage was Amalie Mickelthorpe?

His hands came to rest on her shoulders, and suddenly his mouth brushed hers, soft and pleading. Portia was too startled to resist. He drew her closer, his body hard and urgent against hers. But his lips were still gentle—asking rather than commanding—as he tugged at her lower lip and nipped the corners of her mouth. She felt tiny and precious in his arms, nurtured and cared for and safe... and she melted into him, her hand curving around his neck, her fingertips tangling in the springy curls at his nape.

His tongue explored her mouth. "You taste like coffee," he murmured against her lips.

The rumble of his voice vibrated through her, caressing her breasts and sending a streak of heat through her belly.

"Oh God, Portia…"

As if her name had jolted him, he jerked away, breaking the kiss but continuing to hold her tightly against him. He expelled a long breath, reached up to peel her hand away from the back of his neck, and eased her away from him.

"I'm sorry," he said. "For a moment I forgot myself."

Embarrassment swept over her—then Portia told herself she'd simply been taken off guard by the situation. It wasn't that she'd *wanted* him to kiss her. All right, that was a lie. But it was perfectly clear he'd been overcome by a whim and he hadn't meant anything by it.

They had been living under the same roof, in this forced proximity, for so long now that their defenses had gone down—that was all. Portia had tried to tell Lady Stone at the beginning that this was a dangerous plan… She just hadn't realized exactly where the danger lay, and that was why she'd been taken aback.

Feeling dreary, she said, "What will you do?"

"Make an offer at the ball tomorrow."

The tone of his voice—firm, determined—made Portia feel cold. "An offer for whom? Or does it matter? Perhaps you can just flip a coin as the ball starts, or wait to see which of the ladies on your list greets you with the biggest smile, before you decide."

To Portia's surprise, he seemed to take her question seriously. "Juliana Farling, most likely."

"Amalie Mickelthorpe has a larger dowry." She wasn't sure what had made her say it. "As long as you're going to marry for money, you should make the effort worthwhile."

"I don't think I could bear to hear that voice of hers day after day."

And night after night as well, Portia thought.

"At least Miss Farling is…" He paused, as if he didn't know how to go on.

And perhaps he didn't, Portia realized. What more was there to say? Juliana Farling was a cipher, a nothing. She seemed to have no opinions of her own, no convictions, no beliefs. She wasn't even a woman, really—at least, obviously not to Lord Ryecroft. She would be a body to occupy his bed and give him an heir…

And that was exactly what he had come to London to find. So why should Portia be surprised now—or disappointed by his decision?

❦

Until the moment she let the knocker fall on the front door of Marcus's house in Bloomsbury, Miranda had kept telling herself that she wouldn't go through with her plan. Even when she'd strolled two blocks away from Grosvenor Square before climbing into a hackney… Even when she'd told the jarvey to take her to Bloomsbury… Even when she paid the fare and climbed out… Even when she'd stood on the step with her hand raised…

She could have still backed out. But she didn't.

She had seen Marcus half a dozen times in the past

week, and every time she'd laid eyes on him, her longing had grown stronger. Every time they met, he had suggested an assignation—and he had told her in detail where he would like to take her and what he planned to do there. She now knew that there was a private room at the booksellers and a hidden alcove under the stairs at Lady Sprague's house and a handy corner off a concert hall near Piccadilly Circus.

She even knew that the music room in Lady Stone's house was a favorite with the rakes. Marcus had told her about that one morning when he'd sat in on Carrisbrooke's dancing lessons.

Not that Miranda had gone with him to all the places he described. At least, physically she had not. But in her dreams…

And twice she had given in to temptation. In a thickly curtained window embrasure in St. James Square, he had kissed her so thoroughly that she was astounded afterward when no one seemed to notice. And after the dinner party they'd attended last night, he'd served up the most memorable dessert of her life by intercepting her in their host's conservatory and taking her behind a dense screen of palm trees, where he'd knelt and used his tongue to bring her to climax.

Then he had taken her back to the party. She'd still been quaking from the aftershocks, but he had asked nothing for himself.

Not that he hadn't wanted more. That had been abundantly clear from his body's responses and the way he had kissed her afterward. Miranda had not been able to sleep because of the guilt she'd felt about being satiated by that incredibly powerful climax, while knowing that he must be frustrated beyond bearing.

She told herself it had been his choice to visit the conservatory and his fault if he was disappointed, for she hadn't encouraged him. Except she knew in her heart she hadn't exactly *discouraged* him either. That was why, after her largely sleepless night, she had come to Bloomsbury. She would restore the balance by satisfying him as he had satisfied her last night. Then she could truly declare an end—and this time she would mean it.

The manservant answered the door. Without a word, he stepped back to invite her inside. As he was showing her to the same small reception room where she had waited last time, a door opened farther down the hall, and Marcus looked out. "Evans, have you seen…?"

Miranda stepped out from behind the manservant and stood, silent and still, in the center of the hall.

Marcus blinked as if he didn't believe what he saw. He gestured the servant away, and Miranda started toward him.

The hallway seemed very long, and the closer she got to him, the more urgency she felt. But she kept her steps short, because she noticed the way his eyes had widened as he watched her walk toward him with her hips swaying and her head high.

She reached him and glanced over his shoulder into a small, cozy library set up as a businesslike office. There was a big desk at the center of the room and two large chairs in front of the fire.

"This will do," she said primly and saw disappointment in his eyes. No doubt he'd hoped she would suggest they go straight to his bedroom. Now he probably thought she'd come for a talk... perhaps to beg him to stop seducing her with every word he spoke to her, every brush of his hand.

"What brings you here this morning, Miranda?"

She waited until he had closed the door, and then she began to unbutton her gloves. "It seems unfair that recently you have only been able to watch my pleasure, not feel your own."

"I assure you, I enjoy our encounters, Miranda."

"But surely not as much as you would under other circumstances." She laid her gloves aside and ran her fingers down his chest, over the embroidered waist-coat to the front of his pantaloons, where his erection jutted, and she smiled as she loosened the fastenings and took him between her hands.

He drew in a short, sharp breath.

"I don't know why I didn't think of this last night in the conservatory." She knelt, brushing her lips against the velvety tip of his penis. "I suppose because I've never done it before." Her touch was tentative, exploratory. He tasted salty. In a way, she thought, he reminded her of caviar.

He groaned, and his breathing grew uneven.

She pulled back. "Am I hurting you?"

"Yes," he said roughly, and she hesitated. But she didn't believe him, so she gave a tentative lick to the soft skin.

He flung out one arm and, with a single sweep, cleared the desktop of papers, inkwell, and candle-stick—fortunately not lit at the moment. Then he lifted her and set her on the edge of the desk. "I'll happily allow you to experiment some other time." His voice was harsh. "But after a full week of teasing, I want—I need—to be inside you. Right now." He fumbled with her skirt—the first time, Miranda noted almost calmly, that he'd been anything but suave and controlled. Then he parted her legs, and with a single long, hard thrust, he buried himself deeply inside her.

She should have felt violated. He had not been gentle, and he had not taken time to make certain she was ready for him.

Then she saw the relief on his face as he realized that she was wet and slick and welcoming. Tenderness swept over her, and she threw her head back and gave herself up to the pleasure of his possession.

"Tell me this is what you want," he whispered, and Miranda had to admit that she had lied to herself. She had thought she could come here and coolly minister to him as he had to her... but the truth was that she needed more. She wanted him above her and inside her. She wanted to feel once more the heat and power of his lovemaking. She needed to be swept away by what they were doing together, not only because of what he did to her.

Her last coherent thought fled in the sensations he aroused as he began to move inside her.

She clung to him as he rocked with her, faster and faster, and she whispered his name as she toppled over the edge. An instant later he drove even deeper into her and groaned in release.

In the aftermath, he leaned over the desk, bracing himself with one hand, his other arm still cradling her, his face buried in the curve of her neck. The harsh gasps of his breath seemed to scour her skin.

"You're not as shy as you used to be, Miranda." He still sounded breathless as he slowly—almost reluctantly—withdrew from her.

She felt shy right now—sitting there like a hussy, her skirt creased around her waist, her body still aflame, too embarrassed by the power of her response and the wantonness of her conduct to answer.

"I wish I had time to take you upstairs and finish this properly."

She wondered why he couldn't, and then told herself crisply that it was none of her business. In any case, she couldn't afford to disappear from Grosvenor Square for hours again, raising questions about where she had been.

She slid off the desk and shook out her skirts. "That's all right," she said as calmly as she could. "Though that wasn't what I intended to happen today, I believe you found the encounter satisfactory."

"Satisfactory?" His eyes narrowed. "What are you up to, Miranda?"

"Just what I said. Things between us have seemed… unfair… in the last few days. I've been weak, and I have allowed you to believe that we could go on indefinitely. Now we're even."

His jaw tightened.

Miranda was not frightened, for she could never truly be afraid of him. But she had to admit she was the least bit uneasy about what he might do next.

"Shall I see you tonight at Lady Emerson's soiree? Not that it matters, really," she added lightly. "I don't want you to think I'm feeling possessive, for I'm not. I was just making conversation."

"Ever a lady," he growled. "The hell with my appointment. We're going to sort this out right now."

"Your clothing is still undone," Miranda pointed out. While he was pulling himself together, she picked up her gloves and walked out.

The manservant was at the front door. He looked startled to see her, and he responded only with a nervous nod when she thanked him for opening the door for her. With her head high, she went out into the morning sunlight to look for a hackney.

She should have asked the manservant to find her one, she supposed. But she couldn't have waited inside Marcus's house, even for a few minutes. She didn't know what kind of sorting out he had in mind, but she suspected she wouldn't have liked it. Far better to leave under her own terms and her own power.

She would walk toward Mayfair, she decided. The exercise would be good for her, and sooner or later she would see a hackney she could hail.

She barely noticed a curricle moving slowly down the street, until the driver pulled his horses to a halt and leaped down from the high seat, leaving his groom to hold the team as he came toward her.

Of all the bad luck, she thought, it would have to be Robert Wellingham passing at the moment she left Marcus's house. But perhaps he hadn't seen which direction she had come from. "My goodness," she said with false cheerfulness. "What a coincidence it is to run into you here."

"I have a house just a few streets away. Lady

Ryecroft, why do I find you here alone? Has your carriage been detained?"

It must have been. The socially acceptable lie trembled on her lips, but she told the truth instead. "No."

He looked closely at her, and she saw compassion in his eyes. "May I be of assistance? Perhaps I might escort you home?"

He really was kind—so much different than she had thought on that first day when he had appeared in her drawing room at Ryecroft Manor. "If it is not too much trouble. But I do not wish to take advantage."

"My business will wait."

He helped her up into the curricle. In the moment before the groom let the horses go, Wellingham touched the handle of his whip to the brim of his hat in a salute. Miranda glanced back at the house and saw Marcus standing on the top step.

Glowering.

Knowing that Marcus would see—and well aware that she was toying with danger—she turned to Wellingham with a bright smile. "What a happy chance it is that we have this opportunity to get acquainted."

The corner of his mouth turned up. "Do you know, Lady Ryecroft, I was thinking exactly that myself."

Sixteen

EACH PARTY SHE HAD ATTENDED IN THEIR SHORT WEEKS in town had been special, and Sophie had enjoyed them all. But this was to be her very own ball—or at least, hers and Rye's—and though only a country miss would admit to being excited, even the most jaded of debutantes must confess that it was pleasant indeed to be the center of attention.

So it was puzzling for Sophie that she didn't feel particularly exhilarated as the evening approached. Even after she was dressed in her white lace ball gown, with her mother's pearls at her throat and a charming ostrich-feather fan—a gift from Rye—in her hand, she didn't feel as if it was real.

She wandered down to the ballroom. It smelled of beeswax and lemon oil, of candles and roses. The windows and mirrors gleamed, and the floor was smooth and inviting. The days were growing longer now, and sunset still spilled through the windows at the back of the ballroom when Portia came looking for her.

"I'm glad to see you're already dressed, Sophie. You don't want to be late to your own ball."

Portia herself looked lovely in burgundy silk, with a narrow black flounce at the hem and a neckline that was cut low and wide to show off her lovely shoulders. Her only ornament was a small cameo on a black ribbon at her throat.

"Lady Stone would like you to come to her room," Portia went on. "And your mother wants you for a moment as well."

"What have I done now?"

Portia smiled. "I think Lady Ryecroft only means to talk to you about who will lead you out to start the ball. It should be Rye, of course, since he's your guardian, but the two guests of honor can hardly take the floor for the first dance together."

Sophie wrinkled her nose. "It's hard luck to have a guardian who's only a few years older than I am." But Portia was in fact only half correct; a young woman's first dance at her debut ball should be with her father. Sophie wondered if that was what was wrong with her today. Might she be missing the father she had never had a chance to know?

I suppose next you'll be turning into a sentimental watering pot over something you never had.

Obediently, she went upstairs to Lady Stone's boudoir. Despite living in the house for weeks, she had not been summoned there before, and she felt suddenly timid as she tapped on the door.

Lady Stone's maid was still working on her hair, but with the ease of long practice, she kept pinning curls even as Lady Stone craned her neck to get a better look at Sophie.

"Oh yes, I see Miranda was right about how you'd

look in a froth of white lace. But your ears look fright-fully bare, child." Lady Stone scrabbled among the mass of cosmetic pots on the dressing table and came up with a small blue velvet box. "Try these on for size."

Sophie's gaze went to Lady Stone's earlobes. Each of them held a garish, showy amethyst surrounded by bright yellow diamonds, matching the wide collar of gold and jewels that lay around her throat.

Lady Stone cackled with laughter. "No, my dear, don't fret that I'd choose the same sort of jewels for you that I like for myself."

Still wary, Sophie popped the box open and gasped. Lying on a bed of blue satin were a pair of dainty pearl eardrops, each set in a dusting of tiny diamonds—the perfect match for the necklace she wore.

She stammered her thanks, which Lady Stone brushed off. "Hurry and put them on," she ordered. "The gentlemen will be waiting."

Sophie hurriedly fastened the eardrops into place, and Lady Stone laid a hand on her arm as they descended the stairs.

Rye was already in the drawing room, chatting with Carrisbrooke and Marcus Winston, while Portia was having a low-voiced conversation in a corner with Robert Wellingham.

Sophie knew he had been invited; it was, after all, Lady Stone's house, and that made it—as Lady Stone had said—her own damned business and no one else's who she invited there. But Sophie hadn't been convinced he would appear, so she was pleased to find that he had come after all.

Carrisbrooke broke off in the middle of a sentence to

rush across the room to her. "Miss Ryecroft—*And on that cheek, and o'er that brow/So soft, so calm, yet eloquent.*"

Sophie thought, *Whatever that means.*

"May I beg the favor of your first dance?" he said eagerly.

Lady Ryecroft had followed her in so quietly that Sophie hadn't noticed her at all, and she'd completely forgotten about her mother wanting to talk to her. Now she was stunned at the sight of Lady Ryecroft in a gown of bittersweet red. It was the lowest-cut neckline Sophie had ever seen her wear, showing off a magnificent bosom and creamy white shoulders that were, Sophie admitted, prettier than her own. Lady Ryecroft's neckline was bare of jewels, but she wore a single diamond in each ear.

"Mama," Sophie said in awe, "no wonder you were willing to loan me your pearls tonight! You are magnificent. If that dress is what has been taking you out to the shops on so many mornings—"

"Hush, child," Lady Ryecroft said. "The gentlemen do not want to hear your views on my gown."

Sophie thought the gentlemen could not have cared less what she said; they were all too busy looking to listen—and with good reason. Lady Ryecroft wearing something besides half-mourning colors was a sight to behold, and they were drinking her in.

Except for Carrisbrooke, who took one more step toward Sophie. "The first dance—will you share it with me, Miss Ryecroft?"

Sophie heard her mother suck in a breath. Before Lady Ryecroft could interfere, however, Sophie said smoothly, "Regrettably, my lord, I cannot, because

I have already promised the first set to…" Oh, *why* hadn't she remembered to seek out her mother for a moment's counsel before coming downstairs? What did Lady Ryecroft expect her to do?

Sophie glanced around the circle in something like despair. Then her gaze met a pair of steady silvery-blue eyes, and she relaxed. Yes, there was safety there… "I have already promised it to Mr. Wellingham."

Carrisbrooke's mouth dropped open in disbelief.

No one made a sound, until Lady Stone finally broke the silence. "What an unpredictable child you are."

Sophie couldn't decide if she sounded pleased or shocked.

Lady Stone shooed them all toward the door. "Now, come along, everyone. Let's get this ball under way!"

❧

Lady Stone's predictions of a crush had been right on the money. Guests poured into Grosvenor Square, and Rye couldn't see how they were to find enough room for dancing.

His feeling of being smothered by the crowd was made even stronger, because every heiress on Lady Stone's list made it a point to drift past him, sending sultry smiles in an obvious invitation for him to ask for a spot on their dance cards.

When, he wondered, had there gotten to be so many of them? Or was he only imagining there were more possibilities than he'd thought, because he'd set his mind on making an offer tonight?

He was still trying to remember what had made him conclude that his only viable choices were Amalie

Mickelthorpe and Juliana Farling when the orchestra struck up a long note to summon the dancers for the first set. He made his bow before Lady Stone to begin the ball.

She tapped him on the arm with her ivory fan. "You're looking smug, my lord."

Rye realized that he was smiling. He'd been remembering Portia at luncheon today as she'd slyly pointed out that Lady Stone's infirmity came and went at her convenience.

No, he would not think of Portia. Though there was no reason he shouldn't daydream about her, for he was still perfectly free—for now. After the ball, once his offer had been made and accepted, then he must put Portia aside and devote his thoughts to his intended bride. It would be only fair.

But until then, he was free to remember how it had felt to hold her in his arms, the sweetness of her lips against his, the way her body had seemed to match his own...

She was just down the set from him, with Carrisbrooke as her partner. The young earl had eyes only for Sophie, who was still greeting the latest arrivals, except for the moments when he was glaring at Wellingham instead. *That may be a problem*, Rye thought. Though Carrisbrooke's dancing skills had improved remarkably in the last week, while he had been treading on the toes of every female Lady Ryecroft could coerce into practicing with him, he was not yet expert enough to move through the set without focusing his full attention on the figures.

But if anyone could keep him in line, it would be

Portia. She was a woman in a million, and it was too
bad Lady Stone didn't truly appreciate how special her
companion was.

Sophie and Wellingham took their places in the
set, and Rye felt a shock sweep through the dancers as
they realized the banker was not only present, but was
also going to take part. Sophie felt it too, obviously,
but she merely looked around as if daring everyone
present to object to her choice.

Rye wanted to cheer. He settled for catching her
eye with an approving smile.

Wellingham apparently did not notice the reaction
at all. The man seemed to be truly unflappable—so
used to being snubbed that he was armored against it.

Between Rye and Portia, his mother was partnered with Marcus Winston. Rye still wasn't certain
what to make of Winston, but tonight it was Lady
Ryecroft who had seized attention. It would be a
wonder if any man could make it through the figures
without losing his place the moment he came in
range of that scandalously low neckline. If Rye had
had any idea *that* was what his mother was about on
her shopping trips...

But she didn't look pleased with herself. She looked
tired instead, and her face was pale against the brilliant
color of her dress. Given the slender elegance of her
figure and the beauty of her face, it was easy even for
Rye to forget that his mother was no longer exactly
young. She'd had too many late nights. Too many
parties. Too many days of having to watch every word
and every action, not only for herself, but for Sophie
as well...

It was time to go home to the manor, he told himself. Time to make certain that his mother was provided for in her declining years.

He steeled himself to the decision he must make by the end of the evening. Amalie Mickelthorpe or Juliana Farling? Or was it foolish to think at this late date that perhaps one of the others would do as well?

As long as you're going to marry for money, Portia had said, *you should make the effort worthwhile.*

It was true that Amalie Mickelthorpe's portion was larger. The additional money she brought to Ryecroft Manor would allow him to renovate the dower house, so his mother would have her own home.

On the other hand, Juliana Farling was a gentle, unassuming soul who would surely be pleased to have Lady Ryecroft continue to live with them. And Sophie as well, of course. If his sister didn't settle on Carrisbrooke—and after getting to know the young man better, Rye was inclined to think it would be a disaster if she did—there seemed to be no one else who stood out among her covey of suitors.

If he didn't have to rebuild the dower house to provide a home for his mother and sister, then Juliana's smaller dowry would go just as far as Amalie's larger one.

Portia had suggested he flip a coin. Rye was beginning to think he might have to do exactly that.

✒

After Portia had survived the first set with Carrisbrooke as her partner, the rest of the ball should have been a pleasure. Instead she felt as if the dance floor was coated with molasses. It was impossible to truly feel the gliding joy of a waltz when she was in Marcus Winston's arms instead of in Rye's—no matter how much she told herself that she must not think of him.

When Robert Wellingham walked her through a country dance and once more took up the topic he'd broached in the drawing room before the ball began, she shot him a fulminating look.

"It's a romantic night," he said. "You should go after what you wish for."

"You're assuming a good deal about my wishes," she said coldly and then ruined the effect by adding, "I could make the same point about you."

"Mine is a different case."

She would have argued, but the steps took them away from each other, so she moved on with all the grace she could muster.

When the set finally ended, she caught a glimpse of Rye with Amalie Mickelthorpe, just leaving the floor. Miss Mickelthorpe was wearing green tonight; it made her look like an olive, Portia thought uncharitably. But the young woman's smile held both satisfaction and triumph.

Portia had to assume that their exit meant Lord Ryecroft had not only made up his mind but had whispered as much to Amalie during that last dance.

Bile rose in her throat. She tried to tell herself that it was hardly fair of her to blame him for doing what she'd advised. He'd chosen the larger fortune, exactly as she'd told him he should.

But that only confirmed what she'd known all along: when it came right down to the end, only money mattered. And as for what he had told her long ago—that it was just as important to him to choose as his bride a woman he could learn to care for—well, at the time she'd thought that was pure rubbish, and she'd been right.

Portia looked around for her next partner, intending to make some excuse, because she hardly felt like waltzing. Instead her employer waved her over.

"Quite a success we have tonight," Lady Stone rasped. "All due to you, my girl. There will be a nice bonus for you in pulling this ball off with such style. Would you care to have a wager?"

"On what, ma'am?"

"I say we'll have at least one match to announce before the end of the evening—and possibly two."

Portia followed Lady Stone's gaze to Sophie and Carrisbrooke, at the edge of the dance floor, and then on to Rye, who was bowing before Juliana Farling. "Those particular two couples, you mean?" She kept her voice steady with an effort. "I'm inclined to think not, but—"

Lady Stone beamed. "I never thought I'd see the day when *you'd* be willing to take a sporting chance! Done, my girl. I'll lay a diamond bracelet against…" She considered and said slyly, "What would you like to give me when I win?"

Portia started to point out that she'd only been offering an opinion, not agreeing to a wager. Then something cracked deep inside her, and a surge of recklessness swept through her veins. She was tired of acting sensible and practical—of always being the voice of reason. If Lord Ryecroft was cork-brained enough to offer for Amalie Mickelthorpe despite knowing that the sound of her voice already grated on him—as though he thought that rasp would get better with increased intimacy!—Portia might as well benefit to the tune of a diamond bracelet.

"I'll stake that bonus you were talking of, ma'am. But since it must be a large bonus, in line with the amount of work this ball has been, you'll need to make it a nice diamond bracelet."

Lady Stone chuckled merrily. "Done. I like a wager that's got some spirit to it. Oh, now, look at that."

Portia glanced over her shoulder, just in time to see Rye lean down to Juliana Farling and say something that made the young woman go all soft-faced and starry-eyed.

She felt her heart drop to her toes.

"Yes." Lady Stone clicked her tongue with satisfaction. "One match at least before the evening's out... Unless you'd you care to raise the stakes and bet on two?"

❧

Carrisbrooke's dancing lessons had helped a great deal to keep his partners from being trampled on, but in Sophie's opinion, he now had a great deal more self-confidence than his skill warranted. She hadn't been able to refuse him a waltz, but accepting him as a partner was a great deal different from looking forward to dancing with him, she thought wearily, spotting him standing at the edge of the floor waiting for her to finish a set.

He had obviously been watching her and her partner, the Earl of Swindon, as they progressed through the country dance that preceded the second waltz of the evening. As Carrisbrooke presented himself, Swindon said in his cool, bored way, "Such enthusiasm must not be denied, I believe." He strolled away.

"If you're so excited about dancing," Sophie said, "I don't know why you haven't asked someone else instead of simply standing there watching me all evening."

Carrisbrooke beamed. "You've been watching me as well, then. It's because I only want to dance with you, Miss Ryecroft, not any of the other girls. I still don't understand why you wouldn't have me as a partner for the first dance."

"It's not that I *wouldn't*," Sophie said with more diplomacy than truth. "I *couldn't*. To have led off the ball with you would have been as good as making a declaration that we were betrothed."

"But what would be wrong with that?"

Everything. The instant mental protest made her feel guilty, so she kept her voice light and amused. "To begin with, you haven't asked me."

"Only because your brother and my uncle felt it was too soon. But since you're expecting my offer… shall I get down on one knee?"

"In the middle of a ballroom? Have you no sense at all?"

He seized her hand instead and raised it to his lips. "*Have I caught my heav'nly jewel…?* That's by Sir Philip Sidney, by the way."

Irritated beyond measure, Sophie snapped, "Oh, do please stop behaving like a child!"

Carrisbrooke went silent, and suddenly, under the boyish enthusiasm, she could see the man he would someday be.

"I didn't mean…" she began warily.

"A child, am I? I've noticed you seem to prefer older men."

"I prefer sensible ones," Sophie admitted.

"My uncle was right. You *are* a heartless Beauty, thinking only of yourself. *And* you have a want of breeding, to prefer a moneylender to me."

She was outraged. "Your uncle said I lack breeding? I cannot believe that Mr. Winston said any such thing!"

"No, I saw that part all on my own." He sounded proud of himself. "And I don't want to dance with you anymore."

Clearly his moment of maturity had passed. "Good. Go away, my lord."

All she wanted was to sit for a while, anyway. Perhaps even—if there weren't so many people about—put her head down on her mama's shoulder for a moment and be soothed.

But though Lady Ryecroft, in her bittersweet dress, was not difficult to spot even in the crowded ballroom, she obviously hadn't seen Sophie's distress, for she was otherwise occupied. She had just left the floor after a country dance with Robert Wellingham, and she was laughing with him as if they were the most intimate of friends.

Sophie barely noticed when Carrisbrooke stomped off. But she felt the ripple when others in the ballroom realized that she was suddenly standing alone at the edge of the floor.

Marcus Winston strolled up and handed her a glass of lemonade. "It seems my nephew has yet to learn tact."

"And a great many other things as well." Sophie caught herself and added primly, "But knowing a man's faults is a positive thing, for then a woman understands what adjustments would be necessary in herself, should they decide they suit."

"There's nothing wrong with the boy that time won't cure. Give him a year or two." He watched Carrisbrooke move across the floor. "Or, more likely, five. It will take him longer to grow up than it has your brother."

He had a point, and Sophie knew it. Carrisbrooke *was* simply young. With time he'd be less foolish, less flighty, less silly. Also more self-confident, a great deal harder to manipulate, and a far better bargain as a husband.

"I don't have a year or two to wait," she said, almost to herself.

"I believe you are mistaken, Miss Ryecroft. There *is* time. I urge you to take it—and to make no decisions that you cannot later modify."

"My brother cannot afford a second Season for me."

"Circumstances change—and not only for your brother."

Winston wasn't looking at her. She followed his gaze across the ballroom to her mother, who had just laid a hand on Wellingham's arm.

Obviously Winston recognized the peculiar intimacy of that combination just as clearly as Sophie did. He beckoned, and Wellingham nodded, lifted Lady Ryecroft's hand to his lips with a courtly gesture, then left her standing with a group of matrons and crossed the room toward them.

"Miss Ryecroft needs a partner for this waltz," Winston said. "I should be the one to oblige, since it is my nephew who so rudely left the belle of the ball standing alone, but I regret that I am already committed."

"It would be my pleasure," Wellingham said. "Miss Ryecroft?"

She had noticed long ago how beautiful his voice was, but never before had she realized that he could turn her name into a poem far more powerful than the lines Carrisbrooke spouted with such facile ease.

The music began, and Sophie found herself floating onto the floor. When her fingers trembled in his grasp, he closed his warmly and reassuringly around them. His hand at the small of her back exerted just the right pressure to tell her which direction to move. She could close her eyes and still never miss a step.

She felt as if she had waltzed with him many times before—and as if she could dance on forever.

His gaze was steady, sober, as he studied her. "I must admit to being puzzled. Why did you choose me to lead you out in the first dance?"

Because I was thinking of my father…

But that wasn't the reason at all, Sophie realized. Though she hadn't forgotten for a moment what Wellingham had said, days ago now, about her looking at him as a father figure, it was not that image that had influenced her tonight. It had been the overwhelming feeling of safety she'd experienced when she'd looked at him there in the drawing room.

Or were those two things simply different sides of the same coin? Did she trust him because he was trying to marry her mother or in spite of it?

Sophie was feeling confused, but before she could puzzle it out, he'd swept her around the room again.

He really was an astoundingly good dancer, she mused, for someone who was seldom included in society balls. Sophie thought if every young woman in the room tonight could waltz with Robert Wellingham, he'd be so swamped with invitations that he'd never again have time for banking. Not that she was going to suggest it; she'd prefer to keep him for herself. There would be at least one more waltz of the evening… though regrettably, she'd already promised it to someone else.

Just as well. A third dance with the same man in an evening would have all the gossips twittering—and when the young woman was the guest of honor and the man was Robert Wellingham, everyone would notice.

"Those are lovely eardrops," he said. "The diamonds are almost as bright and as beautiful as your eyes."

"Oh, don't *you* start being poetical at me," she scolded.

He laughed so merrily that Sophie found herself smiling back. "They were a gift from Lady Stone. At least, I think they were a gift, but perhaps she intended them only as a loan. I must remember to ask."

"It's not the sort of thing she'd wear, so you can assume she intended you to keep them. Miss Ryecroft, I wish to host a picnic next week. Can you think of anyone who might like to help me plan it?"

Her eyes widened. "You know I love picnics."

"That fact had slipped my mind." But the twinkle in his eyes told her that he hadn't forgotten at all.

"If you're trying to win my favor, Mr. Wellingham"—for the first time, he looked just a little discomfited, and Sophie was pleased to have made a dent in his armor—"you're going about it all wrong, you know. It's not me you need to impress; it's my mama."

"Indeed?"

"And you can't do that by walking away from her when Marcus Winston merely raises a finger to summon you. It's not at all flattering to Mama that you were paying so little attention to her that you saw Mr. Winston beckoning." She lifted her chin a little. "In fact, I can't help but think that you may not be at all the thing for her."

He laughed. "I am sliced to the quick, Miss Ryecroft."

His laughter really was a beautiful thing. No wonder her mother had looked as if she was having such a good time...

Still, there was something about the idea Sophie didn't want to think about.

Seventeen

PORTIA WATCHED FROM THE SHELTER OF A PILLAR IN the corner of the ballroom as Carrisbrooke stormed away from Sophie, leaving her standing alone beside the dance floor. "*Two* matches to announce this evening, my lady?" she murmured. "Perhaps you'd like to back down from that prediction?"

"We only wagered on one," Lady Stone pointed out. "And it's early yet. Where are you going?"

"To get Sophie. She can't just stand there alone." But Portia realized Marcus Winston had already come to the rescue—had he been watching that scene play out?—so she settled back in her chair. "Is there anything I can do for you, Lady Stone? Would you care to lean on me for a stroll around the ballroom?"

Lady Stone's beady eyes gleamed. "I'm feeling remarkably fit tonight. Making a winning wager does that for me, you know—it's so uplifting to watch it play out. This must be your partner for the waltz, coming to claim you, so go and dance."

Portia's intention had been to sit out the waltz, but she knew that staying at the edge of the floor would only give her the opportunity to watch every fleeting expression on Rye's face. It would be far better to be occupied, so she couldn't wonder what he might be saying to Juliana Farling as they swirled around the room.

She turned to greet her partner and stopped abruptly, for instead of the young man who had asked for this dance, it was Lord Swindon who bowed and offered his arm. "I do not think your name is on my card, my lord."

"Your partner is indisposed. I've come to offer myself as substitute."

Portia hesitated, but with Lady Stone right there, she could hardly point out that she didn't like the way Lord Swindon had held her when they waltzed. Then she remembered that soft, starry look on Juliana Farling's face, and she threw caution to the winds. If she was going to live on the edge tonight, why not dance with the rake as well? At least it would keep her mind off what might be happening on the other side of the ballroom…

As they took the floor, Swindon said, "Lady Stone is full of crochets and odd notions."

"That's what I like about her."

"It's a good thing you get on well with her, with a lifetime stretching ahead of you as a companion."

A lifetime…

As the orchestra struck up the waltz, Portia let her gaze sweep across the ballroom and saw Rye and Juliana Farling strolling out into the hall. Surely they would not be going down for a cool drink, with the waltz about to begin. And the supper hour was still some time off.

No, they were clearly slipping away to some private spot. He wouldn't go off alone with Juliana unless he intended to propose. Or perhaps he had already spoken, and that starry-eyed look of Juliana's meant that she had said yes, and now the newly betrothed couple simply wanted privacy...

But what about the triumph on Amalie Mickelthorpe's face? Could Portia have been so wrong?

Stop it. It doesn't matter who he marries; it's over.

The ache in her chest would not let her deny the truth any longer. She had fallen in love with Rye.

But she quickly realized that only the admission was new. The pain of loving him was not fresh at all; it was a dull ache that must have been lingering inside her for weeks, waiting only for her defenses to drop.

The music started, but her feet seemed not to want to leave the floor at all. It took effort for her to fall into the rhythm of the waltz. At least Swindon seemed willing to obey the proprieties, and he didn't try to draw her into a closer embrace.

"There are options, of course," Swindon said.

Options? What was he talking about? Telling Rye what she'd discovered about herself?

As if that would make a difference. Not without a fortune to go with her feelings.

And even if she could conjure up enough money to rescue his beloved manor for all time, Portia was certain she would have been just another name on the list he and Lady Stone had assembled—a name to be kept in reserve, in case his first choices didn't work out. She would like to think she would have been high on that list, but that was only vanity speaking. If Amalie

Mickelthorpe's voice bothered him enough that he'd opted to settle for a slightly smaller dowry, then Portia's outspoken opinions—along with the lack of deference she had shown him from the beginning—would no doubt have kept her out of consideration entirely.

Unless, of course, she had more money than Juliana Farling and Amalie Mickelthorpe put together. If that were the case, he'd no doubt convince himself he was besotted, at least long enough to win her hand… and that would be even worse.

No. Portia would not marry a man who made no secret of the fact that money was more important to him than anything else, for she would never be able to trust anything he said.

"You don't have to be a companion forever," Swindon said. "At least, not a companion to an old lady."

Lost in her thoughts, she didn't follow what he was saying. "What do you mean?"

Swindon laughed and drew her closer. "You don't really want to dance right now, do you?"

"No," she said honestly.

They were at the edge of the dance floor, near the doorway, and with a gentle sweep of the music, he urged her out into the hallway.

Portia was so relieved to be away from prying eyes that, for a moment, she didn't realize he wasn't stopping there. Instead his hand tightened at the small of her back, and he urged her on into Lady Stone's music room and closed the door.

She wouldn't have been surprised to come face-to-face with Rye and Juliana Farling, but the room was empty, which left her with an entirely different problem.

"You're difficult to get alone long enough to ask a question," Swindon said, and for once he sounded serious.

Portia was startled. Everyone in London knew that Lord Swindon was seeking a bride this year. But he had showed no partiality to any of the debutantes. Was it possible his eye had fallen on Portia? He'd told her he liked her spirit...

She should be flattered, of course, and pleased. But truly the last thing she wanted to deal with just now, with her senses in turmoil, was how to politely let down a gentleman who had worked up the courage to make an offer.

Wasn't it odd, though, that she'd had no hint of this before? He had sent that huge bouquet of yellow roses, of course... but surely a man who was developing a *tendre* for a woman gave off hints. Had she simply been so caught up in thinking about Rye—*no,* she argued to herself; she'd been caught up in thinking about Lady Stone's ball, not Rye—that she'd missed the signs?

Inside the music room, where only a single lamp glowed, his hold tightened. He caught her chin and turned her face up to his, then gave a low chuckle and kissed her, long and slowly.

Portia's body tightened in protest, and deliberately she forced herself to relax. What was so wrong about a stolen kiss, anyway? She'd made up her mind to live a little dangerously tonight—why not test this too? Perhaps she simply liked to be kissed, and that accounted for how she'd reacted when Rye had kissed her. And if Swindon was making her an offer...

No. Stealing a kiss, just to find out what it felt like to slip off with a rake, was one thing. But committing herself to such a man was something else entirely.

Swindon growled a little, pulling her even more tightly against his body. One hand pressed hard against her spine, grinding her against his pelvis. The hard contact jolted Portia out of her daydream. This was not a man to toy with. She leaned back, pushing against his chest, but she couldn't escape the steel of his grip.

He touched the cameo trinket at her throat, making it sway between her breasts. His eyes dilated; his fingertip trailed down her breastbone and under the edge of her neckline, rubbing the sensitive skin of her breast.

"My lord," she said sternly.

"I will give you jewels to replace this trinket—rubies, I think, for the fire in you—and all you have to do is be nice to me." He dropped his head to her breast and nuzzled her nipple. "I need a new mistress, and you'll do very well."

Portia braced her hands against his waistcoat and pushed. "Let me go, sir."

"How I will enjoy having you get starchy with me like this when we're in bed."

She clenched her fist and swung at him.

He caught both her hands and mercilessly dragged them behind her. "You were willing enough a moment ago."

"I thought…" She stopped herself too late.

He laughed. "You thought I was offering marriage? To *you*? A penniless companion? You're nothing but a tease, making promises with your eyes and then holding out for more. I've heard the stories about how you've led men on to think you had some kind of fortune—from a sugar plantation in the Caribbean, wasn't it? How convenient that it was so far away. One of them told me himself how lucky he was to discover the truth before he married you."

"I never said—"

"You only hinted, didn't you? It was your aunt who spread the rumor. We'll take care of this right now, *Miss Langford*. After tonight you won't be so high-and-mighty."

She struggled, but her efforts to break free of his punishing grip only pushed her harder against him, and she could feel his arousal growing. She opened her mouth to scream. But if they were discovered here...

"Go ahead and yell," he said, "if you want to have society witness your shame."

When she hesitated, he backed her against the wall, and his mouth came down hard on hers, muffling her protest.

She couldn't see past him, and she could barely hear over the pounding of blood in her ears. But suddenly there was a creak, and a shaft of light from the hallway cut through the gloom as the door opened.

❧

The ball should have been a joy. Miranda had looked forward to it, eager to see Rye and Sophie not just as guests at other people's parties, but as the central figures of their own. But when the first dance was finished and she retired from the set, all she could think of was how much she wanted the evening to be finished, so she could go to her room and try to sleep.

She had shared that first country dance with Marcus, and he'd said barely a word to her. As soon as the music ended, he bowed and went off to finish filling his card—at least, she assumed that was what he was doing, for after that, he was out on the floor for every dance—with Sophie, with Portia, with Juliana Farling, with Lady Flavia Summersby. When he stood up for a country dance with Amalie Mickelthorpe, Miranda turned her back.

After everything he had said about wanting her to wear colors, he hadn't even seemed to notice her dress. Oh, he'd been appropriately quiet when she'd walked into the drawing room, before the ball started, but his eyes hadn't popped—as she must admit she'd hoped for.

Of course, they hadn't exactly parted on good terms yesterday, when she'd left him standing on his doorstep while she rode off in Robert Wellingham's curricle.

She calculated. The supper dance was still a long way off; the ball would go on for at least three more hours. She didn't know if she could stand up so long, but she didn't want to sit down, for fear she'd nod off.

"I know it is not the polite thing to say," Robert Wellingham told her, "but you seem tired, ma'am."

"Truth is often not polite, Mr. Wellingham, but that doesn't make it any less true. Sometimes one devotes so much time and energy to getting ready for an event that the occasion itself does not live up to one's expectation." She surveyed him. "It was kind of you to lead my daughter out in the first dance."

"It was kind of her to include me by asking. She is an excellent dancer—like her mother, I suspect. Is your card filled, ma'am?"

"No. I could hardly refuse to take part in the opening set, but as for the rest of the evening…" She shrugged a little, forgetting for a moment exactly how low-cut her dress was—until Lord Swindon, passing with his partner, paused to take a good look. Miranda felt suddenly naked under the intensity of his gaze.

Without haste, Wellingham moved between them, presenting his back to Swindon to shield her from the rake's stare. "I find myself without a partner for the next set, ma'am. Will you do me the honor?"

If she refused him, he would think she was another of the snobs who thought less of him because of his livelihood. Besides, he had just done her a good turn. "Of course."

"I find that staying busy helps the time pass. And it is more entertaining to take part, not just watch."

He was right about that; she enjoyed following the complexities of the dance, and she was almost energized by the time it was finished, not only from the exercise, but from his dry wit and the droll observations he made each time they joined up again. The only bad moment was when she made a turn and came face-to-face with Marcus…

"Winston has seemed out of sorts all evening," Wellingham said as the dance finished. "I must find an opportunity to apologize to him for missing my appointment yesterday. I was on my way to his house to discuss a business matter when I encountered you, and I did not get back to Bloomsbury until far too late to call on him. I fear he must have thought I was enthralled with you and forgot him entirely."

Miranda couldn't stop her little gurgle of amusement. "You didn't tell him that all you did was to drive me straight home?"

"No. I've been letting him think whatever he likes. It amuses me far more than it seems to entertain him. But I see he is summoning me. Miss Sophie seems to have been deserted."

"What?" Miranda looked around. She put a hand on his sleeve. "Bring her to me."

"It would be better if she continues with the evening's entertainment, as if nothing important has happened."

She stared up at him for a moment. "You're right, of course. You're very wise, Mr. Wellingham. And compassionate as well. You do realize that, do you not?"

"Ah yes." His voice held a note of irony. "The tendency toward compassion makes my profession difficult to practice sometimes, you understand."

She laughed at him, and he kissed her hand and strolled across the room without hurry toward her daughter.

With Sophie once more in safe hands—and what an interesting conviction *that* was, Miranda thought—she went looking for a chair.

Marcus fell into step beside her, offering his arm. "Did you see that our cubs have had a falling-out?"

"That's good news, surely."

"I have some ideas about how to capitalize on it." His voice was low and intimate—every bit as much a caress as if he had run a hand across her bare shoulders.

Wellingham must have explained to him about

yesterday, she thought, since Marcus was back to his normal self. "And I suppose you want to discuss this in private? You have ideas about everything, and they all seem to end in the same place."

"Is that why you were not at Lady Emerson's soiree last night after all? Because you were afraid you would succeed in tempting me into a dark corner?"

"That *I* would tempt *you*? That's the outside of enough, sir."

"It's true. You're a dangerous woman, Miranda."

"In any case, I was simply tired last night. I was not avoiding you." She spotted a chair behind a potted palm. "It seems I must thank you for the opportunity to know Robert Wellingham better. Such a pleasant man. Very gentle. He tells me he was on his way to an appointment with you yesterday when I encountered him."

A smile tugged at the corner of Marcus's mouth. "Then he didn't tell you the entire truth. He had already knocked, and Evans told him that I was with a caller. A few minutes later you came out."

"So he knows I was…" She bit her lip.

Marcus nodded. "Alone, in my house, with me."

"But he didn't mention it just now."

"He won't ever mention it to anyone—if I ask him not to. As you said, he's a pleasant man, and very gentle."

"And what must I do in return?"

"I'm sure I can think of something." His eyes lit with mischief. "Something exciting. Admit it, Miranda—he's not at all right for you. You should give up the idea of marrying him before it comes back to embarrass you."

She couldn't deny that he was correct, though it made her feel sad. It would have been such a practical match.

"I'm planning an outing next week," he went on. "A visit to Vauxhall. It's so temptingly full of dark passages and private spots where one isn't interrupted. Will you come? If you turn me down, I shall cancel the party."

She felt longing and desire pool between her legs at the mere idea of trysting with him in a dark corner of the pleasure gardens. "I'm amazed you'd trust yourself with me there."

"Oh, we'll let the youngsters chaperone us. I'm inviting them all—and Lady Stone too—as an excuse."

Suddenly weariness swept over her. "Goodness," she said, looking down at her hem. "I've torn a ruffle. You must excuse me while I go and repair it."

"What's wrong, Miranda?" The teasing note was suddenly gone from his voice. "You're tense, you look tired, and your face is drawn as if you're ill."

"How ungallant of you to tell me so. Now I must go up to my bedroom and fix my ruffle." He frowned, but she ignored him and circled the ballroom. She was so tired she didn't know if she could climb the stairs to her room.

In the hallway, she almost collided with Rye and Juliana Farling as they came up from the dining room, where refreshments had been laid out. Juliana was still clutching a glass of punch.

"Mama," Rye said. "What's wrong?"

Miranda shook her head. "Just a minor repair. I didn't see Portia in the ballroom. Will you ask her to keep an eye on Sophie while I'm gone?" She didn't wait for Rye's nod but grasped the newel post and began hauling herself up the stairs.

In her bedroom, her maid was sitting by the fire, repairing the delicate lace edging on the cuff of a morning dress. She jumped up when Miranda came in. "Ma'am?"

"It's nothing, Mary. I just need to rest for a few minutes."

"And a cup of tea, perhaps?" Mary tucked her up on the chaise longue and left the room to fetch a tray.

Miranda turned her head to look at the fire. The room was dark, and the crackle of the embers was soothing. She was soon lulled into such a state of relaxation that when the door opened, she barely noticed. Perhaps Mary would think she was asleep and not bother her with tea.

A chair scraped as Marcus set it between her and the fire, directly in her line of vision. Miranda sat up so quickly that her head spun. "What are you doing in my bedroom?"

"Talking to you, unless you have a better idea to suggest."

"Get out."

"No. You walked away from me yesterday; this evening you were careful not to appear until we were surrounded by people, and one cannot have a serious conversation at a ball. But when you leave your daughter unsupervised..."

"She is not unsupervised. Portia will look after her, and Lady Stone."

"And when I dare to point out that you look ill,

you make an excuse and leave the room. You didn't tear a ruffle, did you?"

"No." She leaned back against the cushions. "I just needed—"

There was a scratch on the door, and Miranda shot up again. "That's my maid. She can't find you here!"

Marcus didn't move. "She's the one who told me which room was yours."

"Go!" Miranda pointed toward the dressing room.

The door opened, and Sophie peeked in. The light of the candle she carried fell across her face and reflected off the white lace of her dress. "Mama?" she said anxiously.

Miranda shot a look toward Marcus, but he was no longer by the fire. She could barely see him lurking in the shadows of her dressing room. He'd moved across the dark, unfamiliar bedroom in absolute silence—a truly handy talent, acquired through years of practice, no doubt.

"Oh, please, Mama," Sophie wailed. "You *have* to be here. We need you!"

❧

Though Rye would have only one dance with Juliana tonight, she had saved one of the few precious waltzes of the evening for him, and he took it as a sign that his offer would be accepted. He wouldn't get a better opportunity than that waltz. As they danced, he would ask her for a moment alone. Then, in private, he would tell her that if she was indeed receptive to his offer, he would call on her father tomorrow to set the formalities in motion.

It was not the accepted protocol, to ask the young lady before presenting himself to her father to request formal permission. But Rye had hashed out the plan with Lady Stone, who agreed that he had only one shot at pulling this off. When a man asked a young lady's father for permission to court her, word got around, so Rye needed to be certain that the first heiress he asked would accept him, and only then carry on to the next step.

He presented himself to Juliana when the preceding country dance was finished, and she suggested that they go down to the dining room for a cold drink. He was mentally rehearsing his question as she slowly sipped her ice, and twice he had to ask her to repeat a comment. The second time, she said crisply, "If you don't wish to talk to me, my lord, we may as well go back up to the ballroom. Perhaps the waltz is still going on." She picked up her reticule and her glass and started off without him.

"It's not that, Miss Farling," he said as he caught up with her by the stairs. "I *do* want to talk to you. I *need* to talk to you. I just—I'm not sure how to say…" They reached the upper hallway, and his mother almost bowled him over as she came out of the ball-room. "Mama, what's wrong?"

"Just a minor repair," Lady Ryecroft said. "I didn't see Portia in the ballroom. Will you ask her to keep an eye on Sophie while I'm gone?"

Rye nodded, but she had already started up the stairs. He looked after her, frowning. *A repair*, she'd said, but it looked a great deal more serious than that to him, to cause her to rush off as if something were chasing her.

He took a deep breath and turned to Juliana. Instead of looking at him, she was gazing up the stairs to where the last glimpse of Lady Ryecroft's dress was disappearing onto the bedroom floor. Her eyes were narrowed.

There was no point in postponing further, and for the moment they were entirely alone in the hallway. "Miss Farling, I wish to ask you a question."

"Yes?" she cooed and set her iced punch on a handy table.

"I wish to ask you..."

He paused as a maid came out of the ballroom, balancing a tray of empty glasses. She picked up another from a plant stand just outside the drawing room and then came toward them on her way to the door at the back of the house that blocked off the servants' staircase. As she passed, she bobbed a little curtsy and reached for the glass Miss Farling had just set down.

"Leave it," Miss Farling said sharply and raised her hand as if to strike the girl. "Can't you see I wasn't finished with it, you fool?"

The maid stammered an apology and hurried off.

"Servants are so annoying." Miss Farling gave an irritated little sigh and picked up her glass again. "Yes, my lord? Do go on with what you were saying."

Rye told himself it was a small thing, the sort of display of temper that anyone might show when nerves were taut and important questions were interrupted. In any case, it was her upbringing that was at fault, not her nature. Perhaps she hadn't been taught to treat servants well. She could learn better...

But the words felt hollow.

"I don't recall just now," he heard himself say. "I'm sorry, but I must do as my mother requested."

She tossed her head. "Oh yes. Such a good boy you are, to go looking for that tiresome Miss Langford. No doubt you will always obey your mama's wishes above all else... unless a wife makes it clear that she will not live under your mama's thumb. If you *happen* to remember what it is you wanted to ask, my lord, you may call on me tomorrow—and rest assured, none of my mother's servants would dare to interfere in a private conversation." She thrust her empty glass into his hand and walked off with her head high.

If the gentle Juliana Farling had suddenly turned into a cobra, Rye couldn't have been more startled. He would never have dreamed her voice could be so cutting, her entire bearing so sarcastic. As for the notion of her happily sharing Ryecroft Manor with his mother—how had he fooled himself so completely?

She'd be waiting a good long time before he paid a call or requested a private conversation. But with her out of the running... perhaps Miss Mickelthorpe's voice wasn't so unbearable after all.

He set the empty glass down on a table outside Lady Stone's music room and heard a rustle from inside. There wasn't supposed to be anyone in there, but no doubt a couple had slipped away for a moment's privacy.

Only... had that been a protest he'd heard, or just a passionate sort of gulp?

Rye quietly opened the door. He wouldn't look at who was inside, he told himself. He was only going to

make certain that both of them were willing partici-
pants, and then he'd go away.

The couple was veiled in shadow and entwined
embarrassingly closely. As the light from the doorway
fell across his shoulders, the man said something that
sounded like a curse.

Swindon. That was no surprise. Rye looked more
closely. "Portia?"

"Go away," Swindon muttered.

"Gladly," Rye growled. "Your pardon—both of you."

Portia gave a little squeak and jammed her fist into
Swindon's ribs. As he jerked back, she slid past him
and flung herself at Rye. She slammed hard into his
chest and dug her face into his shoulder. Automatically
his arms closed around her. She was shaking.

"It's all right," he whispered into her hair. "It's all
right now. You're safe."

Swindon snorted. "Before you challenge me to a
duel, Ryecroft, you should know that I didn't drag
the... lady... here against her wishes. She's no better
than she should be."

"You will say nothing of this, Swindon," Rye ordered.

"Definitely not. I wouldn't want my future bride—
whichever of this year's brainless broodmares I eventually choose—to know about my mistress. So I'll keep
my tongue between my teeth. Unless Miss Langford
refuses me."

He ran a hand over his neckcloth, opened the door
carefully to glance out, and was gone.

Portia huddled against Rye. Even as he held her
close, he felt his temper hit the boiling point. "You
came in here with him *willingly*?"

She sniffed, but only once, and stood up straight. "I must thank you for your timely intervention, my lord."

Her bodice had been pulled askew, and one nipple peeked temptingly out over the black lace at the edge of her neckline. Rye tried not to look, but the sight of the pert little peak was almost enough to undo him. He had dreamed about her breasts, but even the most powerful fantasy could never quite capture the dainty shape or the exquisite smoothness of her skin. "Dammit, Portia, what were you thinking, to toy with a man like that one?"

"Naturally you would believe that it must be entirely my fault!" Her voice quivered on the edge of hysteria. "Will you please just go away?"

She tried to fix her dress, but her hands were trembling too much. He saw a shadow on her wrist, just above the edge of her glove—the mark of a strong man who had held her against her will. Fury burned through him, along with a primitive urge to call Swindon out and kill him—slowly.

"Oh, Portia, of course it's not your fault." He pulled her close, cradling her like a child. "I'm sorry. I'm sorry." She sagged against him, and Rye buried his lips in her hair and held her tightly. It was a long time before she sighed and stepped away and began a feeble effort to tidy herself up. Rye's palms itched with the desire to help her.

Just then the door swung wide, and suddenly the room seemed to fill with people. But there were really just a few—Lady Stone and Lady Brindle, with Lord Randall trailing behind.

Shock ricocheted through the room.

Lady Stone lit a candle and held it up. The wavering yellow light fell across Portia, showing her hair falling down and her bodice still askew. Hastily, Lady Stone moved the light aside. "Who did this, Portia?" she asked sternly. "Tell me. He must make things right."

Her voice sounded like doom. Rye had no doubt she would do it too; as soon as Portia whispered Swindon's name, Lady Stone would drag him back and insist that he restore Portia's honor by giving her his name. By marrying the woman he had tried to violate…

"I should think it's obvious who's responsible," Lady Brindle said. "I never thought it of Miranda, but there's bad blood somewhere in that family, for the daughter's a hoyden and the son's a cad."

Just behind Lady Brindle, Sophie had suddenly appeared—her eyes wide and horrified. Lord Randall looked as if he wished he were anywhere else. Lady Stone's gaze skidded from Portia to Rye.

There was only one thing he could do.

Rye shrugged out of his coat and draped it around Portia's shoulders. "Sorry to have gotten carried away like that, my sweet. I know it's not the way you wanted to announce it, but it's done now, and we have to face the music. Lady Stone"—he faced her squarely—"I have just asked Miss Langford to be my wife."

Eighteen

THEIR WALTZ HAD FLOWN BY AS SOPHIE PLANNED Wellingham's picnic, and long before she had run out of ideas, the music ended. "I don't see your mother," he said as they left the floor.

And of course he would be looking for Lady Ryecroft. All Sophie's joyful anticipation of the picnic suddenly fled.

"I don't see Miss Langford either. Would you care to sit with Lady Stone while I get you a cold drink?"

"How kind of you, sir. But you must not trouble yourself."

Preoccupied with her aggravation, Sophie was only feet from Lady Stone when she realized she'd walked into a low-voiced argument. "Then by all means go and look for her," Lady Stone said. "She can't have gone far; she was here for the last set."

"I merely asked if you had seen her go," Lady Brindle said haughtily. "And though perhaps *you* wouldn't hesitate to go poking around in a private home, I would! However, we shall take your refusal to help as permission to look behind closed doors. Come, Lord Randall."

She actually calls her son Lord Randall? Sophie wasted a moment remembering how foolish she'd been to think of Lord Randall as a potential mate. It was a note in Carrisbrooke's favor that his only family was an uncle whom she found both witty and wise.

"If you're looking for my mama," Sophie said, "I'm sure she'll be returning at any moment."

Lady Brindle stared at Sophie through her quizzing glass. "Why would we be seeking Miranda? It's Lady Flavia who has gone missing."

"Mama." Lord Randall looked around, as if checking for spies. "Keep your voice down, I beg you."

"She's missing too?" Wellingham murmured. "There seems to be a lot of that going on tonight."

Lady Brindle dismissed him with a glance and laid a hand on her son's arm.

Lady Stone gave a little snort. "Oh, very well, I'll come and help you look. Though I think it would be wiser for you to merely blink and let the young woman have her fun. There'll be little enough of it in her future." She stalked off after the other two.

"If you would care for that cold drink after all," Wellingham said, "we could go down together. The ballroom feels stuffy."

"It's less so after those two left," Sophie said frankly.

They were at the head of the stairs when Lady Stone opened the door of her music room, and the sudden and dramatic silence drew Sophie like a magnet. She arrived in the doorway just as Lady Brindle's opinion of her and Rye rang out—and then Rye spoke, and Sophie stared at him in disbelief. Surely he couldn't have done this—not to Portia! She turned to flee, and

Wellingham took her by the shoulders. "Stop and think, Sophie, before you make this worse."

"I'm trying to make it better." She stared up at him. "Help me find Mama. Maybe she can fix this."

Lady Ryecroft's bedroom was only the second place they checked. Sophie felt her heart lift when she saw movement on the chaise longue by the fire, for Mary wouldn't sit there in the dark. "We need you, Mama," Sophie said, and when Lady Ryecroft answered, she went running across the room to throw herself into her mother's arms. Then she sniffed, and her eyes went wide as she smelled cologne. "Mama! Do you have a *man* in here?"

❦

The entire episode felt like a nightmare, but Portia was all too aware that there would be no waking up. It wasn't what Swindon had done that made her feel like casting up her accounts; the worst part was realizing that her idiocy had trapped Rye.

She was betrothed to a man who had been given no choice in the matter. If he didn't offer for her, his reputation would be ruined; five minutes of Lady Brindle's tongue running loose and he'd be forever known as the man who had destroyed a lady and then refused to marry her. It was incredibly unfair. All Rye had done was rescue her, but this was his reward.

She could have cried—except that she was far beyond the point where tears would do any good.

For Portia, the saddest part of the entire episode had been when Rye had made one last desperate effort to escape his fate by begging the witnesses not to talk.

He'd done it in a gentlemanly manner, of course—she expected nothing else from him. He'd said that since announcing the betrothal right away would only call attention to Portia's disarray, he hoped that they would all keep the secret until tomorrow.

Lady Brindle had looked mutinous, but at that moment Lady Ryecroft had arrived, summed up the situation with a glance, and swept Portia and Sophie up to her bedroom before either of them could say another word. It took both Portia's maid and Lady Ryecroft's Mary to put her back together enough to reappear in the ballroom just as the supper dance was ending.

Rye didn't come near her for the remainder of the evening, but that was no surprise. He would hardly want to conduct the first conversation of their betrothal in a public place, especially after she'd so efficiently snared him...

Portia watched him across the room, however, dancing with one of the minor heiresses. That reminded her of Juliana Farling, and her heart sank.

The moment the ball was finished, Portia pleaded a headache. She was silent as her maid brushed her hair and braided it and helped her into a nightgown. Then she sent the maid away and sank down by the fire to wait. Once the house was quiet, she tightened the belt of her wrapper as if it were armor and tiptoed down the hall to knock timidly at Rye's bedroom door.

Rye had taken off his coat and his neckcloth, and he was holding a brandy glass when he opened the door. "Do come in, my dear. I was wondering when you'd be along."

"Are you foxed?" Portia asked.

"Not yet."

She winced. "I came to tell you that, of course, this can't be allowed to stand."

"What do you propose to do about it?"

"I don't know. But you obviously can't marry me. What about Juliana Farling? If you offered for her tonight…" Maybe that was why he'd pleaded so eloquently for silence—to give him time to make some kind of excuse to the woman he'd actually *asked* to marry him.

"I didn't. Then this little wrinkle got in the way." He didn't meet her gaze.

So Lady Stone had been right after all in betting on that particular match. The reminder of the wager only made Portia feel worse.

"What the hell were you thinking of, putting yourself in danger like that?"

Portia reminded, "You said once that you wouldn't swear at me."

"Well, that was when I still believed you'd never do anything so flea-brained as to go in a room alone with that cad!"

Portia looked down at her clasped hands. "I've really dumped us in the sauce, haven't I? I'm sorry, Rye. Truly. But can we just figure out how to get ourselves out of this? You don't want to marry me; I don't want to marry you…"

He grunted and went to refill his goblet, then held it out to her. "Have a sip—or several. I've found it helps."

She took a gulp. He was right; the liquid burned all the way down, but it distracted her for a moment.

"Lady Stone could stop this disaster; I'm sure of it. I shall ask her, in the morning."

"Ask her to do what? Make Swindon marry you? If you still want him after all that, then why on earth didn't you just tell me to go away a couple of hours ago?"

"Are you fool enough to think I'd want to marry him?"

The anger in his face died. "Portia, you were found in a room alone with a man, with no hope of an innocent explanation. You have to marry someone."

"And so you're caught in a trap, simply because you rescued me."

His mouth quirked into a reluctant grin. "Well... you rescued me first, from Miss Mickelthorpe. So we're even."

"Hardly. That was a different thing."

"And tonight you rescued me from Miss Farling, and a lucky escape that was too." In the fireplace, a coal cracked and settled. "I know this isn't what you want, Portia. It's a bad situation. But we'll have to make the best of it—as people have always done."

Make the best of it. It was hardly what she wanted from a marriage... and now that it was too late to change what she'd done, she realized how much she had longed for the very thing that had happened tonight. But she hadn't wanted it to come about like this. She wanted Rye, yes, but she had wanted a husband, a lover... not a man who had been backed into a corner.

Yesterday, when he'd kissed her, she'd dared for just a moment to hope that the young Lord Ryecroft might look beyond money to seek a woman he could grow to love, and see Portia. But tonight she'd ruined any possibility that he might ever look at her with anything other than disdain. Every time he saw her, he would remember exactly why she was his wife—and recall it was her foolishness that had destroyed his plans.

A soft tap sounded on the bedroom door. Portia looked wildly around for an escape. It would be just too ironic to be caught in Rye's bedroom barely two hours after the debacle downstairs.

"Draw the bed curtains," Rye whispered. He opened the door an inch, blocking the view with his body, while Portia scrambled onto his four-poster and pulled the blue velvet hangings at the foot.

"Rye?" Sophie said. "Oh good, you're still dressed. Well, almost dressed. Do you have Portia in here?"

"Why would you ask such a thing?" Rye sounded nearly as pompous as Lord Randall. Under other circumstances, Portia would have wanted to laugh.

"Because she doesn't seem to be anywhere else. I just checked her room, and she's not there, but her ball dress is. And she's not downstairs either, or with Mama. Speaking of Mama, you should know that I'm nearly certain I smelled a man's cologne in her room tonight."

Portia had no trouble visualizing the way Rye rolled his eyes. "*Nearly* certain? There are scents aplenty at a ball. You probably got cologne on your gloves while you were dancing, and that's what you smelled. Go to bed, Sophie—and take your imagination with you."

"You don't think she's run away, do you? Not Mama, of course; I mean Portia. To avoid the disgrace of having to marry you."

"I'm certain she has not."

"That's a relief. Night, Rye." She gave him a noisy, childlike smack of a kiss on the cheek and called, "Night, Portia!"

"Good…" Portia clapped her hand over her mouth, but it was too late.

Sophie gave a gleeful little laugh. "Next time, Rye, make sure the bed curtains aren't still swinging," she advised, and the door closed behind her with a click.

Portia buried her face in her hands. The blue velvet hangings whooshed open, the rings rattling above her head. She didn't look up.

"You do have a gift for this sort of thing." Rye sounded almost grim. "What do you think now? A little too late to ask Lady Stone to fix it?"

❧

There was no justice in the world, Miranda thought as Mary brushed her hair. She'd spent the better part of the last two weeks carrying on a torrid affair, but the one time that she *wasn't* doing anything disreputable—well, aside from the obvious misstep of having a gentleman present in her bedroom—she had been caught.

She'd have to talk to Sophie in the morning and explain. Of course, it would have been better to say something immediately—something casual or funny. Tomorrow, when she brought the subject up again, it would assume even more importance in Sophie's mind, but that was the best she could do.

She must have heaved a heavy sigh, for Mary clucked sympathetically and said, "You'll feel better soon, ma'am. It never lasts more than a few weeks."

"What never lasts?"

"The tiredness. Remember? You never had morning sickness with the others either, but practically the minute you were *enceinte*, you'd start nodding off at dinner or in the middle of a conversation. It'll only last a few weeks, and then you'll have your usual energy back."

Miranda gulped. The floor seemed to shake under her.

"Ma'am?" Mary turned pale. "I'm sorry. You didn't realize…?"

The possibility had not occurred to Miranda. If she'd given it a thought at all, she would have assumed she was too old to fall pregnant. But now that Mary had pointed out the obvious, she could no longer deny the facts.

It appeared she was going to have a baby. Marcus Winston's baby. An illegitimate half brother or half sister for Rye and Sophie…

And she'd thought explaining the scent of a man's cologne in her bedroom would be difficult!

⚜

Portia looked absolutely disconsolate. Not the look a man wanted to see from his promised bride, Rye thought.

"Where would you like to be married?" he asked in the hope that planning a ceremony would distract her.

She shook her head. She was still kneeling on his bed. She must not have realized that the belt of her wrapper had come loose, allowing the shadows cast by the candlelight to caress the hollow at the base of her throat and the cleavage below. Her nightgown was made of fine lawn, and the finicky little vertical tucks and stitches on the bodice only encouraged his gaze to drop a few inches more, to where her breasts swelled enticingly under the sheer fabric, reminding him of the nipple he'd glimpsed downstairs. Resolutely he looked away, but that didn't help either, for his gaze only slid down to the outline of her legs and the interesting little crevice between them…

Rye thought it would be a good idea for him to sit down before she noticed evidence of the direction his thoughts were taking. She was already flighty enough without his reminding her that this marriage would have a physical side.

He could have used a nice solid chair right now—big enough to hold Portia on his lap and cuddle her. Or a chaise longue wide enough for two to recline and explore each other's bodies…

And there he went, posting off into dangerous territory again. He really couldn't continue to stand at attention, so to speak; if she saw how aroused he was, she'd probably scream and flee. And since the only chair in the room was a spindly little thing he didn't trust to hold him, the bed would have to do.

He sat down next to her. "Come now; let's not start that again. I've made up my mind to it, Portia, so why can't you?"

"That's the problem. *You've* made up your mind, so you think that's all there is to be said about it."

"Isn't it? Would you have preferred me to just stand there and let you explain what really happened?"

She looked for a moment as if she was about to say yes.

"It's not as bad as that, surely. I won't beat you." He half expected the comment to win a smile, but when it didn't, he said gloomily, "It won't be any different, really, than the sort of marriage I was contemplating before."

"Except for the money." Her voice was low and taut.

"Oh. The money. Well, yes." For a while he'd almost managed to forget that little problem. He expected, now that he'd been reminded, that it would come crashing down on him once more. But it didn't; at the moment none of it seemed to matter. Perhaps he'd been sensible enough all along not to let himself count on ending up with a fortune. Or perhaps he was still too stunned by the turn of events to really take in what had happened tonight.

This unexpected betrothal was hard to forget, however, when Portia was right in front of him, for all practical purposes, occupying his bed. Even if she was, in Rye's opinion, definitely on the wrong side of the blanket at the moment.

"My lord—"

"You've been calling me Rye for some time now. And if you're going to marry me..." He shouldn't have said *if*.

"I understand, of course, that you have a duty to produce an heir." She spoke softly.

It took Rye a moment to hear what she'd said—because from his new position he could look almost directly down the neckline of her nightgown, which only served to remind him once more of the glimpse of rosy, eager-looking nipple he'd had downstairs...

An heir? Oh yes. A wonderful duty, that one. Looking forward to it.

"I know that men can"—she stopped to lick her lips, sending a surge of hot blood to Rye's groin—"men can perform adequately, even when they're not particularly attracted to the woman, to make a child. That was, after all, what you expected with Miss Mickelthorpe or Miss Farling. So why would it be any different with me?"

Rye was feeling seriously at sea. "What makes you think I'm not attracted to you?"

Her face flushed, and she looked away.

This discussion was getting to be seriously interesting. Rye leaned a little closer. She smelled good too. Like rose water. Maybe lavender. Something sweet, anyway.

He wanted to pull her down under him and show her exactly how attracted he was.

"Because when you kissed me yesterday, you stopped."

He couldn't keep from smiling. "You think I ended that kiss because I found it distasteful?"

"I know that I am not at all what you were looking for in a wife."

"Well, that's true enough, and I'm sure if I climbed into a marriage bed with Amalie Mickelthorpe, I'd have to think of her money in order to perform my husbandly duty. Portia, the truth is any man would find you tempting."

She shook her head.

Rye's heart sank. Had he missed the point entirely? "If what you're really saying is that you don't find me appealing, and you don't want to give me an heir…"

She looked down at her hands, which were clasped hard together. "I *do* want a family, Rye. But not if… Of course you'd say that you… like me. What else could a gentleman say?"

A tiny voice in Rye's brain whispered, *This is the foundation of the rest of your life. You have to get it right.* "So you're saying if I had to force myself in order to get an heir with you…"

"Then I would much prefer not to marry you. Even if it means being ruined."

She had been right about one thing, Rye thought. She was absolutely *not* what he'd been contemplating in a wife. And he was beginning to think he was the luckiest fool in England.

"Portia, kiss me again the way you kissed me yesterday."

She hesitated, and for a moment he thought she was going to refuse. Then she leaned toward him, and her lips brushed gently against his—a mere butterfly kiss. A kiss his sister might have pressed on him.

"No, that wasn't it at all. Let me show you." He wanted to crush her against him—and under him—but he limited himself to kissing her, licking and nipping and tasting her lips, slowly working up to exploring her mouth. When her tongue finally darted out to sample him, a jolt of pure lust rocked him, and he had to back off to keep himself from spreading her out across the coverlet and taking her right then.

"That was… pleasant." There was a quiver in her voice.

"So is the rest of what men and women do together, Portia. I stopped kissing you yesterday because if I didn't, I wouldn't have been able to stop. And that's why I'm going to take you back to your room now—even though I want to make love to you."

She looked at him thoughtfully. "Don't stop."

"Portia, you don't know what you're asking. If I go any further—"

"But that was only a kiss."

"*Only?* Sweetheart—"

"I don't know if you're telling the truth or just being gallant, and I won't wait to find out till it's too late to change our minds. I mean it, Rye. Prove you really do want me, that you're not just saying so. Prove it right now, or I won't marry you, no matter what happens to me."

She pulled away from him, but instead of climbing off the bed, she insinuated herself under the coverlet. Only after she was covered to her shoulders did she wriggle out of her wrapper and toss it aside.

Watching her was like setting a torch to tinder. All she'd really done was to get between his sheets, but her innocent, modest little maneuver was the most sensual dance he'd ever seen. The most practiced courtesan couldn't have inflamed him more completely.

"As the lady wishes." He barely recognized the rasp of his own voice.

Rye held her gaze as he undressed, and he was rewarded with a little gasp when he dropped his breeches and his erect penis sprang free.

He climbed onto the bed and stripped the coverlet back so he could look at her. Without her wrapper, the fine lawn nightgown was almost transparent. The dark circles around her nipples and the shadowy triangle between her legs were even more alluring for being veiled. He didn't bother to remove her gown; instead he leaned over to kiss her again. After a long, hot, deep exploration of her mouth, he let his lips wander slowly down her throat, touched the tip of his tongue to her cleavage, cupped her breast in his palm, and slowly took her nipple into his mouth. The fine fabric went completely transparent as he licked and nipped and sucked.

Her breathing grew taut.

He shifted to the other breast and then unlaced the fastenings and spread the gown wide, feasting his eyes for a few seconds before tasting her once more. Her skin was soft as velvet, and he took his time, toying with her nipples until they peaked and trembled, while his hands wandered on to her waist, to the curve of her hip.

The hem of the long nightgown had ridden up as she slid under the blankets, leaving a good deal of leg bare. Still, it took all his ingenuity to get her out of the nightgown, and he thought about just ripping it before he managed the feat. But finally she lay before him, completely exposed.

Her gaze dropped to his erection. Her eyes were wide and a little fearful.

"Are you still worried that I might not be interested enough in you to perform adequately?" he asked dryly. "Portia, I promise you'll like this. I'll make sure you do." *Even if it kills me.*

Slowly, she relaxed, and he spread her knees and

knelt between them. He kissed her navel, darting his tongue into the little depression, and briefly nuzzled the sweet little birthmark just over her right hip bone. Was it truly the shape of a heart? He'd have to check... some other time.

He parted her curls and bent closer to inhale her scent—spicy, clean, earthy. He held her open to expose the little pleasure nub and breathed on her. She said something incoherent.

Good, he thought. *She's losing her mind just as surely as I am.*

He settled back to taste and to stroke her with his tongue. Her first orgasm terrified her—he could see her apprehension—so he cradled her against his chest and held her till the tremors passed, whispering nonsense in her ear, and used his fingers to bring her to climax again. He watched the awe in her face and reminded himself that there was all the time in the world to enjoy her. He could wait till she was ready.

Only when she was limp and gasping did he once more move over her. This time he nudged with the head of his penis, slowly sliding into her slick, wet heat, inch by inch, then waiting until she had adjusted to him before moving again. When he came up against her maidenhead, he said, "This will hurt, but only for a moment," and thrust firmly past the barricade.

She gave a tiny yelp and tried to pull away. He held her tightly, and after a moment she eased and he slid deeper. His head was beginning to feel fuzzy from the effort to restrain himself, and when she gave a tentative little thrust to meet him, he wanted to cheer. He began to move, slowly stroking her until he felt her muscles start to tighten around him. He pulled back just enough to be able to watch the fierce concentration in her face as she reached for her satisfaction—and just as she found it, he drove deep inside her and came, whispering her name.

⤜⤛

After her maid left her tucked into bed, Sophie relit her candle, propped herself against a mass of pillows, and began to contemplate the Ryecroft family's future.

Because someone has to, she thought pragmatically.

She liked the idea of having Portia as her sister, and she thoroughly approved of her as a wife for Rye. But lovely as it would be to officially add Portia to the family, she wasn't any help when it came to the financial conundrum.

In fact, Sophie admitted, the marriage would actually make things worse.

The money Robert Wellingham had paid to lease the manor wouldn't last forever. Rye was going to need a good chunk of whatever was left to purchase a special license—for clearly he couldn't wait for the banns to be read before he married Portia.

And it was Sophie's opinion that the remainder should be spent to brighten up the manor for its new mistress. A bride should at least have new sheets and bed hangings, along with a few bits and pieces to make her feel the house was truly hers.

Feeling both noble and practical over that decision, she moved on. There were, after all, two more Ryecrofts. And Sophie, who was far more realistic than her brother, wasn't entirely discounting their mother.

Until she had seen Lady Ryecroft and Robert Wellingham together in the ballroom, she hadn't put much faith in the idea of a match between the two of them. But she'd gotten a jolt tonight as she'd observed them. Only then had she realized that while it was eminently sensible for Wellingham to marry so far above himself, it was just as sensible for Lady Ryecroft to marry a fortune as it was for Rye to do so, or Sophie herself.

Then she'd gotten a second rude awakening when she'd gone to her mother's room. Whatever Rye said, Sophie was certain that she'd smelled a man's cologne. She'd almost recognized it—the scent had been familiar, but she couldn't be certain where she had encountered it before.

She was positive, however, that it wasn't the scent Wellingham used. Besides, he'd not only been standing right behind her at the time she smelled the mysterious cologne, but he'd been with her since long before her mother had left the ballroom.

Whatever Lady Ryecroft was up to—and Sophie had her suspicions—she wasn't likely to be bringing Robert Wellingham's fortune into the family.

So everything came down to Sophie.

There was still Carrisbrooke, of course—assuming that he'd ever speak to her again after she'd accused him of acting like a child.

Sophie decided that she could bring him around with a judicious amount of flattery, mixed with some eyelash batting, a charming giggle, and a few glimpses of a well-turned ankle. And if she were to allow him to steal a kiss, she was fairly certain she could be wearing an engagement ring within the week and be married by the end of the Season.

But then she would spend the rest of her life with a boy who might never grow up. A boy who would have good reason to believe she was a heartless Beauty who thought only of herself, because she would have married him for all the wrong reasons.

But what else could she do? Wait and see what happened?

Conditions change, Marcus Winston had said. *And not only for your brother.*

Well, he'd hit that nail right on the head. Conditions had changed, all right, but not in the direction he'd expected. Despite all Marcus Winston's platitudes about taking her time, the truth was Sophie had only a few more weeks to accomplish her mission.

And a desperate shortage of options.

Nineteen

Rye's voice held a wicked edge. "Did I perform adequately and to my lady's satisfaction?"

They might have already made a child tonight. Portia felt herself grow warm at the thought. Or was she feeling that sensation because of Rye's hands on her? He'd spooned her body against his, with his palms cupping her breasts and her head tucked under his chin. Every breath he took stirred her hair. He had grown hard again almost at once too, and his penis nestled insistently against her derriere...

"Or do you think I need practice?" He sounded hopeful.

Portia, who was rapidly losing her innocence, knew that she had to act quickly. "Rye, there's one more thing."

He pushed himself up on his elbow and looked down at her warily. "The last thing you wanted nearly wore me out."

"Liar."

He grinned. "All right, I admit it. I could do that every hour for the next week and not be satisfied. My dear, will you mind having my mother living with us? And my sister, if she doesn't marry? I had hoped to fix up the dower house, but—"

"I should not mind it at all, but perhaps you'll find that Lady Ryecroft has plans of her own."

"Plans? Oh, you mean that nonsense of Sophie's? She gets these notions; ignore her. I don't mean that you'd be living under my mother's thumb…"

The sole candle still lighting the room popped and sputtered. It had burned almost down to the socket.

Rye pushed back the blankets. "It's almost morning, sweetheart. We need to get you back to your room before the servants begin stirring. We'll talk tomorrow— no, *today*—and plan our wedding. I wonder how soon we can be married."

He insisted on helping her back into her night-gown—a process that took far longer than if she'd done it herself, for he seemed to think he needed to check every part of her body to be certain it was in good condition before he covered it, and he much preferred using his mouth to do the inspection. By the time he was finished, Rye was looking very satisfied with himself, and every square inch of Portia's skin was quivering with delight.

Tomorrow, she thought. *I'll tell him tomorrow.*

❧

The household was slow to stir on the morning after the ball. But when Sophie came into the breakfast room, expecting that she would be the first to appear, Rye was already there and tackling a sizable pile of eggs and ham.

She fixed her own plate and sat down across from him. "A night like that does give one an appetite." She reached for the toast rack.

Rye leveled a stare at her.

"All that dancing." Sophie kept her voice innocent. "What did you think I meant?"

He cut a bite of ham. "You told me you don't have any particular interest in Swindon, Sophie."

"Not a whit."

"You're never to be in a room alone with him."

"I know. Portia told Mama what happened while I was helping fix the damage last night. You're quite the hero, Rye, stepping in to save the damsel in distress. Oh, don't look at me like that. I'm *glad* you're marrying her—she'll make you laugh, which is far more than any of the heiresses could do."

"I doubt they'd have even tried."

"Anyway, I told you long ago that if it came down to a choice between your marrying someone like Miss Mickelthorpe or my marrying a gentleman who amuses me"—Sophie noticed that her hand was shaking and put down her fork—"the answer is perfectly clear."

"No, it isn't, Sophie. You are not to marry Carrisbrooke just because he's rich. We'll get along somehow. In any case"—he hesitated—"I think you should know that after Mama took you and Portia upstairs last night, Lady Brindle finally located Lady Flavia. She was in that little room at the far end of the hall—and Carrisbrooke was with her."

How odd, to feel almost relieved... "Was she kissing him? I'm sure he could use the practice."

Rye glared at her. "And how would you know he lacks experience?"

"Talk about the pot calling the kettle black! I only meant that a man who can't dance probably hasn't learned how to kiss either."

From the doorway, Lady Stone said tartly, "This seems to be an edifying conversation for the breakfast table."

Sophie's jaw dropped. Their hostess had never, during their entire stay, come downstairs for breakfast. For her to do so on the morning after a late party was unthinkable.

Lady Stone went on, "I don't suppose Portia has made an appearance as yet?"

Sophie darted a glance at Rye and said virtuously, "I haven't seen her since the ball ended last night." It was true; she *hadn't* seen Portia in Rye's bedroom— only heard her.

Lady Stone eyed her speculatively.

Rye got to his feet and took a deep breath. "Ma'am, I know you're not best pleased about how things have turned out. You undertook to help me find an advantageous match, and I failed to follow your advice. Worse, I've treated you badly by stealing away your companion. But I hope you will believe that I will do my best to make her happy."

Portia came in just then. She turned pink when Rye leaped to hold her chair.

Lady Stone snorted. "From the look of things, you'd best be off to get a special license this morning, Ryecroft."

"I had thought to finish my breakfast first," Rye

said mildly. "But yes, that is my intention." He kissed Portia's hand and gave it back to her with every appearance of reluctance.

Sophie was fascinated.

Lady Stone set her cup down with a crash. "This tea is cold. Sophie, ring for a fresh pot. Where do you wish to be married, Portia? St. George's, Hanover Square?"

Portia gave a little shiver. "Must it be so public?"

Sophie mused, "I always thought it would be most romantic to be married in the village church at Ryecroft."

Portia's eyes lit up. "I'd like that. But is it possible?"

Padgett, standing in the doorway, cleared his throat. "My lady, Mr. Wellingham sends his compliments and asks—"

"Bring him in, Padgett." Lady Stone said.

"—asks if Lord Ryecroft will see him," the butler finished.

"Well, he can see him over breakfast, since Lord Ryecroft is eager to finish eating so he can go and get a special license." Her tone was acerbic. "And send in a fresh pot of tea."

"No, I'm finished." Rye made a coolly formal bow to Lady Stone, kissed Portia's hand again, and completely ignored Sophie as he left the room.

Lady Stone pushed her untouched plate away. "Good. Now that he's no longer here to distract Portia, perhaps we can make progress. Sophie, go and ask your mother when she's coming down. We have a great deal of work to do."

❧

Wellingham was waiting in the smallest of the reception rooms, warming his hands at the fire. "Let's go into the library," Rye said.

Wellingham shook his head. "I need only a moment, my lord, and my business is not private. First allow me to express my congratulations on your betrothal."

"Thank you. But does everyone know already?"

"I think not. Lady Stone confided in me late last night, but she swore me to secrecy."

"She's not best pleased with me," Rye admitted. "I'm thinking it's a good thing I have an excuse to take myself out of her sight this morning."

"It occurs to me, my lord, that Miss Langford will want to see her new home at the earliest possible date, but I thought you might hesitate because of the small matter of the lease."

"I hadn't got that far, to tell the truth. But thank you."

"In fact, if you would prefer to be married from the manor, I understand. It is your home after all, and if you wish to take your bride there immediately, I will happily relinquish the remainder of the lease."

Rye remembered the glow in Portia's eyes when Sophie had mentioned being married in the village church. "Unfortunately, I'm in no position to refund your payment—it has all been spent."

"And in a good cause. Winning Miss Langford's hand and establishing Miss Ryecroft. In any case, I would not dream of accepting a refund. You may consider it a wedding gift."

It was ironic, Rye thought, that the man seemed to be more of a romantic than anyone else he knew. But Wellingham had no shortage of funds and no estate to drain his pockets. He could afford grand gestures like writing off a quarter's lease payment…

Rye couldn't accept the offer, of course, because it would feel too much like accepting charity. Yet Portia had said it would be lovely to be married at Ryecroft… and it wasn't as if Wellingham was actually using the house. "If you really don't mind, then let us agree that as soon as I am able to repay you, I will do so."

"Let us agree, instead, that we will discuss it when that time comes. Perhaps, my lord, if you truly wish to avoid Lady Stone for a while—"

"I do," Rye admitted.

"Then go on down to the manor today and set things in motion. I intended to go myself, but there are a few things I must do in town, and you will be able to arrange things far more efficiently than I could."

"Now that is a damn fine idea." Except, of course, that if he was at the manor, and Portia remained in London, there would be no more opportunities for her to slip into his bedroom. His body stirred at the memory.

Clearly the faster he could arrange a wedding, the better.

∞

The breakfast room was quiet for only a moment after Sophie left, before Lady Stone said sternly, "In case you're thinking I'm going to cough up that diamond bracelet we spoke of last night, Miss Langford, you're wrong."

Portia was startled. "A diamond…? Oh." She hadn't given a thought this morning to the wager, for it seemed so long ago. She started to agree, then noticed her employer's expectant gaze. Lady Stone was spoiling for an argument, and it would be better to tussle over a bracelet than something else. "That's right. You wagered a diamond bracelet against my bonus that Lord Ryecroft would offer for Miss Farling. I'd say you lost."

"Not at all. I said we'd have at least one match to announce before the end of the evening. And you made certain of that, so I win."

"You obviously meant Miss Farling. Changing the terms of the wager is cheating, ma'am."

Lady Stone's eyes were even beadier than usual. "And you would know all about cheating, miss, since you're the one who made certain Miss Farling was out of the running!" She smiled suddenly. "Oh, my dear, let an old lady have her fun. We'll call the wager a draw. You earned the bonus, and I'll throw in the diamond bracelet as a bride gift."

Portia smiled ruefully. "It would be a great deal more than I deserve."

"That's the truth. Deserting me like this... You're the only companion I've ever had who wouldn't let me bully her, though I thought for a moment this morning that you'd gone soft. But except for losing you, I am far from displeased. I must admit, in fact, that I'm quite proud of how it all worked out. Have you told Ryecroft yet?"

"Told him what? About Lord Swindon, you mean? He was right there; he knows what happened."

"No, no. I mean the sugar plantation."

Portia toyed with her teacup, trying to play for time, but Lady Stone's gaze was merciless. "You knew, ma'am?"

"I would hardly take an employee into my house without investigating her history. And it's remarkably difficult to keep that sort of information completely quiet."

"But you never gave a hint..." No, perhaps that wasn't entirely true. There had been a moment here or there when she'd thought there was an edge to Lady Stone's voice or a possible double meaning in what she said. But each time, the moment would pass with no further comment, so Portia had assumed it was her guilty conscience speaking.

"I thought it was your own concern," Lady Stone said, almost gently. "And by the by, it's not at all a bad way to test whether a gentleman is fond of you or only of your money—to persuade him that you have none. However, now that Ryecroft has proved himself—"

"It's not an enormous sum, ma'am. Respectable, yes, but not nearly the sort of fortune Miss Mickelthorpe has, or even Miss Farling."

"You haven't answered my question, Portia."

"No, ma'am. I haven't told him."

"Why not?"

Because he was making love to me, and I couldn't think straight... "There hasn't been much opportunity."

"Make one. The gentleman stepped in and offered for you, even though he was giving up a fortune in the process. He didn't have to rescue you."

"It would have ruined him if he hadn't. He... he was trapped either way."

"And he's being remarkably sanguine about it. He's a good man. He deserves to know the truth."

Rye *was* a good man, Portia thought, to have accepted the ruin of his plans with such cheerfulness. "Yes, ma'am." She went to look for him.

He was not difficult to find, for he and Wellingham and Marcus Winston were all three in the entrance hall. Wellingham was leaving, Portia deduced, and Marcus Winston was just arriving, but the three of them seemed to be having a wonderful time. Rye was laughing as he accepted congratulations.

"You'll come to the wedding, Winston?" he asked. "We're going to be married at the manor, as soon as I can arrange it. Wellingham's agreed to let me buy back the lease, so I'm going down now to get everything in order."

Buy back the lease? *With what*? Just a couple of days ago he'd told her that his money had all been spent.

"We've been talking about possible improvements at the manor," Rye went on. "Wellingham's going to drive down to give me his opinion. But I'd like your advice as well, Winston. Your experience at Carris Abbey would be helpful to me in deciding where investment would give the best return."

Improvements? *Investment*? Portia felt frozen. All that would take money—and it sounded like large sums of money. But Rye had none at all. At least, yesterday he'd had none. And only one thing had changed in the meantime...

He must have known about her money after all, and he'd made a deliberate choice. He'd said something last night about how she had rescued him from Miss Farling—*and a lucky escape that was*.

Had Portia been on his list of heiresses, and he'd

simply worked his way down the roster till he'd reached her?

And then, by making love to her last night, he had made certain that she no longer had the smallest whisper of choice about whether to marry him...

That was your own doing, she reminded herself. *You practically forced him into it.*

She heard a rustle above her on the stairway. The men looked up as Lady Ryecroft came into view, and Rye spotted Portia in the hall and came quickly toward her, his face alight.

He was contented at how things had turned out—but not, as she had thought, because of her.

If I climbed into a marriage bed with Amalie Mickelthorpe, he'd said last night, *I'd have to think of her money in order to perform my husbandly duty.*

Had he been counting Portia's money in order to perform his husbandly duty?

Swindon had known about her past, though he'd had the details wrong. But others could have been closer to the mark. For that matter, Lady Stone herself could have told Rye—the wily old woman had practically admitted to engineering the outcome she preferred. And it would have been to Rye's advantage to pretend not to know...

Only long practice kept her from shuddering away from Rye as he brought her hand to his lips. His gaze on hers was warm, and the message was clear—he was thinking about kissing much more than her hand. Or at least he wanted her to think he was.

"We'll be married at Ryecroft, darling. Wellingham has offered to give up the lease for us."

Interesting, she thought, that he didn't mention paying for the favor.

"I'll go down today to set things in motion, and you can follow as soon as you're ready. Portia"—his voice dropped to a whisper—"don't be long."

She didn't trust herself to speak, but she nodded.

She would marry him, for she had committed herself last night, and now there was nothing else she could do.

⤜⤏

Miranda was not yet dressed when Sophie came to her room, and she was startled when her daughter delivered Lady Stone's message and then simply went away.

Was the child moping over Carrisbrooke? Miranda hoped not, but only time would tell.

She was halfway down the stairs on her way to join Lady Stone when she saw Marcus standing near the front door with Wellingham, and her foot faltered on the tread. She hadn't prepared herself to encounter him—not so early in the morning and not before she'd had a chance to adjust to the news that had burst on her last night.

She pasted on a smile. "Good morning, gentlemen. You show great courage to enter a house where there's a wedding being planned. There will be time to discuss nothing else until the festivities are over."

She was painfully aware of Marcus's gaze, dark and intent on her, and she knew he understood the message underlying her words—that she had no intention of talking to him until after the wedding, and it would do him no good to persist in the meantime. She looked at Rye, standing with Portia in the shadow of the stairs. "Did I hear you say you've decided to be married at the manor?"

Rye nodded. "Just as soon as we can accomplish it, Mama. I've got some business to tend to this morning with these gentlemen, but as soon as that's finished, I'm off to Surrey."

"What business? Surely a special license doesn't require all three of you—and confirmed bachelor that you are, Mr. Winston, I doubt you're an expert on the subject."

"Together, I'm sure we can work it out," Marcus said. "Unless you'd rather I stay here and help the ladies plan the wedding."

She eyed him coolly. "Hardly. By all means, enjoy the experience, since it's no doubt the only time you'll visit Doctors' Commons." She brushed past him and turned into the passage toward the breakfast room and heard Marcus laugh softly behind her.

"Ryecroft," he said, "if your invitation to the wedding stands, I shall consider it my honor to escort the ladies to Surrey whenever the preparations are complete."

≈

The trip from London back to Ryecroft Manor seemed, to Sophie, to take an immense amount of time; they moved ever so much more slowly than on their journey up to town. They even stopped to rest the horses at a coaching inn in Staines rather than changing to a new team, because Lady Stone preferred not to use post-horses when her own would do perfectly well.

"Don't look so woeful, Miss Ryecroft," Marcus Winston told her. "It's not only horses that must stop to rest and eat, and at any rate, the wedding isn't until tomorrow."

"Yours don't seem to need rest at all," she said, looking back over her shoulder at the glossy blacks, still harnessed to his curricle, that were being led away by a groom. Unlike the team that pulled Lady Stone's traveling carriage, the blacks were still spirited and playful.

"Would you like to come up with me on the next stage instead of riding in the carriage?"

Sophie felt herself start to glow. "May I? And will you teach me to drive them?"

"Don't get above yourself," he advised.

For the rest of the drive—for once she was in the curricle, Sophie refused to return to the closed-in carriage—she had the benefit not only of a better view from the high seat, but she could enjoy the sunshine and the spring breeze, which was bracingly fresh against her face.

"You don't seem to be mourning over Carrisbrooke's defection," Winston observed.

"Is it true he's taken up with an opera dancer?"

"Who dared to tell you such a thing?"

"Lady Brindle whispered it to Lady Stone. But I'm nearly certain she intended me to overhear."

"Ann Eliza was always generous that way, making certain that hurtful gossip was heard by the people who were most concerned in it. I'm glad to see it didn't throw you off your stride."

"Then he *does* have an opera dancer? No, it didn't

break my heart. Only"—*only I don't know what to do now*—"she also told Lady Stone…" Sophie hesitated.

"Give over, brat. What scandal was she passing along this time?"

"She said it was such a shame that Lord Swindon fell down the stairs at his town house on the morning after the ball. And Lady Stone laughed and said that it wasn't a shame; it was two black eyes and a broken nose for a good cause."

"What an odd thing for her to say," Winston mused. "Lady Stone, I mean."

"Yes, especially since Lady Brindle hadn't told her what his injuries were. She looked quite shocked that Lady Stone already knew."

"That does seem strange," he agreed.

"I think it must have been Rye who blacked Lord Swindon's eyes."

"My dear Miss Ryecroft, I'm shocked at your suspicions. Wellingham and I were with your brother all that morning, and I can swear to you—"

"That Lord Swindon didn't fall down the stairs."

He smiled, and it was answer enough. "My goodness, is that the village already?"

"Yes, and it *is* good to be home, even though Mama says…"

"What does your mama say?" His voice was edgy, as if this topic troubled him far more than Lord Swindon's injuries.

Sophie sighed. "That we aren't going back to London at all."

"Does she, indeed? Perhaps she intends to stay at Ryecroft Manor to supervise the newlyweds."

"No, she'd never do that. She said we might go to the seaside. But I'd much rather be in London, even if…" Her voice trailed off as the picturesque little village opened out before them.

Sophie couldn't help remembering the last time she had ridden through here, holding a sweet bun as carefully as if it had held an explosive, not simply a message from Robert Wellingham. How innocent she had been, only a few weeks ago—plotting how to transport herself to London, thinking that merely being in the city would open the world to her, and then she could choose a means to support herself and have enough left over to save Ryecroft Manor.

She supposed she should count herself fortunate that it had been Wellingham she had approached. Another man might have outright laughed at her for being so bird-witted. Or worse, assumed that she was offering herself up as his mistress and simply picked her up and carried her off right then and there.

Winston shot a look at her. "Sophie, what are you up to now?"

They were well through the village. "Oh look—the gates of the manor. Just another mile across the park and we'll be home. And there's Rye up on the hill with his favorite hunter. I once took Admiral out for a gallop without permission, and Rye read me such a lecture I never dared touch that horse again."

Her voice was airy. Winston laughed, and as the moment eased, Sophie returned to her thoughts.

She might just have a plan left to her credit after all.

⁂

Portia couldn't deny a healthy curiosity as the carriage swung between the gateposts, past a stone gatekeeper's cottage, and around a long, sweeping bend that showed off a grand view of Ryecroft Manor.

Sophie had described the house to her—or tried to at least; she kept wandering off into descriptions of the stables or the woods or the gardens, so Portia had never managed to get a good picture in her mind of the manor itself. It sounded ramshackle, to tell the truth, so she hadn't pushed for a more complete description.

The reality took her by surprise. Ryecroft Manor was larger than she'd expected, an Elizabethan stone mansion with superb mullioned windows stretching across the deceptively simple facade. Smooth, rolling lawns led up to the front door. Ivy climbed one corner and wandered over the stone, though it had been neatly trimmed back from the glass. A puff of smoke rose from one of a dozen-or-so chimney pots atop the gabled roof.

"It looks like a home," she whispered.

"You're seeing it at the best time of year, my dear," Lady Ryecroft said. "In the winter, all those windows get drafty. There's Rye, coming to meet us."

Portia looked out again and saw the black hunter trotting across the lawn. The horse reached the front door just as the carriage halted, and the rider swung down and tossed the reins to one of the postboys.

Portia found herself wishing for an instant that she hadn't overheard that conversation in the hall at Lady Stone's house, so she could arrive here with nothing but happiness and hope in her heart, looking forward to a lifetime with a man who could send her soaring, as he had on the first night of their betrothal.

But that was cowardly. And she was not a coward.

She swallowed hard and braced herself to come face-to-face with her future husband.

Twenty

IT HAD ONLY BEEN THREE DAYS SINCE HE'D SAID good-bye to his promised bride in London. How, Rye wondered, was it possible that she could look so different now? Beautiful, of course, for Portia could never be anything else in his eyes. But she also looked frightened as he handed her down from the carriage.

"I'd like a word in private, my dear, before we join the others." He ignored Lady Stone's knowing smile. "I'm sure everyone would prefer to freshen up after the drive, anyway."

Carstairs was there to open the front door, and Mrs. Carstairs came bustling forward to greet the newcomers. Rye took two steps toward the library before changing his mind. As he drew Portia toward the staircase, Mrs. Carstairs gave a squeak of protest, and Rye turned on her. "Are you attempting to warn me that the rooms are not ready as ordered, Mrs. Carstairs?"

She said meekly, "They're ready, my lord."

The outburst made him feel better, though he'd have some fence-mending to do with the housekeeper later, he suspected. Especially if his mother had happened to be within earshot. But this was one conversation that was not going to be interrupted.

"You'll be in the viscountess's rooms," he said. "It seemed silly to put you in a guest room, with the wedding tomorrow."

Portia's voice was tart. "You're very thoughtful to the servants, my lord, considering how busy they'll be."

He opened the door to the viscountess's suite and ushered her into the sitting room. She looked around, and he felt his pride prickle. Though everything was scrupulously clean—Mrs. Carstairs would have stood for nothing less—the room was far from matching the expensive luxury of Lady Stone's house. Was Portia noticing how worn the upholstery was and how the draperies were carefully arranged to conceal the worst of the fading?

"And you?" she said. "Your room is…"

"Through there. But I'll retire somewhere else tonight if you don't care for the idea of my being next door before we're wed." That was not at all what he'd meant to say. "Portia…"

She looked at him with one eyebrow raised.

Rye felt his temper slip. "What do you have to say for yourself, ma'am?"

Sparks flared in her eyes. "I have no idea what you're talking about, but I will not be treated this way. You will not coerce me by yelling, sir."

It was past time to bring the facts into the open. "I suppose you believe because you are the one who brings money to this marriage, you'll rule the house? Well, you're wrong!"

Her face went pale. "You admit, then, that you knew." Portia took off her bonnet and laid it aside. "I have no idea why it seems to upset you, unless you were anticipating a fortune the size of Amalie Mickelthorpe's, my lord—and in that case, you must lower your expectations. Whoever led you to think that I am wealthy had it entirely wrong."

"Really? I think it unlikely that Wellingham is mistaken about the extent of your resources, since he's your trustee. Though perhaps, since you have left your business affairs entirely in his hands all this time…"

She was obviously shocked. "*Wellingham* told you?"

"He expected that I already knew. Dammit, Portia, how could *you* not have told me?"

She was staring at him with her mouth open, but rather than appearing awkward or foolish, she simply looked delectable. Rye had to swallow hard to keep from stepping forward and taking that tempting mouth and everything that went with it…

Because if he did, he suspected, they would never sort this out.

He watched with regret as her mouth thinned to a tight line. "When?" she asked.

Given a little time and patience, he could coax her to open it again. "I beg your pardon?"

"When did he tell you?"

"Yesterday. We were riding over the estate, and he kept suggesting ways to invest to improve the land—good ideas too, every one of them—until I finally said that would all be well and good if I had any real money to spend, but could he confine himself to things I could afford, ones that would turn a profit quickly, and he said…" Rye frowned. "What the hell do you mean, *when did he tell me*?"

"I thought perhaps it was… before." She swallowed, and Rye watched the little flutter at the base of her throat and wanted to press his lips there. "You said as you were leaving Lady Stone's that he'd agreed to sell back the lease. But I knew you didn't have any money to buy it. So I thought…"

Pieces clicked together in his mind. "You thought I knew even before the ball that you were wealthy, and that's why I seized the opportunity to marry you."

She nodded.

His fists clenched. "You thought I was capable of that?"

"You *are* capable; you can't deny it, Rye. You'd have married Juliana Farling, or even Amalie Mickelthorpe."

"Instead I ended up with a woman I thought was a feisty, penniless companion. Imagine my surprise when I find you're swimming in riches!"

"Hardly swimming," Portia said coolly.

"*Definitely* swimming—so I couldn't even fool myself about how I'd made a noble sacrifice in marrying you. It put me squarely in my place."

"Well, at least the money is some compensation for a bad situation that we must make the best of—as people have always done." There was a painful little twist in her voice.

His mouth went dry at the words. "Is it such a bad situation? You didn't seem to feel so that night we spent together." *I should never have left you, my darling.*

I should have stayed right there... and convinced you every moment that this isn't a calamity after all.

"You said all that yourself—about having to make the best of it."

"What else could I say to you right then, when you'd had such a blow? At least I'd had the choice to speak up, but once I did, you had no options at all."

"Neither of us did," Portia mused. "You must have been furious, being trapped like that."

"Perhaps I should have been upset at having all my plans washed out, but I wasn't. Still, I could hardly confess that I was happy when you'd just had the roof dropped on you."

"Happy?" she whispered. "You were *happy* about it?"

"I'm a fool not to have seen it long before I did. I would not have married any of those girls, Portia—and not because of a braying voice or a habit of speaking harshly to servants or an inclination toward being rude to my mother. If it hadn't been for those things, I'd have found something else that disqualified them. I would never have married anyone but you."

She was biting her lower lip. He wanted to make her stop so he could kiss the injured spot. No, he just wanted to kiss her... But she didn't quite look convinced.

"The last thing I expected that night was for you to seduce me," he said. "But you were the most perfect thing that's ever happened in my life."

She turned a promising shade of pink.

"Of course, there was still the problem of how to make the manor support us. I dragged Wellingham down here in the hope that he'd invest enough to help me turn the estate around—and he's agreed to do so. It may be a long time before I can pay him back, especially if Sophie needs a second Season. But if I'm very careful—"

Portia's eyes widened. "You're *not* going to mortgage the manor."

"No, for we worked out an agreement. Portia, I can't promise that Wellingham didn't take your fortune into account when he agreed to help me, but I assure you *I* didn't. The only thing I want from this marriage is you—my feisty, sassy, opinionated companion. And I'll rebuild the manor without a cent of your money if that's what it takes to convince you."

"That would be foolish." She dug into her reticule and pulled out a small rectangular metal box. "This is my father's snuffbox. It's the only thing I have of his."

"Aside from the sugar plantation, of course. Was he really the bookkeeper?"

"To start with, yes." She opened the lid and handed him the box.

Inside was a dried-up, weedy-looking purplish object. Rye squinted at it. "Is that a violet?"

She nodded. "From the first day outside Lady Stone's house, when you accidentally showered me with them. Even then, Rye, I knew you were special. I knew I could care about you if I wasn't careful. But you seemed so determined to marry a woman who had money, even if you could never love her—"

"Oh, I love you, all right. Did I forget to tell you that?" He reached for her cautiously—not wanting to frighten her. "Portia, are you finished with being careful? Will you try to love me in return?"

"I don't have to try… my lord." Her eyes were

brilliant, and she came willingly into his arms. Her mouth was just as sweet as he remembered. But her body was taut and even more eager than before—now that she knew what making love could be like.

"The wedding's tomorrow," he said, as much to remind himself as her. "We shouldn't."

She smiled up at him. "The wedding's tomorrow," she repeated softly. "So why not?"

❧

Sophie's maid exclaimed in horror that her face was windburned from the drive, and insisted on slathering her with cream and settling her for a rest. The moment the maid was out of sight, Sophie wiped the cream off on a handy towel and settled on the window seat to look out over the park.

She'd only been upstairs for a few minutes; the coach was still standing in front of the house, while a swarm of servants unloaded baggage. But already she felt as if she'd never been gone at all. The view from her window was one of her favorite things about the manor, one she would miss if Lady Ryecroft insisted on removing herself to the seaside…

But Sophie wasn't going to think about that just now. She had a plan to put into operation. She'd begin in just a few minutes, when everyone gathered downstairs.

A curricle swept around the side of the house and drew up by the front door. Not a visitor, for the vehicle had come from the stable block. It wasn't Marcus Winston's, and it wasn't Rye's. But she had seen it before.

Her eyes widened. A tall man in a lightweight coat

with capes on the shoulders came out of the house and climbed up onto the driving seat. The groom who had been driving leaped down, then swung onto the perch at the back as the driver lowered the reins and let the horses free. Sophie spotted a small trunk strapped to the back, next to the groom's seat. With a spray of gravel, the curricle pulled away.

Wellingham was leaving the manor.

Sophie almost flew down the stairs and out the front door. But he was wasting no time; the curricle was already at the bend in the drive and gaining speed. Last time, she had run across the lawns and through the woods and barely managed to catch him before he reached the gate. But today he had a longer start.

She looked around wildly. *Why* was there never a horse saddled and waiting by the front door at the moment when she needed one?

But there was; Rye's hunter had been left standing, reins looped around a post, because the grooms were all helping to unload the carriage. Sophie untied Admiral and led him over to the largest trunk she could see, stepped up onto the lid, and scrambled into the saddle. The skirt of her traveling dress was too narrow to ride astride, and it split under the strain. The stirrups were too long, but she managed to get her balance without them and leaned forward, nudging the horse with her heel.

She *had* to catch Wellingham before he reached the gate, or she might never see him again.

❧

Miranda leaned back on the chaise longue while Mary massaged her temples. "Everything appears to be well in order, ma'am. Mrs. Carstairs says the house ran just as you like it the entire time you were away. Mr. Wellingham seems not to have changed anything."

"That might be because Mr. Wellingham was scarcely here at all. Thank you, Mary. I think I'll rest."

"Yes, ma'am." Mary covered her with a light blanket and tiptoed away.

Miranda was already drifting off, when she sensed someone standing over her, and opened her eyes to see Marcus beside her. "Oh no."

"In the last three days, you've used up every possible excuse not to talk to me, Miranda. And I've offered you a wide range of reasonable options to have this conversation—such as inviting you to ride in my curricle on the drive down here. You avoided every one of them. So I'm taking advantage of this *un*reasonable option and invading your nap."

Miranda didn't stir. "And if I choose not to talk to you now?"

"Then I'll return in the middle of the night, and I'll make sure your son, or Lady Stone, discovers me here."

"You would not, for either of them would attempt to make you marry me."

"Do you really think I would shame so easily?"

"No," Miranda said wearily. "I don't. Trying to force you is a futile exercise."

"I'm glad you recognize that. You were about to tell me, that night in your bedroom at Lady Stone's when Sophie so inconveniently interrupted, what has made you ill and tired and out of sorts."

"*You.* So now that I've answered the question, go away."

He pulled the chair away from her dressing table, turned it to face her, and sat down. He should have looked foolish, sitting there on the small flowery seat, but instead he commanded the room. "Sophie tells me you're not planning to go back to London."

"Sophronia should learn not to gossip."

"The Season is barely half gone. You would take her away from all her success?"

"Once Rye is married, Portia can deal with Sophie and see her through the rest of the Season."

"And you?"

"I'm going away. I don't know where—and if I did know, I wouldn't tell you."

He was silent for a moment. "Are you so tired of me, Miranda?"

"No, just tired." Too tired, in fact, to think up any more stories, so she told the truth. "I'll find some little village where I can live quietly. Where no one will realize, when the widowed lady's child is born, that her husband died years ago, not within the last few months."

Marcus went very still. "A baby—and you weren't going to tell me?"

She felt a twinge of guilt, because she'd considered keeping her secret. "I don't know for certain. And I'm telling you now."

"Only because I've twisted it out of you. Why wait so long?"

"I couldn't risk the scandal, for Sophie's sake and Rye's."

"You thought I would make this a subject of gossip?" His fury was obvious, though he didn't raise his voice.

"Of course not. But I expected you would behave differently as soon as you knew, and it would cause talk if you suddenly didn't come around anymore or dance with Sophie or…" Her voice trailed off. "I was going to tell you tomorrow—after the wedding. I thought it would be better that way, and then I could just go away directly. Make a clean break of it."

"You think it won't cause talk if you just disappear?"

"I don't see why it should."

Marcus shook his head. "You're incredible, Miranda."

"I told you I'd be a terrible mistress," she said irritably.

"I don't recall your saying anything of the kind."

"Well, perhaps I only thought it. But it's true enough—what kind of a mistress doesn't consider that there might be consequences?"

"And that's really what you want to do? Go away? Have your baby alone?"

Your baby. Not *our* baby. "What other option is there? I can't exactly move through society, unmarried and with a child. And I won't trap you into a marriage that neither of us wants."

"No," he said softly, "you most certainly will not." He reached into the inner pocket of his coat. "Oddly enough, I suspected I might need this today." He drew out a sheet of parchment and dangled it in front of her, inches out of reach. "It's a special license, Miranda—for you and me."

She gaped at him.

"It was your idea," he reminded. "You suggested I go along with Rye to Doctors' Commons, to enjoy the experience."

"*Rye* knows you have this?"

"No. I went back the next day." He refolded the page and put it safely away. "No traps, Miranda, but you will marry me. Unless you truly want our child to be a bastard? And before you flare up at me for saying that— no, I do *not* play fair. Not when it's this important."

She sank back on the chaise. "I'm not good at marriage. I never considered marrying again."

"Nonsense, darling. You told me you had your eye on Robert Wellingham."

"Not that it bothered you in the least." She knew she sounded bitter.

Marcus's tone was meditative. "It's true that if you had threatened to become his mistress, I would have been far more worried."

Miranda felt her breath catch in horror at the idea of such an intimate relationship with anyone but Marcus. "In any case, marrying him would have been different. No one would have been confused about love, and so…"

"Love. Yes, Miranda—tell me about love. You loved Henry, yet you weren't happy. Were you?"

"Neither was he," she admitted painfully. "First love doesn't last. As soon as the bloom wore off, and we stopped being in love… If he had continued to love me, he wouldn't have gambled. He wouldn't have gone around in a drunken haze. He wouldn't have risked his children's future—and mine."

"Yes, he would. I knew Henry too, and because he was my brother's friend, I saw sides of him that you didn't. But you were too blinded by his title, and his elegant manners, to listen to me—especially when all I could offer then was to run away with you."

Perhaps there was an element of truth in what he said, but it didn't matter now. "At any rate, that's why I didn't want Carrisbrooke for Sophie."

"Because first love doesn't last? I think it was because Carrisbrooke is a great deal like Henry, and you saw that. The truth is, first love *does* last, when it's truly love and not the sort of infatuation you and Henry felt. I've loved you forever, Miranda."

Her heart skipped a beat.

"I just didn't know whether you were still the woman I loved, or if I'd only imagined her—not until I saw you again. When you visited me at Carris Abbey and offered to be my mistress, I have to admit I wanted to punish you a little for not caring enough to come to me after your husband died. I'm sorry, my darling. I should have asked you to marry me that day. But I don't think you would have agreed. And after that, any time we weren't actually making love, you were too busy pushing me away for me to ask."

Her throat was too tight to speak.

Marcus stood. "Sleep now. I'm going to go hunt up your son and ask his permission to pay my addresses to you. Or something like that."

Sadness washed over Miranda, and tears threatened to overflow. "I can't help but feel… You haven't even touched me. You don't really want this, Marcus. Perhaps you suspected—about the baby—and that's why you got the license."

"I hoped, and there was a note in your voice when you talked about Rye's special license…"

She was past the point of hearing. "But you don't

truly want a wife, and I won't be of much use as a mistress when I'm big as a house!"

"And you're too emotional at the moment to realize that you're making no sense at all. But since you need convincing…" He settled himself beside her on the chaise and gathered her close in his arms and stopped her protests by kissing her until she forgot what she'd intended to say. "Now, do you really think I'm being forced into this?"

She wriggled a little against him. "I still can't believe it. If it hadn't been for Lady Stone, and Wellingham taking a wild notion to lease a house in the country, you and I might never have…" She snapped her fingers. "I was right, wasn't I? There *was* something fishy about his leasing the manor. Did you…?"

But he kissed her again, and suddenly nothing else seemed important enough to pursue.

"I'm marrying you because I adore you," Marcus whispered finally. "And you'll marry me, because if you don't, I'll stand up at Almack's next week and announce that you're to have my child. Besides, you gave yourself away just now."

She frowned.

"You said marrying Wellingham would have been different than marrying me, because with him, love wasn't involved. You do love me, don't you?"

"I always have," she whispered, and the admission sent a wave of peace over her.

"Then it's perfect. You're going to be my wife *and* my mistress. Forever."

His kiss was tender, but the expression in his eyes

was wickedly suggestive—and Miranda knew the choice was hers.

"Today," she said shyly, "I'd rather be your mistress."

Marcus laughed and granted her wish.

⤫⤬

Sophie took the path across the park and through the woods as fast as she dared, and she was breathlessly clinging to the back of Rye's hunter when she plunged down the bank and into the carriageway just as Wellingham's horses came around the last bend. She turned Admiral to face his team and held up her hand.

The curricle came to a gentle halt just a few feet from her, and Wellingham looked across at her from the driving seat with polite inquiry.

"I need to speak with you, sir," Sophie said.

He nudged the team closer, until the front wheel of the curricle almost brushed Sophie's foot. "Come here." He shifted the reins into one hand and held the other out to her.

"The word *please* would not come amiss," she said. He did not seem amused. Or perhaps he didn't remember saying it to her the first time she had held him up here.

It was the most awkward dismount of Sophie's life, and she had to admit she felt safer once she was off the back of the hunter and perched in the curricle. Though not a great deal safer, she realized as she faced the blazing wrath in Wellingham's eyes. There would be no pleasantries this time about holdups and masks and pistols.

"Take the hunter back to the stables, Henry,"

Wellingham told his groom. "I will make sure Miss Ryecroft gets home."

"But I don't want to go home. I want to talk to you."

"Speak quickly, then. You have until we reach the front door."

This was not going at all the way Sophie had planned. "I know why you're leaving. It's so you don't have to meet Mr. Winston face-to-face, and it's entirely my fault. I don't know why he was in Mama's bedroom the night of the ball when we went to get her, but I know it was him, because I recognized his cologne today as we were driving—and if I hadn't said what I did in front of you about her having a man there that night, you would never have known, and so—"

"Stop for a breath, Miss Ryecroft, or you shall faint and tumble out."

"And so I'm the reason that you've given up the idea of marrying Mama to improve your social status, and it's only fair that I make it up to you, so I'll marry you instead."

He jerked on the reins as if his muscles had gone into spasm, and for a moment he was fully occupied in correcting the gesture and soothing the team. When he set them back into motion, it was at a gentle walk, and he turned to look at Sophie. "Miss Ryecroft, your willingness to make such a sacrifice is noble indeed. However, I must decline."

"I don't see why."

"Because you think being my wife would be a much more pleasant alternative for you than dancing in a theater."

"Of course it would." Then she frowned, for he seemed not in the least flattered that she preferred him to a career as a performer. "I mean… well, the two things aren't *really* alike."

"Aren't they?"

"Dancing in a theater would be much more like being your mistress rather than your wife. Not at all respectable. But if you don't want to marry me, then I suppose—"

"Marrying someone solely for money is not at all respectable either. Miss Ryecroft, though I am not at liberty to give you the details just now, I can assure you that your family's finances are no longer a concern, so there is no need for you to sell yourself to me or to anyone else."

"Oh." It didn't occur to her to doubt him, for if Robert Wellingham said it, then it was true. And if she no longer needed to bring a fortune into the family, then…

But Sophie didn't feel the overwhelming relief she would have expected. It wasn't a matter of need; the Ryecrofts' lack of cash had only been the excuse to go after what she wanted.

And what she wanted was Robert Wellingham.

The sudden realization shook Sophie to her core. She felt dizzy, and she clenched the edge of the seat to hold herself upright.

No wonder she'd so enjoyed dancing with him and carrying on their verbal fencing matches. No wonder her mood always lightened the moment he appeared. No wonder she felt safe when he was in the room. And no wonder she'd had such mixed-up feelings

when she thought he was courting her mother—
because what Sophie had really wanted was for him to
fall in love with her instead.

The curricle pulled up in front of the manor. She'd
been brought home like a wayward child. Not that
she didn't deserve it; she'd acted like one. She even
looked the part—dress torn, hair falling down, hat and
gloves forgotten, a sore spot on her palm where the
reins had rubbed…

"Thank you for bringing me back," she said with
dignity.

A groom came running, and Wellingham climbed
down and held up a hand to help Sophie out of the
curricle.

At least he wasn't going to drive straight off and
leave her. "I suppose you're coming in to tell my
mother?" Sophie tried to pat her hair back into place.

The corner of his mouth twitched. "I suspect
Lady Ryecroft will notice for herself that something
is awry."

Lady Stone was alone in the drawing room,
drinking a glass of port in solitary splendor. "Looking
for Miranda?" she asked. "Or perhaps for Lord
Ryecroft? I'm sure they'll all be along sooner or later.
However, I'm betting on *later*, so I think I'll go have
a nap." She started to close the door behind her, then
leaned back into the room to whisper, "I look forward
to collecting my winnings, Robert."

"Winnings?" Sophie asked.

"A very poor joke. Should you not go and change
clothes? You've torn your skirt."

"I couldn't possibly abandon you to your own

devices." *Because you might seize the chance to escape.* Sophie settled herself on the sofa, wrapping her skirt carefully around her legs to conceal the split as best she could. From the corner of her eye, she saw Wellingham watching, his gaze intent, so she took her time and smoothed the fabric over her knees until it was just right.

She filled a glass for him from the wine decanter, and with obvious reluctance, he came close enough to take it from her hand. She leaned back on the sofa with her own glass. If she kept him busy, he might not notice for a while that they were alone in a room. "Did you enjoy living at the manor? How long were you actually here, anyway, before the lure of town drew you back? Because I have to tell you, sir, I still think you only pretended to rent the manor so you could give money to Rye without Mama knowing it was a loan."

"Perceptive of you, Miss Ryecroft. But it was not a loan."

"Then what made you act as our benefactor? It can't have been my telling you I wanted to go to London—or at least not entirely, for you'd already made the deal."

"I must admit that meeting you on the carriageway cemented the notion, but you're correct. I acted for a friend."

"Lady Stone, of course—so Rye would have the funds to take us to London." But the idea didn't feel right.

"No. In fact, it was Marcus Winston who asked me to act in his stead. He wanted your mother in

London, I believe, so he made it possible for her to present you."

"It was *his* money you gave Rye?"

"Not entirely," Wellingham admitted. "It seemed to me he'd underestimated the amount required to launch a Beauty."

Sophie studied him. Did he mean he truly thought she was beautiful? No, the twinkle in his eyes was subdued, but it was there; he was laughing at her. "So you added funds of your own. No wonder it seemed such a generous offer. But if you knew how Mr. Winston felt—"

"I knew that he has long cherished a *tendre* for Lady Ryecroft, yes."

Sophie frowned. "If you weren't interested in Mama that way, why did you keep telling me I should look on you as a father figure?"

"I was reminding myself, as well as you, that I'm nearly old enough to be your father."

"That's sheer nonsense; you're not. And if you have to remind yourself of it all the time… Well, it *almost* sounds as if you find me appealing."

"Appealing and enticing and charming and delightful—and very tempting. Does that frighten you, Miss Ryecroft? Because it should."

"Not at all. You told me once that when you've given your word, you do not make a practice of breaking it."

"That's true." He sounded wary.

"Well then. You promised to take me to London, and I demand that you keep your word. If you weasel out of it, I shall tell my brother you have toyed with my affections."

"You're doing an excellent job of proving how very young you are." He picked up his hat. "Miss Ryecroft, *adieu*."

"Not so fast, sir." His stern look almost made her quail, but Sophie steeled herself. "The truth is I am disappointed to find that you don't wish to marry me. Because"—her voice was very soft—"because I find that I want to marry *you*."

Silence dropped over the drawing room like morning fog.

"But if you truly have no desire to make me your wife—"

"I never said I didn't." He sounded as if the words had been squeezed out of him.

Sophie felt something relax deep inside her. "In all this time, I haven't found anyone I like nearly as well as I like you."

"*All this time?* A few weeks of a single Season?"

"I've been out a lot longer than that in Surrey." Sophie noticed the rip in her skirt had opened up again when she felt cool air—and a warm gaze—on her knee. She shifted just a bit, and her silk garter peeked out. She thought she heard Wellingham gulp. "And I have yet to find anyone who makes me feel as safe as you do either." She tipped her head to one side and regarded him thoughtfully. "Though not when you look at me like that."

"Like what?"

"As if you want to consume me," she said frankly. "Except I think, as long as it was you, I shouldn't mind that either." She stood, slowly smoothing her skirt back into place, and moved a little closer.

"If I were to tell you I've lost my entire fortune in a single bad investment—"

"I wouldn't believe you. But if you had, how exciting it would be! Then you'd have to train me as a clerk or something to work with you, so we could start over."

He shook his head as if to clear it.

"Oh, do stop being such a dunderhead, Robert. The truth is I've been chasing after you, one way or another, ever since that first day. I knew then that I wanted you; it just took me a while to admit it." She let her fingertips skim his face. "How long is it going to take you to stop running?"

He caught her hands, holding them closely against his chest. She could feel his heartbeat against her palms.

He took a deep breath. "You're certain, Sophie?"

"Yes," she whispered and stood on tiptoe to press her lips against his.

The kiss might have started out as her idea, but barely an instant later he took control, and Sophie was swept away. She'd had no notion that kisses could be so powerful, so all-enveloping, so *nice*. It was lovely to learn that a man's lips could be soft, gentle, teasing, insistent, warm, caressing, demanding—and that he didn't want to just kiss her mouth, but her eyebrow, her ear, her throat… "Oooh," she said as his hand skimmed over her breast.

Wellingham looked down at her warily, as if he expected to see shock or distaste in her face. Sophie laughed and molded herself closer to him. "Do that again, please—all of it. I didn't know kissing would make me feel so warm all over that I want to tear off my dress."

"What little is left of it. But please don't… Not that it would make much difference if your brother walks in."

"Oh, he'd only blacken both your eyes and break your nose if you refused to marry me." Sophie's voice was airy. "And you *are* going to, aren't you, Robert?"

"Yes, and may heaven help me. Shall you mind very much, I wonder, being married to a banker rather than a gentleman of leisure?"

"That depends. When we're married, will you take me on picnics?"

"Now and then."

"Will you escort me to dances?"

"If we're invited, but I'm not certain marrying *you* will improve my social standing—hoyden that you are."

"Poor Robert. Will you recite poetry to me?"

"Doubtful."

"All the right answers. By the way, if you think I'm letting you leave now, to go to London without me—"

"I was only going as far as the inn in the village. I wouldn't miss this wedding."

"Well, even that's too far to suit me." Sophie tipped her head to make it easier for him to nibble her earlobe. "What was Lady Stone talking about—collecting her winnings?"

"I asked her for a favor, and she finagled me into a wager before she'd agree. She said you were going to marry me despite myself, and I bet her a ruby ring that you wouldn't."

Sophie shook her head. "I thought you were more sensible than that. What was the favor?"

"I wanted you to have something special for your ball, but your mother would never have allowed you to accept jewelry from me."

"And so you didn't even hint that those eardrops were your gift? Robert, it's not very flattering that you seemed to be *trying* to win that wager. I may yet have to save up my pin money for a mask and a pistol."

"I shall give you both as a wedding gift, so you'll be properly equipped the next time. And knowing you, I'm sure there will be a next time."

"Count on it," Sophie said. "But the next time I hold you up, it's going to be forever." And then she didn't talk any more at all.

Acknowledgments

Special thanks to: my writing buddies, Rachelle and Elaine, who held my hand throughout the writing of this story. My devoted agent, Christine Witthohn of Book Cents Literary Agency. My editor, Deb Werksman, and the support staff at Sourcebooks Casablanca, who display more concern for every word and comma in my stories than even I could ask. My good friends Margaret, Sandi, Desiree, and Bev. My family, both by blood and by affection—Linda; Amanda, Ashley and Karina; Irene and Sue. My romance-writing students at Gotham Writers' Workshop—thank you for keeping me on my toes!

And above all, my husband, who listened patiently to every word of this story three separate times and never once fell asleep while I was reading.

About the Author

Leigh Michaels is the author of nearly one hundred books, including eighty contemporary novels and more than a dozen nonfiction books. More than thirty-five million copies of her romance novels have been sold. A six-time RITA finalist, she has also received two Reviewer's Choice awards from *RT Book Reviews* and was the 2003 recipient of the Iowa Library Association's Johnson Brigham Plaque Award. She is the author of *On Writing Romance* from Writer's Digest Books. Leigh also teaches romance writing on the Internet at Gotham Writers' Workshop: www.writingclasses.com. Visit her website at www.leighmichaels.com. She lives in Ottumwa, Iowa.

One

WHEN THE HEAVY BRASS KNOCKER FELL AGAINST THE front door, the crash echoed through the cottage. Olivia ignored it. She wasn't expecting callers; she wasn't prepared for callers; and she didn't want to greet callers.

But barely half a minute later, the knocker dropped once more. She abandoned the bread dough she'd been kneading and wiped her hands on her apron. The baking was late already, and this interruption wasn't going to help.

As she crossed the narrow hall, she noticed a dusting of flour on her blue muslin skirt and brushed feebly at it, but she managed only to make the smear look worse.

The man waiting on the doorstep was short, stout, and past middle-aged. His face was red, as if the warmth of the day was too much for him, or perhaps his neckcloth was just too tight. He looked astounded to see her there. "Lady Reyne, where are your servants today?"

All two of them? Olivia wanted to answer. But she

didn't think Sir Jasper Folsom really wished to know that this was the housemaid's weekly afternoon out or that Nurse was upstairs putting Charlotte down for her nap. And since he hadn't asked about Kate Blakely, who was Olivia's guest, she felt no need to explain that Kate had gone to call at the vicarage.

At any rate, Sir Jasper was Olivia's landlord, not her keeper, so she didn't feel obliged to tell him why she was the only one available to answer her door in the middle of a sunny Wednesday afternoon.

She smiled vaguely. "I find it terribly boring to sit and be waited on, Sir Jasper."

"You are a most unusual lady, ma'am. I have come to collect the next quarter's rent."

"Of course." Olivia hesitated and then stepped back. Better, she thought, not to have this conversation on the doorstep. "Would you care to come inside?"

He looked startled at the invitation, though an instant later he had masked the expression. He bowed and followed her into the tiny parlor, where the single window stood open and a fire had been freshly laid, ready to light in case the evening should turn cool.

Sir Jasper took off his hat and looked around the room. "Quite delightful."

Threadbare was the word Olivia would have used for the furnishings Sir Jasper had supplied along with the cottage, but she supposed there was a certain cozy charm about the mismatched chairs and the way personal items—a smock she was hemming for Charlotte, a shawl Kate had started knitting last night—were sprinkled around.

Don't be so snobbish, she told herself. The cottage

wasn't grand, but it was home in a way that her previous residence had never been, and she was grateful to Sir Jasper for offering it at a rent she could afford.

At least, she had been able to afford the rent until now. She braced herself to tell him that at this moment she could not pay the entire amount she owed, but she found she couldn't come straight out with it.

"I don't keep ale in the house," Olivia said, "since we do not as a rule have gentleman callers. But I can offer you tea."

Sir Jasper smiled, displaying yellowing teeth. "That would be most welcome, my lady."

Olivia poured the tea and drew a breath to begin explaining.

Sir Jasper sipped. "I'm sure you're excited by the news. The entire countryside is agog."

"What news?" She was almost relieved to be interrupted, though also surprised. Rarely did anything worthy of comment happen in Steadham; Olivia found the quiet to be one of the village's greatest attractions.

"The wedding, of course. Lady Daphne's wedding." He looked startled when she didn't react. "You did not receive an invitation? I would have thought... The festivities are to be held here. At Halstead, to be precise."

Halstead—one of the few country houses in England that had only one name, as if the single word made it clear to any audience what was being discussed. The country seat of the Duke of Somervale, the manor house at Halstead lay less than a mile from the village if one walked across the fields and the park. But the estate was so large and self-contained that when the family was not in residence, it was easy for the villagers to forget the manor lay so close by.

In the months since she had arrived in Steadham village, Olivia had seen Halstead only from a distance. Apparently that wasn't going to change in the fore-seeable future. But then, she would have expected nothing else.

Sir Jasper went on, "The wedding itself is to be in the village church, I understand."

He *understood?* Then Sir Jasper must not have received an invitation, either. That surprised Olivia much more than the fact that she had not been included on the guest list—for though Sir Jasper was a mere baronet, he must have been a neighbor of the Somervale family for years.

"I felt sure you would be invited," he mused. "As the widow of an earl... but the duchess is even higher in the instep than I believed."

"It's hardly a snub for me not to be included, Sir Jasper. So far as I am aware, I have never met any of the family, and I doubt the duchess even knows I've taken up residence in the neighborhood." *Or would care in the slightest, if she knew.*

Sir Jasper's face had tightened as if the mere mention of a snub had made his own exclusion sting more. So Olivia hurried on. "Perhaps it's a very small wedding—just the family."

"A *small* wedding? For one of the Somervales? That family doesn't know the meaning of the word."

The firm click of the empty cup as he set it down made Olivia fear for her mother's china; she had managed to save fewer than a dozen good pieces as it was.

"But perhaps you are correct," Sir Jasper went on. "Now I must continue my rounds. The rent, Lady Reyne?"

Olivia's fingers trembled as she took her reticule from under the smock in her sewing basket and opened it. "I can give you half of the rent today, Sir Jasper, but I'm not able to pay for the entire three months right now. I had hoped to make an agreement in regard to the remainder."

He was silent for so long that the rattle of a carriage wheel in the road outside the parlor window seemed to echo through the room. "What sort of agreement did you have in mind?" His tone was low and suggestive.